Praise for Kat Martin

"Martin revs the power from page one of this fast-paced romantic thriller... Fans of romantic suspense won't be able to put this book down until the final page is turned, and Martin is likely to recruit thriller readers as well."
—*Publishers Weekly* on *The Deception*

"An un-put-down-able page-turner that's sure to satisfy fans of romance and thrillers alike."
—*Kirkus Reviews* on *The Deception*

"Martin keeps the twists and turns coming in the sensuous and spirited first Maximum Security romantic thriller.... Readers will find It hard to wait for the next book in this tantalizing series."
—*Publishers Weekly* on *The Conspiracy*

"Kat Martin is a fast gun when it comes to storytelling, and I love her books."
—#1 *New York Times* bestselling author Linda Lael Miller

"[Kat] Martin is a terrific storyteller."
—*Booklist*

"It doesn't matter what Martin's characters are up against—she dishes up romantic suspense, sizzling sex and international intrigue."
—*RT Book Reviews*

"Suspenseful, emotion-packed page-turner... This nonstop, high-stakes adventure stands on its own."
—*Library Journal*, starred review, on *Against the Edge*

KAT MARTIN

THE
ULTIMATE
BETRAYAL

HQN

ISBN-13: 978-1-335-48375-1

Recycling programs
for this product may
not exist in your area.

The Ultimate Betrayal
First published in 2020. This edition published in 2021.
Copyright © 2020 by Kat Martin

Before Nightfall
First published in 2020. This edition published in 2021.
Copyright © 2020 by Kat Martin

This edition published by arrangement with Harlequin Books S.A.

For questions and comments about the quality of this book, please contact us at CustomerService@Harlequin.com.

HQN
22 Adelaide St. West, 40th Floor
Toronto, Ontario M5H 4E3, Canada
www.Harlequin.com

Printed in Spain

CONTENTS

To the brave men and women
of our armed forces who risk their lives daily
to keep us safe.

And to US Army Colonel Thom Nicholson
for his many years of friendship and his help
with this book.

THE ULTIMATE
BETRAYAL

CHAPTER ONE

Dallas, Texas

Too much downtime always made him nervous, kind of edgy as he waited for the other shoe to drop. It had been a week since his last client had headed back to Nashville, Bran's services as a bodyguard no longer required. A week of peace and quiet he should have enjoyed.

Instead, he had a nagging feeling that something bad was coming down the line.

Lounging back in the chair behind his desk at Maximum Security, Brandon Garrett ended the phone conversation he'd been having with Heath Ford, a Dallas police detective. Ford was working a murder case that involved one of Bran's former clients, a white rapper who called himself String Bean. Unfortunately for Bean, when Bran's services had ended after his last concert tour, he had been murdered.

Bran's jaw clenched. String Bean had been a cocky, arrogant little prick, but he didn't deserve to die. The only good news was that Ford was the best detective on the force. He was following a lead that looked promising, and he wouldn't give up till he brought the killer to justice. Bran would do whatever he could to help him. Which might turn into something, but not enough to keep him busy.

The sound of the front door swinging open caught his attention and he glanced up. A gust of cool, late October air swept in, along with a petite, whirlwind of a woman with the prettiest strawberry blond hair Bran had ever seen.

She had a sweet little body to match her fiery long hair, he noticed, enhanced by the dark blue stretch jeans curving over her sexy ass and the peach knit top that hugged her breasts.

It wasn't tough to read the anxiety in her big green eyes as she surveyed the room, gripping a wheeled carry-on, probably coming straight from the airport. But instead of walking to where the receptionist, Mindy Stewart, sat behind the front desk, she paused.

Her glance slid past the dark red, tufted leather sofa and chairs in the waiting area, over the antique farm tools decorating the walls, to the rows of oak desks where Jonah Wolfe, Jaxon Ryker, Lissa Blayne, and Jason Maddox were all hard at work.

Those green eyes landed on Bran, and as she started toward him, there was something about her that rang a distant bell. Interest piqued, he rose from his chair. "Can I help you?"

"You're Brandon Garrett, right? You were a friend of my brother's. Danny Kegan? I recognize you from the photos Danny sent home."

The mention of his best friend's name hit him like a blow, and the muscles across his stomach clenched. Daniel Kegan had been a member of his spec ops team, a brother, not just a friend. Danny had saved Bran's life at the cost of his own. He was KIA in Afghanistan.

Bran stared down at the girl, who was maybe five foot four. "You're Jessie," he said, remembering the younger sister Daniel Kegan had talked so much about. "You look like him. Same color hair and eyes." An image of Danny's face arose along with a painful memory of the day he died.

Bran forced away the images of blood and death and concentrated on the woman.

Nervously she licked her lips, which were plump and pink and fit her delicate features perfectly.

"My brother said if I ever needed help, I should come to you. He said you'd help me no matter what." She glanced back toward the door, and his mind shifted away from the physical jolt he felt as he looked at her to the worry in her eyes.

"Danny was my closest friend. Whatever you need, I'll help. Come on. Let's go into the conference room and you can tell me what's going on." When her gaze shot back to the door, his senses went on alert.

"I didn't mean I needed your help later," Jessie said nervously. "I meant I need your help right now."

Gunshots exploded through the windows. "Get down!" Bran shoved Jessie to the floor behind his desk and covered her with his body as glass shattered and a stream of bullets sprayed across the room.

Ryker popped up, gun drawn, and ran for the door. Maddox and Lissa were shuffling through their desks, arming themselves. Wolfe drew his ankle gun and ran for the rear entrance, ready for any threat that might come from there.

"Black SUV with tinted windows," Ryker called back. Six feet of solid muscle, dark hair and eyes, Jax was a former navy SEAL, currently a PI and occasional bounty hunter. "Couldn't get a plate number." Jax's gaze swung to the front of the room. "Mindy, you okay?"

She eased up from beneath her desk. "I—I'm okay. Should I call the police?" Around here, it was never good to jump to conclusions.

Bran hauled Jessie to her feet. He could feel her trembling. Her eyes looked even bigger and brighter than they had before. "Are they coming back?" he asked.

"I—I don't know. It could have just been a warning."

Bran turned to Mindy. "Unless someone's already phoned it in, let's wait to call the cops till we know what's going on." His attention returned to Jessie. "We need to talk."

She just nodded. Her face had gone pale, making a fine line of freckles stand out on her forehead and the bridge of her nose.

Bran took her arm and urged her toward the conference room. "Keep a sharp eye," he said to The Max crew. "Just in case."

JESSIE SANK UNSTEADILY into one of the rolling chairs around the long oak conference table. The man she had come to see, Brandon Garrett, sat down beside her.

"Okay, let's hear it," he said. "What's going on?"

She thought of the men who had just shot up his office and her pulse started thumping again. "Danny said if I ever needed help—"

"Yeah, I get that. Your brother knew he could count on me. Like I said, I'll help you any way I can, but I need to know what's going on."

Bran was taller than Danny, around six-three, she guessed, with a soldier's lean, hard body, V-shaped, with broad shoulders and narrow hips. Powerful biceps bulged beneath the sleeves of his dark blue T-shirt. With his slightly too-long mink-brown hair, straight nose and masculine features, he was ridiculously handsome, except for the hard line of his jaw and the darkness in his eyes that contrasted sharply with their beautiful shade of cobalt blue.

"Start at the beginning," he said.

Jessie took a shaky breath and let it out slowly, giving herself time to think. "I'm not exactly sure where the beginning actually is. My father was Colonel James Kegan, Commander, US Army Alamo Chemical Depot."

Bran nodded. "Danny mentioned that. He was very proud of his dad."

"Dad was proud of Danny, too. He was a great father."

Bran's gaze narrowed on her face. "You said *was*. When did he die?"

"He died on August 15. I still have trouble believing he's actually gone."

"I'm sorry."

"My father is the reason I'm here. Just before he died, a little over two months ago, he was removed from active duty. He was charged with larceny—the theft of military property, specifically chemical weapons stored at the depot. Because the army believed he was selling the weapons to a foreign entity, he was also charged with espionage and treason, and confined to the stockade at Fort Carson. At the hearing he pleaded not guilty to all charges, but he died before he could prove it."

Bran leaned back in his chair. "The timing's unfortunate to say the least."

"That's the thing. My father didn't just conveniently have a heart attack five days after they arrested him. He was murdered. The perfect scapegoat for the real criminals."

Bran's gaze sharpened. "How do you fit into the picture, and why were those men shooting at you?"

"I'm a freelance journalist. I investigate unsolved crimes, environmental disasters, political scandals, celebrity misdeeds, anything that makes an interesting story and maybe does some good. Mostly the articles are published digitally in online magazines. But I have a certain reputation for thoroughness and honesty that has helped me grow a sizable audience. In other words, I'm good at my job."

A corner of his mouth edged up. She remembered her brother telling her that Brandon Garrett was a heartbreaker and that if Danny ever brought him home, she was forbidden to go out with him. Not that she ever paid much attention to her older brother when it came to dating. But now that she had met Bran, she understood her brother's warning.

"I'm guessing you decided to investigate the theft of chemical weapons from the depot," Bran said. "The crime your father was charged with."

"The crime my father was *wrongly accused* of committing."

"All right, we'll assume for now that's true."

"It's true. I know my father. He was a soldier's soldier, army all the way. Add to that, he was a patriot. He would never do anything to harm our country or the people in it. Those munitions stored at the depot? The contents are deadly. God only knows how many people could be killed."

Bran's dark eyebrows drew together. "Are you saying the army never recovered the stolen property?"

"That's exactly what I'm saying. They're still searching, but as far as they're concerned, the man responsible for the theft is dead. They claim that's the reason they haven't been able to find the munitions, or even a link to anyone else involved."

"But you believe they can't find a link because your father wasn't the guy behind the thefts."

"Exactly."

"Did you talk to him before he died?"

Her throat tightened. She missed him so much. "No. He never called me. He didn't want me to know anything about it. I think he was sure he could prove his innocence and it would all go away."

"But that didn't happen."

"No, and without his help, it makes all of this even more difficult." She inhaled deeply, needing a moment to compose herself.

"I was devastated by my father's death," she continued. "It took a while for me to accept that he was actually gone and decide to investigate what really happened. Once I started, I was determined to prove his innocence. I had just begun asking questions and trying to get answers when I realized I was being followed and that perhaps my life was in danger."

Bran seemed to be watching her closely. "Are you sure what you're doing is worth that kind of risk? Your dad wouldn't want you to die trying to save his reputation."

"It's worth it to me. I'm not giving up—which is the reason those men were waiting for me at the airport when my plane landed. Or I'm assuming that's how they found me. I'm pretty sure somebody's been watching me for weeks, but this is the first time they've openly threatened me."

"Who's *they*?"

Jessie gripped her hands tighter beneath the table. "I don't know. I'm hoping you can help me find out."

CHAPTER TWO

BRAN COULD TELL by the dark look on Chase's face when he walked into the office and saw the broken windows—his brother wasn't happy. He took a look around and headed straight for Bran. At least the glass on the floor had been swept up.

"What the hell, little brother?" Chase propped his hands on his hips as he surveyed the jagged shards left in the window frames, all that remained after the shooting.

"Take it easy. I've already called the glass company. They're sending a guy out to take measurements and replace the panes. I'll take care of the cost."

"It's not the money and you know it." Considering they were each worth millions, thanks to the extremely profitable oil-and-gas business their father had left them and the great job their brother, Reese, as CEO, had been doing to grow the company.

"Someone could have been seriously injured or even killed," Chase said. He was the oldest of the Garrett brothers, brown eyes, dark blond hair, a hard jaw rimmed by a short, dark blond beard. Chase was newly married and extremely happy. Well, until today. "What's going on?"

Bran tipped his head toward the woman quietly sitting in the oak chair next to his desk. "Chase, meet Jessie Kegan. She's a journalist from Colorado. And Daniel Kegan's younger sister." After the shooting, there had been no more problems, but the back door was now locked and Jax was keeping an eye on the front just in case.

Chase's dark gaze went to Jessie, but he didn't have to ask who Daniel Kegan was. He knew how close Danny and Bran had been, knew Danny had been killed in the war—killed saving Bran's life. Knew the pain his friend's death had caused.

"It's nice to meet you, Jessie," Chase said. "I assume all of this has something to do with you."

"I came to ask for Brandon's help. I didn't mean to bring trouble down on all of you."

Chase's expression softened. "Trouble kind of goes with the territory when you're in the security business." His gaze returned to Bran. "I take it you're going to help Ms. Kegan solve her problem."

"I'll keep her safe. But the problem won't be solved until we track down the people involved. To do that, we're going to need to go back to Colorado."

"When are you leaving?"

Bran glanced toward the broken windows, his hand automatically going to the custom grip on the Glock 19 now clipped to his belt. "I'd say the sooner the better."

"How are you getting there?"

"It's too far to drive. Less than three hours by plane."

"Less than that if you take the company jet."

"If I fly us down in the Baron, I'll have a little more flexibility. Not sure where we might end up. That is if you aren't planning to use it."

"I don't have anything planned. But keep me posted, and if you need help, call me."

"Will do."

Chase headed for his office. So far the cops hadn't shown up, and it looked like they weren't going to. Reporting the

incident without any info or even a plate number on the vehicle wouldn't do jack, so it didn't really matter.

"You own a plane?" Jessie asked.

"Technically, it's Chase's, but my brothers and I all
share it. We don't know where this thing with your father
is headed. With the plane, we'll be able to move around
more easily, depending on what we find out."

"That sounds good. When are we leaving?"

"First thing in the morning. I've got a couple of loose
ends I need to take care of before we go."

"I took a taxi straight here from the airport when I realized those guys were following me. I need to find a hotel
to spend the night."

Bran felt a trace of amusement. "You won't be needing a hotel room, Jessie. You'll be staying at my place tonight. You're Danny's sister. From the moment you walked
through that door until this is over, you're under my protection."

She blinked. "Wait a minute. I'm not sure what I expected when I came here—your help clearing my father's
name, for sure. But I certainly wasn't expecting you to act
as my bodyguard."

"Until today, you didn't know you needed one. Now
you do."

She looked as if she might argue, but since he was right,
she stayed silent.

Bran closed the laptop on his desk and shoved it into its
black neoprene sleeve. "Ready to go?" he asked.

"What if they're watching?"

Bran flicked a glance toward the rear entrance leading
to the parking lot. "I hope they are. Better for everyone if
they know you're no longer here."

"But—"

"Don't worry. We'll lose them long before we get any-where near my condo. Let's go."

JESSIE STEPPED BACK as Bran grabbed the handle of her carry-on and started for the back door, stopping several times to speak to one of his colleagues. They were all good-looking people, and amazingly fit; even the receptionist up front was a pretty brunette with a sunny disposition. Another woman walked toward her, a stunning blonde who looked to be in great physical condition.

"You don't have to worry," the blonde woman said. "Bran won't let anything happen to you."

"Jessie, this is Lissa Blayne," Bran said. "Former police detective, currently a private investigator."

"It's nice to meet you," Jessie said. "I'm just hoping Brandon can help me clear my father's name."

Lissa smiled. "If anyone can, it's Bran."

Jessie didn't mention the theft of the chemical weapons or that they would be trying to find them before some-thing terrible happened. She figured the fewer people who knew, the better.

Bran nudged her forward and they started moving again, her carry-on rolling along in his wake. He paused at the back door and handed over the bag. "You take it from here. I need to keep my hands free."

Remembering the gunfire that had erupted only a short time ago, she felt a rush of nerves. "All right."

"Stay here till I check things out."

She nodded. Bran pulled the door open enough to scope out the parking lot, then stepped outside. He wasn't gone long before she heard the rumble of a car engine starting, pulling to a halt outside the door.

A moment later the door swung open again. "Let's go."

Pulling the carry-on behind her, Jessie followed Bran out to where a black Jeep Wrangler idled in the lot. He helped her into the passenger seat and closed the door, rounded the vehicle, and slid in behind the wheel. He pulled into the street more slowly than she would have expected.

"Did you see anyone?"

Bran shook his head. "No sign of them. They might pick us up later, but I'm thinking you were right. They were sending you a warning."

"You mean like, *this is what's going to happen to you if you keep asking questions*?"

"Yeah, that's about it." He started driving, constantly checking the rearview mirror, the side mirrors, his head swiveling right to left, left to right as he swept the area around them.

He turned the Jeep at the corner, pulled into the left lane, turned another corner, pulled into the right lane, sped up, slowed down, shot through traffic and drove through parking lots, turned into alleys, and gunned through yellow lights.

After twenty minutes of zigzagging between cars, she was sure anyone who might be trying to keep track of them was not going to succeed.

"You okay?" Bran asked as she clung to her seat.

"How long do we have to keep this up?"

He cranked the wheel, turning the Jeep into an underground parking garage, and pulled into a space marked Unit 1410, next to what appeared to be a brand-new Chevy Stingray, bright red with matte-black trim.

"Home sweet home," Bran said, grinning. Jessie pulled her gaze away from that amazingly handsome face and ignored the little tug of awareness she felt when he smiled, which only made him more attractive. He turned off the engine and cracked open his door at the same time Jessie opened hers.

"Stay there," he commanded, back in bodyguard mode, the smile gone from his face. He checked their surroundings, then came around to her side of the Jeep to help her out. He hauled her luggage out of the back, but didn't offer to tow it up to his condo. Apparently, he didn't believe in taking chances.

Jessie glanced around the parking garage, which was cleaner than most houses, not a trace of oil on the concrete floor. The neighborhood was extremely upscale, and from the looks of the mirrored glass building, perfectly landscaped flower beds, and manicured grassy open spaces, so were the condos.

She'd known the Garretts had money, but she hadn't thought about it when she'd come to Dallas. She just needed help, and she believed her brother's friend would agree.

She towed her carry-on into the elevator and waited as Bran pushed the button for the fourteenth floor. The carriage zipped up as if it had wings, and the doors opened onto a corridor lined on one side with plate glass windows looking out over the city. Opposite the windows, a row of apartments. Bran paused at 1410, swiped his key, and opened the door.

Jessie waited while he disabled the alarm, then reset it to perimeter only. When he turned, she could feel him close beside her, big and male, vowing to protect her. He was former army Special Forces, a Delta operator, just like her brother, one of the most capable and deadly men on the planet. For the first time in days, she felt safe.

"The guest rooms are down the hall," Bran said. "Each has its own bath. Follow me."

She took a look around as he led her beneath the modern glass chandelier in the granite-floored entry. Ten-foot ceilings, hardwood floors, stunning views of the city, big sliding glass doors that opened onto a terrace.

"Your place is lovely."

"Thanks." He flashed another grin. "Long as my brother Reese keeps the family business making money, I can afford it. Besides, I've lived everywhere from a tent in the middle of the Afghan desert to a hammock in the Colombian jungle. I figured it was time for a change."

She smiled. "I'm betting the Stingray is yours, too."

"Recent addition. I've barely had time to try it out."

Jessie felt a pang of guilt. "And now here I am, dragging you off to Colorado, into what could turn out to be a very dangerous situation."

He sobered, walked back and caught her chin, forcing her to look up at him. "I owe your brother my life. In giving it to me, he lost his own. There is nothing his sister or anyone he cared about could ever ask of me that I would not do."

Her throat tightened. She thought of how much she missed Danny, knew how much her brother had admired and respected Brandon. "I'm glad I came to you. When I left Colorado, I wasn't sure it was the right thing to do, but now I am. Thank you for helping me."

"The only thing I've done so far is sweep a pile of glass off the floor of my office. You can thank me when this is over."

Jessie just nodded. Now that they were safely inside his condo, Bran took the handle of her suitcase and tugged it down the hall into one of the guest rooms. The bedroom furniture was modern, dark wood throughout, the bed covered by a pale blue silk comforter, trendy lamps on the bedside tables, a desk, and two pale blue chairs in a small seating area.

"You have very good taste in interior design," she said.

He tossed the carry-on up onto the bed. "Afraid I can't take the credit. A friend helped me."

A friend. The way he looked, there was no doubt what kind of friend. "Female, I imagine."

He just shrugged those wide shoulders. "Women have a knack for that kind of thing."

In today's world, it was a sexist thing to say, but she almost smiled. She had lived with her dad and brother. She knew how military men thought. Since they also tended to be caring and protective, it wasn't a problem for her.

"Some women, I guess," she said. "I was never good at that stuff myself."

"That why you took up writing?"

"Investigating and writing. I like the challenge of digging into mysteries and solving them."

Bran's features turned serious. "That's good because we're going to need your skills *and* mine to figure out what the hell is going on in Colorado."

Jessie stayed silent. Because Bran Garrett was right.

CHAPTER THREE

BRAN SAT DOWN behind the desk in his home office. He booted up his computer, a top-of-the-line iMac Pro with a twenty-seven-inch, 5K, P-3 widescreen color monitor. The room was filled with state-of-the-art equipment, some of it stuff he rarely used and was still getting a handle on figuring out.

While Jessie got settled in the guest room, he used the time to Google *Colonel James Daniel Kegan.*

Bran had met Danny's father several times over the years, a good-looking, distinguished man with very straight posture, a slightly ruddy complexion, and a mane of silver-streaked dark red hair. He had always been cordial, if a bit formal due to his superior rank, but he had clearly loved his son.

Bran had gone to see him several months after Danny's funeral, which he'd been unable to attend. He'd been in the hospital at the time, recovering from injuries he had suffered in the same Afghan firefight that had killed his friend.

He glanced down at the pages of links, began clicking through them. The colonel had graduated West Point and gone on to achieve a sterling military career. Several articles talked about his outstanding record, his service in the Gulf War, in Iraq and Afghanistan, about the medals he had won, including a Silver Star, a Bronze Star, and a Purple Heart.

It was hard to imagine a man like that stealing chemical weapons.

Bran found no articles on the theft, which he had expected, since the information would have been highly classified. The public would not be happy to learn that military-grade weapons had been stolen and not recovered.

He looked up information on the US Army Alamo Chemical Depot, responsible for the safe and secure storage of chemical weapons stockpiled in Colorado, one of only two such installations in the country.

He glanced up as the soft fragrance of flowers drifted toward him, and saw Jessie walking into the study. He told himself the little kick he felt had nothing to do with the way her fiery, red-gold hair fell in soft waves to below her shoulders. Or the way the long-sleeved T-shirt she had changed into hugged the swell of her breasts, just the right size to fit his hands.

Bran jerked his gaze away and turned back to the computer screen. Unfortunately, Jessie rounded the desk and stood close behind him to peer over his shoulder.

His groin tightened. *Not good.* This was Danny's sister, not a woman he could trifle with and just walk away. She was special to Danny, which made her special to him.

"I see you're digging up info on the depot," she said.

"Yeah. I know it's there to destroy the country's stockpile of chemical weapons, but that's about it."

"In a nutshell, they've got fifteen thousand pounds of mustard gas, in seven hundred and eighty thousand recovered munitions. Last I checked, there were approximately fifty thousand 155 millimeter projectiles, three hundred 105 millimeter projectiles, and a hundred four-point-two-inch mortar rounds."

Impressed, he turned in the chair to look at her. "Anything else I should know?"

"The actual destruction of the weapons is contracted to a civilian corporation, Weidner Engineering. They have fourteen hundred employees assigned to the project. Year-to-date they've destroyed over 365 tons of munitions at a cost of over a billion and a half dollars. Of course that doesn't account for the stuff that's gone missing."

"How much?"

"That, I don't know. As an outsider, it isn't that easy to find out."

"Maybe not, but you've obviously done your homework."

"I'm a journalist. I need to be as accurate as possible. Add to that, I want my father's name cleared. I need as much information as I can get."

Bran nodded. "We'll find out more when we get to Colorado. I do know these are the same type of chemical weapons used in Syria against the Syrian people. If you come in contact with the stuff, it's bad news."

"At the very least, it blisters your skin and mucous membranes on contact. Breathing it can result in permanent blindness, or worst case, it reacts with the water in the air to form hydrochloric acid, which causes swelling and blocking of the lung tissue."

"Death by suffocation," Bran said.

"I remember the gruesome pictures from Syria, what it did to the children."

"Yeah. The stuff is brutal and deadly."

"It's horrible," Jessie said.

"I assume you have a file on this, information you've collected."

"I do."

"I need to see it." He rose from his chair. "In the meantime,

I'm getting hungry. Let's go see what my housekeeper's got stored in the fridge."

The look on Jessie's face said that after their gruesome conversation, food was the last thing on her mind. Her stomach rumbled as if it disagreed.

She sighed. "I haven't eaten since I left Colorado. Too much going on."

Bran sobered as he led the way to the kitchen. There was plenty going on, all right. And none of it good. Helping Jessie Kegan was far more than a protection detail. Whatever was going on involved national security.

If Colonel Kegan had been murdered, the men responsible were as deadly as the chemicals Bran and Jessie were hunting.

From now on—as spec ops soldiers liked to say—the only easy day was yesterday.

AFTER ROAST BEEF sandwiches and a cup of Campbell's Cream of Chicken soup, assembled by her ridiculously hot male host, Jessie retrieved the file she had compiled on the case and carried it in to Bran, seated once more behind the desk in his study.

As he accepted the file, he gave her left hand a pointed glance. "You never married?"

She shook her head, suddenly uneasy. "No."

"Why not?"

Tension filtered through her but she managed to smile. "Turns out my judgment of men is lousy."

"Seemed like your folks had a happy marriage."

"They did. Dad loved Mom and she was crazy about him, too. It nearly destroyed my father when she died."

"I remember Danny telling me she had a stroke. He talked about what a great mom she was."

"She really was. She was always there for all of us, kind of the bedrock of the family. I think Dad took her death even harder than Danny's. Being a soldier, he accepted that his son could be killed. It never occurred to him that Mom would die before he did."

Bran leaned back in his chair, his gaze fixed on her face. "So…no husband. No serious boyfriend, either?"

"No. Listen, if you're finished with the third degree, I'm going to bed. It's been a rough day."

His gaze sharpened. "Sorry," he said, not looking sorry at all and even more curious than before—unfortunately. "I'll see you in the morning."

"What time?" she managed to ask calmly.

"We leave at six. We can pick up something to eat on the way to the airport."

"I'll be ready. Good night, Bran. And thanks again. I really appreciate your help."

Bran casually nodded, but his beautiful blue eyes never strayed as she turned and walked away. She shouldn't have let his questions get to her. It was a dead giveaway to a guy as smart as he was that there was more to the story than she was willing to tell.

Far more.

She thought of the man whose brutality had changed her life. Jordan Duran, Jordy, he'd signed his emails, the man who was currently serving a ten-year prison sentence. She didn't like to think about him. She refused to let him control any more of her life than he already had. As she had learned to do, she pushed his image from her mind and just thanked God she was still alive.

Calm once more, she closed the guest-room door and headed over to the desk, where she'd set up her laptop. For the next half hour, she researched the town of Alamo and the surrounding area, saw that the violent crime rate, which included murder, rape, manslaughter, and armed robbery, was the highest in Colorado, one of the highest in the nation.

As a military brat, she and her family had moved from one end of the country to the other. They had been living at Fort Carson in Colorado Springs when she had graduated high school. Going to the University of Denver, only ninety minutes away, seemed a perfect fit. A little distance, a little room to grow, but still close to her family. During those four years, she had fallen in love with the Mile High City and decided to stay after graduation.

She knew a lot about Denver and Colorado Springs, but very little about the town of Alamo and the area around the army Depot. Jessie went back over the crime links she had Googled, hoping something would click in regard to the theft, but nothing seemed remotely connected to stealing chemical weapons.

Yawning, she packed up the computer so she would be ready to travel in the morning. Stripping off the long-sleeved pink T-shirt and soft brown leggings she had changed into, she headed for the bathroom to brush her teeth, then went to bed.

After the drama of the day—being followed from the airport, being shot at, meeting Brandon Garrett and his friends, and escaping a possible tail, she should have been exhausted, and she was. Still, she couldn't seem to fall asleep.

Every time she started to drift away, she saw Bran's perceptive blue eyes and wondered what he thought of her. Wondered if he found her attractive. It had been months since she had been interested in a man. After Jordy, none of her attempts at a normal relationship had worked out, and eventually she had just given up.

But Bran intrigued her. She knew what it took to become a Special Forces soldier. Knew Danny and Bran had both been Delta operators, the most elite soldiers in the world. You had to be way beyond smart, had to speak several languages and pass a battery of physical and mental tests. Their missions were so top secret it was as if Delta soldiers didn't actually exist.

She also knew that getting involved with Bran on a personal level was a terrible idea. He was exactly the heartbreaker Danny had warned her about. He was also ex-military, an adrenaline junkie who loved to be in the middle of the action. Guys like that never changed. Just as before, her judgment sucked.

As she plumped her pillow and tried to get comfortable, Jessie vowed that for once she would take her brother's very sound advice and keep her distance from Bran.

Unfortunately, now that they were working together, it would be nearly impossible to do.

Two hours later Jessie still lay awake. The sound of wind racing past the windows was usually comforting, but tonight it seemed ominous instead of relaxing, sending her thoughts back to the shooting and what she and Bran might face ahead.

Since she badly needed some sleep, she pulled on her short white terry cloth robe and padded down the hall toward the kitchen, hoping to find some chamomile tea or warm a cup of milk. The door to Bran's study stood open, and she spotted him still sitting behind his computer.

He glanced up as she paused in the doorway. "Couldn't sleep?" he asked. His hair was mussed, and the shadow of a beard darkened his jaw.

Jessie shook her head. "You either, I guess."

"No. Come on in."

She walked over to the desk. "What are you working on?"

"I've been going over the file you gave me." He tapped the thin manila folder. "I was hoping to find more in it."

"I wish I had more. The truth is, I waited too long to start digging. My dad's death hit me hard, especially after losing Mom and Danny. I couldn't seem to pull myself together. Once I did, I got angry. I knew in my heart Dad wasn't guilty. That's when I went to work."

Bran rose from his chair, file in hand. "Since we're both still awake, we might as well get started."

Jessie followed him over to a sleek dark walnut meeting table in the corner surrounded by four matching chairs. A fire flickered in the gas fireplace built into one wall. They each pulled out a chair and sat down.

Bran opened the file. "I read the initial report of the investigation—brief as it is."

"It's brief because the CID asked for an extension to delve more deeply into the charges." CID stood for Criminal Investigation Division Command, like the FBI of the military. "Because of the seriousness of the crime and the threat it posed to national security, my dad was confined to the military stockade while the balance of the investigation was completed."

"It says here, a civilian employee who works for Weidner, guy named Charles Frazier, discovered the missing munitions. The details have been redacted in the copy of the report you received."

"It's classified. As I said, being an outsider, it's hard to get information. They don't want anyone to know the quantity of chemical weapons that were stolen."

"According to this, Frazier was a computer specialist working in the division of Weidner in charge of inventory. He discovered a discrepancy and reported it to Colonel Kegan as commander of the depot." Bran glanced up from the page. "It says Colonel Kegan waited instead of reporting it. Frazier got worried. On the morning of the third day, he went directly to your father's superior, Brigadier General Samuel Holloway, at CMA."

She nodded. "That's right. Holloway is the director of Chemical Materials Activity. He oversees both the Alamo Depot and the Blue Grass Depot in Kentucky."

"According to your father's comments, he waited to report the missing weapons because he wanted to be sure the discrepancy wasn't just a clerical error, an accounting mistake of some kind. Which is what he believed, at least at first. He also stated he wanted to be sure he had all the facts. Once he was satisfied the theft was real, he planned to move forward, to find whoever was responsible and bring them to justice, which was why he began an internal investigation."

"That sounds reasonable to me," Jessie said.

"It does. Until you add the fact that Charles Frazier decided it was too dangerous to ignore the theft—which he believed the colonel was doing—and went straight to Holloway with the information. A few days later your father was apprehended—"

"Military jargon for arrested."

"And confined to the stockade at Fort Carson." Bran set the file on the table. "Apparently, CID investigators discovered an offshore account in your father's name. They also found deposits totaling a hundred thousand dollars."

Jessie felt a jolt of indignation for her father. "Someone set him up. I spoke to Charles Frazier. Since the number of missing munitions was classified, he couldn't tell me the quantity, but he said on the black market, they would be worth a great deal of money. I got the impression it was a lot more than just a hundred thousand dollars."

"Frazier tell you anything else?"

"He said it was a fluke that he discovered the theft at all. Some glitch in the system that turned up a discrepancy that most people would have missed. He followed up, and that's when he realized the weapons were no longer in storage. If he hadn't discovered it, the perpetrators would have gotten away clean."

"Why do you think Frazier went over your father's head directly to the CMA?"

"I don't know. Frazier wouldn't say, and no one I talked to was very helpful."

Bran tapped the file. "After reading this report, I have a hunch the reason they aren't being helpful is the same reason the quantity of missing weapons is redacted. The theft was a lot bigger than they want anyone to know."

Jessie felt a chill. Exactly what she was afraid of.

CHAPTER FOUR

THIN RAYS OF sunlight washed over the flat Texas landscape the following morning. Bran sat at the controls of the sleek white twin-engine Beechcraft Baron G58 parked in front of its hangar at the Dallas Executive Airport, south and a little west of downtown.

He had learned to fly after he'd left the military. Barely recovered from the bullet wounds that had forced him to leave the army—one in his thigh, one in his abdomen, and another that had taken out part of his spleen—he'd been bored and unhappy to have lost the job he was trained for.

He'd been trying to figure out what to do with his life when Chase suggested he take flying lessons. Once he'd started, he'd liked it so much he'd considered getting a plane of his own, maybe something like the single-engine Cessna that Hawk Maddox flew.

Chase had come up with the idea that Bran and Reese should share the one he owned, since it didn't get used that often. It was a beautiful plane so Bran had eagerly agreed. Once he discovered private security work was the answer to his career dilemma, the plane had come in handy.

"You belted in?" he asked Jessie.

She nodded. "All set." She settled back in the fawn-colored leather copilot's seat and glanced around the interior. "This is really nice." Besides the two people in the cockpit, the plane was equipped to carry four passengers in comfortable club seating.

"It hasn't gotten a lot of use lately. We've all been pretty busy." He started the preflight, checking the electrical system, looking for any warning lights, checking the GPS navigation, checking the oil and fuel levels.

He'd already done the walk-around, inspecting the body for damage, looking for fluid leaks: oil, fuel, hydraulics.

"We're all set." He put on his headphones and waited for Jessie to put on hers. Settling back, he got on the radio and spoke to the tower, then began taxiing into position on the runway.

Once cleared for takeoff, the plane began to roll down the tarmac, the propellers humming as the engine picked up speed. Jessie studied the landscape outside the window as the plane lifted into the air and climbed to flying altitude. She didn't say much until the city of Dallas disappeared in the distance behind them.

"As a rule, I'm not crazy about flying," she said. "But I have to admit this is great."

He smiled. "Glad you're enjoying it. For me flying's mostly a convenient way to get around. Helluva lot better than going through all the hassle at the airport."

"That's for sure."

It was an easy flight, just a few thunderheads beginning to develop, which he was able to skirt by slight course alterations. The patchwork quilt of farmland below held Jessie's attention, giving Bran a chance to study her.

She really was pretty, he thought, and she was smart. There were plenty of beautiful women in Texas, but when you added brains and a dynamite figure, it was a combination Bran found hard to resist.

But he owed a debt to Danny Kegan that he could never

repay. A one-night hookup with his sister or anything remotely similar was out of the question. His sigh went unnoticed beneath the hum of the engines.

Near the halfway point, he landed at a small executive
airport in Amarillo and had the fuel topped off while they
went into the terminal restaurant for a pit stop and something to eat. Sandwiches and soft drinks and a couple of
bags of chips and they were airborne again. A short flight
north and a little west and he landed at Cutter Aviation, a
private airport a few miles west of Colorado Springs.

The executive terminal, where he'd made arrangements
for a hangar to store the plane, was housed in a log building
furnished with brown leather sofas, photos of the surrounding snow-capped mountains, and bronze sculptures of wild-
life, a place perfectly suited to its location in the Rockies.

Bran had a rental car waiting, a big dark gray metallic
Ford Expedition. He grabbed the handle of his carry-on,
tossed the black canvas duffel that held his gear over one
shoulder, and urged Jessie, towing her own suitcase, toward the parking lot.

"I booked two rooms for us at the Holiday Inn," she said
as he loaded their luggage into the back of the vehicle. "I
hope that works for you."

He paused to take the Glock out of his canvas duffel,
clipped the holster to his belt and pulled his Henley out to
cover it, then loaded the bag into the back.

"Call and cancel," he said. "I've got a suite for us at the
Cheyenne Mountain Resort. It's up in the hills not far from
Fort Carson." Apparently she hadn't figured out that separate hotel rooms weren't an option. People had been shooting at her. He wasn't letting her get that far away.

"It's an hour drive from there to the depot," he said,
opening the passenger door. "But we'll also be spending

time at the base, which is fairly close, so we might as well stay somewhere nice."

"You're spending a lot of money. I didn't expect that. I'll find a way to repay you."

He stopped walking and turned back. "I told you before—I owe your brother my life. You don't owe me anything and especially not money. I've got plenty of it, far more than we'll need." He stared down at her. "All right?"

She shrugged. "I guess so." She was a foot shorter than he was, petite, but she wasn't frail. He usually went for tall, buxom women. They just seemed less fragile, a better fit for a guy his size. But there was something about Jessie that drew him.

"No more talk about money," he said to make the point. "Okay?"

Her chin went up. "Fine."

He bit back a smile. She was really cute. Too bad she didn't look more like her silver-haired father and less like her brother, whose good looks had appealed to women around the world.

They belted themselves into their seats, and he started the engine.

"You don't want to talk about the money you're spending," she said. "So what do you want to talk about? The case, I hope."

He grinned. "Why don't we talk about why you don't have a serious boyfriend. That should be interesting."

Instead of the snarky remark he expected, Jessie's face went pale. She glanced out the window. "It's not a good story."

Bran silently cursed. Dammit, he hadn't intended to make her uncomfortable, and it was really none of his business. "Hey, I'm sorry. I was just kidding around. You don't have to tell me if you don't want to."

She fell silent and he didn't press her, just set the nav system for the Cheyenne Mountain Resort and drove out of the parking lot.

Following GPS directions, he found US 24 East and headed for the hotel.

"Something happened three years ago," Jessie said as the SUV rolled along. "I started corresponding with this guy I met through an online dating site. His name was Jordan Duran."

"Why the hell would you need to go online to meet someone? Any guy with eyes in his head would want to ask you out."

Jessie gave him the faintest smile. "I thought I might meet someone more interesting than the men I seemed to attract."

He kind of got that. Having sex with a good-looking woman wasn't the same as actually enjoying her company. He didn't do relationships mostly because very few women understood him and the kind of life he led, and he rarely understood them.

Jessie leaned back in her seat. "Jordy came from a family of teachers, nice, down-to-earth sort of people. Or at least that's what he said in his emails. He had a way of making me smile, and I really liked that. According to his bio, he was thirty-four, six feet tall, four years of college, looked good in his photo. We were going to meet for lunch but the night before, a man followed me out of the grocery store. I didn't realize what was happening until it was too late."

The muscles across Bran's stomach clenched. "What happened?" Because it sounded as if—Jessie being Danny's sister—it definitely *was* his business.

"I guess he used something to knock me out. I remember struggling, remember him pressing something over my mouth and nose, then nothing. The next morning, I woke up bound and gagged, locked in a basement somewhere. That night and the next, the guy showed up in a ski mask. He... touched me. He described in detail what he was going to do to me after we 'got to know each other better.'"

"Christ, Jessie."

"To make a long story short, the third day, I managed to escape. The police caught him and put him in jail. End of story."

No way was that the end, but he didn't say that.

"So you can see why I don't have a boyfriend and why I don't like to talk about it," Jessie finished.

Oh, he saw, all right. And the fury he was feeling wasn't going to disappear anytime soon.

He turned onto CO 115 and kept driving. "One last question." He had a thousand but for now he'd settle for one. "Was this the same guy you met online?"

"Yes. Jordy wasn't his real name. His real name was Ray Cummings, but it was him."

His hands tightened around the steering wheel. "So where the fuck is this guy now?"

"That's two questions," she said. But his hard look convinced her to answer. "He's serving ten years in prison— where my testimony helped put him. I wasn't the first girl he kidnapped, but I was the last. Now can we change the subject?"

He didn't want to. He wanted to know more about what had happened, what the bastard had done to her, wanted to be sure she'd come out of it all right. But he had upset her enough for today.

"All right," he said. "Let's talk about the case."

She settled in the seat and her shoulders relaxed. She understood he was letting her off the hook. She didn't know he was far from finished with Jordan Duran/Ray Cummings.

In time, she would figure it out.

For the moment, Cummings was in jail, and they needed to find a load of missing chemical weapons. First things first, he always said.

CHAPTER FIVE

THE RESORT, NESTLED at the base of the Rockies, was a lovely spot, Jessie thought as they walked into the suite they had been assigned. Built on two hundred acres, it offered its guests a golf course, tennis courts, a fitness center, hiking trails, and beautiful views of the mountains.

The suite was big and roomy, with a rock fireplace, comfortable overstuffed furniture, and a wet bar with a refrigerator. A coffee maker sat on the counter. Windows wrapped around the living room, overlooking the golf course and mountains beyond.

"You take the bedroom," Bran said. "The sofa unfolds into a bed, and I need to sleep out here where I can keep an eye on things."

Her mind went back to the shooting, and a shudder ran through her. She wondered if the men in the black SUV were still in Dallas. It didn't seem likely they would know she had left with Bran Garrett and that she was currently back in Colorado Springs.

Of course, as soon as she returned to the base and started asking questions, her whereabouts would be more than clear.

Bran pulled the file out of his carry-on, carried it over to the dining table, and pulled out a chair. Jessie joined him. He opened the folder, shuffled aside the investigative report he had read last night, picked up her father's autopsy, and studied the pages.

"I assume you've seen this." He pointed to the report. "Cause of death is listed as a heart attack. I don't see anything here that looks suspicious."

"I know they killed him. I'm not sure how they did it, but my dad had the heart of an elephant. His last physical was only a few months before he died. He called me to brag about how well he had done. He told me the doctor said he was in superior physical condition. Even his cholesterol levels were good. We laughed about it because I had been bugging him to eat less red meat."

"Things like that *can* happen out of the blue," Bran said. "Maybe the shock of being accused of such serious crimes then locked behind bars was too much for him."

"My dad was a soldier. He'd faced enemy fire in combat. He was in charge of a huge operation at the depot. He was used to handling stress."

Bran looked down at the autopsy. "We'll talk to the medical examiner, ask him if there is any possibility the heart attack could have been artificially triggered, see what he has to say."

"Actually, I've been thinking of having my father's body exhumed. The idea makes me nauseous, but I know how important Dad's reputation was to him. He would want me to do everything in my power to prove his innocence."

Bran leaned back in his chair, his brilliant blue eyes assessing. "You understand at this point your theory is purely conjecture. You have nothing to substantiate your claim."

"Even if I'm wrong, at least I'd know."

Bran scrubbed a hand over his face. "The fact you have people willing to shoot you to keep you from investigating is enough to make me think there's a chance you could be right. After we talk to the ME, you can decide if you want to have the colonel's body exhumed. Painful as it's going to be for you, maybe it will help clear the air."

They discussed the case into the early evening, then Bran ordered room service, steak for him, chicken for her, salad for both of them. He also ordered a bottle of red wine. When they finished the meal, he folded out the sofa bed in the living room, which was already made up with sheets, and grabbed a blanket out of the closet.

Jessie helped him spread the blanket over the mattress and retrieve the pillows. "Have a good night," she said when they finished. "I'll see you in the morning."

"Good night."

There was a powder room off the entry for Bran to use, which meant she had privacy until tomorrow when he would need to use the shower in her en-suite bathroom.

She yawned as she closed the door, more exhausted than she had expected. She fell asleep quickly and slept far better than she had the night before, then rose at the first gray light of dawn. She took a shower and got ready for the day, dressed in a conservative dark brown skirt suit and heeled pumps, then quietly cracked open the door to the living room.

Bran was already up, standing with his back to her, one hand on his hip, the other pressing his cell phone against his ear. A pair of white cotton briefs that hugged his round behind was all he had on.

Jessie's mouth went dry. His suntanned back was smooth, except for a jagged scar on one side, and ridged with solid muscle. Bands of muscle defined his shoulders and arms, and long sinewy legs tapered down to toned calves and narrow feet.

She told herself to close the door before Bran caught

her staring at him like a juicy piece of meat, but instead she just stood there, her heart pounding, her breathing a little ragged.

She was just pulling herself under control when he turned, the phone still pressed to his ear. Jessie froze. Her gaze shot to the heavy bulge at the front of his briefs, and she felt a rush of heat so hot it made her dizzy. Muscular pecs and six-pack abs. A lean, hard-muscled chest and amazing biceps. Desire hit her so hard she swayed on her feet.

She didn't move till Bran jerked the blanket off his makeshift bed and wrapped it around his waist, knocking her out of her self-imposed trance and flushing her face with embarrassment.

"Sorry," she managed to breathlessly whisper, then stepped back and slammed the door. *Ohmygod, ohmygod.* She hadn't felt the least attraction to a man for so long she'd forgotten what it was like. Correction, she had never felt the jolt of desire she had felt looking at Brandon Garrett. *Ohmygod.*

She told herself he was probably used to that kind of reaction from a woman, or at least the women who had seen him nearly naked. Jessie sank down on the bed. What could she possibly say to him? How could she explain?

But no words of explanation popped into her head.

Since she couldn't hide in the bedroom all day, and because Bran undoubtedly wanted to take a shower, she inhaled a deep breath, opened the door, and walked out into the living room.

"Sorry about that," she said.

He had pulled on his jeans, but the rest of him was still gloriously bare. "No problem. I should have grabbed one of those terry cloth robes in the bathroom."

She just nodded. "Yeah." Her fingers curled into the palms of her hands as she walked past him toward the counter where he had brewed a pot of coffee.

"Mind if I use the shower?" he asked.

"Of course not. You're paying for the room." When he opened his mouth, she held up a hand. "Sorry, no more talk about money."

"Exactly."

She took a mug down from the cabinet above the sink and filled it with coffee, her hands still a bit unsteady.

"Why don't you order us something to eat?" Bran suggested as he crossed the room toward the bedroom. "I won't be too long."

"Bacon and eggs?" she asked.

"Sounds great." As he disappeared through the door and closed it behind him, Jessie sank down onto one of the chairs at the dining table, coffee mug gripped tightly in her hands. At least now she knew the abduction hadn't completely destroyed her desire for the opposite sex.

Or at least one member of the opposite sex. She grimaced. She just wished the man who had rekindled her long-dead fire wasn't Brandon Garrett.

BRAN TURNED ON the shower, set the nozzle to cold, and climbed in beneath the icy spray. He clenched his jaw, fighting to block a memory of the look on Jessie's pretty face when he had caught her watching him. Trying to block the erection he got every time the image reappeared in his head.

Bran knew women. He knew when a woman wanted him. He swore softly, cursing the fate that had brought the two of them together, putting them both in a situation that could only get worse.

So far he had managed to suppress the desire he'd felt

from the moment Jessie had walked into his office. With her fire-touched blond hair and fine features, she was beautiful. He liked her body and admired her brain. In a softly feminine way, she was sexy as hell, and he wanted her— no doubt about it.

But aside from the erotic dream he'd had about her last night, he'd been doing an admirable job of controlling his lust.

Until this morning. When the flush in her cheeks and the heat in her eyes had made it clear that the desire he felt was returned. She wanted him. Which meant he had to be the strong one because no way could he have her and just walk away.

Jessie wasn't the type he usually slept with, women who didn't require exclusivity and didn't expect to give it in return.

He was fairly sure Jessie hadn't been with a man since she was abducted. He sure as hell didn't want to be the first, didn't want to deal with whatever trauma she had experienced, maybe make it worse.

He turned off the freezing water, reached for a towel and ran it over the goose bumps on his skin. At least the bathroom was warm when he stepped out of the shower and towel-dried his hair.

Instead of thinking of Jessie, he needed to focus on the case. He needed to find the people behind the stolen chemical weapons and clear the colonel's name. Once he'd done that, she could go back to Denver and he could go back to Dallas, to the life he'd had before. Jessie would be safe from him, and he would be safe from temptation.

He'd dish out retribution to Duran/Cummings when the time was right.

Determined to stay focused, he grabbed one of the white

terry cloth robes hanging on the bathroom door and slid it on, walked out of the bedroom into the living room.

"I need the rest of my clothes," he said to Jessie, who sat at the dining table. He ignored the flush that rose in her cheeks, rummaged through his carry-on, grabbed a rust-colored Henley and a pair of clean underwear, and walked back into the bedroom to put his jeans back on.

When he came out again, room service was busily setting breakfast on the dining table. It smelled delicious. He looked at Jessie, noticed sunlight glinting on the ruby strands in her long blond hair, the soft blush in her cheeks, and felt a tightening in his groin. Inwardly he cursed.

Looked like he'd be taking a lot more cold showers before this was over.

CHAPTER SIX

JESSIE FIDGETED IN her seat as Bran pulled up to the main gate of US Army Fort Carson. The base was the home of the Fourth Infantry Division, among various and sundry other units including the Tenth Special Forces Group. Bran flashed his retired military ID, and the solider at the gate looked for his name on the admissions list.

"You phoned ahead," Jessie said to him.

Bran just shrugged the muscled shoulders that were now imprinted in her brain. "10th Special Forces is here. I know some people. I called a few I thought might be able to help us."

"I should have figured," she said. She had called and set up meetings at the ME's office as well as her father's military counsel. Apparently, Bran had made a few calls of his own.

"I see here you'll be checking a weapon," the soldier said.

"That's correct." It was illegal for anyone to carry on base.

"Drive straight to the armory. Do you know where that is?" The guard was short and stocky, in combat boots and military fatigues.

"I've got someone here who knows her way around," Bran said, tipping his head toward Jessie.

But it had been years since she had lived on the base.

She'd come back to Colorado Springs for her father's funeral, then returned to Fort Carson a month ago when she'd started her investigation. At the time, she'd hit nothing but a string of dead ends. Back in Denver, she'd kept working the case, making phone calls out of her apartment, digging up facts on the internet. Now she was back at the base.

The guard waved Bran through and, following Jessie's directions, he drove the SUV down O'Connell Boulevard.

They made a quick stop at the armory, where Bran left his unloaded Glock, then climbed back into the vehicle. He was wearing a dark brown tweed blazer with his jeans and Henley. He looked good. Sexual awareness trickled through her, making her stomach flutter. Too damned good.

"I trained at Fort Bragg," he said as the big SUV rolled down the road. "Never made it to Fort Carson." He glanced at the soldiers marching on the parade ground as they drove past. "Looks like a good place to be stationed."

Jessie shrugged. "Good as any. The population is around fourteen thousand, a town in itself. The scenery is better than most, the weather's good, and there are lots of outdoor activities."

The landscape was mostly flat and arid, but the area around the base was ringed by rolling hills covered with juniper and sage. Snow-topped mountains rose in the distance not far away. The end of October temperatures remained in the low sixties, but at night it dipped into the thirties.

Jessie directed Bran to the Army Community Hospital, where the medical examiner's office was located. He parked in the lot and they walked into a three-story tan building, part of the base medical complex. Jessie had never met the doctor who had done her father's autopsy. She had spoken to him on the phone, but had gotten mostly a recitation of what had been in the report.

Bran held the door open for her, and they walked up to the front desk, where he spoke to the female soldier behind the counter.

"Captain Brandon Garrett, First Special Forces Operational Detachment-Delta, retired. This is Jessica Kegan, Colonel James Kegan's daughter. We have an appointment with Dr. Matthew Dillon."

"Yes, sir. I'll let him know you're here." The woman, a slender blonde in a perfectly tailored dark blue uniform jacket and skirt, headed down the hall. A few minutes later she returned. "Dr. Dillon will see you now."

Jessie followed the woman, Bran walking behind her, into an office with a window looking out on low rolling hills. The doctor rose from behind his desk to greet them. Dillon was a slim, fine-boned man, early fifties, with sandy brown hair.

"Captain," the doctor said to Bran.

"Retired," Bran reminded him. "It's just Brandon now." The men shook hands, and the doctor turned to Jessie.

"Ms. Kegan, it's nice to put a face with the voice on the phone. I'm sorry the circumstances aren't better. Let me start by saying I'm sorry for your loss."

"Thank you."

"Have a seat," the doctor said, gesturing to the visitor chairs opposite his desk.

For the next few minutes, they discussed the autopsy that had been performed on her father, which led to her theory that he had been murdered.

"You read the report, Ms. Kegan," Dr. Dillon said. "Your father complained of nausea and stomach pains and was taken to the infirmary. Less than an hour later, he suffered a massive heart attack and died. There was no sign of anything other than acute myocardial infarction. I'm sorry. I realize, under the circumstances, this has been a very troubling time for you, but you need to deal with the facts."

"Did the autopsy show what caused the stomach pain?" Bran asked.

"The nausea started after lunch. It was assumed to be a digestive problem or an intestinal virus, but it turned out to be a symptom of his impending heart attack. Unfortunately, by the time he was discovered in his room, it was too late to revive him."

A sound of pain slipped from her throat as Jessie imagined her father dying alone. She steeled herself. She had known this wouldn't be easy.

"Is it possible that at some point my father could have been given some kind of drug that could have triggered the attack?"

The doctor frowned. "As I said, the colonel was found unresponsive in his hospital bed. The physician on duty reported cause of death as congestive heart failure. The autopsy supports that diagnosis. There was nothing on his tox screen that would indicate his death was anything other than natural causes."

"But the tox screens you ran were limited, were they not?" Bran pressed. "That would be typical."

The doctor's irritation grew. "Unfortunately, there is no way we can test for every drug on the face of the earth."

Bran wisely let the subject drop. They needed this man's cooperation. No use making him angry unless there was a reason.

"What about security cameras?" Jessie asked.

"There are cameras in the hall outside the cells. Unfortunately, the day he died, the camera inside the cell was temporarily out of service."

Jessie flashed a look at Bran. *See? I told you this was all too convenient.*

"Do you have a list of the visitors who came to see Colonel Kegan while he was incarcerated?" Bran asked.

"I'm sure Major Anson, his military counsel, was provided with a list of all visitors. The major would also have had access to any security camera video." The doctor rose from his chair. "If there isn't anything further…"

Bran rose and so did Jessie. "There is one more thing," she said. "I'd like to request my father's body be exhumed. What procedures do I need to follow to make that happen?"

The doctor's sandy brown eyebrows drew together. Clearly he wasn't happy with the direction the conversation was taking, an implication he might have missed something when he'd done his job.

"You would need grounds for such an action before disinterment could be approved," the doctor said. "I'm afraid at this time, there's nothing I can do to help you in that regard."

Jessie straightened. "If we need grounds, we'll find them. Thank you for your time, Dr. Dillon."

The doctor remained standing as they walked out the door.

"I was hoping we'd get something a little more concrete," Bran said darkly as they made their way to the parking lot.

"Maybe we did. The question you asked about the nausea my father experienced? The way the report read, I didn't really give it that much thought. But what if someone put something in his food that would make him sick enough to get him transported to the hospital? If they planned to kill him, it would be a lot easier once he was out of his cell."

Bran walked her to the passenger side of the Expedition and pulled open the door. "The thought occurred to me. If the heart attack was actually induced, it would almost have to be done away from his cell."

"That's right. Even it they disabled the video camera, whoever gave him the drug would probably have to sign the visitor registry."

Bran nodded, playing the theory out. "So they feed him something that makes him sick and give him the drug at the hospital or on the way there."

"Exactly. Which means until we find out something different, it's still possible he was murdered."

FOLLOWING JESSIE'S DIRECTIONS, Bran turned onto Titus Boulevard, rounded the traffic circle onto Sheridan, and eventually pulled up in front of 1633 Mekong Street. Building 6222, the Judge Advocate's Office, was a no-nonsense two-story white stucco building a little less than two miles from the ME's office.

The military counsel Jessie's father had chosen was a major named Thomas Anson. According to what Jessie had told Bran, she had visited the attorney several times and spoken at length with him on the phone. Fifteen minutes early for their appointment, they were shown into his office to wait.

Both of them took seats in front of his desk, and a few minutes later Anson walked in and closed the door. They both rose to greet him.

"It's good to see you, Jessie." Anson smiled and reached out to take hold of her hand, clasping it in both of his and holding it a little longer than necessary. His greeting held the kind of warmth Bran understood. Clearly, the major, in his thirties, brown-haired and good-looking, would like to get to know Colonel Kegan's daughter a whole lot better.

Not going to happen, Bran thought, feeling an unexpected surge of possessiveness. For the moment, Jessie was under his protection. The look in the major's dark eyes did not sit well.

Jessie made the introductions. "Thomas, this is Brandon Garrett. He was a close friend of my brother's. They served together in Afghanistan."

The major looked him over, taking in his height and build. "I understand Daniel Kegan was Special Forces. Shall I assume you were, as well?"

"That's right."

"It's good to meet you." But it was clear he saw Bran as a rival and he wasn't pleased. The men shook hands, then the major took a seat behind his desk. "What can I do for you?"

"We have some additional questions about the investigation," Jessie said. "Also, we need a list of the visitors who came to see my father, particularly those who were there the day he died. I was told you have that information."

The major released a weary sigh. "I was hoping you'd be able to deal with what happened and move on with your life, Jessie. Obviously that hasn't happened."

"My father was innocent, Thomas. I intend to prove it."

"You must believe I did my best to defend the charges against him. Espionage, larceny, and treason are extremely serious offenses. Everything pointed to your father's guilt, particularly the hundred thousand dollars in his offshore bank account."

"He explained that to you," she said. "That's what you told me. Someone set up the account in his name and put the money in to make it look like he was involved in the theft."

"Yes, that's what he said."

"How did the CID find the account?" Bran asked.

"They had a warrant to search his home. MPs took his

computer, among other evidence. The bank information was found on his laptop."

Bran leaned forward. "Very convenient, wouldn't you say? A secret bank account worth a cool hundred grand sitting right there on his computer—the payoff for deadly chemical weapons possibly worth a hundred times that much on the black market, maybe a whole lot more?"

Anson's jaw subtly tightened. "Even if you're right, there's no way to prove it."

"I guess we'll see," Bran said.

"The ME mentioned you had access to the security camera video," Jessie said. "I assume you've looked at it."

The major's gaze swung back to her and the warmth returned. "Of course. There was only a limited amount of footage, but I didn't see anything unusual."

"What about the stolen munitions?" Bran asked. "Have they been recovered yet?"

"Unfortunately, the weapons are still missing. No sign of them has turned up so far."

"Got any idea how much inventory was taken?" he asked.

"The information is classified so even if I knew—which I don't—I couldn't tell you."

"Who's leading the investigation?" Bran pressed.

"General Holloway, head of CMA. He's working closely with the project manager at Weidner to locate them."

"Weidner Engineering is the civilian operation in charge of weapons destruction," Bran said just to clarify.

"That is correct." Anson's gaze returned to Jessie and softened. "I'm sorry this happened, Jessie. Your father chose me to represent him on the basis of my reputation. He could have hired civilian counsel, but he believed strongly in the military system of justice."

"I know he did. I'm sure he had every confidence in you, Thomas."

"Unfortunately, aside from what he told me, I have no way of knowing whether he was innocent or guilty. Either way, it was my job to defend him. I wish I'd had a chance to dig deeper into his case, perhaps find something that would corroborate his story. As it happened, time ran out."

"I don't believe time simply ran out, Major," she said. "I believe someone murdered him. In order to prove it, we need that list of visitors. We may also need to exhume his body."

Anson blinked, obviously surprised. "You would need some sort of grounds for that."

"I understand. Once we have them, will you handle it for me?"

The major breathed out slowly and rose from his chair. "I'll help if I can. It's the least I can do."

CHAPTER SEVEN

THEY COULDN'T GET in to see General Holloway, her father's superior, until he returned from a meeting at the Blue Grass Depot in Kentucky.

In the meantime, Jessie set up an appointment with the project manager for Weidner, a man named Robert De La Garza, for ten o'clock the next morning. She also hoped to speak to Charles Frazier again. Frazier said he'd reported the missing munitions directly to the CMA because her father hadn't acted swiftly enough. He was concerned the weapons were a threat to national security.

She wanted Bran to question him, see if he could get something more out of him.

Over cheesesteak sandwiches and fries during a late lunch at Charley's on the base, they took a cursory look at the visitors list, but nothing jumped out at either one of them. A few of the names were unfamiliar, people her father knew that Jessie had never met. They needed to follow up on those, but equally important was discovering who had contact with her father before his heart attack.

Kitchen stewards and orderlies, nurses, even doctors couldn't be overlooked.

"You realize you could be following a wild-goose chase," Bran reminded her as they finished the last of their meals and began to pack up paper cups and soiled wrappers.

"I know I could be wrong, but I just don't think I am."

He tossed the trash in the can. "I believe in following

your gut. We'll keep working our latest theory, see what turns up."

Jessie flashed him a grateful smile. "Thanks for sticking with me on this."

He just nodded.

Before they left the base, Bran stopped to pick up his weapon at the armory. It was late in the afternoon when the SUV rolled along Club House Drive, heading back to the resort.

"Besides going over the main list of visitors," Bran said, "we need to find out who else came in contact with your father that last day."

Jessie sighed. "It's not going to be easy."

"We'll start on it tomorrow. I think we've done enough for today."

Weariness washed over her. "It's after five. I could really use a glass of wine." She summoned a tired smile. "Scratch that. I'd kill for a cosmo."

Bran chuckled. "We can do that. Too early for supper, but I could use a snack of some kind." Instead of heading for the building that housed their second-floor suite, Bran drove up in front of the entrance to the resort and parked the SUV.

As they walked into the open, high-ceilinged lobby with its gray rock walls and heavy wooden beams, Jessie was reminded that today was October 31. Jack-o'-lanterns flickered on tables, orange and black crepe paper draped from ceilings, gauzy spiderwebs clung to walls, and the staff all wore costumes.

"Halloween," Jessie said. "My least favorite holiday."

"What?" Bran grinned. "You don't like ghosts and goblins?"

"Devils and monsters and ghouls? Are you kidding me? When I was little, some of the costumes people wore freaked me out. Though I did like trick-or-treating, getting all that free candy."

Bran led her into the bar, which was also decorated in orange and black. They sat down in front of a window looking over the pool toward the mountains. A candle flickered in a minia-ture pumpkin in the middle of the table. The room was about half full, many of the customers wearing costumes or masks.

A waitress dressed as a pirate wench in a low-cut white cotton blouse, black corset, and very short, red gathered skirt came by to take their orders. Long dark hair hung down her back, and her bosom nearly spilled over the top of her blouse.

The waitress gave Bran a thorough glance and smiled. "Happy Halloween. What can I get you?"

Jessie had a hunch the woman was offering more than a drink, but Bran didn't seem to notice.

"Cosmo for the lady," he said. "Club soda with a lime for me."

Jessie's gaze shot to his face. "Seriously?"

He just smiled. "And bring us an order of those wings that guy over there is eating." He glanced at Jessie. "Any-thing else you want?"

She just shook her head.

The waitress smiled at Bran. "I'll be right back." She sa-shayed away, hips swaying, but Bran's gaze didn't follow.

"You're not drinking," Jessie said.

"I don't drink when I'm working. The glass of wine I had last night was it till this is over. Add to that, I'm carrying."

Carrying. For an instant, she had forgotten it wasn't long ago people were shooting at her. That, and the reminder she was nothing more than a debt he believed he owed her brother, did nothing to heighten her mood.

Bran glanced around at their colorful surroundings. "My brothers and I used to love Halloween. Mom would let us pick our own costumes, and we all tried to outdo each other to see which of us could look the scariest."

"I'm more a Thanksgiving and Christmas person my-self. I look forward to the holiday season every year." The thought sobered her. She wouldn't be having Thanksgiving or Christmas with her father this year. Her mom was gone. Her brother, Danny. Now her dad. She would face the holidays alone. She felt a quick burn behind her eyes and glanced away, hoping Bran wouldn't notice.

He reached over and covered her hand where it rested on top of the table. "Hey, I can see where your thoughts just went. You're welcome at our house. Chase and his wife, Harper, are planning to make a big Thanksgiving dinner. They're newlyweds, and Harper is excited to be hosting. There'll be other people there too, friends of the family. For Christmas, we're all flying down to the family ranch out in the Texas Hill Country. It's real pretty out there."

She wiped an unexpected tear from her cheek. "That's really nice of you, but I'm sure I'll find something to do." She managed a half-hearted smile. "I'm just not used to Dad being gone, you know? It doesn't seem quite real."

She toyed with the paper napkin the waitress had set in front of her. "Dad was my rock. He was always there when I needed him. I miss him every day." She looked Bran straight in the face. "I'm going to clear his name, Bran. No matter what it takes."

He squeezed her hand. "We're only getting started. The next few days should be interesting."

The drinks and wings came. Bran helped himself, and they talked and began to relax. She probably shouldn't be drinking because Bran was looking better and better. She wanted to reach out and brush back the curl of dark hair that had fallen over his forehead. She wanted to run her hands over all those glorious muscles beneath his shirt.

Inwardly she sighed. She didn't have sex with men she

had only just met, no matter how attractive they were. After Ray Cummings, she wasn't sure she would ever have sex again—though she had tried on two separate occasions. Guys she had been dating for a while and believed their relationship might be going somewhere. Both attempts had been disastrous, embarrassing for both of them and especially her.

She finished her cosmo and was thinking about ordering another when Bran rose abruptly from his chair.

"Time to go," he said, but the wings he'd ordered were only half gone.

"What is it?"

"Not sure. Couple guys came in after we did. Fellow wearing a Frankenstein mask and the guy next to him with a skeleton face. They're in jeans and sneakers, not costumes, and they seemed a little too interested in us. Don't look at them. Just get up and let's go."

Jessie stood and started walking. Bran tossed some bills on the table to cover the drinks, and a sizable tip, and they crossed the room to the door.

"Keep walking," Bran said. "I'll be right behind you." He held back long enough to see if the men were following, then caught up with her a few paces later.

"They were paying their tab, getting ready to leave. Head for the car." They walked hurriedly in that direction, Bran clicked the door locks, and they climbed inside. His hand went automatically to the Glock clipped to his belt beneath his shirt, then he started the engine.

They drove out of the lot, following the road around the main building to the structure where they were staying. Hurriedly, they climbed the wooden stairs to the outdoor corridor that led to the rooms.

Bran stopped her at the door to the suite. "Wait here."

He pulled his pistol and went inside, came out a few seconds later, his jacket off, his gun reholstered.

"All clear. Go in and lock the door. Don't open it for anyone but me. I'll be right back."

Jessie walked into the room and Bran closed the door. She counted to ten, then turned the knob and cracked the door enough to see what was going on in the corridor. Bran had almost reached the staircase. He took a quick look over the railing, then flattened himself behind one of the wooden pillars supporting the roof.

Jessie could hear the sound of quiet footfalls coming up to the second floor, and her pulse slammed into gear. She glanced around the suite in search of a weapon, wished she had the revolver she kept for self-defense in her apartment. She found a black, long-handled LED flashlight in Bran's gear bag and raced back to the door.

Through the crack, she saw two men top the stairs, one around six feet, with what looked like a tattoo on the side of his neck and dark brown hair pulled back in a man bun. The other guy was way taller, a mountain of a man, thick-shouldered and muscular, with a bald head and straggly blond beard. Each held a semiautomatic pistol.

Jessie's heart raced as Bran stepped out from behind the pillar, grabbed the guy with the tattoo by the arm and twisted, wrenching the gun out of his hand, sending it flying. Bran spun and shot his leg out in a sideways kick that smashed against the bald man's wrist, knocking his pistol into the air. The gun flew over the railing of the balcony, and the fight was on.

Gripping the flashlight, Jessie ran toward the men as Bran threw a series of punches that sent the tattooed guy careening backward, crashing to the floor of the corridor. Bran whirled to face the bald man, ducking a sharp, heavy blow and throwing a powerful punch that buried fist-deep in the man's stomach, doubling him over.

The tattooed man shoved to his feet and charged, and Jessie swung the heavy LED flashlight, hitting him in the head and sending him staggering into the wall. His man bun came loose, and his hair fell down to his shoulders. Swearing foully, he pushed to his feet and rushed her, stopped before he reached her when he saw the fight was nearly over and Bran was winning.

With another foul curse, he spun and ran in the opposite direction, toward a set of stairs at the far end of the hall.

Bran was still throwing punches when one of the doors along the corridor flew open and a slender woman with a little girl in a pink princess costume and an adorable little boy in a plush, black-and-yellow leopard outfit walked out into the hall.

Everything happened at once. A knife appeared in the bald, bearded man's hand. His arm shot toward the little boy and wrapped around his neck, yanking him off his feet.

"Teddy!" his mother screamed as the bald man held the squirming child against his thick chest, the blade of his knife pressed against the little boy's throat.

"Nobody move! Do what I say and the boy won't get hurt!"

So far Bran hadn't pulled his weapon. Jessie thought he didn't want to escalate the situation. Now his hand hovered over the pistol grip.

"The boy is coming with me to the parking lot," the bald man said. In the lot below, a car engine roared to life. "When I get there, I'll let him go. Anybody tries to interfere, I slit the kid's throat." He looked hard at Bran. "You understand?"

Bran inhaled deeply, then slowly released the breath he'd taken and appeared to relax, but Jessie recognized the tension in the muscles across his shoulders and the back of his neck.

"No one will interfere," Bran said calmly. "But I'll be right behind you all the way to the parking lot."

Teddy was crying, calling for his mother as the big bald man hauled him toward the stairs.

"My baby," the woman sobbed, holding on to her little girl, tears streaming down her cheeks. "Please don't let him hurt my baby."

"Stay here," Bran commanded. "Stay with her, Jessie."

Jessie managed to nod, the flashlight shaking in her hand. When the bald man was halfway down the stairs, Bran drew his weapon and followed, and Jessie and the mother ran for the railing to see what was happening.

Tires screeched as a white pickup truck skidded to a stop at the bottom of the stairs and the passenger door flew open.

"Toss your weapon!" the bald man shouted at Bran.

Bran leveled the gun at the man's bald head. "Not gonna happen. Let the boy go and you can leave."

Silence fell. The truck engine idled.

"Holster your pistol and I'll let the boy go. Otherwise he comes with me."

With little choice, Bran holstered his gun. The man tossed the little boy the few feet between them and ran for the truck, and Bran caught the child in his arms. The pickup roared away, leaving the smell of burning rubber in its wake, and Jessie breathed a shaky sigh of relief.

"Thank the good Lord," the mother whispered, smoothing blond curls back from her daughter's forehead and wiping tears from her cheeks.

Bran propped the little boy against his shoulder and started back toward the stairs. "Hey, buddy. Everything's okay." Teddy burrowed into his neck, his chubby arms tight around him. Watching Bran with the child, Jessie felt a pinch in her heart.

"Your mama's right up there." Bran pointed toward the railing. "See her?"

"Mama!" Teddy reached up to her, waving his arms in the air.

"Teddy!"

"Go on," Jessie said to the mother. "I'll watch your daughter till you get back." The woman raced down the stairs, meeting Bran and her son halfway.

"He's okay," Bran said. "Just a little shook-up, is all. I'll carry him the rest of the way up for you."

They climbed the stairs together, and at the top, Bran handed little Teddy into his mother's arms. The little girl wrapped her arms around her mother's legs.

"I'm Kira," the woman said tearfully. "This is Teddy and my daughter is Mary Ellen. Thank you for what you did. Thank you both so much."

Bran said nothing. If the men hadn't come after Jessie, none of it would have happened.

"Shouldn't we call the police?" Kira asked.

"Where's your husband?" Jessie asked.

"He's in a meeting. He's here for a medical conference. We decided to make it a family vacation."

"We're checking out," Bran said. "Those men won't be back once we're gone. Be better for us if you didn't call the cops. They'll want to talk to us, and we need to get out of here."

Kira swallowed and held tightly to her children. "You helped us. It's our turn to help you. Unless something else happens, I won't call."

"Thank you," Jessie said.

"Take care of yourself," said Bran.

"You, too," the woman replied.

CHAPTER EIGHT

JESSIE WALKED INTO the suite, Bran right behind her. For a moment, he stood glaring down at her, his hands on his hips. There was a cut next to his lower lip and a bruise forming on his cheek. She wanted to reach out and touch him, make sure he was okay.

He ran his fingers through his too-long hair. "You were amazing out there."

She smiled. "Thanks."

His expression hardened. "Don't do it again. Next time I tell you to stay put, you do it. You got that?"

Irritation trickled through her. "No, I don't *got that*. I'm an army brat. I don't stand by and let people I care about get hurt. You got *that*?"

Surprise widened his eyes, then they crinkled at the corners and his mouth edged into a smile. She had the most shocking desire to kiss him.

"Yeah, I guess I do. In that case, thanks." He sighed. "Couple of lowlife flunkies. I was hoping to take one of them down without hurting him too much, find out who the hell they worked for."

He was worried about hurting that massive mountain of a man? And she'd thought he needed her help.

"It wasn't your fault he got away," she said. "Kira and her kids walked out at exactly the wrong time."

"The way those guys moved, they're ex-military. The

long hair and beard aren't regulation so they're not active duty. Could be mercenaries, ex-military for hire, but they're definitely not at the top of the food chain."

"The guy with the man bun had a tattoo on his neck. I couldn't quite make it out, but it looked like a gang tat of some kind."

"Yeah, I caught a glimpse, not enough to tell what it was. You're right, it could be a gang tat. Believe it or not, there are gangs in the army, same as anywhere else."

"What about the license plate number? Did you get a look at it?"

"I got the number, but odds are the plate is stolen. I'll run it down, see what I can find out, but don't get your hopes up."

"How did they know we were here?"

A muscle worked in his jaw. "Good question. Either someone at the base put a tail on us or they're tracking you, may have been tracking you all along. I was watching for a tail, didn't see any sign of one, which means…"

He strode over to his black canvas duffel, tossed it up on the sofa, and unzipped it. He pulled out a handheld, black plastic device with tiny lights on the front.

"What is it?"

"Bug detector."

She followed him into the bedroom, watched him check her carry-on, then run the device over the clothes in the closet. Finding nothing, he walked back out and checked her purse. LED lights began to flicker, growing brighter and brighter, and a buzzing sound went off.

"Fuck." Bran grabbed her purse and dumped the contents on the sofa, then started digging around inside. He found a small round chip about the size of a thumbnail in the bottom of one of the pockets and held it up.

"Oh, my God."

Carrying it over to the stone-floored entry, he dropped the disk on the floor and crushed it beneath the heel of his boot.

"There's a good chance your car is bugged, too. That's probably how they knew you were flying into Dallas. Tracked you to the Denver Airport. If they watched you check in, it wouldn't be hard to figure which flight you were on."

"So they called someone in Dallas and had them waiting at the terminal when I landed."

He nodded. "Hired guns. Like you said, they were probably watching for you, followed your taxi to The Max."

Her hand shook as she started putting the contents of her purse back inside. "How did they get the bug into my bag?"

"You were on the base asking questions before you flew to Dallas, right?"

"That's right. Once I decided to look into the theft, I drove down from Denver and stayed overnight. I drove down again right before I left for Texas. Both times I got stonewalled by just about everyone. They wanted me to back off, but I told them I was going to keep digging."

"Who, specifically, wanted you to back off?"

"Thomas Anson, Dad's counsel, for one. You heard what he said. He thought I would be better served to get on with my life."

"Who else?"

"Charles Frazier. I spoke to him about the theft, asked him how many munitions had been stolen. He was evasive, just said the weapons would be worth a lot of money."

"Anson and Frazier both visited your father the day he died."

She nodded. "According to the list, Frazier came in with his assistant, Andrew Horton. He's a young guy, a computer specialist. I met him, but he was on his way out, so I didn't really get to talk to him."

"With any luck, we'll be talking to Frazier tomorrow. Maybe we can speak to Horton while we're there."

"There was also a woman on the list. Mara Ramos. Dad never mentioned her."

"We'll track her down." Bran glanced regretfully around the beautiful suite. "We need to pack up and get out of here before those guys or someone else decides to take another crack at us. I'm sorry to say, the next place won't be nearly so nice. We need to find a spot with a lower profile."

"I can do that while you're driving," Jessie said.

"You could, but you need to take the battery out of your phone so they can't track us. Mine's encrypted. It's also got antitracking software."

Jessie had to admit she was impressed.

"There's a disposable you can use in my gear bag."

She took the battery out of her cell, went over and got the disposable and stuck it in her purse. Quickly repacking her carry-on, she towed it into the living room.

"You ready?" Bran asked.

"Whenever you are."

He grabbed his duffel and slung it over his shoulder. "Time to get the hell out of Dodge."

BRAN'S PISTOL RESTED on the center console as the SUV rolled along in the darkness. While he made evasive moves to be sure no one followed, Jessie brought up Expedia on the disposable phone and found a Holiday Inn and Suites that met their needs but was a little off the beaten path.

The suite Jessie had found was basic, just a bedroom, bathroom, living room, and small galley kitchen. The rooms were decorated with the usual hotel furniture, brown veneered tables, a dark brown tweed sofa in the living room that unfolded into a queen-size bed, a cheap pair of lamps.

Bran figured the sofa bed would be lumpy and uncomfortable, but at least the suite was roomy. They set up their laptops at opposite ends of the dining table, and both of them went to work.

Jessie had told him she made notes every day on the information they gathered. "I document everything, then speculate on what it might mean and decide what actions I should take next."

"Sounds useful," he'd said. And meant it. It was good to keep tabs on the investigation. Since Jessie was handling that part of the job, he didn't have to worry about it.

So far she'd only grumbled a little about having to give up internet access on her laptop for fear of being tracked, while Bran's was even more protected than his phone.

While she worked, he phoned Tabitha Love, The Max's computer guru, a brainy female who knew the ins and outs of the internet like nobody he had ever met.

"Hey, Tab, I need a favor," he said when she picked up.

"Hey, Bran, no problem. What can I do for you?"

"I need you to run a plate number. Got a hunch it's stolen, but I need to be sure." He rattled off the vehicle description and Colorado plate number EQZ-555.

"I'll call you back," Tabby said. Since she also did occasional work for law enforcement, she had access to all sorts of useful information.

"Who's Tab?" Jessie asked from the far end of the table.

Bran noticed the faint slump in her shoulders. After the day she'd had, she had to be exhausted, but Jessie rarely complained.

"Tabitha Love. She's a computer whiz who works for The Max." Tabby wasn't just smart, she was a genius, and distinctly her own person, with short black hair, shaved on the sides and moussed on top. She had enough silver in her nose, ears, and tongue to drive up the price on the stock market.

"She can get a name off the plates?"

"Maybe." He could read the fatigue in Jessie's face. Just thinking about the men who had come after her and what might have happened if he hadn't been with her made his stomach burn.

Nothing he could do about it now. Shoving his concern for her aside, he went back to work on the keyboard, searching for information on paramilitary groups in the area, men who might be willing to hire themselves out for whatever dirty work paid the most. There were five militia units listed, each with dozens of members.

But something about the two men didn't feel right. He wished he'd gotten a better glimpse of that tattoo. Dammit, they needed more intel. The trick was to stay alive until they got it.

He worked for a while, then looked up to see Jessie emerge from the bedroom in her short white terry cloth robe. Her legs were smooth and tanned, her softly curling, reddish blond hair clipped at the nape of her neck, her small feet bare. Bran felt a rush of heat that went straight to his groin.

"I'm totally dragging. Maybe a swim will perk me up."

He shifted to get comfortable inside his jeans, and clamped down on his lustful thoughts. "A swim, huh? In case you've forgotten, tomorrow's the first of November."

She grinned. "This place might not be as luxurious as the last one, but it's got something the other place didn't have."

"Yeah, what's that?"

"An indoor heated swimming pool. I need some exercise. I won't be gone long."

Bran shoved up from his chair. "You won't be gone at all unless I go with you."

She just shrugged. "Fine. Grab your suit and let's go."

"I don't need a suit. I'm on the job." He plucked his pistol off the table and clipped the holster back onto his belt, crossed the room and pulled open the door. The corridor was clear. "After you."

Jessie sighed. "This bodyguard thing gets old pretty fast."

He chuckled. "Yeah, I've heard that one before. Best way to make it end is to find those missing munitions and clear your father's name."

"I'll go for that."

A few minutes later Bran stood at the end of the long, rectangular pool. Being off-season, the pool was mostly deserted, just an older couple sitting on the steps at the shallow end, talking quietly between themselves. Determined to keep his thoughts on the straight and narrow and avoid another cold shower, Bran forced himself to look away as Jessie shed her robe.

He turned to catch a glimpse of her diving gracefully into the pool, skimming along like a fish underwater, her head popping to the surface halfway down the pool. He watched as she began swimming laps with smooth, efficient strokes and tried not to imagine what kind of swimsuit she was wearing, couldn't really tell from the brief glimpses of her body as she carved her way through the water.

At the opposite end of the pool, she made a racer's turn, flipping over and shoving off the wall, then headed back his way. At his end of the pool, she made another turn, her pretty little behind surfacing right in front of him, making him groan. The orange-striped bikini he now knew she wore suddenly seemed way too small, and perspiration popped out on his forehead.

She stroked her way to the end of the pool and back

again, made another turn, and kept swimming. He was hard inside his jeans, unable to look away as she continued to swim, didn't stop until she had completed twenty laps. By then he had imagined ten different ways to have her in the warm, enticing water.

Dammit to hell and back.

To make matters worse, at the final lap, she surged out of the pool right in front of him and came to her feet dripping wet just a few feet away.

He swallowed. Her nipples were hard little pebbles, her legs shapely and trim, her waist so tiny he could span it with his hands. His mouth went dry. He handed her the towel she had brought and prayed she'd be quick about putting on her robe.

Instead, she unclipped her hair and shook it out, spraying him with drops of water and grinning. It was all he could do not to drag her down on the pool deck and bury himself as deep as he possibly could.

"If you're finished," he groused, "I could use something to eat. Let's go back to the room and call for pizza, and you can get dressed."

The words brought up the image of her sweet little ass flipping over in the water, and inwardly he groaned. He couldn't remember such a strong craving for a woman, but maybe it was just that he knew he couldn't have her.

Finally she put on her robe, and he released a sigh of relief.

"Let's go," he said sharply.

She flicked him a sideways glance. "You're awfully grumpy. You should have joined me. The water was really relaxing."

The only thing that would relax him right now was about three rounds in bed with her. Not trusting himself to touch her, he tipped his head to indicate which way to go, and she started walking back along the pool deck the way they had come. Bran fell in beside her.

He had thought this job was going to be hard. Now he knew exactly how hard it was. *Pun intended.* Time to get the job done and get back home before he did something he would regret.

Or maybe he wouldn't regret it at all.

Exactly what he was afraid of.

HALLOWEEN NIGHT. A full moon, the wind howling. People roaming the streets dressed like fucking dead people. It suited Vlad's foul mood perfectly.

Vladimir Petrov wasn't actually Russian. He just liked pretending he was. Vlad's real first name was Janos, and according to his grandmother on his mother's side, he was Czechoslovakian. Ancestry.com agreed—at least 30 percent.

Of course, he'd been born in the States, as American as his friend, Harley Graves, aka Gravedigger, *Digger* to the guys in the White Dragons.

Vlad clenched his fist. He and Digger had fucked up royally tonight. They were being paid a shit ton of money to take care of the girl. Should have been simple, would have been if it weren't for the cocky bastard she was with.

Two against one, he and Digger both ex-army, still in prime condition, training a couple days a week. It should have been easy. But the guy they'd come up against was no average soldier. The way he handled himself, he was spec ops for sure, and as good as Vlad had ever seen.

Thank Christ, Digger had been smart enough to get the truck so they could get the hell out of there.

Vlad clenched his jaw, dreading the report they would have to make to the man who had hired them—not a guy you wanted to disappoint. Guy like that—Weaver, he called himself. Just Weaver. Good chance you could wind up buzzard meat out in the desert.

Vlad scratched his chin beneath his thin blond beard and glanced over at Digger, whose mood was as foul as his own. They were supposed to check in when the job was done, get a location from Weaver to pick up the money they'd earned. But they had failed tonight, and with Weaver, failure wasn't an option.

A shudder of dread rolled down his spine.

He looked over at Digger, who was pacing the floor of the apartment, wearing a hole in the cheap brown-shag carpeting. "I been thinking. There's no reason we have to call in tonight."

Digger paused. He rubbed the side of his neck just above his tat. "What are you talking about?"

"I mean our time hasn't completely run out. If we could find the girl, we could make another run at her and still meet our deadline."

Digger grunted, his features grim. "Odds are she'll still be with her Captain America boyfriend."

"Maybe. Maybe it won't matter. Not if we can come up with a better plan."

"You got an idea that's gonna get us paid and save our asses?"

"We gotta find 'em first, but yeah. We'll get our money and better yet, we won't get dead."

Digger walked over to the breakfast bar, where a six-pack of empty Coors bottles lined up on the counter like dead soldiers. "I'm listening. But this idea better work or instead of the girl, Weaver will be gunning for us."

CHAPTER NINE

AFTER COFFEE IN the room the following morning, they headed back to the base, pulling into a McDonald's drive-through for a Sausage McMuffin with Egg on the way.

Jessie had noticed that Bran's personal clock ran a few minutes early, which put them ahead of schedule for their ten o'clock appointment with Brigadier General Samuel Holloway, US Army director of Chemical Materials Activity, her father's direct superior.

After a brief wait, his assistant, a young soldier with a slender build and wheat-blond hair, led them down the hall to his office, which was pretty much standard military, with framed commendations on the wall and family photos on the desk.

General Holloway rose from the chair behind his desk. He was around five-ten, with graying brown hair, very straight posture, and a severe expression. Jessie had read all about him, fifty-six years old, highly decorated, married, with two grown children who each had two kids of their own. He'd been in charge of both US chemical storage depots, Colorado and Kentucky, for the past four years.

"Ms. Kegan. Let me start by saying I'm sorry for your loss." He turned to Bran. "Captain Garrett, I assume you're here unofficially, as Ms. Kegan's companion."

"Actually, I'm here as Ms. Kegan's bodyguard. So far there have been two failed attempts on her life."

The general's gray-brown eyebrows drew down in a frown. He studied the bruise on Brandon's cheek and the cut next to his lower lip. "I'm afraid I don't understand."

"We believe the attempts have something to do with Colonel Kegan's death," Bran said.

"That's right, General," Jessie added. "Finding the truth about what happened to my father is the reason we're here."

Holloway rounded his desk, giving himself a moment to consider the information. "Why don't you have a seat and tell me what's going on."

"That's the problem, General," Bran said as they sat down in the visitor chairs across from his desk . "We don't know what's going on."

"We're hoping you can help us figure it out," Jessie added.

Seated once more, the general's gaze swung to her. "Do you mind if I call you Jessie? Through your father, I feel as if we've already met."

"I would prefer it, General."

"I must tell you, Jessie, the CID began an investigation as soon as the theft of the munitions was reported. Everything they came up with pointed to your father as the man behind the crime."

"What about after he died?" she asked. "Has the CID continued to investigate?"

"We need to know who else was involved, so yes, the investigation is ongoing. Unfortunately, so far very little new information has turned up."

"How were the weapons stolen?" Bran asked. "I mean, physically moved off-site."

The general's cool blue gaze didn't waver. "I'm afraid that's classified information, Captain."

"So what *can* you tell us, General?" Jessie asked.

Holloway leaned back in his chair. "I can give you a little basic information you might not know. The fact is, chemical weapons were never actually used by the United States. But they were stockpiled after World War II at a number of bases. In 1985, Congress ordered the destruction of all the aging munitions."

"I'm aware," Bran said.

"The Alamo facility was built to eliminate the weapons stored in underground bunkers on the site. When the project is completed, the depot will be closed."

"In the meantime, however," Bran said, "someone was able to gain access and steal an unknown quantity of those weapons—an amount, I'm guessing, that is not a number you would like known to the public."

The general's features tightened.

Bran leaned toward him. "The army needs to find out where those munitions have been taken and recover them. We need to prove Colonel Kegan was not involved in the crime. I suggest we work together to our mutual benefit. What do you say, General?"

Holloway's lips thinned. Clearly he didn't like being pressed. "Knowing you would be here today, Captain, I took a look at your service record. I know you were Delta, that you were in Afghanistan and God knows how many other places around the globe. You have an impressive list of commendations and medals that rival the best of our soldiers. Before you were injured and left the army, you were clearly a valuable asset to your country."

"Thank you, sir."

"Here's what I can tell you. The munitions are normally transported by truck from the bunkers they're stored in to the destruction facility. In this case, the truck carrying the weapons was diverted, plundered, then put back into service. Its payload was missing and not discovered until several weeks later. That's all I can tell you."

"I understand there was a computer glitch," Jessie said. "That's the reason the theft wasn't discovered right away. Clearly someone hacked your inventory system and made changes to cover the disappearance."

The general's already straight posture stiffened even more. "Who told you that?"

Jessie just smiled. "Like you, General, there are things I'm not at liberty to say."

The general rose abruptly from his chair, putting an end to the meeting. "I'm sorry, but I'm afraid I'm out of time. As I said to you before, Jessie, I'm sorry for your loss. On a personal level, I liked your father very much."

She and Bran also rose to their feet. "Then you'll be pleased when his innocence is proven," Jessie said.

A muscle ticked in Holloway's cheek. "In regard to the threats against your life…has it occurred to you that whoever stole the weapons might believe your father gave you information about the theft, something they don't want revealed?"

"Has it occurred to you, General, that the men who are trying to kill me don't want me to continue my investigation because they don't want me to find out who actually stole the weapons?"

The general fell silent. His gaze turned to Bran. "I can talk to the provost marshal, see if I can arrange some sort of military protection for Jessie."

"Since we have no idea who's trying to kill her or who we can trust, at present it's not a good idea."

The general gave a curt nod of agreement. "Perhaps you're right."

He spoke to Jessie. "I can't guarantee how any of this is

going to shake out, but I can assure you of one thing—you won't find a man whose skills make him more capable of protecting you than Captain Garrett."

"I know," Jessie said softly.

"Thank you for your time, General," Bran said. "If there's anything more you can share with us, I hope you will."

The general remained stoic as Jessie left the office and walked next to Bran back to the SUV. He hadn't given them much, but maybe he didn't know a whole lot more himself. Didn't mean she was giving up. She was the daughter of a colonel in the US Army. Retreat wasn't an option.

Jessie sat quietly as Bran pulled out of the parking lot.

"It's almost noon," he said. "Let's get some lunch before we drive down to the depot."

The facility was an hour southwest on I-25, and Jessie had to admit food sounded good. "I like that idea."

Using the disposable phone, she got on the internet as they drove out of town. On Tripadvisor, she found a Mexican restaurant called La Fiesta that had a ton of five-star reviews.

Mexican music played in the background and piñatas hung from the ceiling as they walked inside. A pretty dark-haired woman in black slacks and a white blouse seated them at a corner table and took their orders, a taco and enchilada for Jessie, chile verde with homemade tortillas for Bran. Both of them ordered iced tea.

"I love Mexican food," Bran said, biting into a chunk of pork wrapped in a tortilla.

"Me, too." Jessie snagged a crispy tortilla chip and crunched it down. But as she ate the delicious meal, her mind strayed back to their meeting with the general and his mention of Bran's military record.

She took a sip of iced tea. "I know you left the army after you were wounded in Afghanistan, but I never really knew what happened."

Bran swallowed the bite of chile verde he had taken. Wariness crept into his features. "Your dad never said?"

"He didn't like to talk about it."

"Neither do I."

"Do you think maybe you could, just this once? I'd really like to know."

Bran's features tightened. When he looked at her, pain surfaced in his beautiful blue eyes. With a sigh, he leaned back in his chair. "Being Danny's sister, I guess you have a right to know."

She thought of Danny and her throat tightened. Bran glanced away and she could almost see his mind spinning, flashing backward in time to a day he desperately wanted to forget.

"I was wounded in the same skirmish that killed your brother. Maybe you already knew that. Maybe your dad told you."

"He said you were badly injured in the battle."

A muscle worked in his jaw. "At the time Danny was shot, we were fighting side by side in a remote, abandoned Afghan village. The intel was lousy and the mission went sideways. There was gunfire all around, pinning us down. Danny spotted two enemy soldiers rushing up behind us, like they came right out of nowhere. I should have seen them, but I didn't—not until Danny spun and fired."

Bran fell silent, his eyes fixed somewhere over her shoulder, as if he were watching a movie playing in his head.

"What happened then?" she gently prompted, afraid he wouldn't say more.

Bran looked at her, something dark and terrifying in his

eyes. When he spoke, the words tumbled out frantically, as if he couldn't get them said fast enough.

"Danny took the bullet that was meant for me. He died instantly. I was hit three times before the bastard came at me with a knife. I took him out for Danny. I carved him into pieces and I was glad."

Shock held her immobile.

For several moments, neither of them spoke. Then as if he was coming out of a trance, Bran shook his head. "I made it. Danny didn't. That's pretty much it."

There was far more to it than that. But she could see what talking about it had cost him, could still recall his pain-ravaged face. She wanted to reach out and touch him, make it all go away.

She noticed a faint tremor in the hand that held his fork.

"You make it sound like it was your fault," she said softly.

"It could have been. I'll never know for sure."

"The army didn't think so." Her dad had told her that much.

"No."

She reached out and covered his trembling fingers, stilling the motion. "It was war, Bran. There's no way to know what's going to happen."

The turbulence returned to his beautiful eyes. "We were like brothers, Jess. You don't get much closer than two men fighting together in combat. I would have taken a bullet for him. As it turned out, Danny ended up taking one for me."

She swallowed past the thickness in her throat. "That's what brothers do, Bran. They look out for each other."

He made no reply. When he finally spoke, his voice sounded gruff. "Thank you for saying that."

"I mean it. He'd be glad you're alive." She smiled at him softly. "So am I."

Some of the anguish seemed to fade from the lines of his face. She had read about survivor's guilt. Bran had loved Danny. He would always carry a thread of guilt that he had come home and his friend had not. It made her heart hurt to think of it. She was coming to care for Bran far more than she should, though she knew it was a mistake.

He went back to eating, shoveling in the food with more gusto than before. She hoped their talk had eased his mind a little. The last thing her brother would have wanted was for his friend to suffer.

They finished the meal and headed outside, their thoughts returning to the trouble they were facing. Their meeting at the depot with project manager Robert De La Garza lay ahead.

Jessie hoped the conversation would be more productive than the last time she was there.

CHAPTER TEN

THE ALAMO CHEMICAL DEPOT, fifty miles southwest of Fort Carson, sat on twenty-three thousand acres of flat, arid land dotted with sagebrush. Concrete bunkers beneath mounds of grass-covered earth housed the weapons set for destruction.

The plant itself was an eighty-five-acre facility composed of buildings, storage units, and pipelines created specifically to destroy one of the last two remaining US chemical stockpiles.

Bran had done his homework on the facility, digging up as much as he could off the internet. It helped that Jessie had been to the depot when her father was commander and had learned so much about it.

Carol Mason, Robert De La Garza's administrative assistant, was a dark-haired woman in her thirties, a civilian, like the rest of the employees at the plant. She led them to a beige, flat-roofed, unremarkable structure, where men and women in yellow hard hats, the Weidner emblem on the front, roamed the grounds. Employees working inside the actual destruction facility wore full-body hazmat suits, including gloves and helmets.

"The chemicals are destroyed by a neutralization process," Carol explained as they walked. "Followed by a biotreatment procedure. It's all done with the use of sophisticated robots."

"From what I understand," Bran said, "not all the weapons can be destroyed that way."

"That's right. There's a second procedure, an explosive system that's used for problematic munitions whose deteriorated condition won't allow them to be destroyed by the automated system."

Carol paused in front of a door. "We're here. Mr. De La Garza is expecting you." She opened the door and Bran walked past her into a simply furnished office with a desk, metal file cabinets, and a black ergonomic computer chair. A pair of metal-framed chairs upholstered in beige vinyl sat in front of it. A single window behind the desk looked out on a series of huge stainless pipes and more flat-roofed buildings.

Robert De La Garza rose from behind his desk, tall and lean, with the olive skin and coarse black hair of his Hispanic heritage. Introductions were made and De La Garza shook Bran's hand. "Nice to meet you," he said.

"Thank you for seeing us," Bran said.

De La Garza turned to Jessie. "I'm surprised to see you back here, Jessie. I thought I'd answered your questions when you came to me before, but apparently not to your satisfaction. Have a seat."

She sat down and Bran sat down beside her.

"I was hoping by now you'd have more details on how the theft was actually accomplished," Jessie said.

De La Garza leaned back in his chair, steepling his fingers as he considered his reply. "I suppose you deserve to know as much as I'm at liberty to tell you."

Bran tried to get a read on him, but he was careful to school his features. De La Garza was a powerful man in a powerful position. The theft of deadly chemical weapons was a black mark against him that could destroy his career.

"Our assumption at this point," he began, "is that the operation was carried out by a small number of people. We aren't sure how many. As you probably know, trucks loaded by soldiers at the bunker sites are used to transport the munitions to the destruction facility. On the day of the theft, the truck was loaded as usual, but instead of following the normal routine, the driver simply drove away."

"No one noticed when the truck didn't show up at its destination?" Bran asked.

"A GPS tracker monitors all the vehicles' locations. Twenty-three thousand acres is a huge parcel of land. There was a programming glitch that allowed the truck to go missing without anyone noticing. Apparently it was unloaded somewhere off-site, then returned to the plant."

"Why weren't the missing weapons noticed when the truck finally arrived?" Jessie asked.

"Our facility is highly automated. When the trucks reach the plant, they aren't unloaded manually. A mechanized system does the work. The computer registered delivery of the munitions, and the driver returned to the field for another load, and so on until the end of the day."

"So the vehicle arrived empty," Bran said, "but the weapons weren't discovered missing for more than two weeks."

"That's right."

"That's when Charles Frazier found the computer discrepancy and reported the missing munitions to my father," Jessie added.

"Why didn't Frazier come to you?" Bran asked.

"He was respecting the chain of command. I'm in charge of civilian operations. The weapons belong to the military. Unfortunately, your father decided not to immediately report the theft."

Jessie straightened in her chair. "Because he wanted to be sure it wasn't just another computer glitch."

"So he said. However, Charles Frazier believed it was critical to public safety to make the theft of the weapons known."

"What about the driver?" Bran asked. "Where is he now? He must have been arrested."

"Rollie Owens. He quit before the theft was discovered, said he had a better job offer. Someone was hired to take his place and that was the end of it. The police interviewed a number of individuals and put out a warrant for Owens's arrest, but so far there's been no sign of him. And the fact is, this is primarily a matter for the military."

Bran clamped down on his irritation. "It's obvious the theft was well planned and that some of the people involved work right here at the plant."

"Perhaps. But someone manipulated our computer systems, which could have been done from anywhere."

"You mean it was hacked," Jessie said. "If that's the case, what's to stop these people from doing it again?"

De La Garza's shoulders tightened, a sign he was tired of answering questions. "After the theft, we installed new security software that prevents any sort of tampering. We're confident the munitions are safe until they're all destroyed and the plant is closed." He rose, signaling the interview was over.

Bran and Jessie stood. "Thanks for your help," she said, though he was beginning to know her well enough to catch the hint of sarcasm in her voice.

He followed her out of the office, where Carol waited in the hall to lead them back to visitor parking. They were supposed to speak to Charles Frazier next, but Carol told them something had come up and Frazier had to cancel. His assistant, Andrew Horton, was also unavailable.

Conveniently. It was Jessie's word, but Bran was beginning to see a pattern. It was starting to look like there was a giant cover-up going on that might reach the highest levels.

Maybe it was just a matter of CYA—cover your ass. In this case, everyone covering his own. Or maybe the theft involved a shit ton of money and everyone wanted a cut.

"What do we do about Charles Frazier?" Jessie asked, breaking into his thoughts as he drove back to the Holiday Inn. "We really need to speak to him."

"Yeah, I've been thinking about that. Actually, not being able to talk to him right now might work in our favor. If we talk to Frazier at home, he may be more cooperative."

Jessie flicked him a sideways glance. "By cooperative, you mean we can press him harder to tell us what we want to know."

Press him. That was a polite way to put it. Bran's jaw hardened as he thought of the man who had brought all-hell down on Colonel Kegan, ultimately leading to his death—or murder.

"Yeah," he said. "That's exactly what I mean."

JESSIE SWAM LAPS again that night. Since the pool was crowded with kids and their parents well into the evening, she waited until close to ten, just before the area closed.

After leaving the chemical depot, she had worked on her laptop the rest of the day, writing up notes, putting them into some kind of order.

She made lists of questions, some for Charles Frazier, some for his assistant. Both of whom had *conveniently* not been available that day. The implications were beginning to drive her crazy.

They ordered in Chinese food and Bran turned the TV on in the living room, but neither of them were in the mood to watch. Jessie knew exactly what she was in the mood for. She hadn't thought about sex this much in the last three years. Now, every time she looked at Bran, having sex with him was all she could think of.

Everything about him turned her on. The cadence of his voice, the way he laughed, the way he moved. Just watching him amble across the living room sent a curl of heat into the pit of her stomach.

What would it be like to kiss him? Run her hands over all the lean, hard muscles she had seen and couldn't get out of her head? What would it be like if he made love to her?

Would she ruin it the way she had when she had tried before? Start thinking about Ray Cummings and the intimate way he had touched her? Conjure images of the rape he had planned to carry out if she hadn't managed to escape?

Fidgety and unable to relax, she headed for the pool, Bran reluctantly accompanying her. Exercising in the warm water was the perfect stress reliever. She glanced over to where he paced the deck at the opposite end of the pool, tall and lean-muscled, blue-eyed, and built. Nothing better than swimming—except for hours of erotic sex with the man of her fantasies.

It seemed so outrageous she found herself grinning as she stroked to the far end of the pool. She was still smiling when she came up out of the water, dripping and adjusting her swimsuit, just a few feet away from him.

"What's so funny?" Bran asked, as grumpy tonight as he had been the night before.

She looked into his hard, handsome face and some little devil made her say it. "If you really want to know, I was thinking what it might be like to have wild, uninhibited sex with you."

Hunger flashed in his eyes so quickly she took a step back. "Is that so," he drawled, his gaze running over her, assessing every curve her orange-striped bikini displayed.

Her whole body flushed with heat as she realized she wasn't the only one who'd been thinking about sex.

She swallowed. "I was imagining what it might be like, but I... I know if we tried, I'd screw it up. After Ray, I've got, you know, hang-ups."

His gaze grew more intense. "What kind of hang-ups?"

She picked up her towel off the lounge chair and quickly dried off, then slipped on her white terry cloth robe. Fortunately, the overhead lights began to flash, signaling it was time for the pool to close.

"Time to leave." She started walking back to the room, wishing she'd kept her mouth shut. By the time Bran opened the door and checked inside to be sure it was safe, she was starting to relax.

"What hang-ups?" Bran asked as he closed the door behind them.

Jessie's stomach instantly knotted. What had possessed her to mention it? But Bran had opened up to her yesterday, which meant she owed him the same courtesy today.

Trying to appear nonchalant, she shrugged. "You know, kissing's okay, but if a guy starts touching me, my mind flashes back to Ray Cummings and I, um, I start thinking about the way he touched me, where he touched me, and pretty soon sex is the last thing I want to happen."

Bran's jaw looked iron-hard. "Did he rape you?"

She swallowed and shook her head. "On the third day, just before he got home, I managed to get loose. I couldn't get out of the basement, so I searched for a weapon." Her lips trembled as the memory became all too clear. "I found a wooden crate and pried a board loose. The board had a nail in the end so I held it like a bat, and I waited till he came down the stairs."

"Go on," Bran said so softly she felt a chill.

"He always wore this black knit ski mask with a red ring around the mouth, which made him look even more terrifying. Knowing what he planned to do gave me courage. The minute he stepped off the bottom step, I swung the board as hard as I could and smashed him in the side of the head. As soon as he hit the floor, I starting hitting him over and over with the nail in the end of the board. He was unconscious and bleeding when I took off running."

"Finish it," Bran said when she paused, more a demand than a request.

Her voice trembled. "The woman in the house next door let me in and called the police. Ray was still unconscious when they got there. Turned out he was a serial rapist. He had abducted four other women and locked them up just like me. Eventually, he released them somewhere, but none of them could identify him or the place he had taken them. I was the only one who escaped."

She was shaking. She didn't realize she had tears in her eyes till Bran pulled her into his arms.

"Oh, baby," he said. "I'm so sorry."

Jessie clung to him. She never cried, but she couldn't stop the tears from sliding down her cheeks. "I was so scared. I thought he was going to kill me."

Bran's hold subtly tightened. "He's lucky he's in prison." There was such quiet venom in his words she knew that if Bran had his way, Ray Cummings wouldn't live another day.

Jessie clung to him a few moments more, soothed by the feel of his hard arms around her and the wall of muscle pressing into her breasts. When her body began to heat from the inside out and her thoughts began to shift in a more intimate direction, she took a deep breath and stepped away.

"I'm sorry. I never cry. I don't know why I did now."

He tipped her chin up, forcing her to look at him. "Maybe because you know you can trust me. I'd never hurt you, honey. I'll help you any way I can, and I'll do everything in my power to keep you safe."

She wiped away the wetness and managed to smile. "I know that. The way Danny talked about you, I knew I could trust you. I knew you would help me. I never doubted it."

There was something different in his eyes now, something sober and distant. It occurred to her that the hunger she had seen there before was gone.

He didn't want her anymore. He was worried he would somehow hurt her.

Jessie felt like crying again.

CHAPTER ELEVEN

BRAN'S MOOD FLUCTUATED between concern for Jessie and what she had suffered, and fury that he was helpless to do anything about it.

Fucking Ray Cummings was in prison, exactly where he belonged. He was being punished—not enough as far as Bran was concerned—but punished nonetheless.

And now, knowing the extent of what she had been through put Jessie even further out of his reach. She didn't need more heartache, and having sex with him was exactly where that would lead. She wasn't a one-night hookup kind of girl, and he wasn't a relationship kind of guy.

Jessie deserved a man who was gentle and patient, a guy who would help her deal with the trauma she had suffered. Bran was a rough-and-tumble lover. He demanded a lot from a woman, and the women he took to bed liked it exactly that way.

He sighed as he lay on the lumpy sofa in the living room staring up at the ceiling. If only he could get the look on Jessie's face out of his head, the heat in her big green eyes when she'd told him she was thinking about having sex with him.

Sweet Jesus. He'd been so hard he ached with every heartbeat. Then she'd told him about her *hang-ups*. He wouldn't have a clue how to deal with that. Though in some weird way, he felt an obligation to try to help her.

She was Danny's sister, after all. Or at least that was his rationale for the erotic thoughts he couldn't seem to banish no matter how hard he tried.

He had no idea what had possessed him to extend the invitation to join his family for the holidays, except that he owed it to Danny to look after his sister. Hell, in a way, she was already part of the family. He'd never brought a woman to any family gathering, and knowing his brothers would make more of it than it actually was, he was mildly relieved that she had declined.

He sighed into the darkness. He wished to God this mission was over. Wished he had the evidence they needed to prove Colonel Kegan's innocence. Wished he knew where to find the missing weapons.

In the morning, they planned to talk to the CID special agent who had handled the investigation, see if he had come up with anything new since Jessie's last trip to the base.

Then tomorrow night they were going to pay a surprise visit to Charles Frazier at his home in Alamo. Bran was looking forward to the conversation. He had a feeling Frazier knew a helluva lot more than he was saying. And if he did, he was going to tell them.

One way or another.

Bran rolled over on the lumpy mattress, trying not to listen for sounds of movement in the bedroom, where Jessie slept in a comfortable king-size bed. But the more he tried to banish lustful thoughts of her, the more he failed.

He kept seeing her in her tempting little orange-striped bikini, remembering the ties that held it in place. All he'd have to do was reach behind her and pull the strings and the top would be gone. Pull the bows on each side of the bottom and the fabric would disappear. Jessie would be his, a willing participant in his every erotic fantasy.

A soft groan escaped. It wasn't going to happen. Too many obstacles between them. Instead, it was going to be another long night.

And another cold shower in the morning.

THEIR MEETING WITH CID Special Agent Derek Tripp proved fruitless. Or at least it seemed that way to Jessie. Tripp, a man in his forties with blond hair shaved close on the sides and slightly longer on top, brought her up to speed on what they had uncovered since she had spoken to him last.

Unfortunately, after talking to the medical examiner, to Major Anson, General Holloway, and Robert De La Garza, it was mostly information she already knew.

"What about the offshore account?" Jessie asked. "There is no way my father opened a bank account in the Cayman Islands then made deposits into the account equaling a hundred thousand dollars. My mom handled all the finances when she was alive. After she died, my dad could barely balance his checking account."

Seated behind his desk, Tripp worked the button on his ballpoint pen. "I agree finding the source of the money could be the key to unraveling all of this. It's something I'm looking into. Unfortunately, with your father gone, my superiors want to put more resources toward finding the missing munitions. Since it's a matter of national security, we're working with several other agencies, including counterterrorism."

"What about the FBI?" Bran asked.

"So far we haven't asked for FBI assistance, but that could happen any day. If those weapons fell into the wrong hands, it would be disastrous."

"But you won't just let the investigation into my father's innocence drop," Jessie pressed.

Sympathy surfaced in the agent's eyes. "I'll do what I can, Ms. Kegan. That's all I can promise."

The meeting left Jessie as frustrated as before.

"Tripp is looking into your dad's offshore account," Bran said as they headed back to the Expedition. "Since it isn't his top priority, I need to talk to Tabby, see if she can find out where the money came from. If anyone can figure it out, it's Tab."

"You think she can trace the money back to the source?"

"Maybe. Odds are, she can at least come up with a little more info, something that could point us in the right direction."

"She sounds pretty amazing."

"She is."

Curiosity slipped through her. "So...how old is she?"

Bran's gaze swung toward her. "Late twenties. If you're wondering, Tab's a great girl, but she isn't my type. Besides, she's got a boyfriend."

Jessie smiled, wishing she didn't feel a sweep of relief. It was none of her business who Bran dated. One thing for sure—a man who looked as good as Bran didn't lack for female companionship.

But the subject of Bran's women continued to intrigue her even after they were back at the hotel. "I probably shouldn't ask, but I'm curious. You said Tabby wasn't your type. So what kind of woman is?"

His eyes locked with hers and she was almost sure the heat was back. "Lately I've discovered my tastes are flexible."

"Which means?"

"Which means, under different circumstances, I might be interested in a pretty little strawberry blonde with the sweetest body I've ever seen."

Surprise widened her eyes and desire made her breasts ache. She had never felt this overwhelming lust for a man. It was embarrassing.

"Unfortunately, the circumstances aren't different," Bran said flatly. "And the lady is completely out-of-bounds."

Jessie fell silent. Out-of-bounds because she was Danny's sister? Or because of what Ray Cummings had done to her? The thought depressed her. She wished she had the courage to ask, but she had pushed the subject too far already.

The afternoon slid past. Bran spoke to his tech friend, Tabitha Love, who reported the license plate on the Ford pickup had been "borrowed" from another vehicle. By now, Bran said, it was probably back where it belonged.

Tabby also promised to see what she could dig up on the offshore accounts, though she cautioned it might take some time.

As evening approached, they prepared for their visit to Charles Frazier, assuming he was home when they arrived unannounced.

"You ready?" Bran asked as she walked out of the bedroom in a pair of dark brown leggings, a V-necked cashmere sweater in a soft shade of blue with a cashmere scarf to match, and low-heeled brown suede ankle boots. She liked the look, but she hadn't expected to stay out of town this long and her wardrobe was running thin.

"I hope Frazier gives us something useful," she said on her way out the door.

Bran's gaze hardened. She could tell he was armed by the slight ridge beneath the brown leather bomber jacket he was wearing with his jeans.

A muscle ticked in his cheek. "I got a hunch he will."

CHAPTER TWELVE

CHARLES FRAZIER LIVED in a big two-story beige stucco home in an upper-middle-income neighborhood near the Walking Stick Golf Course in Alamo. It was eight o'clock when Bran pulled up in front of the residence, hopefully after the family had finished supper. Lights burned in a number of windows, both upstairs and down, and the lawn was neatly trimmed.

According to Frazier's Facebook page, the computer specialist had a wife named Tina and three kids, a boy fourteen, a girl twelve, and another son just six.

As Bran climbed out of the SUV and rounded the front to Jessie's side, he scanned their surroundings. So far there'd been no sign of the two men who had come after them at the resort. He'd been watching for a tail, but seen no trace of one.

Losing the GPS tracker had clearly set the men back, but he figured it was unlikely they'd given up. He and Jessie had been to the depot asking questions yesterday, then returned to the base this morning to talk to the CID. There was a good chance whoever wanted to stop Jessie's investigation knew she hadn't given up her quest to clear her father's name.

They were still a threat to her, but things were different now. Now they also had to deal with him.

Bran clenched his jaw as they walked up the concrete

path to the house. They needed answers. Tonight, he planned to get them.

Jessie rang the doorbell and he stepped back to wait. When the door swung open, Charles Frazier stood in the opening, his Facebook photo spot-on. Tall and reed-thin, red-haired and freckle-faced, he was the epitome of a computer geek. His eyes were blue and they widened as he recognized Jessie.

"Hello, Charles," she said.

"Ms. Kegan… Jessie. What are you doing here?"

"Charles, this is Brandon Garrett. He knew my father and he was my brother's best friend. He's helping me… look into things."

Frazier's gaze swung to Bran. "It's nice to meet you." He held out his hand and Bran shook it, felt a faint tremor as Frazier's palm touched his.

"We'd like to talk to you, Charles," Bran said. "May we come in?"

He swallowed, glanced back inside the house. "It's getting late. Tomorrow at the plant would be better."

Jessie's smile looked tight. "You had your chance to talk to us at the plant. You were too busy."

Frazier glanced back inside. "My…my kids are getting ready for bed."

"You should have thought of that before," Bran said, stepping forward, forcing Frazier back into the entry. "A computer guy like you must have a home office. We can talk in there."

Frazier managed to nod. "All right," he said weakly. "Down the hall." As he turned, a petite woman with straight black hair and smooth Asian features came out of the kitchen.

"You didn't tell me you were expecting company, Charles," she said, a little surprised.

"Tina, this is Jessie Kegan and her friend, Brandon Garrett. I worked with Jessie's father, Colonel Kegan. You remember meeting him at the company party last year?"

Tina flashed a look of sympathy. "Yes, of course. I'm so sorry about your father. Charles always spoke of him highly."

"Thank you," Jessie said. Bran could hear kids' voices coming from the kitchen and the sound of small running feet.

"It's nice to meet you both," Tina said. She looked back over her shoulder. "I'm afraid you'll have to excuse me. The kids still have homework, then it's time to get them ready for bed."

"Always plenty to do when you're raising a family," Jessie said. Tina smiled and walked away, and Charles resumed his journey down the hall.

Frazier's home office was dominated by a pair of computers on a desk against the wall. Along with the ergonomic chair at the desk, there were two swivel chairs to accommodate visitors. Bran studied the framed certificates hung on the walls, degrees from Carnegie Mellon, Cornell University, Massachusetts Institute of Technology, and others.

The guy was no dummy.

Frazier closed the door but didn't bother to take a seat. "What would you like to know?"

"We could run through all the usual questions," Bran said. "And you could parrot the same responses we've been given by everyone else. But I prefer to cut to the chase. You're a computer specialist. Apparently a very good one." Bran glanced toward the framed documents to make his point, but Frazier didn't reply.

"You were the guy who found the glitch in the Alamo system that allowed the stolen chemical weapons to go unnoticed for more than two weeks," Bran continued. "Isn't that right?"

Frazier nervously cleared his throat. "I found a discrepancy that indicated an accounting problem. At that point, I didn't know the munitions had been stolen."

"So you reported that a glitch showed an error in the number of munitions that had arrived at the plant."

"Yes."

"What did my father say when you reported the problem?" Jessie asked.

"He was extremely concerned—as of course he would be."

"And?" Jessie prodded.

"And he said that he didn't want to rush to the conclusion the munitions were actually missing until he was certain the computer hadn't made another mistake."

"Didn't that seem like a reasonable thing to do?" Bran asked. "Confirm it wasn't another system error? Maybe the weapons had been logged improperly, maybe they were misfiled, something like that?"

"At...at the time it made sense."

"Did my father ask you to look for the missing weapons?" Jessie asked.

"Yes."

"But instead, you took it upon yourself to go over the colonel's head and report them missing to General Holloway, his direct superior at CMA."

Frazier moistened his lips. "I was worried about public safety."

"Did you tell my father that?" Jessie asked.

When Frazier didn't answer, Bran gripped his shoulder

and forced him to sit down in the swivel chair. "You heard the lady. Did you tell Colonel Kegan that you'd gone to General Holloway? That you were worried about public safety?"

Frazier shook his head. The color had leached out of his face, making his freckles stand out. "I trusted the colonel's judgment." The torment in Frazier's face was unmistakable. He kept glancing toward the door, and Bran had a feeling he knew exactly why the man had gone to Holloway.

"Then what made you change your mind?" he asked.

Frazier looked up at him. "I c-can't tell you."

Bran squeezed Frazier's shoulder, not too hard, just enough to make his point. "Oh, you're going to tell me. Did the colonel ever talk about his son?"

The change of subject had Frazier's head coming up. "His son...? Yes. His son was a Special Forces soldier."

"That's right. Danny and I served together in the same spec ops military unit." Bran's ruthless smile made the rest of the blood slide out of Frazier's face. "So you're beginning to get the picture. You can either tell me the truth, or I can do things to you that will convince you. I don't want to do that. You're a family man with a wife and three kids. Tell me why you went to Holloway. Was it money? Those weapons are worth a small fortune. You told Jessie that when she talked to you before. How much did they pay you to help them frame Colonel Kegan?"

Frazier started shaking. Bran kept his hand firmly on Frazier's shoulder, making the threat clear. He could bring the man to his knees in seconds. "I'm waiting..."

Frazier swallowed. "It wasn't the money," he said shakily. "I respected Colonel Kegan. I had no idea what they planned to do to him."

"If it wasn't the money, what was it?" Jessie asked, but Bran was even more certain he knew.

Frazier looked up at him, his eyes bleak. "They…they threatened my family. By then I was sure it wasn't an accounting error and the weapons had actually been stolen. I needed to talk to the colonel, but it was very late by then so I planned to see him first thing in the morning."

"Go on," Bran urged when Frazier paused.

"As I drove home from the plant that night, a vehicle followed me. Two men in a pickup forced me off the road. They had guns. They said I should report the theft to Holloway the next morning. They said if I didn't, Tina and the kids would have a very bad accident. They knew where I lived, knew that my wife was a kindergarten teacher at Alamo Elementary, knew my kids' names. I believed they would do what they said."

"So instead of talking to the colonel you reported the theft directly to the CMA," Bran said.

Frazier nodded. "I told General Holloway about the missing weapons. It never occurred to me it would lead to the colonel's arrest and ultimately his death."

"Or murder," Jessie said.

Frazier looked as if he had taken another blow. "Dear God."

"We don't know for sure," Bran said. "But it's a distinct possibility."

"We need to know how many weapons were stolen," Jessie said.

Frazier ran a trembling hand over his carrot-red hair. One glance at the implacable look on Bran's face and he started talking. "A truckload. That's three pallets. Each pallet holds five thousand pounds. Fifteen thousand pounds of munitions of various shapes and sizes."

Bran clenched his jaw. "Far more than enough for a terror attack."

"Or to cause a small war," Jessie added.

Frazier's gaze turned beseeching. "Please… I'm begging you. If you tell the army what really happened, those men will kill my family."

"We aren't ready to tell anyone anything yet," Bran said.

"And it wouldn't matter if we did," Jessie added. "The money in the offshore account still makes my father look guilty. Until we can find out who put it there and prove it was done to frame him, nothing will change."

"What about the missing weapons?" Frazier asked. "Someone's got to find them."

"The army is searching," Bran said.

"And so are we," Jessie added. "It's what my father would have done."

Bran didn't correct her, though they were hardly in a position to track down a truckload of stolen chemical weapons—especially since they had no idea who was involved or who they could trust.

But Bran was pretty sure that wouldn't stop Jessie from trying. And since he had vowed to help her, he was in it till they found a way to make it end.

CHAPTER THIRTEEN

THE WIND WAS BLOWING, the temperature dropped into the thirties by the time Frazier walked them back down the entry hall and opened the front door. Jessie waited while Bran handed the man a card with his cell number on it.

"If you need help, you can reach me here anytime," Bran said.

"Thank you." Frazier turned to Jessie. "I'm truly sorry about the colonel. He was a good man. He didn't deserve what happened."

"No, he didn't," Jessie said.

"I was terrified for my family. I just… I didn't know what else to do." Surprise flashed in Frazier's eyes when Jessie leaned over and hugged him.

"It wasn't your fault any more than it was my father's. Whoever planned this—they're the ones to blame."

Frazier managed to nod. "Be careful," he said as they walked out the door.

They were doing their best to stay safe, but they had no idea where the next threat might come from.

They didn't have to wait long to find out.

"Headlights just came on behind us," Bran said, as he turned the key in the ignition. "They must have been watching Frazier's house."

Jessie shot up in her seat. "Oh, God, you don't think they'll hurt Charles's family?"

"Frazier did what they asked him to. I think they came here looking for us. Probably figured we'd show up to ask questions sooner or later." Bran's voice held a steely edge, and what might have been a hint of anticipation.

"You've got your seat belt on, right?"

"It's on," Jessie managed to say.

The Expedition was a big, heavy vehicle, but it had plenty of power. Bran stepped on the gas and the SUV shot forward so fast Jessie slammed back in her seat. He made several turns, slowing then accelerating, weaving his way out of the subdivision toward the main road, then pouring on the gas as the road widened and stretched out into the darkness.

The headlights stayed doggedly behind them, a little farther back now, but closing the distance.

"Can you tell what kind of vehicle it is?" Jessie asked, her heart racing as she turned to watch the road through the rear window.

"I got a look as it drove under the streetlight. Ford extended cab pickup. Gotta be our friends from the resort."

"What…what do we do?"

Bran stepped on the gas. "Well, we aren't going back to the hotel. If we did, they'd find us and we'd just have to move again. Wouldn't want to do that." He grinned. "Not when we both enjoy the pool so much."

Both? She couldn't miss the implication or the flash of heat that burned in his eyes. Her breath hitched, and her mind shot straight to sex. Then the Expedition sharply swerved, straightened abruptly, and all she could think of were the men trying to kill them.

The chase continued through the outskirts of town into the desert, the pickup's headlights getting closer. Bran was letting the truck close the distance on purpose, she realized, and her pulse shot up another notch.

"Hold on," Bran commanded, as if she weren't already clinging to her armrest with a death grip. The Expedition accelerated, swerved, bounced over a drop-off at the edge of the road and shot out into a field, careening down a dirt track into the pitch-black darkness.

The headlights followed their route, the Expedition leading them farther and farther into the desert, both vehicles flying down the dirt road at a breakneck pace for about a mile. A shot of fear hit her when their headlights went off, Bran slammed on the brakes and spun the wheel, and the SUV did a one-eighty so it now faced the opposite direction.

"Get ready," he said, his gaze riveted on the oncoming vehicle racing toward them. Every cell in her body burned with nerves as they waited, the SUV idling like a predator, the truck getting closer, thundering toward them, but in the deep, powdery dirt not able to travel as fast as it had on the highway.

Suddenly the SUV's lights went on, the high beams hitting the pickup windshield dead center as Bran gunned the engine and the Expedition leaped forward. The pickup slammed on its brakes and veered off the road to avoid a collision at the same time Bran hit the brakes, and the SUV skidded to a halt just a few feet away.

"Get down!" Bran shouted, as his door flew open and he leaped out into the darkness. She expected the overhead light to go on, but it didn't. She should have known he would have thought of that.

She crept up in the seat enough to watch events unfolding, illuminated by the headlights. Bran had already reached the passenger side of the truck and jerked open the door. The man inside flew out like a ball on the end of an elastic band, his gun soaring into the air, his body landing in an unmoving heap on the ground beneath the open door. Gunfire erupted, the driver shooting wildly, but his target had already disappeared into the darkness.

Jessie recognized the huge bearded bald man running toward her, his pistol pointed directly at the window where she sat. She clamped down on a jolt of fear, ducked below the seat, reached up and locked the door, though it wouldn't do much good against a bullet.

Crouching in the footwell, her insides trembling, she eased up enough to see Bran run up behind the bald man, grab him by the back of the neck, and spin him around. A brief scuffle ensued, the sound of fists connecting and the bald man's heavy grunts of pain. The next minute the man was sprawled on the ground, moaning.

Jessie opened the door and got out as Bran pulled a zip tie from the pocket of his bomber jacket. He bound the man's wrists behind his back, used another tie to bind his ankles. Then Bran walked back to the pickup to secure the man who lay unconscious on the passenger side of the truck. Jessie caught a flash of light as he used his phone to snap the guy's picture.

A few feet away, the bald man began squirming and shouting, trying to get free, his gaze furious in a face filled with hostility. "You're gonna pay for this, you bitch!" A string of swear words followed, and fury burned through her.

"You think so?" Pulling the cashmere scarf from around her neck, she wound it around the bald man's head several times, till his face was completely covered, his vulgar tirade reduced to a torrent of mumbled words.

Bran walked up grinning. "Nice work."

Her gaze went from the bound man thrashing around on the ground, back to Bran. "Same goes."

His smile faded as he knelt and rolled the man onto his back. "We need answers—and you're going to give them to us."

"Muff you!"

Bran just smiled. "You've got two choices. You can tell us who hired you, or I can shoot you and bury you right here. I really don't care which you choose. If I kill you, your friend over there is going to realize he's next and decide it'd be a good idea to cooperate. Either way, I'll find out what I need to know."

Bran pulled his Glock from the holster on his belt and pressed it against the side of the bald man's head. "What's it going to be?"

The guy stared up at him for several long seconds, pondering his fate. Reading the deadly threat in Bran's eyes, he started nodding. "O-hay, o-hay."

"I think you mean okay," Bran said. His gaze went to Jessie. "It's a pretty scarf. You can always wash it."

She nodded. Her mouth was dry. She wasn't sure if Bran would have pulled the trigger or not. It was a question she would never ask. She wasn't sure she could handle the answer. Unwinding the strip of pale blue cashmere, she backed away.

Bran holstered his weapon, grabbed the bald man by the front of his shirt, and hauled him upright. "What's your name?"

"Petrov. Vladimir Petrov."

Bran dug into Petrov's pockets but found no wallet. Never a good idea to carry ID when you were committing a crime.

Pulling out his cell, he took the man's picture. Bran

tipped his head toward the pickup, whose headlights streaked past sagebrush and desert, tunneling into the darkness. "What about your friend?"

"Harley Graves. We call him Digger."

"Who hired you and Digger to kill Jessie Kegan?"

Petrov shook his head. "We didn't have to kill her. We just had to convince her to quit sticking her nose into other people's business."

"And if you couldn't convince her?"

Petrov shrugged his thick shoulders. "Then we'd have to do something that would." He was built like a bull, and with that pale, scraggly beard, he was ugly.

"What? Like make her dead?" Bran pressed.

Petrov didn't answer, just gave another shrug as if killing her was no big deal. Jessie shivered. She gasped when Bran drew back his fist and punched Petrov hard in the face, sending a spray of blood into the air and his body flying backward into the dirt.

"Bran, stop!" Jessie grabbed his bicep, which was bunched hard as steel, ready to deliver another brutal blow.

He shook his head, fighting for control. "He's lucky I don't kill him." Instead, he jerked Petrov upright. "I need a name. Who hired you?"

Petrov spit out a wad of blood. "Weaver. That's his name. Just Weaver."

"How do I find him?"

More blood trickled from Petrov's nose. The way it was swelling, by tomorrow both eyes would be black.

"I don't know. He phones us on a burner, tells us what he needs, we call him back after the job's done. Weaver tells us where to pick up our money. That's the way it works."

Bran swore foully. "What's going to happen when Weaver finds out you didn't finish the job?"

Petrov grimaced. "He ain't gonna like it, that's for sure."

"Then I'd strongly suggest the first chance you get, you and your buddy leave town. I've got friends on the base. I'll be texting them your photos. You don't leave, I'll know, and you'll be dealing with me instead of your buddy, Weaver. You won't have a second chance to walk away."

Petrov stared up at him. Jessie knew Bran was talking about soldiers in the 10th Special Forces stationed at Fort Carson, where he had friends.

"You understand what I'm saying?"

Petrov swallowed and nodded.

Bran turned to Jessie. "Time to go."

"What about them? We can't just leave them out here. They could die of exposure."

"We'll call the sheriff once we're on the road."

"I thought you were letting us go," Petrov complained.

"You're lucky you're still alive." Bran closed Jessie's car door, rounded the hood, and slid in behind the wheel.

"Maybe we should call the MPs instead of the sheriff," she suggested as the engine roared to life. "Since it involves a CID investigation."

Bran shook his head. "These guys aren't active duty, plus we don't know who we can trust on the base."

Unfortunately, that was true. Her dad had been murdered on the base. The military was somehow involved.

As soon as the SUV reached the highway, Bran called 911 and anonymously reported that two men had assaulted him and were now tied up in an empty field. He gave the location using GPS coordinates.

"Sheriff will be there in ten," he said, ending the call. "We need to be long gone by then." He punched the gas and the Expedition picked up speed, heading back to Colorado Springs, forty miles away, and their hotel.

"What will the sheriff do to them?" Jessie asked.

"For starters, they're probably driving with a stolen license plate. There's also a good chance there'll be warrants out for them. Guys like that…could be anything from a speeding ticket to a felony. Might get them locked up for a while."

There were few cars on the back road Bran was driving toward town. The wind had picked up, blowing dust and dry leaves into the air. The night was dead black, no moon and no stars. Jessie shivered, though it was warm in the SUV.

She thought of the men who'd come after them. "Once they're released, do you think they'll actually leave town?"

"I'd say chances are better than good. Men like that go after the easy money." He cast her a glance that held a trace of arrogance. "Turned out getting to you wasn't as easy as they thought."

She almost smiled. No, not nearly as easy with Bran Garrett acting as her bodyguard.

"I'll text those photos to a couple of SF guys I know, have them spread the word to their buddies, keep a lookout, give me a heads-up if anyone spots them."

She nodded. At least they might get some kind of warning if the two men stayed in the area.

Silence began to stretch between them. Neither spoke until town drew near and Bran's gaze slid back to her.

"You okay?"

Was she okay? Men had been hired to stop her—one way or another—from finding out what had happened to the stolen munitions and clearing her father's name. Since she had no intention of quitting, no, she wasn't okay. But she didn't say that.

"I will be. Once we clear my father's name."

"Be smarter to quit before things get worse."

"You think they will?"

"Good chance they will."

She fixed him with a stare. "You sticking?"

His mouth faintly curved. "If you are."

As Jessie leaned back in the seat, she found herself smiling. "Glad that's settled."

Bran just shook his head. "Well, you sure as hell aren't boring." He flashed one of his devastating grins. "Can't remember when I've had a better time with a lady."

Jessie scoffed. "Not counting sex," she said dryly.

His look turned scorching the instant before he glanced away. "Yeah," he said. "Not counting sex."

Jessie's whole body went warm, and in that moment she made a decision.

She decided she was going to seduce him.

CHAPTER FOURTEEN

IT WAS LATE when they got back to the hotel. Jessie went straight into the bedroom, but Bran was too jacked up to sleep. He rubbed his bruised knuckles and chuckled to imagine what story the two men had told sheriff's deputies when they arrived to find them tied up like a pair of stuffed turkeys.

He thought about finding a late show on TV, but instead went over to his laptop and downloaded the photos he had taken of the men. A separate picture showed the tattoo on the side of Digger's neck. A shamrock with *666* inside.

It didn't take long to find the symbol on Google. Aryan Brotherhood prison tat, not really much of a surprise.

He glanced up as the bedroom door swung open, and Jessie walked into the living room in the short white terry cloth robe she had worn over her swimsuit. A memory of her in the orange-striped bikini popped into his head, and his mouth actually watered.

"Pretty sure the pool is closed," he said a little gruffly.

Jessie glanced at the clock as if she had no idea it was almost midnight and walked right up beside where he sat in front of his laptop at the dining table.

"That's too bad." She smiled. "Since we both enjoy it so much."

She was tossing his words back in his face. It had been torture to watch her in her tiny bikini and not be able to touch her. But it was sweet torture.

When she didn't back away, Bran came up out of his chair, which put them just inches apart. "What's going on?"

Instead of answering, she untied the sash on the robe and let it fall to her feet, leaving her in the orange-striped bikini he fantasized about every night. His pulse kicked up and arousal stirred through him. She had left her hair loose around her shoulders, a mantle of gleaming fire-touched gold. He wanted to run his fingers through it, see if it felt as silky as it looked.

He stood frozen as her palms flattened on his chest and she went up on her toes and settled her mouth over his. A groan locked in his throat, and for an instant he could only stand there, entranced by the feel of those plump pink lips moving over his and the brush of her breasts against his chest. His arousal strengthened, turned rock hard.

The groan broke free as he gave in to the need pounding through his blood and kissed her back, taking control, slanting his mouth over hers, tasting her, allowing himself a few forbidden moments of pleasure.

Then reality struck. This was Danny's sister. Aside from that, she had suffered enough trauma already. Setting his hands on her shoulders, he eased her away, reluctantly ending the kiss.

"We can't do this," he said.

Jessie smiled up at him. "Why not?"

She was so damn pretty with her lips moist from his kiss and her big green eyes liquid with desire. He clamped down on a fresh shot of lust.

"You know why not. You told me yourself you have hang-ups. I don't want to make them worse."

"What if you can make them better?"

An idea he had actually considered. "What if I can't?"

Jessie reached behind her and pulled the strings holding

her bikini top in place. His eyes widened as the striped top tumbled to the floor.

"Jesus," he said, automatically reaching out to cup the enticing fullness that tilted slightly upward, his thumb stroking over the hard little berry at the tip. *Perfect.*

He wanted to settle his mouth there, taste that smooth perfection. He wanted to lay her down on the sofa and bury himself to the hilt.

Jessie cupped the back of his neck and pulled his mouth back to hers for another searing kiss, this one slow, deep, and lingering, making his erection throb.

Christ, he wanted her.

Jessie just kept kissing him and he kept kissing her. He was kneading her pretty breast, lifting and caressing, when he felt her stiffen against him. Too far gone to think clearly, he cupped the other breast and stroked her nipple till it hardened, slid his hand into the back of her bikini bottom to cup her sweet little ass and pull her closer, fitting her snugly against his erection. Damn she felt good.

"Bran..." she whispered. "Bran... I'm sorry, please... don't." Through the haze of his lust, the pain in her voice finally reached him. It hit him like a bucket of cold water that she wanted him to stop.

Sucking in a breath, he forced himself to move away, his body aching from the strength of his arousal. "Christ, Jess, I shouldn't have done that. I'm sorry. I knew better. I don't know what I was thinking."

Her lips trembled. She gathered up her white terry robe and slipped it on. "Don't say that. It wasn't your fault and you know it. It was my fault. I planned it. I tried to seduce you. I thought I could make it work."

She looked at him and tears glistened in her eyes. "I'm

the one who's sorry. I just… I've never wanted anyone the way I want you."

He told himself not to touch her. That she would probably pull away if he tried to hold her, comfort her, but the next thing he knew he was easing her against his chest, her arms were around his waist, her head tucked beneath his chin. He felt a faint tremor move through her body as she fought to hold back tears.

"It's okay, baby, don't cry. I wanted you, too. So much." He kissed the top of her head, felt fine strands of red-gold hair against his cheek. He wanted to say that if it were anyone's fault, it was Ray Cummings. But he didn't want the specter of Cummings's past deeds anywhere near her.

"I shouldn't have done it. I knew better. I just… I wanted to feel normal again." She shook her head. "At least now I know the truth." She turned and started walking.

"Jessie, honey…"

But Jessie just kept walking. Disappearing into the bedroom, she firmly closed the door.

The sound was like a gunshot straight to the heart.

JESSIE LAY AWAKE in the darkness. She had taken a risk tonight and she had failed. She brushed a humiliated tear from her cheek. In a way, it was worth it. Because now she knew for sure that she would never be a normal woman again. She wanted Bran Garrett with a soul-deep hunger unlike anything she had ever known. If her body couldn't convince her mind to accept him as a lover, no other man stood a chance.

She rolled onto her side and looked at the red numbers on the digital clock. Nearly 3:00 a.m. She needed to get some sleep, but every time she started to drift off, she remembered the heat in Bran's amazing blue eyes, remembered the way he had looked at her, as if she were the only woman in the world.

She remembered the exact taste of his kiss, the soft-firm feel of his lips melding with hers, the warmth of his tall, hard body. She remembered the touch of his big hand caressing her breast, his thumb sliding over her nipple.

Yearning arose, swift and unrelenting, coming from somewhere deep inside her. She didn't understand it, couldn't figure out how she could experience such intense sexual desire and not be able to act on it.

In time, she would learn to accept things as they were, to deal with the reality—just as she'd dealt with the trauma of surviving three days with Ray Cummings.

Instead of thinking of him, she fixed her thoughts on Brandon and eventually fell into a deep, drugging sleep. It was late morning when she emerged from the bedroom in skinny jeans and a forest green cable-knit sweater to find him working on his laptop at the dining table.

She looked like crap and she knew it. She was beyond embarrassed about what had happened last night, and yet, as she watched him, a curl of heat tugged low in her belly. It seemed none of the lust she'd felt for him had disappeared.

"Good morning." Determined to brazen it out, she walked toward him. "What are you working on?"

Bran leaned back in his chair. With the scruff of beard along his jaw and those amazing blue eyes, he looked like every woman's fantasy, especially hers.

He crossed his arms over his chest. "So I guess we aren't talking about last night."

Warm color rose in her cheeks. "No."

Bran made no comment. She couldn't tell if he was relieved or disappointed. She wandered over and poured herself a cup of coffee from the pot on the counter and took a sip. "So where are we in the investigation?"

He straightened in his chair. "I've been going over some of the things we've found so far, and I've come up with a theory."

Picking up his cell, he brought up a photo he had taken of the tat on Digger Graves's neck and held it out to her. "Shamrock with a 666 inside. You were right about it being a prison tat."

"Really?" She moved close enough to see. "Have you figured out which gang?"

"Aryan Brotherhood. One thing we know, stealing those weapons took a helluva lot of planning. Everything from computer hacking to murder—if you're right about your father, and I think there's a good chance you are."

She ignored the ache of grief that moved through her.

"Money seems to be the common denominator," Bran continued. "The one thing necessary to make everything work."

"I see what you mean. They needed an initial investment of capital in order to get everything done."

"Exactly. Even if they were expecting a big payoff from the sale of the weapons, somebody put up a lot of cash in advance. The driver of the truck had to be paid. Someone deposited a hundred grand into a phony offshore account in your father's name. And if my theory's correct, there were others."

"Someone in the prison kitchen was paid to put something in my father's food to make him sick. Someone in the ambulance or at the hospital was paid to administer the lethal drug that caused his heart attack."

"The question is, how would you find enough people willing to do that kind of dirty work and keep their mouths shut?"

Her mind spun. She thought of the tattoo and the obvious answer hit her. "They all share some kind of bond. In this case they're all in the same gang."

He nodded. "That's right. Maybe not all, but a lot of them. Aryan Brotherhood has members in the army stockade where they were holding your dad, as well as people on the outside. Gang members, former gang members, they all live by the same rules. Number one being, if you talk you wind up dead."

"You think Aryan Brotherhood gang members pulled off a theft this complicated?"

He snorted a laugh. "Hell, no. I think they're in it for the money. I think those weapons were sold in advance. I think whoever planned to steal them got at least a partial up-front payment, enough to buy the help they needed to make it happen."

"What about this guy, Weaver?"

"He's involved up to his neck, but I don't think he's the mastermind. More like he's at the top of the Aryan food chain. We need to find him, figure out what he knows."

"How do we do that?"

"We start by calling Tabby." He picked up his phone and punched a contact number, then put the phone on speaker and set it back down on the table.

"Hey, Bran," Tabby answered in a buoyant female voice. "I'm glad you called. I've got something for you."

"Tab, I've got you on speaker. Jessie Kegan is with me."

"Nice to finally meet you, Jessie," Tabby said.

"You, too, Tabby."

"Listen, Bran, I've got some info on that money deposited into Colonel Kegan's offshore account. I was hoping I could track the money backward, find out where it originated, but it was transferred from another offshore account, one that was highly protected. I wasn't able to get in so I can't give you any names."

"That's not good news."

"No, but I was able to track the deposits to an email address. It's closed down now, but I followed the messages and get this—the messages indirectly led to an online auction on the dark web."

"An auction," Jessie said, her gaze shooting to Bran. "That's how they sold the chemical weapons?"

"That's right," Tabby said. "The digital black market allows buyers to access a large assortment of arms and explosive material. Crypto bazaars, social media channels, e-commerce sites, that kind of stuff. Lot of potential buyers out there, Pakistan, Iran, Republic of South Africa, Somalia. In this case, the terms of the auction required twenty percent up front, the rest on delivery."

"How much did they sell for?" Bran asked.

"Either of you wanna guess?"

Jessie tried to imagine what such an amount of deadly weapons would be worth on the international market. "Let's see...fifteen thousand pounds of mustard agent stored in projectiles and mortar rounds. I'm thinking...fifteen million dollars?"

"Nope. These days fifteen million is chump change."

"Twenty million," Bran guessed.

"Try twenty-five million dollars. Five mil up front, the rest on delivery."

Bran scrubbed a hand over his face, rasping over the dark scruff along his jaw. "So someone has twenty-five million dollars' worth of chemical weapons. Enough to kill hundreds of people or maybe start a war."

"A thought that gives me nightmares," Tabby said.

"It's got to be terrorism," Jessie said. "I wonder why they haven't used them already."

"An attack takes planning," Bran said. "Planning takes time."

"So all we have to do is find the buyers before they're ready to execute their plan," Jessie said, drawing a grim look from Bran.

"Believe me, I'll stay on it," Tabby said.

"Listen, Tab, there's something else we need. There's a guy named Weaver. No first name. It looks like he's a leader in the Aryan Brotherhood. Ex-con, most likely. Could be connected to the military. Chance he's in Colorado somewhere, but there's no way to know for sure."

"Pretty tall order," Tabby said. "Finding a guy with only one name."

Bran smiled. "Yeah, but you're up to it, right? No challenge too big for the Tabinator."

Tabby laughed.

"I'll send you a couple of photos, Vladimir Petrov and Harley Graves. Graves has an Aryan gang tat on his neck. Might get lucky, turn up a connection to Weaver."

"All right, I'll see what I can find out. If that's it, I need to get to work. Stay out of trouble, you two." The line went dead.

"I wonder how you get someone to give you five million dollars in exchange for weapons you don't have," Jessie said.

"Good question. Might not be that hard if you have something the buyer really wants."

"Like a truckload of chemical weapons."

"Yeah." Bran rose from his chair. "I'm going to shower. If you need the internet, now would be a good time."

She just nodded and watched him walk away, all broad shoulders, long legs, and a sexy male behind. She couldn't help wishing last night had gone differently.

She sighed as she sat down at his software-protected computer to check her email. Knowing her best friend in Denver would be worried, she dropped her a note. She and Hallie Martinez had been best friends since college, both students at the U of Denver. They had met when they dated two men who were close friends, discovered they had a lot in common, and stayed close over the years. They hadn't seen each other since Jessie had left for Dallas in search of Brandon Garrett.

Jessie told Hallie she was back in Colorado, still working to prove her father's innocence, now with Bran's help.

When she finished updating her friend, she worked on her article for Kegan's Korner, the blog she wrote for the digital website, Factfinders.com. Several other sites also usually picked up her work, which was how she made her living.

The article she'd been writing before her father had died concerned a small Colorado town with an aging water system similar to the one in Flint, Michigan. Many of Drover City's health problems were the same. Her research was completed. She just needed to write the last few pages and summarize her conclusions. With everything that had happened, she had put it off far too long.

At least money wasn't a major factor. Her dad had left her a small inheritance, giving her the freedom to work at her own pace. It also gave her the time she needed to find the men who had murdered him and stolen twenty-five million dollars' worth of chemical weapons.

She needed to finish the article and send it off so that she could get back to the urgent job of trying to save lives—hers and Brandon's included.

Jessie put her head down and went to work.

CHAPTER FIFTEEN

SHOWERED AND DRESSED in jeans and a clean dark brown Henley, Bran returned to work on his laptop while Jessie sat at the opposite end of the table, typing away. At the moment, finding Weaver was his priority.

Bran searched Google, Facebook, LinkedIn, Twitter, all the social media websites, trying to find someone named Weaver connected to the Aryan Brotherhood. Coming up with zip.

He looked up at the sound of Jessie's chair sliding across the vinyl floor. He could smell her soft perfume as she walked up behind him, something slightly sweet but sexy enough to stir his blood. Sweet and sexy, that was Jessie. The last time she'd been this close, she had ended up in his arms half naked. His groin tightened before he could push the lust to the back of his brain where it belonged.

"I assume we're calling the CID to tell them what Tabby found out," she said. "We can't risk letting the buyers use those weapons in a chemical attack."

"Yeah, well, that sort of poses a problem. Tabby doesn't exactly go through channels. Technically, there's no way we could have accessed the info she gave us."

She cocked a reddish gold eyebrow. *"Technically?* I'm guessing that means legally."

"Yeah."

She sighed. "We need someone on the base we can trust.

I think we should take a chance on Agent Tripp. He wanted to go deeper into the offshore account. Maybe he'd be willing to overlook where the information came from in favor of getting important facts."

"Maybe. Then again, maybe he'd have us all arrested."

She blew out a breath. "There is that." Wandering over to the counter, she poured herself another cup of coffee from the fresh pot she had brewed. "You want another cup?"

What he wanted was to take up where they'd left off last night, but that wasn't going to happen. "I'm good."

She sipped from her mug. "So where do we go from here?"

Bran reached over and picked up the file he'd been constructing, took out the list of people who had visited the colonel while he was incarcerated.

"I've been going back over the visitors list your father's attorney gave us."

"Good idea. With so much going on, it's kind of fallen to the bottom of our priorities. Did you find anything interesting?"

"There isn't much. Mostly just lawyers and investigators we've already talked to, a couple of officers who were the colonel's friends."

"I talked to them when I started my investigation. They didn't know much about the charges. They just came by to support my dad."

"Unfortunately, the orderlies who brought his meals aren't listed, neither are the EMTs who took him to the infirmary. But there is one thing we can check out." He glanced in her direction, tried not to look at the curve of her ass in her skintight jeans.

"Remember the name Mara Ramos? You said your dad had never mentioned her."

"I've never heard of her. I was going to see if I could find out something about her, but then Petrov and Graves were trying to kill us, and I never got around to it."

He turned the computer so that she could see the screen. "According to Mara's Facebook profile, she's forty-five years old, a retired schoolteacher, no husband, no kids, lives right here in Colorado Springs."

"She's beautiful."

Mara's profile picture highlighted her long, thick black hair, black eyes, nice smile. Jessie was right. Mara was a very pretty woman.

"I've got her phone number and street address. We could phone her, but I think we should make a house call."

"Great, I'll get my purse."

It wasn't far from the hotel to Mara's unimposing apartment on Sandalwood. Bran parked in front of a sprawling three-story, gray-and-white building complex, and to save time headed for the manager's office.

A stout gray-haired woman in a flowered dress and house slippers answered the door. "May I help you?"

"We're looking for apartment 13-C," Bran said. "The tenant's name is Mara Ramos."

The woman looked back over her shoulder. "Cyrus! You got a nice young couple here looking to rent 13-C."

"I'm comin'! Just need a minute to fetch my readin' glasses."

"I'm sorry for the confusion," Bran said. "We aren't here to rent the apartment. We're looking for the tenant, Mara Ramos. Are you saying she doesn't live here?"

Cyrus walked up to the door, early seventies, snow-white hair and small wire-rimmed glasses.

"This is my husband," the woman said. "He's the manager. He can help you better than me." She waddled a few steps away, but stayed within hearing distance, eavesdropping clearly her primary source of entertainment.

"If you're lookin' for Ms. Ramos, she moved out a couple months back. Took a job in a city somewhere. Denver, I think...or maybe it was LA."

Interesting timing, Bran thought. Just after the colonel's death, and no mention of the move on her Facebook page. "She leave a forwarding address?"

Cyrus shook his head. "Nope. Just packed up, dropped off her key, and moved out one day. Had to charge her credit card an extra month's rent, her leavin' without givin' her thirty-day notice."

"How long did she live here?" Bran asked.

"Only here a couple months, real nice lady."

Jessie took her wallet out of her purse and slid out a photo of her father. "Did you ever see this man around her apartment?"

He nodded. "Sure did. Thirteen-C is just over there." He pointed to a building across a small, grassy open space. "Some military guy. Started coming round to see Ms. Ramos a month or so before she moved out. Spent the night so I guess he was her boyfriend."

Bran almost smiled at the look of horror on Jessie's face, like she couldn't believe her dad could possibly have a sexual relationship. If the colonel was anything like his son Danny, a high sex drive was in his blood. If the implications of Mara's sudden departure weren't so dark, it would have been funny.

He tipped his head toward Jessie. "The military guy you were talking about? This is his daughter. We'd like to find Mara if we can. I don't suppose you'd have a copy of the credit card receipt you have on file for her? I'll make it worth your while."

Cyrus shook his grizzled head. "Sorry. Company policy. We gotta destroy the records soon as a tenant moves out. Don't want to end up in a lawsuit, you know."

Bran sighed. "I get it. These days you can't be too careful. Could you at least tell us the date she moved?"

"I'll check." Cyrus ambled back into his apartment, then returned a few minutes later. "It was August 18. Housekeeping shampooed the carpets the next day."

Bran glanced at Jessie, whose shock was now tinged with anger. Colonel Kegan had died just a few days before Mara Ramos packed up and left town. The coincidence was worrisome at the very least.

Of course it could just be coincidence.

If he believed in coincidence, which he didn't.

"Thanks anyway, Cyrus." Bran waved at the older man over his shoulder as they left, then stopped a few minutes later at the rapid sound of footsteps shuffling after him.

"Wait!" Cyrus called out. "Wait just a second."

Bran turned to face him. "What is it?"

Cyrus took a couple of winded breaths. "Just remembered. I got her license plate number. Had to put it on the application so she could park her car in the lot." Cyrus handed him a piece of paper: 6EQS505. "Don't know if it'll help, but I thought it might."

Bran smiled. "You did good, Cyrus." He took out a fifty and handed it over, and the old man beamed.

"Now I can buy my Betty somethin' nice for our weddin' anniversary. Be fifty years. Fifty years puttin' up with me, she deserves somethin' nice."

"Glad I could contribute," Bran said, smiling.

The old man shuffled back the way he had come.

"I can't believe Dad never mentioned he was seeing someone," Jessie said, still looking dumbstruck as she clicked her seat belt into place and Bran pulled away from the curb.

"He's a man, honey. And as you said, Mara is a beautiful woman."

She hooked her fiery hair behind an ear. "Odd timing, though, her leaving just days after he died. You think the plates will help us find her?"

"Maybe. I noticed there weren't any recent posts on her Facebook. Now I think I know why. I'll text Tabby with the number, see what she comes up with."

"CID was trying to find the missing chemicals. They would have interviewed everyone on the visitors list. I'll call Agent Tripp, see if he'll tell me what Mara Ramos had to say."

"Sounds good."

Jessie sighed. "I wish we knew more about her."

Bran flicked her a sideways glance. "Oh, we're going to. You can count on that."

THE AFTERNOON SLID into evening. Agent Tripp was out and hadn't yet called her back. She had ordered a pizza, but by the time it was delivered to the hotel, it was cold, which didn't really matter since Jessie's appetite was gone.

She still couldn't believe her father had been involved with a woman and hadn't told her about it. Surely he would have said something if Mara Ramos was anything more than a sexual fling. Her dad's sex life wasn't something she wanted to dwell on, but there was an aspect of it she couldn't ignore.

Her gaze slid to Bran. He was sitting at the dining table, but he wasn't working on his computer. Instead, all evening, his intense blue eyes seemed to seek her out wherever she was in the room.

She had the strangest feeling he was thinking about last night, thinking about what it might have been like if she hadn't rejected him. Dear God, watching him all evening, she hadn't been able to think of anything else.

She clamped down hard on the desire she didn't want to feel and forced her mind in another direction. "Do you think Mara Ramos was involved?"

Bran leaned back in his chair. "My instincts say yes. I think she might have helped whoever planned it set your father up. She was sleeping with him. That would give her access to his military ID, his social security number, credit card information, things that a bank might require to open an account."

"God, I hadn't thought of that." She got up from the sofa and walked toward him. "Do you think it's possible she could have...? I mean, a woman as pretty as she is could seduce a man into doing things he...um...otherwise would never consider."

"Like stealing chemical weapons? If you're asking me if I think Mara Ramos seduced your dad into going along with the theft, I'm going to say no. I didn't know your father that well, but I knew Danny. He had a will of iron, and he would never break his code of honor, not for a woman he cared about or anyone else. From what Danny told me about your dad, I have to think he'd feel the same way."

Relief swept through her. "My dad was the most honorable man I've ever known."

Bran rose from his chair, his lanky strides crossing the distance between them, coming up behind her.

"A man will do a lot for a woman he wants." He set his hands on her shoulders and began a gentle massage. She could feel the heat of his body and warmth slipped through her, settled in her core.

"A man might be willing to trust a woman he cares about in a way he usually wouldn't," Bran continued. "He might do unexpected things for her. He might ask her to trust him in return." He turned her into his embrace. "Kissing's okay, right?"

Her body flushed with heat and unconsciously she moistened her lips.

"I'll take that as a yes." Bending his head, he settled his mouth over hers. It was a gentle kiss, no pressure, giving her every chance to pull away. The soft touch of his mouth over hers brought the sting of tears. She wanted him so badly, and yet she knew his tender seduction was going to fail.

"I can't," she said, breaking the contact. "I'll only let you down again."

He kissed her once more and she let him, responding to the hunger he kept carefully controlled, fighting the same hunger in herself. She wondered if she had ever wanted anything as much as she wanted Bran Garrett.

Bran just kept kissing her, softly but firmly, a gentle demand that made her desire swell until she trembled. His hands slid into her hair to cup the back of her head, holding her in place as his lips moved hotly over hers. He kissed her until her body burned and her legs felt as if they were going to give way at any moment.

"He never kissed you, did he?" He kissed the side of her neck.

"No..." she whispered.

Bran kissed her again, long and deep, a scorching kiss that had her quietly moaning.

"I want you," he said. "So much."

"Oh, God, Bran." She rested her palm against his cheek. "I wish I could give you what you want, but—"

"Do you trust me?"

She swallowed past the lump in her throat and managed to nod. He was Danny's best friend. Of course she trusted him.

"Say it. Tell me you trust me."

"I trust you, Bran. But I—I don't think—"

He cut off her words with another deep kiss. By the time he stopped, her palms were under his shirt, pressing against his warm skin. Hard muscle bunched everywhere she touched, and her body heated and dampened even more.

He reached for the hem of his long-sleeved T-shirt and stripped it off over his head, letting her look at him, stare at all that hard male muscle, as she had wanted to do since the morning she had walked in on him nearly naked in the living room.

"I've got an idea," he said, trailing a finger gently down her cheek. "But I need you to trust me."

She stared at his chest, his gorgeous pecs, six-pack abs, the fine dusting of dark hair that arrowed down and disappeared into his jeans. She reached out to touch him, ringed his belly button with her finger, and he groaned. She wanted to press her mouth there, trace the indentation with her tongue.

She looked up at him, read the blazing desire in his eyes. And his iron control. "I trust you," she said.

Bran scooped her up in his arms and carried her into the bedroom. It felt so good to be held by him, to feel his power and strength. But when he set her on her feet beside the bed, fear began to churn in her stomach.

He must have sensed the change because he bent his head and very softly kissed her. "I'm not going to touch you. I promise. Not unless you want me to."

Reaching into the pocket of his jeans, he pulled out a zip tie like the one he had used to restrain the two men who had attacked them. Before she had time to panic at the thought of being tied up, he pressed the thin strip of plastic into her hand.

"It's for me, not you. You're gonna tie me up. I'll be completely at your mercy. You can do anything you want to me. You can take all the time you need. If you want to stop, you can. If you don't, then we'll both get what we need. What do you think?"

Her eyes stung. She looked at his magnificent body, read the heat in his eyes. He was doing this for her. Any red-blooded female would jump at the chance to sleep with him. Instead, he was putting himself out there for her, willing to try something that might help her.

"Have you done this a lot?" She prayed this wasn't some sort of kink, something he'd done with any number of women. Couldn't imagine a guy like Bran letting anyone restrain him.

His sexy mouth edged up. "No. It's not really my kind of thing. But I thought in this situation, it might work."

Relief filtered through her. She went up on her toes and kissed him. "I have no idea what will happen, but if you're willing, I'd like to try."

Bran traced a finger down her cheek and grinned. "Go ahead, honey. Have your way with me."

CHAPTER SIXTEEN

BRAN COULDN'T BELIEVE he was actually doing this. He'd put it mildly when he'd told Jessie this wasn't his kind of thing. He was a man and she was a woman, and that's the way he liked it, especially in the bedroom.

But Jessie meant a lot to him, and he had a feeling she just needed a little help to get her head back on straight.

He started by turning on the bathroom light and partially closing the door, leaving it open enough to illuminate the room in a soft yellow glow.

Taking a condom from his pocket, he tossed it up on the nightstand, sat down on the edge of the bed, and took off his low-topped leather boots. Standing to unzip his jeans, he slid them down his legs, leaving him in his white cotton briefs. He made no effort to hide his erection. He'd told her he wanted her. He just didn't want to scare her by telling her how much.

"You ready for this?" he asked. She nodded, but he couldn't miss the trepidation that had crept into her eyes. Leaning down, he kissed her long and deep, then stripped off his briefs, lay down on his back and stretched out on the mattress. Reaching up, he grabbed the post at the end of the padded headboard.

Jessie's hand shook as she looped the zip tie around the post and his wrists. Bran spread his hands a little as she tightened the loop, a trick to give him enough room to get free whenever he wanted.

Hell, no way he was actually letting anyone tie him up. He was a soldier and Jessie's bodyguard. That wasn't going to happen.

Didn't matter. All that mattered was giving her the illusion of control. It would work or it wouldn't. He prayed to God it would and inwardly groaned to think how bad he was going to ache if it didn't.

Jessie stood next to the bed staring down at him.

"Be nice if you took off your clothes and joined me," he said. "I'm beginning to feel a little self-conscious."

That made her smile. She took off her clothes one piece at a time, and with every inch of her lovely body she revealed, his lust expanded. Her pretty breasts and tiny waist, the perfect little ass that had intrigued him from the moment she had dived into the warm pool water. Jessie must have sensed the effect she was having because she removed each garment with more and more confidence.

Or maybe it was the perspiration she saw on his forehead just thinking about what she might do to his body.

Naked at last, she settled herself on the bed beside him, leaned over and kissed him. Her silky hair tumbled around her, enveloping him in a fiery cocoon and driving him crazy.

The kiss went on and on. He was beginning to wonder if he had miscalculated and she didn't have the courage to do more than kiss when her hands began to slide over his chest. His abdomen contracted as she explored his biceps, his pecs, the indentations over his ribs. When her tongue ringed his navel, he bit back a groan.

Her lips followed her hands, pressing soft butterfly kisses across his heated skin, making him so hard he hurt.

She paused when she reached the scar from the bullet that had plunged into his abdomen, pressed her mouth there, then kissed the scar near his spleen.

There was something about it so tender it made him want her even more. When she returned to kissing him again, it took every ounce of his will not to free his wrists, lift her up and settle her astride him, surge into her until he found release.

He called on his Delta training in a way he had never imagined, fighting the overwhelming need to take her.

Just when he thought he couldn't stand a moment more, Jessie tore open the condom and gently sheathed him. He closed his eyes at the rush of pleasure and clenched his jaw to stay in control.

Jessie straddled him, raised herself up, and took him deep. Brandon's eyes slid closed on a wave of bliss. Sweet Jesus, nothing had ever felt so good. He let her set the rhythm, fought not to move until his body rebelled and he had no choice. She was riding him now, taking what she wanted.

He clamped down hard on his control until he felt the first ripples of her climax and heard her moan. Triumph burst through him, followed by a rush of incredible heat. Unable to stop himself, he freed his hands and gripped her hips, surged up into her and began to take what he so desperately needed.

Bran took her and took her, drove her up to a second peak, before his muscles went rigid, a fierce groan escaped, and he followed her to release.

Long moments passed with Jessie slumped over his chest, her silky hair spread out around them. Still hard inside her, he ran a hand down her back, praying he hadn't hurt her, praying she had enjoyed it as much as he had. Praying she was okay.

When he felt the wetness of her tears on his chest, everything inside him constricted into a hard, tight ball of regret.

He drew in a ragged breath. "Jessie, honey. I'm so sorry."

Instead of the sob he expected, Jessie shot into a sitting position, a huge grin on her face. "We did it!" She wriggled, still astride him. "We did it!"

They were tears of joy, he realized. Joy, not sorrow.

Relief hit him hard. Swallowing past the knot in his throat, he managed to smile. "Yeah, baby, we did." Easing her off him onto the mattress beside him, he leaned over and very softly kissed her. "You were amazing."

He left her long enough to dispose of protection and returned to find her still smiling.

"It worked," she said as he lay down beside her and curled her into his side. "We made new memories to replace the old ones. I might have a relapse once in a while, but next time I have a problem, I'll just close my eyes and see you. I'll remember how good it felt when we were making love."

Bran chuckled. "Glad I could be of service."

Jessie laughed, a carefree sound, unlike he had heard before. "You were never really tied up, were you?"

He just shrugged. "I'm your bodyguard. I'm supposed to protect you. I couldn't do that if my hands were tied."

She rolled onto her side to look at him, ran her fingers through the fine mat of hair on his chest. "Do you think we could…um…try it again? I mean just the…you know… regular way?"

His body stirred and his blood began to pound. He'd tried to convince himself not to push her, that she was still recovering from Cummings, but he hadn't had nearly enough of her.

"If you're up to it." Which he hoped like hell she was. He retrieved a couple more condoms, then returned to the bed. "Anything special you need me to do?"

Jessie leaned over and softly kissed him. "I just want you to make love to me like a normal woman. I just want to be a woman Bran Garrett took to bed."

But she was way more than that. It worried him to think how much more.

He was already hard. He leaned over and kissed her pretty breasts, tasting the sweetness he had craved from the start. "Just tell me if you need me to stop."

She nodded.

But Jessie never stopped him, and he didn't quit until they had both reached another earth-shattering climax.

He took her once more in the middle of the night.

Tomorrow would be soon enough to worry about chemical weapons, finding a murderer, and trying to stay alive.

CHAPTER SEVENTEEN

THE SOUND OF Bran's phone signaling on the nightstand awoke her. Jessie sat up as he fumbled, grabbed it, then cursed softly and swung his legs to the side of the bed.

The red numbers on the digital clock read 6:45 a.m. Bran was usually up by six, a little before she was, but they hadn't gotten much sleep last night.

Heat slid through her as she thought about what they had done. She'd only had a couple of serious boyfriends. Sex with them was nothing like sex with Bran. There was just something about him.

Maybe his amazing body, or maybe just that he was such a virile male. He had taken his time, been careful not to push her too hard. She'd never flashed back to her abduction. Her mind was too full of Bran.

She sighed into the morning light seeping into the bedroom. She was going to have a very hard time forgetting him when all of this was over.

A thought that had her good mood slipping away.

Yawning, she focused on the call that had just come in.

"Thanks for the heads-up," Bran was saying. "I'll get right on it. I owe you one, Tab." The seriousness of his tone as he ended the call snared her attention. He slid on his jeans while Jessie slipped on her terry cloth robe and followed him into the living room.

"What's going on?"

"That was Tabby. She's been looking into Petrov and Graves, trying to find Weaver. Petrov's real name is Janos, not Vladimir." He raked back his sleep-mussed dark hair. "Yesterday afternoon Janos Petrov turned up dead."

"Oh, my God."

"It gets worse. The murder was reported on the local five o'clock news. At the end of the broadcast, the sheriff put out an appeal to the public, looking for any information on the victim. According to an internet news site, the woman from the resort recognized his picture, called in and told them about the fight. I checked us into the resort under my name, so now the sheriff has a BOLO out on me as a person of interest."

"They think *you* killed Petrov?"

Bran just shrugged. "They're looking for me, which means unless I want to dodge police cars all over the state, I need to turn myself in."

"I'm your alibi. I'm going with you."

"Oh, you're coming with me. People are still hunting you. I need you where I can keep you safe. We've got time to shower, but we need to get going."

Jessie cast him an interested glance and he grinned.

"As much as I like the idea, we definitely need more time for a shower like that."

She laughed.

"While you're gone, I'll see what I can find out on the internet."

Jessie spun and headed for the bathroom. "I'll hurry."

Thirty minutes later Bran pulled into an angled parking space in front of the El Paso County Sheriff's office on East Vermijo Avenue. He got out and checked their surroundings, which was probably second nature after so many years in the army, then motioned for her to join him.

They shoved through the front doors and walked up to the counter, where an eager young deputy in a dark gray uniform shirt and black uniform pants sat behind a computer.

"May I help you?" he asked.

"My name is Brandon Garrett. This is Jessica Kegan. I'm her bodyguard. I understand the sheriff is looking for me in regard to a man named Janos Petrov."

The deputy, Hillman, his badge read, looked up at Bran in surprise and quickly came to his feet. "Yes, sir. You said bodyguard. Are you armed, Mr. Garrett?"

"Not at the moment."

A second deputy appeared to assist Hillman. They definitely weren't taking any chances, and as Jessie thought of what Bran was capable of doing, she didn't blame them.

"If you'll both come this way." The second deputy, Crowley, was older, a slight paunch over his belt.

They passed through a metal detector that showed Bran had been telling the truth about the weapon, which he had left locked in the SUV. Crowley checked Jessie's handbag and motioned for them to follow.

"Right this way," Deputy Hillman said.

But the man waiting in the interview room wasn't the sheriff. He was the sheriff's deputy in charge of the Petrov murder case, Detective Mace Galen.

"Thank you for coming in," Detective Galen said, a broad-shouldered blond man, rather imposing, Jessie thought, with a thick mustache that curved around his mouth, and intense dark eyes.

"No problem," Bran said.

Galen turned to her. "Ms. Kegan, is it?"

"That's right."

"I'm afraid you'll have to wait in the other room. I'll need to speak to you after I'm finished with Mr. Garrett."

Jessie's gaze snapped to Bran. On the drive over, they had reviewed the details of the fight at the resort and also the attack that had left Petrov and Graves tied up in the desert.

"Just tell them the truth," Bran had said. "Can't screw up too badly if you're being honest."

"What about all the other stuff? My dad, and the reason we're here?"

"You're a journalist. You're working on a story. That's all you need to say."

Now, walking out of the interview room, her mind raced as she followed Deputy Hillman into a second interview room next to the first.

"You might as well have a seat," the young deputy said. "It could take a while."

The door closed, and Jessie sat down in a pale blue padded vinyl chair at the metal-framed table in the middle of the room. It was cold in there. The room was stark, except for a big rectangular mirror on one wall, a two-way mirror, she figured, just like on TV.

Jessie thought of what might be happening to Bran and shivered.

"So the cuts and bruises all over Petrov's body were delivered by *you*?" Detective Galen sat across from Bran on the opposite side of the metal-framed table.

"I don't know. I'd have to look at the body."

"What kind of weapon do you carry?"

"On which particular day?"

Galen glared.

"Mostly a Glock 19. If I need it, a Smith & Wesson

.38 revolver ankle gun for backup." Among others, but he didn't say that.

"Petrov died from a .45-caliber bullet wound. He was shot right between the eyes."

"Whoa, brutal."

"Yes, it was. We know you were army Special Forces. Highly decorated before you were wounded and had to leave the service."

He didn't bother to answer. It wasn't his favorite subject.

"A special ops soldier. That makes you more than capable of delivering a kill shot like that."

"I could do it, but I didn't. What about his buddy, Graves? Maybe Graves got tired of playing second fiddle."

"Is that the way it was? Petrov ran the show and Graves just went along for the ride?"

"I'd say Petrov was the alpha dog, but truthfully, I didn't pick up that kind of friction between them."

"We're still looking for Graves. They both had rap sheets, but Graves had no outstanding warrants so he was released the same night we brought him in. Petrov's background was a little more sketchy. Plus he was using an alias so we kept him in lockup overnight. When nothing interesting turned up, we released him the next morning. A teenager found him dead in his truck a few hours later."

"Graves could have been waiting for him."

"He could have been. What about you? The woman at the resort described a rather spectacular fight on Halloween night."

"We fought," he said. "Petrov and Graves were hired to silence my client, Ms. Kegan."

"By silence, do you mean kill?"

"If necessary."

"And why is that?"

"She's a journalist. They wanted to stop her from writing a story she's working on."

"What kind of story?"

"Look, what Ms. Kegan writes is none of my business. I'm her bodyguard. Keeping her safe—that's what I'm paid to do." Not that he was actually getting any money.

"And the night we picked up Petrov and Graves out in the desert? That was you? You're the one who assaulted them and called 911?"

"They made the mistake of coming after Ms. Kegan again. All I did was protect my client. They were lucky I called the cops instead of leaving them to freeze their asses off in the desert."

Galen grunted and leaned toward him across the table. "So you aren't the guy who killed him."

"Hell, no. If I'd wanted Petrov dead, he'd be dead and buried and you never would have found a trace of him."

Galen's chair grated as he slid it backward, got up, and began to pace the tight quarters of the stark white room. The faint smell of stale fear-sweat lingered in the stuffy air.

"Tell me why you believe Petrov was hired to take out your client."

"I told you…she's doing a story someone doesn't want her to write."

"But I'm guessing you don't know who that someone is."

"I wish I did." He straightened, liking the detective's no-bullshit style and coming to a decision. "If you want to know who killed Petrov, I'd suggest you look for the guy who hired him to go after Ms. Kegan. Petrov mentioned someone named Weaver. That's all I know."

"Weaver. What's his first name?"

"No idea."

"So that's it? That's all you're going to say?"

Bran leaned back in his chair and looked up at him. "I can tell you this much. Ms. Kegan's late father was a colonel in the army. Some of what she's working on is of a highly sensitive nature. At this time, neither of us is at liberty to talk about it."

Galen's jaw tightened. He reached into his pocket, pulled out a business card, and flipped it on the table. "Call me when you're ready to talk."

Turning, he opened the door, stalked out, and slammed it behind him. Bran picked up the card and tucked it away just in case. He almost smiled to think what would happen when the detective questioned Jessie.

"You know I can hold you for forty-eight hours without pressing charges." Galen stood on the opposite side of the table, his palms flat as he leaned down and glared at her.

"Seriously? You're going to arrest me? Petrov and Graves came after *me*. All my bodyguard did was protect me. If anything, he restrained himself from hurting the men even worse."

"Why didn't he reveal his identity after the attack when he called 911 and gave the men's location?"

"Because he didn't want to go through exactly what he's going through right now."

A muscle ticked in Galen's cheek. "You said Petrov and Graves were trying to stop you from writing the story you're working on. What's the story about?"

"I'm sorry, that's my business. I'm an investigative journalist. Sometimes researching the subject matter involves a certain amount of risk."

Galen blew out a frustrated breath. "You and Garrett, you're a real pair."

She smiled. "Thanks."

The detective shook his head. He'd been asking her the same questions for the last half hour, getting exactly the same answers. "All right, you can go. Just don't leave the area. We might have more questions for you."

"Fine."

Bran was sitting on a bench along the wall waiting for her when she walked out of the interview room. She smiled. "We can go."

He smiled back, clearly relieved. When they arrived at the SUV and climbed in, there was a note under the windshield wiper on the driver's side. Bran reached around and grabbed the slip of white paper.

"What's it say?" Jessie asked.

"'You want info on Weaver, meet me at the Rooster, at ten o'clock tonight.' There's a cross at the bottom and the initial G."

She leaned over to read the note. "It's supposed to be a grave. Gravedigger. Harley Graves."

He nodded. "He must have seen the news and heard they were looking for me, figured I'd come in to talk to the sheriff sooner or later."

"The Red Rooster. I've driven past it. Kind of a seedy country Western bar." She grinned. "Looks like we're going honky-tonkin' tonight."

Bran cast her a glance, clearly unhappy with the idea. "I can't leave you alone so I guess you're right."

Since it sounded like Graves might have useful information and she was tired of being cooped up in the hotel room, no matter how roomy it was, she was looking forward to the evening.

On the other hand, Petrov was dead. Whoever killed him was likely still after her.

"You think it could be a trap?"

Bran turned the corner, checking the mirror and taking a roundabout route as he drove back to the hotel. "It's possible. But Graves's note mentioned Weaver. If Weaver killed Petrov for not getting the job done, then he's probably gunning for Graves, too."

"How does Graves know we're looking for Weaver?"

"Either Petrov told him or he heard me asking Petrov about him that night."

"So you think Graves might be willing to trade information in exchange for our help."

"Could be."

It was crazy. Helping a man who'd been trying to kill her. Or at least hurt her badly enough to convince her to stop her investigation. But the way things were going, nothing surprised her.

Her stomach growled, reminding her they hadn't eaten breakfast, and it was well past noon. "I'm starving. Let's stop and get something to eat."

Bran cut her a look. "Yeah... I'm hungry, too." But the hunger in his eyes as they fixed on her mouth had nothing to do with food. Her insides curled. Maybe staying at home tonight wouldn't have been such a bad idea.

CHAPTER EIGHTEEN

THE AIR WAS crisp and cold, the night pitch-black as Bran pulled into the big asphalt parking lot. The Red Rooster Bar and Grill on B Street out I-25 was a single-story flat-roofed structure at the back of the lot, a cross between a cowboy bar and a bikers' roadhouse. Dirty pickup trucks, motorcycles, and paint-faded beaters were parked haphazardly out front.

As Bran pushed open the door and surveilled the dimly lit interior, he noted the array of vehicles exactly matched their owners. Frayed jeans, scuffed boots, and battered cowboy hats at one end of the bar, bikers in studded black leather at the other.

It was an uneasy mix that undoubtedly kept everyone entertained.

Bran urged Jessie toward a pair of empty wooden bar stools. The decor was part Old West saloon with a long bar and a carved wooden backbar, but the neon signs, mostly Jack Daniel's, Shiner Bock, and Coors, were pure twenty-first century.

A bartender with greasy black hair and a black T-shirt that said Come Back with a Warrant walked over to take their orders. "What'll you have?"

Bran glanced over at Jessie, who looked a little too fetching in her skinny jeans and ankle boots and low-cut sexy pink sweater. He'd tried to talk her into something a little more modest, but she'd rightly pointed out she'd fit in better in what she had on. Since she was right, he'd sucked it up and escorted her out of the hotel room.

"I'll have a Lone Star," Jessie said.

"Same for me," Bran said. The beers arrived, not as cold as he liked, but he wasn't there to drink so it didn't really matter. He tipped up the bottle as he scanned the room for Digger Graves. They'd arrived early so he'd have time to do a little recon before Graves showed up. No sign of a trap, but he hadn't really expected one.

He figured Graves was in deep shit with Weaver. He needed their help to stay alive.

It was a little after ten o'clock when Graves walked in, brown hair slicked into a man bun, worn jeans, and a long-sleeve camouflage T-shirt under a khaki vest.

"That's him," Jessie said, tipping her head toward the door. She had pulled her hair up in a ponytail, which made her look younger and even more tempting. Half the bar had been staring since she'd walked in. Reading the lust on their horny faces, Bran clenched his jaw against an urge to start throwing punches.

It was a new sensation, this possessive feeling for a woman. He didn't like it, but he couldn't seem to get a handle on it.

Graves spotted them, made eye contact, and headed for a table at the back of the bar. He ordered a drink from a big-haired, buxom blond server and leaned back to survey the room.

"Let's go." Bran tossed money on the bar for their beers and set a hand at Jessie's waist, making it clear she was with him as they began weaving their way through the battered wooden tables scattered around the room.

When they reached Graves's table, Bran pulled out a

chair for Jessie and one for himself. Graves's order arrived, a boilermaker. He tossed back the shot of whiskey and chased it with a swallow of beer. Bran ordered two more Lone Stars just to fit in.

He waited till the server walked away, then turned to Graves. "So I guess you know your buddy Petrov is dead."

Graves tipped up his beer and took a long swallow. The shamrock on the side of his neck seemed to glow in the red neon lights as his throat moved up and down.

"Weaver had him killed," Digger said, setting the bottle back on the table.

"He didn't do the job himself?"

"Can't. He's in prison."

Probably should have seen that one coming, but he hadn't. "Which one?"

"Federal Correctional Institution, Florence. It's about forty miles southwest of here."

"Why does that name ring a bell?" Bran asked.

"ADX Florence," Jessie said, her voice so soft his gaze shot to her face, which looked paler than it had before.

"ADMAX," she continued. "They call it the Alcatraz of the Rockies. I wrote a series of articles about it. The most hardened criminals in the country are locked up in there, or people who pose a threat to national security. Remember Zacarias Moussaoui? He helped plot the September 11 attacks. Dzhokhar Tsarnaev, the Boston Bomber, is also an inmate at ADMAX."

Her gaze swung to Graves. "Leaders of violent gangs are sent there—men who continue to issue orders to their members even after they're put in prison."

Bran looked at Graves. "That what's going on here? Weaver is issuing orders from inside?"

Digger shifted uneasily in his chair. "Pretty much." He

made a visual sweep of the room, on the lookout for any threat. "Weaver murdered three black cops in Georgia, got sentenced to life without parole. Slowed him down a little but didn't stop him. He just kept running the Brotherhood from his cell. When they found out he'd ordered hits on two more men, they moved him to ADMAX."

"So he's there now?" Bran asked.

"He's there, but two years ago, he got transferred out of maximum security for good behavior. He's in a medium security facility in the same complex, which means he's able to give orders again. Weaver says jump, the Brotherhood says how high."

"Nobody's figured it out?"

Graves took a swig of beer. "Big money in looking the other way. Bribes, threats, payoffs. Whatever works."

"And you can't go to the cops because talking's a death sentence for sure."

Graves nodded.

Jessie leaned toward him. "So the reason you're giving us Weaver's location is because you want us to intercede. Find a way to prove Weaver was involved in Petrov's murder and maybe get him moved back to ADMAX maximum security where he's locked up twenty-three hours a day and no longer able to communicate outside the walls of his cell."

Digger looked at her as if she were the smartest person in the room. "That's the idea."

"If you want Weaver off your back," Bran said, "tell us who paid him to order the hit on Colonel Kegan."

Graves shook his head. "I don't know anything about any colonel. You want to know who hired him, get the goods on Weaver. Maybe you can get him to tell you."

Bran ignored a trickle of irritation. "If you want Weaver taken down, we're going to need something to go on."

Digger swallowed the entire second half of his beer in a few long swallows. Bran figured he was trying to work up his courage. Being a rat in the Brotherhood wasn't the recipe for a long healthy life.

Digger set his empty bottle down on the table. "The way the hit on Petrov went down—a .45-caliber bullet dead center between the eyes—I'd look for a guy named Tank. Rides with the A-BOYZ out of Denver. That's Tank's signature, and it's all I know."

Graves set down his empty bottle, dug money out of his pocket for his drinks, and started to rise from the table.

Bran caught his arm as he walked past. "I don't know how this is going to come down, but my advice is you get as far from Colorado as you can."

Graves nodded. "I hear you, man." Turning, he strode out the door without looking back.

Bran tossed down a few more bills, waited a couple of minutes, then he and Jessie followed. Unfortunately, two of the guys who'd been eyeing her earlier rose and followed them outside. The bastards had decided to try him on, find out how serious he was about protecting her.

His jaw went iron-hard. Leading her farther away, he handed her the keys to the Expedition. "Get in the car and lock the doors."

Her glance went from him to the men lining up outside the front door, three of them now, big and ugly. *Perfect*. He needed to work off a little stress.

"No way," Jessie said. "I'm not abandoning you."

A muscle jumped in his cheek. "Go on, Jessie. Dammit, do what I tell you."

"We go together or not at all."

His jaw went tight. "I swear to Christ…"

She lifted her chin. She wasn't budging. He wanted to

paddle her sweet little ass or kiss her. He wasn't completely sure which. He'd never had a woman willing to put herself out there for him the way Jessie did.

"Fine," he said. "Have it your way." Reaching inside his bomber jacket, he pulled his Glock, turned, and aimed it at the three approaching men. "The lady says she doesn't want me to bruise my knuckles, so I guess I'll just have to shoot you."

Jessie gasped. The three men stopped dead in their tracks.

"He's a former Special Forces soldier," Jessie rushed to tell them. "You'd be smart to go back inside."

They grumbled something between them. One of them started forward, but another pulled him back. "Don't come around here again," the third man warned as they sauntered back into the bar.

A relieved smile broke over Jessie's face. "Now, see how easy that was?"

Bran just shook his head. He couldn't hold back a grin. "You are really something, lady."

She glanced back over her shoulder, saw more people drifting out of the bar. "I think we'd better go."

He followed her gaze. "Good idea."

Neither of them spoke as he drove back toward the hotel, watching his mirror and checking their surroundings, making sure he wasn't being tailed.

"There's something I haven't told you," Jessie said as the lights of the Holiday Inn appeared up ahead.

Bran slanted her a glance. Her uncertain expression didn't bode well. "Yeah, what's that?"

"Those terrorists locked up in ADMAX? One of them is a domestic terrorist named Joseph Konopku. He instigated power blackouts in Wisconsin. He was also involved in a thwarted attack using potassium cyanide and sodium cyanide in the Chicago subway system."

"Chemical weapons."

"That's right."

Bran considered what would happen if the missing munitions were detonated in an underground facility like a subway.

"Fuck," was all he said.

BRAN HAD BEEN in a foul mood ever since they got back to their modest hotel suite. He was worried, she knew, about what steps to take next. A wrong move could get both of them killed.

And because she was Danny's sister, he felt a deep sense of responsibility for her safety. After their conversation in the Mexican restaurant, she knew he still carried a great deal of survivor's guilt. He blamed himself, at least in part, for Danny's death. She could see the weight he carried on his usually straight shoulders. But just because she had gone to him for help didn't mean she expected him to carry all the burden.

It was well after midnight, and he was still sitting in front of his laptop. Jessie came up behind him and slid her arms around his neck.

"Let's go to bed. I'm pretty sure I can take your mind off criminals and murder, at least for a while."

He looked at her over his shoulder, and she saw a flare of heat in his amazing blue eyes. "I've still got some work I need to do."

"I was thinking maybe we could start again in the morning."

The heat turned to flame as he shot up out of the chair

and swung her up in his arms. "Jesus, I think I've created a monster."

She arched an eyebrow. "Really?"

He grinned. "I think I'm the luckiest guy in Colorado." Cradling her face between his hands, he kissed her, long and deep, and carried her into the bedroom.

Their lovemaking was slow and easy, both of them exhausted after such a long day. She was sure Bran was still being careful with her, making sure he didn't do anything to upset her. But nothing about him reminded her of Cummings, and she was beginning to want more, want the demanding lover she sensed beneath his careful concern.

Still, when she awoke the next morning, she felt content in a way she hadn't in a very long time. Bran was on his phone when she walked into the living room in her white terry robe, following the aroma of freshly brewed coffee. She yawned as she poured herself a cup and refilled Bran's mug on the table next to his computer.

"Looks like you've been hard at work while I've been sleeping the morning away," she said, picking up on his serious expression.

"I talked to Tabby, told her we found Weaver, that he's locked up in ADMAX but still giving orders. She hasn't come up with anything more on the offshore account, but she's still working on it. Mara Ramos's plate number checked out. Belongs to a white Toyota Camry, but her address is in San Diego, California. Apparently, Mara never changed the registration when she moved to Colorado."

"Or maybe San Diego is still her primary location."

"We'll find out," Bran said. "I also talked to my brothers, Chase and Reese. They tend to get cranky if I don't check in once in a while."

She took a sip of coffee. "So what did your brothers have to say?"

"Chase said not to worry about the plane and to call if I needed any help. I told him at the moment we're better off keeping things on the down-low."

"And Reese? He's the middle brother, right?"

"Reese just said to let him know if I needed anything— he's a genius at getting things done. Said to stay safe and he'd see me at Thanksgiving if not before."

Thanksgiving. October had turned into November. The holidays were coming. Jessie glanced away, suddenly missing her family. Her brother was gone, now her dad. She had lost her mom some years back, but she still missed her. She hoped Bran knew how lucky he was to have a family who cared about him so much.

She heard the chair scrape as he rose to his feet, then his arms slipped around her. "I told you you're invited to Thanksgiving dinner."

She smiled a bit sadly. "I know and I appreciate the offer. I'll be fine. It's just...thinking about your brothers makes me miss my family."

"Yeah, I get that. Sometimes I think about my mom and dad. I'm lucky to have Chase and Reese."

"Yes, you are."

Bran kissed the top of her head and let her go. Missing the warmth, she reached for her coffee mug and took a sip. "So are we going after this guy, Tank?"

"Seems like the best option at the moment."

"According to Digger Graves, Tank is supposed to be in Denver. We can stay at my apartment if you don't mind being a little cramped. My friend Hallie has been watering my plants, but I could really use some clean clothes."

"Might be risky. There's a chance they'll be staking your place out."

Her shoulders slumped. "It's possible, I suppose. But I've only been home off and on for weeks. Hallie's never mentioned any problems, and I can't imagine they're just hanging around in case I show up."

"We'll check it out. If it looks okay, we can at least go in long enough for you to get some clothes."

"Great."

"We also need more info on Mara Ramos."

Jessie had talked to Agent Tripp, but according to him, Mara's social security number and personal information at the time of her visit to the prison had all checked out. Since then she had moved away, and they had no way to contact her. Bran had gotten lucky with the apartment manager. Now Tabby had tracked Ramos's plates to California.

"Maximum Security has an office in San Diego," Bran said. "I'll call one of the PIs, have him check, see if Ramos showed up at her old address."

Bran's phone signaled just then. Jessie set her empty mug on the kitchen counter. "I'll hit the shower while you answer the call."

He flashed her a hot look that held a trace of disappointment. Jessie laughed as she disappeared into the bedroom, leaving Bran to answer his cell.

CHAPTER NINETEEN

THE CALLER ID read *Jailbird*. Bran chuckled. Tyler Folsom. Same name as the prison in California made famous by Johnny Cash. Ty was one of the SF Airborne guys at Fort Carson that Bran had texted with photos of Petrov and Graves.

He pressed the phone against his ear. "Hey, Ty. You get my text?"

"Reason I called, bro. Saw them looking for you on the news. That guy in the photo, Petrov, is dead. Sheriff is looking for you as a person of interest. Figured I'd see if you needed some help."

"Old news, my friend. I'm square with the law, at least for now."

"If you haven't heard, I'm out of the army. Didn't re-up this last time."

"No kidding. I figured you for a lifer."

"That was my plan, but my sister and her husband got killed in a car wreck. Their two kids were in the car. Little nephew ended up in a wheelchair. And his sister, Sarah, is only four years old. Somebody had to raise them, and I figured it ought to be me."

"That's rough, man."

"In some ways it's great. I love those kids, and their grandmother has a ton of money. She insisted we move into the guesthouse on her estate in Denver. Dude, it's bigger than most people's homes. She takes great care of the kids when I'm working, so everything is good."

"You don't miss the army?"

"Only every minute of every day."

Bran laughed. "Listen, I might have a way you can help. I'm headed to Denver with a client. She's going to need protection while I'm tracking down the SOB who killed Janos Petrov. Can you handle it?"

Excitement shaded Ty's voice. "You bet I can. I'm working security, but it's pretty routine. You want the truth, except for the kids, most of the time I'm bored out of my skull."

"So I guess you miss jumping out of a perfectly good airplane."

Ty chuckled. "You better believe it."

Bran smiled. "We'll be in late this afternoon. We'll let you know where we're staying once we get there."

"Why don't you stay here? This place is like Fort Knox. Guarded gate, the whole bit, plus it's up in Evergreen, a little ways out of the city. Safest place your client could be."

Bran mulled over the idea. His first concern was the safety of Ty's kids, but at the moment Weaver's crew had no idea where they were and no way to track them. Being somewhere outside the city would make it even harder. And with any luck, they wouldn't be there long.

"Sounds great. I'll phone you when we get close." Bran ended the call and glanced toward the bedroom. The water in the shower had just started running. His pulse kicked up. He started peeling off his clothes as he headed toward the bathroom.

He was naked by the time he pulled open the door. The plastic shower curtain wasn't an obstacle. Jessie's big green eyes widened as he stepped in with her, his erection already rock hard.

He reminded himself to go easy, that she was still getting used to him. Reaching for the soap, he lathered his hands and began to spread thick white bubbles all over her delicate curves. Jessie moaned as he gently soaped her breasts, slid his hands down to her sex.

Sweet Jesus, he hoped the hot water didn't run out because he didn't plan to hurry.

THE HOTEL WASN'T MUCH, but the shower was pure luxury. At least when Bran Garrett was giving her his personal spa treatment.

Jessie bit back a moan. Those big hands were all over her, gently spreading soap bubbles across her rapidly heating skin. He seemed to know exactly where to touch her, exactly what to do to make her burn.

He soaped her breasts and between her legs until she was panting, the shower making her muscles loose and pliant. She wanted more, wanted all of him, wanted to feel his heavy erection inside her.

A deep, scorching kiss had her insides quivering. She barely noticed when he lifted her, wrapped her legs around his waist.

"Hang on to my neck," he softly commanded, cupping her bottom to hold her in place. He propped her shoulders against the shower wall to steady her, eased himself inside, and dear God, he felt good. Big and hard and amazing. He slid even deeper, taking it slow and easy, until she started begging for more. Bran hissed in a breath and began moving faster, deeper, harder, setting off every nerve ending in her body.

Warm water ran down his magnificent chest, sluiced

seductively over her breasts. He set up a rhythm that sent heat and need pouring through her, sank deliciously into her core.

When she pulled his head down for a deep, erotic kiss, a growl slipped from his throat. Tightening her legs around his waist, she took even more of him and realized he was fighting for control.

A surge of pure feminine power rose inside her. She was no longer victim, but victor, an equal partner in pleasure, as she had been from the first moment that she had been with Bran.

His pace increased as he drove into her, and the first ripples of climax struck, sweet and hot and delicious. A soft whimper escaped as her body clenched around him. Bran growled low in his throat and followed her to an earth-shattering release.

He tipped his forehead against hers and took several steadying breaths. Long seconds passed before he let go and she slid weakly down his body.

A last lingering kiss, and he stepped out of the shower, grabbed a towel, and wrapped it around his waist. He pulled another towel off the rack and bundled her up in it.

"Even better than in my dreams," he said with a grin, then took care of the condom, and headed out of the bathroom to dress for the day and give her a chance to get ready.

Jessie leaned against the bathroom sink, limp and sated. She loved sex with Bran. He was every woman's fantasy. Handsome, strong, intelligent, protective. Great in bed.

She thought of her brother's warning. *He's a real heartbreaker, sis. Bran Garrett's my best friend, but he's the last guy you ever want to get involved with*.

Danny assumed she and Brandon would meet sooner or later, which they would have if Danny hadn't gotten killed.

Her brother didn't want her getting hurt, and now that she and Bran were spending so much time together, she understood what he meant.

She needed to put things in perspective, keep tabs on her emotions. She told herself it was just sex. It didn't really mean anything to either one of them. They'd become friends, and Bran was just trying to help her get over the hang-ups she'd told him about. She wasn't the kind of person to have meaningless sex, but there was a first time for everything.

Or at least that's what she was determined to believe.

One thing was certain. She didn't want to fall in love with him.

Jessie prayed it wasn't already too late.

THEY LEFT FOR Evergreen that afternoon, driving instead of flying. Making the hour and a half trip by car was easier than moving the plane, then having to rent another vehicle.

Ty had given Bran directions up the winding road to his home in the hills overlooking Mount Evans. The weather was cloudy and cold, the temperature down in the thirties with a storm moving in, but the drive through the forested mountains was beautiful, a sea of pine trees that stretched as far as the eye could see.

When they arrived at the property, a uniformed guard in the gatehouse opened the tall wrought iron gates to let them pass, and they continued up the winding drive.

"Look at that," Jessie said as the huge house came into view, modeled after a French château, with balconies and turrets and a circular drive out front. An ornate fountain sat in the middle of the drive, though the water had been turned off for the winter.

"The guesthouse is out back," Bran said, following the

road deeper onto the property. He glanced around. "Ty sure didn't oversell the place."

The guesthouse looked like a smaller version of the main house, two stories, with a turret on one side and an arched, ornately carved front door.

Ty, who was about six feet tall, with light brown hair and a lean, solid build, walked out as Bran drove up. He was pushing a wheelchair and flanked by a little girl with pale blond hair. The little boy in the chair had features similar enough to hint at a relationship, and the same sandy brown hair as Ty's.

Jessie noticed one of the two garage door bays stood open. Ty motioned for them to drive inside, and Bran parked next to a silver Subaru Forester.

"Good to see you, buddy," Ty said as Bran climbed out of the SUV.

"You, too." Bran leaned in to bump shoulders. "Appreciate the help."

"No problem. Let's get you two inside where it's warm, and I'll introduce you to my kids."

Knowing the story of the car accident that had killed the children's parents, Jessie's gaze ran over the two smiling faces and she felt a pinch in her heart.

She and Bran grabbed their bags and their jackets and went into the house through the garage. The kitchen, a chef's fantasy, had the latest stainless appliances, white cabinets, black-and-white granite countertops, black-and-white marble floors. A white kitchen table and six ladderback chairs sat in a turret that looked out big glass windows into the forest.

Aside from a few plush animals and a stack of games on one end of the counter, the kitchen was immaculate.

Jessie figured someone probably cooked and cleaned for the family.

"Ty, this is Jessie Kegan," Bran said. "Jessie, meet Ty Folsom, former Green Beret and one of the craziest wind dummies in the army."

Ty grinned. "Nothing better than the rush of air in your face and the bloom of a canopy overhead. Pleased to meet you, Jessie."

She grinned back. "You, too, Ty."

He turned to the little dark-haired boy in the wheelchair. "This is Christian. He's seven. Say hello to Bran and Jessie, Chris."

"Hello," the boy said shyly.

"And this is Sarah." She had softly curling blond hair and blue eyes. "How old are you, sweetheart?"

Sarah held up four chubby little fingers. "Thwee."

Ty laughed and so did Bran.

"She just turned four. She's only starting to learn her numbers. They both had a bit of a setback, you know, with…what happened to their folks."

"They've got you now, so they'll be fine," Bran said.

Ty seemed pleased by the words. "Yeah, they will. They had a day off from school today, some teachers' function, but they're back in class tomorrow."

The children were darling. And Ty clearly loved them. Jessie had always wanted a family, but the timing never seemed right. Or more likely, it was the person who wasn't right. She wanted kids with a husband who loved her, a man who would love their children as much as she did. Watching Ty with his kids tugged at her heart.

Ty grabbed the handle of Jessie's carry-on. "Come on. Let's get you two settled."

Ty led them through a big, comfortable family room

with a manteled fireplace and overstuffed brown furniture, obviously the center of the household, past a dining room furnished with a mahogany table and eight elegant chairs, and a living room decorated with gold velvet furniture and French antiques.

"Two bedrooms downstairs and a bathroom," Ty said. "Me and the kids are upstairs. This wing's all yours."

"Great. This is perfect," Bran said.

Ty's gaze went from Bran to Jessie and back. Maybe it was how close he was standing, or a look that had passed between them. "She'll be safe with me," Ty said to him.

Bran nodded. "I know."

He was leaving her with his friend, going after Tank by himself. They had argued about it on the drive down, but once Bran had talked to Ty and felt sure she'd be safe, there was no convincing him to take her along.

"I can't deal with this guy and worry about you at the same time. Tank's a killer. I need to find him and figure a way to take him down. I can't do that if you're with me."

Since she was pretty sure he was right and she'd be putting him in even graver danger, she had conceded. Not that he'd ever intended to give her a choice.

Ty left the two of them to get settled in, Jessie in one bedroom, Bran in the other. She glanced at the queen-size four-poster bed beneath a snowy eyelet comforter and mound of matching white pillows and thought how much she would miss Bran's warm body curled around her that night.

She unpacked her toiletries in the adjoining bathroom and walked back into the bedroom just as Brandon opened the door. He looked different, harder, colder, a man on a mission. He hadn't shaved in a couple of days, which made him look even tougher. Dressed in jeans and combat boots, he wore a faded, slightly tattered olive-drab jacket with military patches on the shoulders.

"Time to go," he said. "I don't know how long it will take me to find this guy, but I'll text and let you know what's going on. If trouble comes, do what Ty tells you. He knows what he's doing."

She swallowed and nodded, suddenly afraid for him. "I will, I promise." She looked up at him. "Please be careful."

Eyes as blue as the Colorado sky locked on her face. Bran hauled her into his arms and kissed her, quick and hard. "I'll be back," he said a little gruffly, and her gaze followed him all the way out of the room.

He's a soldier, she reminded herself. *Just like Danny. Just like Dad.* She had never even dated a military man. She didn't want to fall for one, didn't want that kind of life.

Still, she couldn't stand the thought of something happening to him. As she walked out of the room, Jessie said a silent prayer that he would be safe.

CHAPTER TWENTY

IT TOOK BRAN the rest of the day to track the A-BOYZ motorcycle club to the town of Aurora on the outskirts of Denver. The first call he'd made had been to Hawk Maddox at The Max. Hawk was one of the best bounty hunters in the country, one of the most connected guys he knew.

Hawk had made some calls and phoned him back. Tank's full name was Wayne Conrad Coffman. He was ex-army, born in Denver, joined the military right out of high school, dishonorably discharged, gone from the city for years, only recently returned.

By early evening, Bran had the info he needed. He didn't have Tank, but Hawk's informant had given him a place to start looking.

It was ten o'clock by the time he pulled into the dirt parking lot in front of Mack's Roadhouse out on East Colfax Avenue. The lot was about half full, a few battered, mud-splattered pickups, a row of customized bikes, mostly Harleys, a couple of BMWs, and a few crotch rockets.

Bran turned the SUV around and backed into a place in the darkness at the edge of the lot. Always better to be ready if you needed to leave in a hurry. He could hear a band playing country rock a little off-key as he strode toward the entrance.

Two guitarists and a drummer pounded away on a stage on one side of the room. Old plank floors, motorcycle parts on the walls, photos of scantily clad women in various poses and bare-chested bikers in leathers. A shuffleboard clacked in the background.

Bran made his way to the long bar and sat down on one of the black vinyl stools. The bartender, a sleazy looking dude whose shoulder-length brown hair needed washing, mopped the counter with a dirty rag.

"What'll ya have?"

"Lone Star and a shot of Jack." You didn't drink just beer in a place like this. Not if you wanted information.

The bartender set the drinks in front of him and Bran shot the whiskey back. "Thanks. I needed that."

"Haven't seen you in here before."

"Haven't been in before. Just passing through unless I find a reason to stay."

The bartender's wet rag made a circle on the bar. "You a vet?"

"That's right."

"Afghanistan?"

"Kandahar, Helmand Province, a few other scenic spots."

"Fun times." The bartender chuckled and relaxed, headed for a customer at the other end of the bar. Bran sipped his beer and let the time spin out. He had no idea what Tank looked like and only a slim possibility that he would get lucky and the guy would actually show up there tonight, though Hawk's informant had said he was a regular.

He made a trip to the men's room, which was down a long hallway out of sight. A back door at the end of the corridor opened into the parking lot, locked with a dead bolt but no alarm. The two-stall men's room might prove useful. It was close to the exit, and the women's room was on the other side of the hall so noise wouldn't be a problem.

He filed the info away, returned to his bar stool, finished

his beer, and ordered another. He checked his black army wristwatch. Three minutes till time for the phone to ring.

He sipped his beer and set the bottle back down on the bar. Right on time, the phone jangled and the bartender walked over and grabbed it off the wall.

"Mack's Roadhouse."

Bran could almost hear Jessie's feminine voice on the other end of the line asking for Tank. He had called her earlier and set up the scam, hoping to draw the guy out.

"Sorry, lady. Tank ain't here. Got a regular pool game on Tuesdays. Probably be here then. You want I should tell him you called?"

As planned, Jessie told him she'd call back, and the bartender hung up the phone.

Bran felt a rush of anticipation. Tank wasn't there tonight, but he was definitely a regular and tomorrow looked good. He waited just in case, figuring the bartender would mention the call if he spotted Tank coming through the door, but it never happened. It was nearly closing when he left and started home.

Jessie would be in bed by now. Just thinking about her sleeping in one of his T-shirts, her pretty breasts forming soft mounds beneath the fabric, made him start getting hard. He clamped down on the unwanted shot of lust and concentrated on the road.

Jessie's door was closed when he headed down the hall toward the bedroom next to hers. He told himself to just keep walking. It was late and she needed her rest. He'd texted her earlier and thanked her for the help, and she'd texted back, telling him to stay safe, but it wasn't the same as talking.

Arousal slipped through him. Not that talking was all he had in mind.

He sighed and kept moving, had just opened the door to his room, when Jessie's door cracked open and a head of sleep-mussed, fiery blond hair popped into the hall.

"You're home," Jessie said. "I was worried."

He only had so much willpower. Walking back, he stopped in front of her, wished he wasn't so glad to see her. "You should be sleeping."

"I wanted to be sure you were safe."

"I'm okay." He ran a finger down her smooth cheek. "You did good tonight. With any luck Tank will show up tomorrow night, and we'll get this thing done." He told himself to turn around and go back to his own room, but he couldn't make himself move.

"I missed you," Jessie said, looking up at him with those big green eyes he found so appealing.

"I missed you, too, baby." Bran bent his head and settled his mouth over hers. His groin tightened as hunger clawed through him with surprising force.

"Stay with me," she whispered.

He kissed her again, slow and deep. "I was afraid you wouldn't ask." She led him into her bedroom, helped him undress, and they slid beneath the covers. He loved kissing her, loved the way her plump lips sank so softly into his.

The sex was good, better than good, the way it always was between them. It scared him a little. He'd had only a couple of serious relationships, and they hadn't ended well. Women seemed to expect more from him than he knew how to give. Better to keep things on a strictly physical basis. In Jessie's case, he valued her friendship as much as he enjoyed her luscious little body. He didn't want to lose it.

Or her.

The thought surprised him and made him even more wary. He didn't want to think about it so he just leaned over and started kissing her again. Jessie responded, welcoming him into her sweetly feminine warmth. Afterward they slept curled together.

The gray light of dawn slanting through the curtains awoke him. Reaching across the mattress, he realized the bed was empty and Jessie was already gone. Needing to get to his own room before the kids got up, he pulled on his clothes and slipped quietly into the hall, drawn toward the kitchen by the sound of children's laughter.

Jessie sat at the table with Chris and little Sarah playing Fish, a card game he remembered playing with his brothers.

Jessie laughed at something Chris said, and the little boy grinned ear to ear. It was the second time in two days Bran had felt a pang just looking at her.

"Okay, you two, time to get to school," Ty said. "Say goodbye to Jessie and let's get going."

"Bye, Jessie!" Chris and Sarah both called out as Ty helped them collect their things.

"Bye, guys." Jessie smiled. "See you this afternoon."

Ty loaded the little boy into his wheelchair and Sarah fell in beside him as he pushed the chair off toward the garage where the Subaru was parked.

Bran's attention returned to Jessie, whose gaze followed Ty and the kids. Her wistful smile held a softness different than he had seen before. She would want that for herself, he realized, a family, at least a couple of kids. Most women did.

What kind of father would he make? Not the spend-every-weekend-at-home, never-miss-a-PTA-meeting kind of dad. Not the go-to-work-at-eight-and-be-home-by-five kind, either. He rubbed a hand over his unshaven jaw. He had no idea why he was even thinking about it, since he was never going to have any children.

Still standing in the hall out of sight, he watched Jessie moving around the kitchen, cleaning up the cereal bowls left from Chris and Sarah's breakfast.

His mood darkened. Instead of heading into the kitchen to pour himself a desperately needed cup of coffee, Bran turned and walked back down the hall to the bedroom he should have slept in last night.

CHAPTER TWENTY-ONE

JESSIE STOOD AT the door of the garage as Bran drove down the curving lane toward the tall wrought iron front gate and the road down the mountain that lay beyond. He had talked to her, filled her in on Wayne Conrad Coffman before he'd left, *Tank*, the man Digger Graves believed had killed Janos Petrov.

"We bring Coffman in on murder charges, we can leverage him against Weaver," he'd said. "No way Weaver wants to go back into the high security side of ADMAX. Nobody wants to stay locked up twenty-three hours a day. If we can offer Weaver something he wants—like staying where he is—maybe we can get him to give us what we need."

"The name of the person who paid him to use his connections to kill my father before he found out who stole the chemical weapons."

He nodded. "That, and who made sure the colonel took the fall for it."

"How can we be sure Tank is the guy who killed Petrov?"

"No way to know for certain. But according to Graves, that shot between the eyes is Tank's MO. Graves is doing his best to stay alive. I'm betting he's right about Tank."

"Are you sure you can do this on your own? Maybe we should call the police, let them bring him in."

"We don't have enough evidence. Not yet. We'll see how tonight plays out."

He gave her a quick hard kiss and left her there to worry. Since they hadn't made it to her apartment, Jessie busied herself washing their dirty clothes, then used her disposable phone to call her best friend. Hallie picked up on the second ring but didn't recognize the caller ID, since it wasn't Jessie's cell.

"This had better not be some phony credit card sales call," she said, making Jessie laugh.

"Nope, not a sales call, I promise."

"Jessie! Where in the hell have you been, girl?"

"It's a long, not the least bit boring story, some of which I told you when we talked the last time, some you will not believe." Hallie knew about her investigation into her father's death. She'd been at the funeral. She knew Bran was in Colorado helping her, didn't know Jessie was sleeping with her self-appointed bodyguard.

"Where are you?" Hallie asked. "Are you back in Denver?"

"Actually, I'm in Evergreen. It's a long story."

"I want to hear it. I desperately need a best friend fix."

"So do I. I can't begin to tell you how much." She glanced around for Ty, who was never far away. Like Brandon, he took his job as her protector extremely seriously. "Hold on a minute."

She covered the phone. "Ty, would it be all right if I invited a girlfriend up to the house? I haven't seen her in ages, not since the trouble began. You'll like her, I promise."

Ty frowned. "I don't think it's a good idea. It's my job to keep you safe, and your friend is an unknown factor."

"She's not connected to what we've been doing. She actually knows very little about it. She's my best friend since college, Ty. I really need to see her."

He scrubbed a hand over his face. "All right, I guess. I

don't see how it could be a problem. Hand me the phone and I'll give her directions."

Jessie handed him the burner, and Ty gave Hallie instructions on how to find the house up in the hills. "I'll leave word with the guard at the gate."

Hallie must have said something funny because Ty laughed. "You got it." He handed Jessie the burner.

"Is that guy as sexy as he sounds on the phone?" Hallie asked.

Jessie cast him a glance. She hadn't really thought of Ty that way but... "Actually, yes. And he has the cutest two kids you've ever seen." Hallie had always loved children. She couldn't wait to have some of her own.

"Single?"

"At the moment."

Hallie laughed. "I'm on my way."

Forty-five minutes later Hallie's little red Mazda CX-3 drove up in front of the guesthouse, and Jessie hurried outside to meet her. Splashes of sunlight appeared between the clouds, but the temperature had only reached the midthirties. The weather was getting colder, with light snow showers predicted for tomorrow.

The two women hugged. They were close to the same size, both of them petite and around five-four, but Hallie was half Latina, with glossy straight black hair to the middle of her back and velvet-brown eyes. She was wearing black leggings and knee-high boots with a red wool sweater, and she had some very nice curves.

"I've called you like a thousand times," Hallie said. "But the phone went straight to voice mail every time. I would have been really worried except I know the kind of work you do for your blog. I was really relieved when I got your last email."

"It's a long story. I'll tell you over lunch. I made soup and sandwiches for all of us."

Hallie looked over at the man standing on the front porch steps in jeans and a pair of heavy work boots. If Jessie's life hadn't become so crazy, she might not have noticed the bulge of a pistol at his waist beneath the long-sleeve T-shirt he was wearing under a gray hoodie sweatshirt.

He'd given strict instruction to the gate guard to keep a close watch for trouble, and made several trips around the perimeter of the estate that morning. Neither Ty nor Bran expected trouble here in the mountains, but Ty knew the situation and it was always better to be safe.

Jessie made introductions. "Hallie, meet Tyler Folsom. Ty's a friend of Brandon's."

Hallie smiled up at him. "It's nice to meet you, Ty."

"You, too, Hallie."

They went inside where a warm fire burned in the family room, and Jessie finished getting lunch ready, tuna sandwiches and cream of tomato soup. The three of them ate at the kitchen table while Jessie gave Hallie an update on her investigation. She mentioned Bran but only briefly. She was saving that for when they were alone.

Hallie's gaze fixed on Ty. "So you're acting as Jessie's bodyguard while Brandon is out trying to catch bad guys?"

Ty just shrugged. "I guess you could put it that way."

Hallie's dark eyes ran over him. "Well, you look like a man who can handle the job."

Jessie thought she saw Ty's chest expand a little. "Bran wouldn't trust me to keep his woman safe if I couldn't."

Jessie's eyes widened nearly as much as Hallie's.

By the time they had finished the meal, Jessie had filled her friend in on the last few weeks of her life, and Hallie and Ty were chatting as if they had known each other for months instead of only a few hours.

Ty shoved up from his chair, a little reluctantly, Jessie thought. The warmth in his eyes was unmistakable as he looked at Hallie. "Since it doesn't appear you're here to assassinate your best friend, I'll leave you two alone. If you need me, I won't be far away."

Hallie flicked him a last assessing glance as he left the kitchen. "You were right. Ty's yummy."

"I think he likes you. Why don't you give him your number?"

"Maybe I will." Hallie's gaze went from Ty's retreating figure to Jessie. "What about you? From what Ty said, I'm guessing you and Brandon are involved?"

Nerves bloomed in Jessie's stomach. She hadn't discussed Bran with anyone. "We're...um...sleeping together. I never thought I could handle a strictly physical relationship, but that's what it is."

Hallie set a hand over hers on the table. "The last time we talked, you were afraid you'd never be able to be intimate with a man again. All you could think about was Ray Cummings and what he'd done to you. Brandon must be pretty special."

"I've never met anyone like him. Bran's gorgeous and sexy. I wouldn't have thought he could be sweet and thoughtful, but he is. He wanted to help me get over Ray Cummings. He was patient and understanding and it worked." She smiled. "Of course he's a man, so he isn't perfect, but whatever happens, I know Bran will do his best to protect me. He'd give up his life before he'd let someone hurt me."

"Wow. You sound like you're falling in love with him."

Jessie glanced away. "God, I hope not."

"Why not?"

"My brother warned me about him. I don't think Bran could be happy with just one woman. Danny didn't think so."

"You think he'd cheat on you?"

She shook her head. "Bran's far too honorable for that. He'll just end things when they get too complicated. Or I will. I know it, accept it. I'm sure Bran knows it, too. So we're good—at least for now."

"The way you talk about him it sounds like more than just casual sex."

It was more—a lot more—but it didn't really matter. "Even if he fell madly in love with me, Bran's a warrior. He isn't in the army anymore, but he still thinks that way. I don't want that kind of life. Never knowing whether or not he'll be coming home. Always worrying about him. I don't want to live with the same uncertainty my mother did."

"You always said your mom and dad were really happy."

"They were."

"I guess if you love someone enough, the risk doesn't matter."

Jessie stayed silent. She knew better than most how hard it was to lose someone you loved.

Hallie sighed and leaned back in her chair. "It's kind of sad, you know? I was sort of hoping for a happy ending. For one of us, anyway."

In a way it *was* sad. And thinking about it was making her chest ache. "Maybe you'll have better luck with Ty."

Hallie's gaze went to the family room, where Ty perched on an ottoman in front of an overstuffed chair, clearly on alert. "Why don't we go find out?" she suggested.

Relieved at the change of subject, Jessie smiled. "Good idea."

CHAPTER TWENTY-TWO

IT WAS LATE in the afternoon when Bran got a phone call from Ty. "How's the hunt going?" Ty asked.

"I've got the area reconned, got all the intel I need. I'm ready to take the guy down. I just need him to show up tonight."

"If this guy's as bad as his rep, you're gonna need some backup."

"Not happening, bro. You got two kids to think of and now you're their dad. You can't afford to risk winding up dead."

"You're right, so I'm not gonna argue. Colt Wheeler's in town. As I recall, you guys went through spec ops training at Fort Bragg together."

"Colt's a good guy," Bran said. Big and blond and good-looking, a real ladies' man. At least he had been before he'd been wounded in Kabul and lost his right eye. "Now that you mention it, I remember he came from Denver."

"That's right. I gave him a call, told him you might need backup. He's looking for something to do. Colt's even more bored than I am."

It wasn't a bad idea. "You got a number?"

"I'll text it to you."

Bran got the text and phoned Colt's cell. They scheduled a meet an hour later at a café in Aurora called the Chuck-wagon, not far down the road from Mack's.

Ty was sitting in a booth near the back when Colt walked through the door. The black patch over his eye and the scar along his jaw caught the attention of every woman in the room. Apparently his injuries hadn't lessened his appeal to the opposite sex.

Bran rose to greet him. "Hey, buddy, long time no see." They leaned in and gripped each other's shoulders.

"Been a while for sure." Colt sat down across from him. The waitress appeared, and they both ordered coffee and a piece of apple pie.

While they waited for their order, they caught up on each other's lives, both of them still single, neither seriously attached.

Bran didn't mention Jessie though he wasn't sure why. Just that he wasn't interested in sharing, and he didn't want a guy like Wheeler sniffing around his woman.

His woman? He wasn't sure where that had come from, but still…

The waitress returned. The coffee was hot and strong and the apple pie tasted homemade. Bran explained why he was in Denver and the strategy he hoped would net him the information they needed from the big fish in ADMAX, a guy known simply as Weaver.

"ADMAX. The worst of the worst. You really think you can flip this guy, Tank, to get to Weaver?"

"If I can nail him for murder, I'd say there's a solid chance."

"How do you plan to do that?" Colt took a drink of coffee.

"Not sure yet. I need to find him, get a handle on the situation. I'll have to figure it out as I go."

Colt leaned back, stretching his long legs out in front of him. "Sounds interesting. Count me in. Just tell me what you need me to do."

It was after 9:00 p.m. when Bran walked back into Mack's Roadhouse. He figured Tank's weekly pool game would either be in progress or just getting started—if the guy showed up to play.

Wearing a dark green down vest in concession to the weather, he sat on a stool at the bar, same as before, and ordered the same drink, a Lonestar and a shot of Jack. He tossed the whiskey back and set the glass down on the bar. The clatter of pool balls on a table in the rear caught his attention. Bran picked up his beer and wandered in that direction.

A group of men stood around the table, one with greasy hair to his shoulders, another in a frayed denim vest and camo pants. A guy in black leather chaps turned around, and Bran caught the symbol of a 666 inside a shamrock on the back of his leather jacket. The letters A-BOYZ were printed in an arch above.

One man stood out from the rest, tall and thick-chested with a head the size of a cannonball covered by a shaggy mane of thick blond hair. Biceps the size of tree trunks stretched the sleeves of his long-sleeved black T-shirt. From the way the hard-looking women in the bar were watching him, he didn't lack for female companionship. The men deferred to him, marking him as the alpha dog. Bran had a bad feeling the big guy was Tank.

Pool balls clacked against each other and rolled across the green felt table. The four, six, and ten all went into side pockets.

"Hey, Tank, you think you still got a chance?" The guy with the greasy hair grinned at the shot he'd just made.

"You better hope you run the table, Rider, or your ass is mine."

Yup, the guy with the cannonball head. With a name like Tank, Bran wasn't surprised. He was big and rough, and like every guy around the table, he was carrying. Small arms in jeans pockets, a gun holstered inside a jacket. When Tank bent over to take his shot, Bran glimpsed a semiauto holstered at the small of his back.

Not good news, but again, not really unexpected. He ran through his options, chose plan B but didn't completely toss A and C in case he had to improvise. Whichever worked, he needed to get the guy out of there. Bran was damned glad Colt Wheeler waited in his shiny black Mustang out in the parking lot.

Carrying his beer back to the bar, Bran sat down and sent a text, told Colt that Tank was there and it looked like taking him out through the back door was their best option.

Will text when he goes to the john, he added.

Tank must have had a bladder as big as his head because he didn't leave the table for nearly two hours. When he did, Bran tossed money on the bar to pay for his drinks, texted Colt to come in through the back door, which he unlocked, then headed for the men's room.

Tank was zipping up his fly when Bran walked in behind him. Surprise being his only advantage, he moved fast. A kidney jab doubled Tank over with a grunt. Bran slammed an elbow under his chin, knocking him backward into the wall, grabbed the back of his neck and pulled his head down into the knee Bran shot into his face.

He jerked the gun out of Tank's belt as he staggered away, mumbling unintelligible words, rummy but not unconscious. Which was good since 280 pounds of deadweight was bad news. Bran tucked the gun into his waistband as Colt pushed through the bathroom door, and the two of them managed to half drag, half carry Tank out into the hall, which fortunately was empty.

The cold outside air revived the guy a little but Colt's

quick jab, knocking his head back, had his chin drooping back down on his chest.

Bran slapped a piece of duct tape over Tank's mouth while Colt used zip ties to bind the guy's wrists and ankles. Loading him into the back of the Expedition on his belly, Bran bent his legs up behind him and zip-tied his ankles to his wrists. Colt tossed a blanket over his massive body as Bran slid in behind the wheel.

"I'll be right behind you." Colt strode off toward his Mustang.

They were out of the lot and hauling ass down the highway when Tank began to wake up. He was shouting muffled curses behind the duct tape, death threats, Bran was sure, and thrashing around in the back, but the way he was tied, there wasn't much he could do.

Bran turned off the main road onto a farm road, then made a couple more evasive turns before pulling onto a road parallel to the highway heading south. He took out his cell and hit the contact number he'd entered for sheriff's detective Mace Galen, put it on speaker, and set it on the console next to the driver's seat.

A groggy Galen picked up on the third ring. "Whoever the hell this is, it better be important."

"Brandon Garrett. I've got a little present for you, Detective. Made a citizen's arrest on a guy named Wayne Conrad Coffman. Calls himself Tank. He's the man who murdered Janos Petrov. Where would you like me to drop him off?"

Galen cursed foully. "You realize you're interfering in a sheriff's investigation, right?"

"He was carrying a SIG P220 .45 cal. When you run ballistics, I'm pretty sure you'll find it matches the bullet that killed Petrov. Worst case, you'll have him for carrying an illegal firearm. That'll give you some time to check things out."

Galen swore again.

"I'm heading south out of Aurora. Tank's only a little banged up. I'd really like to get him off my hands before his friends show up to rescue him." He checked the rearview mirror, saw Colt's headlights, but so far no one else. It wouldn't be long before his buddies realized their friend wasn't in one of the bathroom stalls getting a blow job from one of the busty blondes who'd been giving him the eye all evening.

"Get him to the county line," Galen said. "Closest is probably Highway 83 at Palmer Divide. I'll have deputies waiting to pick him up. What are you driving?"

"Dark gray Ford Expedition." Bran punched the destination into the GPS. "Unless I run into trouble, I'm forty-five minutes away." Give or take, depending on how many evasive turns he needed to make or if Tank's crew showed up.

Bran ended the call and hit the gas. He punched Cole's contact number and hit the speaker button. "We're heading south to the county line at Highway 83 and Palmer Divide. Sheriff's deputies will take it from there."

"Damn. Just when things were getting interesting."

Bran chuckled. "They still may, if those bastards figure out what happened to their buddy."

"I've still got your back."

"I know. Thanks. Listen, when we get close, I want you to pull over. I need you to take my gear bag. Lot of toys in there the cops won't appreciate. It's legal—mostly—but I don't need the hassle. I'll pick it up when I get back."

"Copy that."

"Once you've got my gear, I want you to head back to Denver. No need for you to get balled up with the sheriff."

"You sure?"

"Affirmative."

The Expedition rolled down the road at a speed hovering around the limit. Under the circumstances, getting pulled over would not be a good idea.

He gazed through the windshield into the darkness illuminated by the headlights. Minimal traffic, the terrain open and hilly, covered with grass and scattered pines. Tank continued to swear muffled curses but finally, thankfully, fell silent.

The GPS showed the county line a few miles ahead. Bran pulled over and stopped, and Colt took his canvas gear bag. The Mustang's headlights flashed a couple of times, then turned and disappeared down a side road into the darkness.

A few miles farther down the highway, Bran spotted a row of sheriff's SUVs lined up like piano keys along both sides of the road.

He set Tank's .45 in the passenger seat, unloaded his Glock and set it next to Tank's weapon. The instant he pulled over and stopped, half a dozen cop cars swarmed around him. As he turned off the engine, he thought the dozen deputies pouring out of their cars, guns drawn, was a bit of an overkill.

"Raise your hands and get out of the vehicle!"

He cracked the door and raised his hands. "I'm licensed to carry." Working everywhere from Texas to California, he had permits for a number of states. "My weapon is unloaded on the seat. There's a loaded .45 on the seat beside it that belongs to my cargo."

"I said get out! Get down on your knees and wrap your hands around the back of your neck!" Deputies rushed forward as he complied. Two officers held him at gunpoint while another did a weapons search and another collected the pistols, bagging them both as evidence.

"No other weapons?" a stony-faced deputy asked.

"No."

"Keep your hands where they are."

"You know I'm the good guy here," he said as one of the officers gripped his arms, twisted them down, and locked a pair of handcuffs around his wrists. "The bad guy is in the back of the car."

Deputies opened the cargo door and hauled Tank out of the Expedition. He started swearing at Bran as they ripped off the duct tape and cut the tie binding his wrists to his ankles. It took five deputies to get him into the back of a sheriff's SUV.

Detective Mace Galen walked up to him. "For your sake, Garrett, I hope you're right about this guy."

Behind them, Bran watched the sheriff's car pull out onto the road and drive away, Tank's big head filling half the rear window. "I guess we'll find out."

Galen turned to a pair of deputies. "Take him away. Call for a tow truck to impound his vehicle. We're going to need it for evidence."

Bran grunted. "Real f-ing nice. I do your job for you and this is how you repay me?"

"Nobody asked for your help."

Bran had hoped Galen might give him a pass, but he wasn't really surprised. The detective had rules to follow. That was the way it worked. It was the reason he worked for himself.

The detective turned back to his men. "Let's get this done. Maybe I can still get a couple hours of sleep."

Bran thought of his nice warm bed at Ty's house. Good chance Jessie would be waiting up for him, same as last night. If she asked him to sleep with her, he wouldn't have the will-power to resist. At least now he wouldn't have to feel guilty.

CHAPTER TWENTY-THREE

JESSIE LAY AWAKE staring at the ceiling, her ears cocked for the sound of Bran's footfalls coming down the hall. Instead, her cell phone started ringing. She sat up in bed and grabbed it off the nightstand, didn't recognize the number, and fear shot through her.

It was 4:00 a.m. and no sign of Bran. She pressed the phone against her ear with a shaking hand. "Who's calling?"

"Jessie, this is Chase Garrett."

"Oh, God, what's happened? Is Brandon…is he okay?"

"He's all right. He's in a holding cell at the El Paso County Sheriff's Office. He only got one call so he used it to phone me. He knew you'd be worried. He gave me this number, asked me to call and tell you what's going on."

Her heart was beating a thousand miles an hour. "Why is he in jail? What happened?"

"He picked up Wayne Coffman and turned him over to the sheriff's detective in charge, but the cops need proof Coffman murdered Petrov. Bran thinks the guy has used the murder weapon before. He thinks Tank's arrogant enough not to toss his piece after a hit. If he's right, he'll probably be okay."

"And if it isn't the same gun?"

"Then we got a problem. So far no charges have been filed, but they can still hold him for forty-eight hours, and unless something turns up, it looks like that's what they'll do. I talked to Reese. He's lining up an attorney, but we can't get him bailed until they formally arrest him. Just stay where you are, and I'll keep you up-to-date on what's going on."

"Thank you, Chase. I really appreciate the call." The line went dead but Jessie was already out of bed and moving around the room, getting dressed and packing her things.

She needed to help Bran, and to do that, she had to get to Fort Carson. She hurried out of the room and down the hall into Brandon's bedroom. His gear bag was gone, the room empty except for his shaving kit and his carry-on. She tossed the kit into his bag, zipped it up and towed it and her own bag down the hall. Then she went into the kitchen to call an Uber and leave a note for Ty.

He must have heard her moving around because he appeared in the doorway in a pair of sweatpants and a white cotton T-shirt. His hair was mussed, and he needed a shave.

"What's going on?"

"Bran's been arrested. I've got to get to Fort Carson. I know someone there who can help. My car is parked at the Denver Airport. It's been there since I flew to Dallas. I've already called an Uber." There was a chance her Honda Accord had been bugged along with her purse. But most of the time, the car was locked in the garage she rented under her building, so there was a chance it wasn't. Either way, it was a risk she had to take.

Ty shook his head. "No way I'm letting you go by yourself."

"Bran needs help. I don't have any choice." She reached over and touched his arm. "No one knows I'm in Denver and once I get to the base, I'll be all right. You have two darling kids who need you. That's what you have to think about."

"I'll drive you to the airport. My mother-in-law can watch the kids. I'll tell Vera it's an emergency. She thrives on excitement. She'll be right over."

Clearly, he wasn't going to back down. She sighed. "All right, if you're sure it's okay."

"Vera's great. It'll be fine."

Thirty minutes later the kids had a sitter, and she and Ty were on their way to the long-term parking lot at the Denver Airport where her Honda Accord was parked.

"So...are you going to call Hallie?" she asked as Ty's Subaru pulled into the lot.

He smiled. "She gave me her number, so yeah. I liked her. I'd really like to see her again."

Jessie grinned. "That's great."

Her white car was covered with a fine layer of dust, dimpled by rain. Ty loaded the bags into the trunk and closed the lid.

"I need to look for a bug," she said.

"Seriously?"

But she was already searching beneath the bumper and along the side of the car. Ty started checking the other side, feeling along underneath. "Didn't find anything," he said. "But they can be hard to locate."

She felt a little better. "We did our best, now I have to go."

"Fine, but there's been a change of plans."

"What do you mean?"

"I'm following you down. It's only ninety minutes. I'll be back before the kids leave for school. I'll be armed, and if someone gives you trouble, I'll be right behind you."

She smiled broadly. "I'd be stupid to turn down an offer

like that, and I'm not stupid. Tank's connected to crucial information the army needs. With any luck, General Holloway will step in and get Bran released."

With any luck, she silently repeated, praying she could convince him.

"All right, then we'd better get going," Ty said.

She leaned up and kissed his unshaven cheek. "Thanks for this, Ty. Thanks for everything you've done."

He just shrugged. "Didn't really do much, and the kids enjoyed your visit."

Her car started right up. She stopped at the kiosk near the gate to pay the exorbitant fee for parking for so many days. She didn't like using her credit card for fear they might be able to track her, but she didn't have that much cash. It was comforting to know Ty was right behind her.

Fort Carson was almost due south out of Denver down I-25. Without much traffic this early, they made good time. She waved goodbye out the window as she pulled up to the front gate of the army base.

While Ty turned around and headed back the way he'd come, the uniformed soldier in the security guardhouse phoned General Holloway's office. As director of Chemical Materials Activity, Holloway was the man who most wanted the stolen weapons found. And he had the kind of authority it would take to arrange for Bran's release.

"The office won't be open yet," the guard said, "but I can always reach someone if necessary."

"I'd appreciate it." She took a deep breath, praying the general was in Colorado and not Kentucky. If not, she'd find someone else. She wouldn't give up till Bran was out of jail.

BRAN SAT ON the bunk in the holding cell he'd occupied since sheriff's deputies had arrested him. It smelled like stale beer and bad breath. Galen had questioned him, but he'd only repeated what he'd said before. *Check Coffman's pistol.* A match would implicate the man in Petrov's murder.

After that he'd stayed silent. During his phone call to Chase, his brother had warned him to keep his mouth shut until he had an attorney. Since he respected his oldest brother's opinion, which was usually right, he clammed up. Let them interrogate Tank and see what they came up with.

In the meantime, they'd be running ballistics on Coffman's .45 and checking the guy's alibi for the night of Petrov's murder. With any luck, something would click. The sheriff would find enough evidence to arrest Coffman on murder charges, and once army brass got involved, he could be pressured to roll on Weaver.

The long game for Bran.

And he would be out of jail.

He stood up as one of the deputies arrived and his cell door slid open with a noisy clang. The deputy, heavyset, with a slight paunch, motioned for him to follow. He wound up down the hall in the stark white interrogation room he'd been in before.

It felt like an hour passed, but it was only a few minutes before Detective Mace Galen walked in. Galen slapped a manila file folder down on the metal-framed table, ran two fingers over the blond mustache beneath his nose, and gave Bran a hard stare.

"You want the good news first or the bad news?"

He leaned back in his chair and stretched his legs out in front of him. "I could use a little good news for a change."

"Ballistics matched the bullet that killed Petrov to the gun we got when we picked you up at the county line."

Bran felt a sweep of relief. "I figured." But he hadn't been sure. "What's the bad news?"

"Bad news is Coffman claims the gun belongs to you. You planted the pistol, set him up to take the fall. He's just an innocent victim."

Bran snorted a laugh and sat up straighter in the chair. "Don't tell me you're buying it. The guy probably has a rap sheet as long as your arm."

Galen ignored him and tapped the file. "You admitted to having a beef with Petrov before he died. You assaulted him. Now we have the murder weapon and your finger-prints are all over it."

"The assault on Petrov was self-defense. I told you that at the time. He was hired to murder my client. You have the murder weapon now because I brought in Petrov's killer. I took the gun off him at the roadhouse. Coffman's prints are bound to be on it, too."

"Anything you want to say before we officially bring charges?"

"Yeah. I've got a lawyer on the way. Be easier for all of us if you just arrested Coffman. You and I both know he's guilty."

"What I know is you're not helping yourself with that attitude. Maybe a few more hours of cooling your heels in a cell and you'll feel a little more like talking."

Bran clamped down on his temper, reminded himself Galen was just doing his job.

"Maybe a few more hours and you'll have what you need to make a case against Coffman, and I can get back to protecting my client."

So far he'd been able to keep thoughts of Jessie out of his head. She was with Ty and he would keep her safe. The problem was, Jessie was a wild card. When she found out he'd been arrested, she'd wouldn't stand by and do nothing, and whatever she did might put her in danger.

Never good at waiting, Bran fidgeted in his chair. Maybe he should make another run at Galen, try once more to persuade the guy to let him go.

He blew out a frustrated breath. Knowing his brother was right, he stayed where he was and kept his mouth shut.

JESSIE SAT IN the waiting room outside General Holloway's office. His assistant, Lieutenant Dickerson, had gotten the call from the gatehouse, and fortunately he remembered her. She'd told him she had crucial information she could only reveal to the general. The lieutenant had spoken to Holloway, and he had agreed to see her as soon as he arrived.

She'd been waiting an hour. It seemed like a week.

Finally Lieutenant Dickerson approached. Jessie recalled his sandy hair and slender, boyish features.

"Ms. Kegan? General Holloway is ready to see you. Please follow me." He led her down a hall into the general's office. Holloway stood up behind his desk as she walked in. The lieutenant closed the door behind her, leaving them alone.

"Good morning, Jessie. I understand you have something important to discuss."

"That's right, General. I appreciate your seeing me on such short notice."

"I'm assuming this is in regard to your father's death."

"It's in regard to the missing chemical weapons, sir. *And* my father's death. As you know, I believe the two are connected."

His eyes remained on her face. "I expected to see Captain Garrett here with you."

"Captain Garrett is currently in jail. That's part of the reason I'm here."

Holloway's interest sharpened, driving up his graying brown eyebrows. "I'm listening."

"Brandon was arrested for bringing in a man named Wayne Conrad Coffman. Coffman is connected to a man named Weaver. Weaver arranged my father's murder through his contacts in the army prison. He was hired by someone who wanted to frame my father for the theft of the weapons. If you want to find the stolen munitions, Wayne Coffman is the man who can help."

The general rounded the desk and motioned for her to join him at the table in the corner. "I think we had better take a seat, and you can start from the beginning."

Jessie took a deep, hopeful breath as both of them sat down.

BRAN PACED THE interrogation room from one wall to the other, anything was better than just sitting there. With every turn, he cursed Mace Galen. The guy had to know the charges against him were bullshit. The gun belonged to the scumbag who'd killed Janos Petrov. The two were birds of a feather. Vultures.

Tension slid through him as the door cracked open and Galen walked back into the Spartan room. Bran wondered how long he and his men had been watching him through the two-way mirror.

"We got some interesting news. I figured you deserved to know."

"Good news or bad news?" he asked, parroting Galen's earlier words.

The detective's mustache kicked up at one corner. "From your standpoint, very good news. Wayne Conrad Coffman was arrested for assault in Atlanta three years ago. He's also been arrested in Memphis and Phoenix. He's got a history of violent crimes, but the charges never seem to stick."

Bran wondered if the Brotherhood had played a part in keeping Tank out of jail and if killing Janos Petrov was the kind of work he did for them in return. He wondered if killing Jessie had been next on his list. "I'm still waiting for the good news."

"The good news is he was questioned as a person of interest in the murder of a federal judge in Nevada last year. There wasn't enough to arrest him, but the MO matches the Petrov murder—.45 caliber gunshot between the eyes. And just like Petrov, the bullet recovered from the crime scene matches the one from the SIG P220 you took off Coffman."

Thank Christ for that.

"Since you were working in Dallas at the time of the judge's murder—verified by several people in your office— it looks like you're going to walk."

The tension in his shoulders relaxed. "About damn time."

Galen smiled. "Guy with your skills needs a little set down once in a while. Keeps you humble."

He almost smiled at the backward compliment, decided to take his brother's advice instead. "So I'm free to go?"

"There'll be some paperwork for you to sign on the way out. You can pick up your phone and your personal items before you leave, but yes, you can go."

"What about my rental car?"

"CSIs are still working on it. Might find something on Coffman we can use. You can pick it up from the impound lot in a day or two. We'll let you know."

It wasn't the best news. He was anxious to get back to Jessie. He'd Uber to Hertz and rent another vehicle, figure a way to get the SUV picked up. He rose from his chair as the door swung open and one of the deputies stuck his head in.

"We got a problem, Mace. Army MPs are here for Coffman. They got a warrant, something about terrorism. They want him now and they mean business."

Galen flicked a glance at Bran. "I don't know whether to be happy about this or pissed." He followed the deputy into the corridor.

Terrorism. One way to get the bastard to talk. Bran couldn't help wondering if Jessie had a hand in this. He caught up with Galen as he walked down the hall.

"Any idea where they're taking him?" Bran asked.

Galen turned. "Wherever it is, the guy will be lucky if he ever sees the light of day again."

Worry settled over him. A terrorism charge was bad news. What if the army made Tank disappear into a dark hole somewhere. They needed him to get to Weaver. Jessie wouldn't be safe until whoever stole the weapons was arrested. The thieves wanted her silenced. There were millions of dollars at stake. Tank was out of the picture, but there was always another killer for hire.

He collected his things, signed the release papers, and walked toward the front door. His mind was on Jessie and the fastest way back to her when he heard a familiar, softly feminine voice.

"Hey, soldier. Need a ride?"

The oddest sensation stole over him, a warm glow, like a long-awaited homecoming. He turned and smiled, thinking how pretty she looked even with her fiery hair mussed and no makeup. "Yeah, sexy lady. I do."

The minute he reached her, he wrapped her in his arms. "Thanks for coming," he said against her cheek, then he tipped her face up and very thoroughly kissed her.

CHAPTER TWENTY-FOUR

AT THE WARMTH she'd seen in Bran's eyes, a lump formed in Jessie's throat. She returned his kiss, clinging to him tighter than she should have. She'd been so worried. The relief she felt now made her eyes sting.

She forced herself to step away. It was dangerous to allow her feelings for Bran to grow, and yet she couldn't seem to stop them. She managed to smile and tried to make light of the situation.

"You realize you smell like the inside of a sleazy bar, right?"

He laughed. "Yeah, I do. Not much I can do about it at the moment. Let's get out of here so I can get cleaned up, and you can fill me in on what's been going on." He stopped at the top of the front steps, his dark brows pulling together. "How'd you get here?"

"Ty drove me to the airport and I picked up my car. I almost passed out at the long-term parking fee."

"Dammit, Jess, what if the damned thing's bugged?"

She just shrugged. "Ty and I took a look but didn't find anything. Besides, I had to get down here. There were things I needed to do."

"Where'd you park?"

She pointed. "The white Honda Accord just down the block."

He grabbed her hand and started tugging her in that direction, careful to keep an eye out for any sign of trouble. Now that Petrov was dead, Graves most likely on the run, and Tank under military arrest, he had no idea what situation they might be facing.

His Glock had been returned unloaded, along with two full magazines. When he reached the car, he pulled the gun out of the plastic bag that held his personal items, shoved one of the mags into the grip, then clipped the holster onto his belt beneath his Henley and dark green down vest.

Feeling a little more secure, he glanced around, checking for a possible sniper or anyone who might have managed to figure out where Jessie was. He made his own brief check of the car, looking for anyplace a tracker could be easily hidden, but didn't find anything.

He stuck out a hand. "I need the keys."

One of her rusty-gold eyebrows went up. "It's my car. I should be the one to drive."

"No way I'm letting you drive," he said.

Jessie huffed out a breath. "Fine. If it's that much of a threat to your masculinity, you can drive." She tossed him the keys and flounced around to the passenger side, jerked open the door, and climbed in. She looked so cute he couldn't stop a grin.

Still smiling, he slid in behind the wheel, having to move the seat all the way back to fit. "Where are we going?"

"If you'd let me drive, you wouldn't have to ask. We've got an appointment with General Holloway. He wants to ask you some questions."

He slanted her a look. "Long as you promise he's not going to throw me in the brig."

"If he does, he'll probably arrest me, too."

He smiled. "At least this time I'd have company."

She stopped just short of a return smile and pointedly wrinkled her nose. "We've got some time. Our suitcases are in the trunk. I washed everything so at least it's all clean. I figured since you've been busy playing bodyguard I owed you that much."

"Great," he said. "Thanks."

"Don't get used to it."

He laughed. "Wouldn't think of it." He pulled onto the road. "Why don't you find us a room so I can shower and change. No way I'm talking to a general smelling like I spent the night in a gutter."

She laughed.

He changed lanes, then turned the corner. "The weather is getting colder. We need some warmer clothes. You know a place we can buy some?"

"I remember passing an REI on Woodman Road." A smug smile curved her lips. "If I were driving—"

"Okay, I get it. Just tell me where to go."

It took less than thirty minutes to pick up some Under Armour, a couple of sweaters, two superlightweight puffy jackets, and whatever else struck their fancy. Since they'd never made it to Jessie's apartment, Bran insisted she buy thick socks and a pair of winter boots.

From there, they pulled into an IHOP for a quick breakfast. While they ate, Bran phoned Ty to let him know he was out of jail.

"Glad to hear it," Ty said. "I called Colt after I got back from the airport and told him you'd been arrested."

"I'll call him, let him know I'm not still cooling it in a cell. Thanks for taking care of Jessie."

"She's a keeper, dude."

"I know," Bran said softly, wishing he was the kind of guy who could make her happy, knowing he wasn't. He shoved the dark thought away, phoned Colt and asked him to bring his weapons.

"Didn't figure I'd end up back here—at least not last

night. Sorry to put you to the extra trouble, but I don't like being here without my gear."

"No problem," Colt said.

"We've got an appointment on the base. How about later this afternoon?"

"I'll be there."

Bran gave him the location of the Homewood Suites that Jessie had booked, nothing fancy and no pool, but with a living room and bedroom, it was spacious, the way he liked. Once he'd showered off the grime of the jail cell, he felt a helluva lot better.

Towel-drying his hair as he walked out of the bathroom, his gaze shot to the king-size bed. He thought of Jessie and his groin tightened, his mind sliding right back into the gutter.

"What time's our appointment with Holloway?" he asked, walking into the living room wearing nothing but a towel around his waist.

Jessie rose from where she sat in front of her laptop, her gaze moving over his bare chest and suddenly sparking with heat. He was already aroused. When she moistened those full pink lips, he went rock hard.

"I wasn't sure how long it would take to get you released from jail. I told him I thought we could be there by 1:00 p.m."

He didn't miss the pulse fluttering at the base of her throat or the flush in her cheeks. "That doesn't give us much time."

Her eyes locked with his. "No...it doesn't. Especially since I'm... I'm already dressed. We'd...um...have to be creative."

"Yeah." He moved toward her. She'd put on makeup, pulled her hair into a thick twist behind her head, and changed into the dark brown skirt suit she'd worn the first time they had gone to the base. "You game for that?"

She swallowed. Nodded.

Bran drew her into his arms, bent and nipped the side of her neck. "I missed you last night," he said softly, then took her mouth in a hot, wet kiss.

Jessie moaned.

Bran kissed and tasted, slid his hands inside her jacket, inside her blouse to tease her nipples through the thin silk of her bra. He kissed her until she was running her hands over his naked chest, gripping his shoulders and repeating his name like a plea. Shoving up her skirt, he slid down a pair of pink bikini panties that had him groaning, then kissed her again and turned her around. In her high heels, the table was just the right height to bend her over.

And didn't she look just fine exactly that way.

"Beautiful," he said as he ran a hand over her sexy curves and began to stroke her. Never one to pass up an opportunity, he'd grabbed a foil packet before he'd left the bedroom, sheathed himself now, tossed the towel, and slid into her welcoming heat.

Jessie moaned and arched her back, taking him even deeper. He always worried she might relapse to her days in confinement, but instead, she gripped the opposite side of the table, making it better for both of them.

Clenching his teeth against the pleasure, he increased his pace until she was making soft little sounds in her throat. A few seconds later she started coming, her sweet little body clenching around him, and Bran completely lost it.

Lightning struck, or it felt that way. He gripped her hips and pounded into her, and Jessie came again. By the time he'd finished, both of them were sprawled on the table, limp and sated. Bran pulled her up with him, turned her into his arms, and kissed her.

He smiled. "You're going to kill me, I swear."

Jessie pressed a last kiss on his lips. "Whatever happens, I'll always be grateful to you for saving me."

He knew what she meant, that he had helped her deal with her trauma. It was the *whatever happens* part that bothered him. He liked being with Jessie, liked it way too much. Sooner or later, it would have to end. Both of them knew it, accepted it.

His mood darkened. Apparently he wasn't ready for that to happen.

"It's getting late. We need to get going." While he left to deal with the condom and get dressed, Jessie freshened up and rearranged her clothes. She was ready to leave when he returned. Only the flush in her cheeks gave away what they had been doing. It made him want her all over again.

Disgusted with himself, he scraped a hand through his hair. He needed to stop thinking about Jessie and focus on his upcoming meeting with the general.

Fortunately, life-and-death matters had a way of dulling his sex drive.

JESSIE FOLLOWED LIEUTENANT DICKERSON down the hall to General Holloway's office, Bran right beside her. She managed not to think about the amazing sex she'd just had by telling herself it would be okay if it happened again.

The general rose from behind his desk, spine straight, short, silver-touched brown hair perfectly groomed. He greeted Jessie, then turned to Bran.

"Captain Garrett. I gather you suffered a rather unpleasant night."

"The deputies were just doing what they're paid for, trying to keep all of us safe."

Holloway nodded, seemed satisfied with his words. "I've got questions I need answered. Why don't we sit down?"

They sat around the same table and chairs Jessie had been seated at earlier that morning.

Holloway focused on Bran. "Let's start with you explaining what led to the conclusion that the man we now have in custody, Wayne Conrad Coffman, is linked to terrorism. You understand the risk I took in acting on the information Jessie gave me."

"I do, sir. Completely." Bran started from the beginning, describing the chain of events that had led to the murder of Jessie's father, progressed to attempts on Jessie's life, followed by the murder of Janos Petrov and the arrest of Wayne Coffman, a member of the Aryan Brotherhood. Bran made the case that if Coffman could be induced to implicate Weaver as the man who had hired him, they could pressure Weaver into giving them the name of whoever hired him, someone directly involved in the theft of the chemical weapons. It was the same case Jessie had made, but the general would want to hear from them both.

"Near as we can tell," Bran said, "Weaver used his Aryan Brotherhood connections to arrange the colonel's murder. That, combined with someone planting money in a forged offshore account, deflected the investigation away from the real thieves."

"Weaver was moved from the penitentiary in Georgia to ADMAX because he found a way to continue giving orders to the Brotherhood," Jessie said. "We believe that's exactly what he's still doing."

"After I spoke to you this morning," the general said, "I received a call from Special Agent Tripp, CID. Weaver's first name is Edgar. He's been convicted of three brutal murders and been implicated in half a dozen more."

"Fits what we were told," Bran said.

"CID investigators specifically asked Coffman about

Weaver, but he insists he's innocent of all charges and says he's never heard of anyone by that name."

"Apparently, he's more afraid of the man who hired him than being held on terrorism charges," Jessie said.

"Which gives you an idea of the kind of man we're dealing with," Bran stated.

The general sat up a little straighter. "Our people are good at what they do. They'll be pressing Coffman hard, but from what they tell me, I'm not convinced anything short of waterboarding will get him to talk—and you know the odds of that happening."

Jessie thought of the fifteen thousand pounds of missing chemical weapons and the hundreds of lives at stake and understood the moral dilemma.

The general rose from the table. "I'll let you know if anything changes. I'd appreciate if you'd do the same for me. Should you run across information that might give us a break in the case, I want you to call me." He handed Bran and Jessie each a card. "My direct number is listed at the bottom."

"Thank you, sir," Bran said.

"In the meantime, unless we can come up with a credible link between Coffman and the missing weapons, he'll be released back into civilian custody to face multiple murder charges."

Bran's jaw clenched. "I'd appreciate if you'd hold him as long as you possibly can."

The general nodded. "I'll do my best."

CHAPTER TWENTY-FIVE

BY THE TIME they left Fort Carson and headed back to the motel, the temperature was sliding toward freezing. To the north, the sky had turned an ominous shade of bluish purple, a harbinger of snow.

Jessie was driving. Bran fidgeted occasionally, not used to someone else being in control. She might have smiled if she weren't so worried and disappointed. As it was, unless Coffman talked, they had reached a dead end.

"So what do we do now?" she asked into the gloomy silence muted only by the hum of the Honda's engine.

"I talked to Hunter Brady," Bran said. "He's one of the PIs at The Max in San Diego. Hunt ran a check on Mara Ramos, says the DMV address for her is still valid. Mara lives in an apartment in La Jolla."

"We really need to talk to her." Though she definitely wasn't looking forward to meeting her dad's...what? Paramour? Mistress? Hookup? Or was she someone who'd been involved in the conspiracy that got him killed?

If Bran was right, Mara could have slept with her father to gain access to his credit cards and other personal data in order to help the thieves deposit money in an offshore account in his name.

Bran stared out the window at the overcast sky. "Storm's sweeping down from the north. I'll check with FAA flight service, see if I can figure a way to fly south before the bad weather hits. If we can get out of Colorado, we should be able to make sunny California easy enough."

"Sounds good."

"As soon as we get back to the motel, we'll check things out and make a plan. Colt may be there by now with my gear."

Bran's tall blond friend was there, indeed. Waiting inside their room though he didn't have a key. Bran seemed unfazed.

"Jessie, this is Colt Wheeler. We met in the army. He's the guy who helped me bring Tank in." Blond and blue-eyed, even with a black patch over one eye and a scar along his jaw, the guy was beyond good-looking. Or maybe the war wounds were part of his sex appeal.

Jessie had more than she could handle with one hot male. "Nice to meet you, Colt. Thanks for helping Brandon."

He just shrugged. "No problem." He had a broad-shouldered, V-shaped build similar to Bran's, probably from years of the same kind of training. "Just glad he's out of jail."

"Me, too," Jessie said. While they talked, Bran phoned FAA flight service, but Jessie couldn't hear the conversation.

"So where does your investigation go from here?" Colt asked her.

"If the weather holds, Bran's flying us down to California to talk to a woman my father was dating when he was killed. She disappeared just days after he died and no one's seen her since."

Bran ended the call. "We've got about a two-hour window to get the plane in the air. After that, the weather'll keep us grounded."

"Then you better get going," Colt said. "Your gear bag's on the bed. You coming back this way?"

"Jessie lives in Denver, so yeah, eventually we'll be back."

Or at least she would be. Bran would be going back to Dallas. The weight that suddenly pressed like a steel ball on her chest was not a good sign.

Colt took off, Jessie changed into jeans, winter boots, and a sweater, and they checked out of the motel. No use keeping the room not knowing how long they'd be in California or where the investigation might lead next. As they loaded the stuff in her car, Bran made a sweep of the vehicle with the bug detector he'd retrieved from his gear bag. Jessie breathed a sigh of relief when the car came up clean.

Bran had called ahead and had the twin-engine Baron towed out of its hangar. Gleaming white with a narrow blue stripe, it sat waiting, fueled and ready for takeoff. It seemed Bran spent an inordinate amount of time doing his exterior flight check, and it occurred to her he was looking for more than GPS tracking devices. Her stomach knotted as she realized he was searching for explosives.

Eventually, he seemed satisfied and they climbed into the cockpit. Jessie didn't like the thought of flying in rough weather, but she had faith in the pilot. They settled themselves in the seats, strapped in, and put on their headsets. Bran completed the flight check, cleared with the tower, the engine revved, and the plane began to roll down the tarmac.

"How far will we be going today?" Jessie asked, communicating through the mic on her headset as the Baron lifted into the air.

"It won't be too long before dark and the weather starts closing in. We'll stay out of the mountains, head south over the valley, then turn west to Albuquerque. It's a little less than a two-hour flight. We'll spend the night there, get an early start, fly on down to San Diego in the morning."

She relaxed back in her seat. It sounded like a good plan.

Or it did until the plane flew into a cloud bank a few miles south of town and started pitching and shaking.

"Hang on. It's just turbulence. We'll be out of it in a minute."

The plane battled through the rough air and flew on. Eventually, the flight smoothed out enough for her to enjoy the view over the flat, arid landscape. Mountains rose on both sides, some covered with snow, but they were miles away. She was just beginning to relax when the engine started sputtering, and an odd shudder rippled through the cabin.

She flashed Bran an uneasy glance, saw that he was wearing the same expression he'd worn the night he'd gone after Tank, and her heart began to beat a little faster. Bran toggled switches and checked a panel of gauges, flipped more switches, then the wings suddenly tipped sideways as the left engine coughed, sputtered, and died.

Oh, my God!

"Fuck."

Hysteria threatened, but she battled it down. Features grim, Bran worked to level the wings and attempted to re-start the engine, adjusting the throttle and working levers, but the engine never fired.

"Something's wrong with the fuel." He cut the gas to the now silent engine and continued working switches and checking gauges. "If we lose the other engine, we're in trouble. I need to find a place to set down."

She swallowed, her heart racing, trying to pound its way through her ribs. She wondered if her face was as blood-less as it felt.

Bran nosed the plane downward, his gaze searching the vast open landscape beneath them. Jessie started looking, too, though she wasn't sure what kind of spot he needed to land a twin-engine plane.

"Sh-shouldn't we radio for help?"

Bran didn't answer and she realized the other engine was sputtering, threatening to fail. Fear gripped her. Her stomach rolled with nausea. She had never liked flying. Now she knew why. Bran worked the controls, dropping altitude as fast as he dared, his gaze still scanning the ground below.

"There!" He pointed to a flat stretch of open land covered mostly with short, dry grass. The second engine was gasping and choking, the stall light buzzing, but the propeller was still spinning. She felt the landing gear lock into place and then he was lining up, leveling off, descending, the ground rushing up with frightening speed.

"Put your head down and brace yourself!" he commanded. The wheels barely missed a barbed wire fence and the second propeller went deadly silent.

Jessie jerked off her headset, braced, and covered her head. All she could hear was the whistle of wind as the wheels hit the ground with bone-jarring force, then the plane bounced into the air for a few terrifying seconds, fell to the ground again and kept rolling, skittering and bumping across the uneven landscape.

When the plane veered sideways, Bran fought the controls, keeping the nose straight ahead. Then one of the wheels hit something solid, bringing everything on that side of the plane to a sudden jarring halt, spinning the wings around in a half circle and flipping the plane into the air then down on its nose. The propellers chewed into the ground. One of the blades snapped off and a piece of metal flew through the windshield, shattering the Plexiglas. Jessie screamed as the world went black.

THEY WERE DOWN. Bran shook his head to clear it, then forced himself to focus on what he needed to do. Hurriedly cleaning the board, he turned everything off to prevent a fire or explosion. As he finished the crucial task, he flicked a glance at Jessie, saw her sprawled unconscious in her seat, blood streaming down the side of her head. His insides clenched into a terrified knot, and everything inside him went cold.

"Jessie! Jessie!" His world seemed to tilt sideways as he popped his seat belt and leaned over her, checked for a pulse with a shaking hand. Feeling a soft, steady heartbeat, he told himself the burn behind his eyes was only a rush of relief.

Jessie moaned. He had to get her out of there, get her somewhere safe until he was sure the plane wasn't going to explode into an inferno. He managed to open the bent cabin door and climb out, hurried around and opened the door on her side of the plane. Easing her down into his arms, he carried her a safe distance away and placed her carefully on the hard-packed earth.

"Jessie. Talk to me, baby." Inspecting the streak of crimson on the side of her head, his mouth went dry. His usual control abandoned him, replaced by gut-wrenching fear. "Jessie!"

Her eyes fluttered open. She looked into his face, reached up and touched his cheek. "You're...bleeding."

His stomach unclenched, some of his fear receding. "I'm okay. We're down. Everything's okay." He touched his forehead, came away with crimson streaks on his fingers, hadn't realized some of the broken bits of Plexiglas had nicked him.

He looked at Jessie and took a shaky breath. "A chunk of the propeller came through the windshield and creased the side of your head. You were out for a couple of minutes so you've probably got a concussion. No idea how bad it is. How are you feeling?"

"My head hurts, but I'm not dizzy or anything."

He held up three fingers. "How many do you see?"

"Five." She grinned at the look on his face. "I'm kidding. Three fingers."

He didn't laugh, just unzipped his down vest and tore a chunk off the bottom of his Henley, folded it and pressed it gently against the side of her head. His eyes closed for a moment. If she'd been hit squarely instead of just grazed, she'd be dead.

"Hold this until the bleeding stops." But it looked like the cut was shallower than it had first appeared, head wounds being notorious for bleeding. The trail of scarlet near her hairline was already drying. "I'd feel better if I could get you to a hospital, but I don't think that's going to happen anytime soon."

"I've hit my head harder falling out of the trees my brother convinced me to climb. I'll be okay."

He tipped her face up and softly kissed her. Since he couldn't find words for what he wanted to say, he looked away, back at the plane. He needed to make sure the fuel tanks hadn't been ruptured when they ground-looped. If it looked safe, he needed to get their gear.

"What happened up there?" Jessie asked, some of the color back in her face.

He worked a muscle in his jaw. "Someone doctored the fuel. I don't know what they added, maybe a pellet of some kind, something that didn't dissolve right away. No way to check for something like that."

She shivered. "They want to kill me that much?"

His mouth edged up. "Looks like we've both made the bad guys' hit list."

She tried to smile, but didn't quite make it. "Is that why you didn't radio for help?"

"Someone at the airport got paid to look the other way. I didn't send out a Mayday because I figured I could get us down in one piece and I didn't want whoever fucked up the fuel knowing where we ended up. With any luck, they'll think we're dead—at least for a while."

The hard truth was, they were still on the run, still being hunted by people connected with the theft of the chemical weapons.

"What now?" Jessie asked.

"I need to check out the plane. Doesn't look like it's going to explode so I'm going to get our gear and get us the hell out of here. If you're up to walking, there's a highway about three miles away. We'll catch a ride as far as the first town we come to. Get a room and spend the night."

He needed some downtime himself. With the impact of the plane, every part of his body felt battered and bruised, and with no sleep last night, he was tired clear to the bone. He knew Jessie had to be feeling the same. "Soon as I get cell service, I'll call my brother, let him know what happened."

Jessie's gaze swung across the open field to where the Baron sat at a cockeyed angle, tipped up on its nose. "Chase was upset about the broken windows in his office. He's really going to be mad about his plane."

Bran laughed and some of the tension he was feeling slid away. "The insurance company won't be happy, but

I'm pretty sure my brother will just be thankful we're both still alive."

He took a last look at Jessie and prayed she wasn't hurt any worse than she seemed. They had to get going. If they didn't, it would be dark by the time they reached the highway.

Bran returned to the plane, and it took two trips to get their bags out of the cargo hold, including the medical kit, survival gear, and his weapons bag, and carry it all back to where Jessie sat on the dry grass.

He took a few precious minutes to put a butterfly bandage over the wound on her head, then they layered up and Jessie helped him condense their stuff down to the basics: laptops, his cell phone, weapons and ammo, the emergency kit, and survival equipment. The stuff went into his black canvas duffel, clothes in a single carry-on.

Bran clipped his Glock to his belt. "You ready for this?"

She nodded. "At the moment, walking beats the heck out of flying."

He chuckled. He couldn't resist cupping her cheek, bending his head to press a soft kiss on her lips. They started walking, heading for the highway in search of a ride, hoping the men who brought down the plane weren't out there somewhere waiting.

Knowing there was a damn good chance they would be.

CHAPTER TWENTY-SIX

As ANXIOUS AS he was to get away from the downed aircraft, Bran kept his pace slow, not wanting to press Jessie too hard. The uneven ground was rough and taxing, the temperature dropping by the minute.

They were both cold, tired, and hungry, their bodies battered and bruised by the brutally hard landing. No choice but to keep going. There was nothing behind them but trouble.

Relief trickled through him when he spotted the highway up ahead, only to discover it was nothing but a two-lane road with almost no traffic.

It was nearly dark, just a thin line of purple on the horizon, and ball-freezing cold as they stood bundled up at the edge of the pavement waiting for a ride. Bran hated the thought of Jessie having to spend the night out in the elements, especially with a concussion, but it was looking more and more likely.

He'd already spotted a place to make camp, off to the west at the base of a granite outcropping. He'd have to check for snakes denned up out of the cold, but at least the rocks would provide a decent windbreak. He'd give it another fifteen minutes before heading over. Then he'd dig out the survival gear he'd taken from the plane.

Resigned to the cold night ahead, he glanced down the road, his adrenaline spiking when he spotted two distant headlights bumping over the uneven asphalt. As the lights grew near, he stepped into the lane and started waving his arms, but the vehicle wasn't slowing. Then Jessie stepped out and started waving.

The ancient Chevy pickup slowed to a rolling stop and pulled over to the side of the road a little ways in front of them.

"Nice work," Bran said, smiling.

Jessie smiled back as she hurried along beside him. "There are definitely some advantages to being female."

He nodded. "A universal truth."

As they approached the pickup, a white-haired, white-bearded Hispanic man leaned his head out the window, his face as wrinkled as the truck was battered. "Where are you going?" There were three other men inside, crammed tightly together.

Bran eyed the bed of the truck—it was better than a night in the cold. "We rolled our car. My wife and I are going to the first town where we can get a room."

The old man's eyes took in the bloodstained bandage on the side of Jessie's head and the cuts on Bran's face. "*Sí, señor.* I will take you. Get in the back."

Bran loaded the duffel and carry-on into the truck bed, which was stacked with old furniture and several crates of chickens. He pushed one of the crates aside enough to make room for them, ignored the smell, and helped Jessie climb in. He settled an old wooden dresser in front of them to help block the icy wind and sat down as the pickup rolled off down the highway.

"I apologize for the accommodations," he said with a smile, squeezing in beside her. "Maybe we'll get lucky and find a Four Seasons in the next town we come to."

Jessie rolled her eyes. There wasn't a town of any size

for miles in any direction. "At this point, a Motel 6 would be a luxury."

"You got that right." He settled her more snugly against him, his arms around Jessie, her head on his shoulder. "How are you feeling?"

She sighed. "I've been better, but I'm okay."

"How's your head?"

"Still hurts, but my feet hurt worse. New boots, remember?"

"Yeah, they never feel good the first day. We'll work them over when we get into the room." Assuming they could find one.

The truck rattled and bumped along the road, the chickens occasionally flapping their wings and squawking. Jessie dozed for a while and he let her, waking her occasionally to make sure she was okay.

They'd been on the road for an hour when the pickup made a turn onto a smaller paved road, and he spotted a sign that read Walsenburg. He knew where it was on the map, knew it wasn't far off I-25, which he would have preferred, but at least they would be out of the cold.

When the pickup pulled into the parking lot of the Sands Motel, he breathed a sigh of relief. He tossed out their gear, helped Jessie out of the truck, and spoke to the old man through the window.

"*Gracias, senor.* We really appreciate the ride." He'd been deployed to South America, spoke fluent Spanish, but sometimes it was better not to show all your cards.

"*Sí, senor*, no problem. *Buena suerte, amigos.*"

Bran waved goodbye, didn't offer to pay for the ride though he would have liked to. Letting strangers know you were carrying cash was never a good idea.

"I'll go get us a room," Jessie offered, spotting the Sands's front office.

He glanced around. "Hold on a minute." There were three motel signs he could see along the road. He hated asking Jessie to go any farther, but his survival instincts were something he never ignored.

He handed her his encrypted cell phone. "Call the Mountain Pines. See if they've got a room. I'd feel better if no one knows where we are, including our new friends."

She nodded and made the call, spoke to the desk clerk, then handed back his cell. "I told them we'd be there in five minutes. That way we can pay cash when we arrive."

"Good idea." From here on out, he wasn't using his credit cards. He had no idea what capabilities these people had. Considering they had just crashed his plane, he wasn't taking any chances.

The motel was a single-story concrete-block building, all the rooms opening onto the parking lot. As soon as they were settled in room number 8, he phoned Chase.

"Hey, big brother."

"Bran. About time you checked in."

"First chance I've had to call."

"I'm damn glad to hear from you. Reese has been bugging me to find out what's going on. You called off his lawyer so I assume you're out of jail. Both of us have been worried sick."

"I'm afraid we got a problem." Bran ran a hand over the roughness along his jaw. "They crashed your plane, bro. Tampered with the fuel. Nothing I could do."

A long pause. "You okay? You and Jessie are safe?"

"Made an emergency landing in a field south of Colorado Springs. Plane's a mess but it didn't explode. You'll have to send a truck to haul it in for repairs."

"I don't give a damn about the frigging plane. It's you two I'm worried about. What the hell happened?"

He was surprised at the comfort that came with his brother's concern. "Piece of the prop came through the Plexiglas when the nose went into the ground. I'm bruised and a little banged up, but I'm okay. I'm monitoring Jessie for a concussion. She definitely got the worst of it."

"Jesus, Bran."

"We're in a little town off the highway." He purposely didn't say the name. He trusted the encryption only so far. "They'll be looking for us. I didn't file a flight plan or send a Mayday so we won't be that easy to find."

"Christ."

"I know. But we're making progress. If we weren't, they wouldn't be coming on so strong. We're heading for California tomorrow. There's a woman named Mara Ramos. She's ass-deep in this thing. Or at least that's the way it looks."

"You put Tabby on her?"

"Tabby found her after she disappeared. Now that our other lead has stalled, I'll get back with Tab, see if she can go deeper."

"You guys need to get out of there. I'm calling Reese. He'll send the jet. I need your location. I'll call you back as soon as we figure the closest airstrip that'll work."

Hoping the phone wasn't being monitored, Bran gave him the name of the town and ended the call. It was worth the risk to bring in the jet. They really needed to get out of Colorado and get to California. They had to make this end. At the moment, Mara Ramos was their best chance of that happening.

He glanced over at Jessie, who was sitting on the bed, shoulders slumped, looking tired and pale and worried. "What did Chase say?"

"He's worried about us. He's sending the jet to pick us up, take us to California."

Her eyes widened. "You have a *jet*?"

He grinned. "Company jet. Cessna Citation CJ4. Comes in handy sometimes."

"Now that I think about it, Chase mentioned it that day in your office." She cocked an eyebrow. "So I guess he wasn't mad about the plane."

"Like I said, he was worried. Of the three of us, Chase is by far the better pilot. I always paid attention when we flew together." He smiled. "I mentally channeled him when I made the landing."

"I think you're a pretty damn good pilot yourself."

He sat down on the bed beside her, took hold of her hand and brought it to his lips. "You were great today. No one I would rather have crash-landed with." He leaned over and softly kissed her.

Jessie kissed him back. "Me, either."

Bran urged her to lie back on the bed and rest, then used his phone to find a pizza place that delivered. But Jessie was too tired to eat. He was sure her head was still pounding like a hammer inside her skull.

"Get some sleep, baby." He smoothed her hair back from her face. "I'll wake you every once in a while so we know you're okay."

"What about you? You were up all night last night. Today has been exhausting. You need sleep as much as I do."

"I'll sleep once we're safe." Which they wouldn't be until they were long gone from the Mountain Pines Motel.

JESSIE STIRRED AS Bran gently shook her awake for the second time that night. "I'm okay," she said groggily, then yawned, curled up, and closed her eyes. Her head still throbbed, but she was so exhausted she was able to ignore the pain and go back to sleep.

At dawn Bran nudged her awake again. It was barely light outside. "You have to get dressed. We've got a ride coming to take us to the jet. It'll be landing at the Cuchara Valley Airport in half an hour. That's about a twenty-minute drive from here."

She tossed off the covers, swayed a little as she rose to her feet.

Bran caught her waist to steady her. "Easy. You don't have to rush. The jet won't leave if we're a few minutes late."

She took a deep breath and the dizziness receded. "I'm all right." Making her way into the tiny bathroom, she hurried through her morning routine, then dressed in a clean sweater instead of the bloodstained one she'd worn on the plane, with the same jeans and boots. She noticed the boots felt a little better.

"I took a hammer to them," Bran said. "Old army trick. Usually helps."

She smiled. "Thanks." She drank a cup of hot water instead of the coffee he'd made in the small pot on the dresser. No caffeine, he'd said, until her head felt better.

She was definitely not looking forward to another plane ride, but a run-in with the men who were trying to kill them would be far worse.

Ten minutes later, dressed and ready, she jumped at a knock at the door. Bran drew his weapon, checked the peephole, and pulled it open.

"I'm Alejandro Nunez," the man on the front step said. "Your brother Reese asked me to pick you up." He looked like a local, midfifties, fine threads of gray in his thick black hair, a sun-browned, weathered complexion.

Bran holstered his weapon. "I talked to him. He said he was sending someone. How do you know my brother?"

"I own the Double Eagle Ranch. A couple of years ago, Reese came to the ranch to go fishing with my son, Luis."

Bran tipped his head in her direction. "This is Jessie Kegan. We appreciate your help."

Nunez smiled, digging lines into his sun-darkened forehead. "Your brother gave Luis a job when he first got out of college. He is a friend." Nunez reached down and grabbed the carry-on sitting just inside the door, while Bran picked up his duffel and slung the strap over his shoulder.

Since the room had been paid in advance, they crossed the parking lot to a newer model, extended cab Dodge Ram pickup with mud on the tires. Bran helped Jessie into the front passenger seat and climbed into the backseat behind her.

The radio played country music as the pickup rolled along the road to the rural airport, apparently the closest around with a runway long enough for the jet to land.

The plane was waiting when the pickup drove onto the airstrip, a sleek white jet with a red stripe down the side. Its powerful engines were running, the steps down, waiting for its passengers to arrive.

Nunez extended a weathered hand to Bran and then to Jessie. "Perhaps you will come back sometime and go fishing. It is beautiful up here in the spring."

Jessie glanced at Brandon. With luck, their investigation would be over long before spring. She would be safe back in Denver and Bran would be at work back in Dallas.

His eyes found hers an instant before his attention returned to Nunez. "You never know," he said. "Maybe we'll do that." But they both knew it wasn't going to happen.

"Thanks, Mr. Nunez, for everything," Jessie said.

"It's Alejandro and both of you stay safe."

A young blond steward met them as they started across the tarmac. He took the carry-on and Bran's duffel and fell in behind them. Jessie's gaze went to the black-haired man who appeared at the top of the stairs, quickly descended, and enveloped Bran in a big bear hug.

"Damned glad to see you, Bran."

"Reese! What the hell, bro? You didn't have to come."

Tall, with a lean, solid build, eyes an even more intense shade of blue than Brandon's, and the face of a fallen angel, Reese Garrett, CEO of Garrett Resources, exuded power and authority.

"I'm glad to see you're actually mobile," Reese said, smiling. "The master of understatement I know you to be, I figured *a little banged up* could be anything from busted ribs to a broken neck."

A corner of Bran's mouth edged up as he turned to introduce her. "Reese, this is Jessie Kegan. She actually got the worst of it. Pretty bad cut on the side of her head, and it looks like she's got a concussion."

Reese nodded. "We'll take care of it once we're aboard." He extended his hand to her. "I'm Reese. It's nice to meet you, Jessie."

"You as well, Reese. I can't thank you enough for coming to help."

He just shrugged. "The plane belongs to the family. Let's get aboard and get the hell out of here before trouble finds us."

She nodded, turned, and climbed the stairs, liking the middle Garrett brother on first meeting. Bran got her settled in one of the honey-colored, butter-soft leather seats, then took the seat across the aisle.

Configured the way it was, the cabin was roomy, with

club seating for four and a sofa along one wall. Two pilots manned the cockpit.

"Once we're in the air," Reese said, "Dr. Chandler will take a look at both of you." He sat down in a seat opposite Jessie, across the aisle from a distinguished-looking gentleman with thinning silver hair. Even before their seat belts were in place, the plane began taxiing down the runway.

Bran looked out the window as the jet gathered speed, the landscape soon roaring past in a blur. "You sure this strip is long enough to get this little beauty in the air?"

Reese grinned, and suddenly Jessie saw the resemblance between the two brothers.

"That's the nice thing about a Citation. Requires shorter runways, ranges over two thousand nautical miles, and cruises at five hundred miles an hour. Plus it's more economical to run a light jet as opposed to a midsize, which we don't really need."

Bran chuckled. "Count on you to think of saving money."

Reese smiled. "Goes with the job." Silence fell as the jet engines roared and the plane tilted upward, pressing them back into their seats.

For an instant, Jessie's mind strayed to the moments yesterday before the plane hit the ground, and her heart started racing. Bran reached across the narrow aisle and his hand covered hers, lacing their fingers together. She released a slow breath. Bran was there. Everything would be okay.

Twenty minutes into the flight, Dr. Charles Chandler had diagnosed her with a slight concussion and put three stitches in the side of her head. Bran carried miscellaneous cuts and bruises, but he was okay. Reese retrieved ham-and-egg croissants, fruit, and coffee from the refreshment center.

Bran declined the coffee but quickly downed a couple

of croissants. As soon as he'd finished, he headed for the sofa, feeling safe for the first time in days. In seconds, he was asleep.

Jessie's heart squeezed as she watched him, this man she had come to respect and care for, a man willing to protect her with his life.

Feeling Reese's eyes on her, she turned in his direction. "You're worried about him," he said.

She felt a stinging behind her eyes, quickly blinked it away. "People have tried to kill him. He was thrown in jail. He survived a plane crash. He hasn't slept in days. All because of me."

Reese's gaze held hers. "Your brother was his best friend. As far as Bran's concerned, you're family. Besides, it's what he does."

She swallowed past the knot in her throat. "I know. I just… I wish this was over." Except that as soon as they found the men who had killed her father and stolen the munitions, Bran would go back to Dallas and she would never see him again.

"He'll feel better when he wakes up," Reese said.

Her gaze swung back to the man on the sofa, far too tall to actually fit comfortably. Still, she had never seen him sleep so deeply. "He trusts you to protect us."

Something moved over Reese's dark features. "He's my brother. He needs me to keep you both safe, and he knows that's what I'll do."

At any cost were the unspoken words. She thought of her brother, Danny. They had shared that kind of bond.

"Thank you," she said. "Thank you for everything."

CHAPTER TWENTY-SEVEN

BRAN DIDN'T WAKE UP when the wheels touched down, not when the jet taxied to the executive terminal at Gillespie Field and the engines shut down. Not until his brother gently shook his shoulder.

"We've landed."

Bran snapped instantly awake, as he had learned to do. Unclipping his seat belt, he sat up on the sofa.

"There's a car and driver waiting," Reese said. "He'll take you to your suite at the Grant. The hotel's about a half mile from The Max in the Gaslamp District. Jessie says you need to talk to a detective there named Hunter Brady."

"That's right."

"When you get to the hotel, there'll be a rental car waiting for your use whenever you need it."

Bran rubbed a hand over his several days' growth of beard and smiled. "You can make my travel arrangements any day, bro."

Reese just nodded. "You can thank my new assistant, McKenzie Haines. She's a real find."

Bran's gaze went in search of Jessie, who waited near the exit. They left the plane and Reese walked them into the terminal.

"Your bags are already loaded in the limo. I'd suggest you get a few more hours' sleep before whoever's after you figures out you're not dead."

The flight had lasted only a couple of hours. He could definitely use a little more sleep. "Good idea."

"Take care of him, Jessie," Reese said to her.

Jessie went up on her toes and kissed his cheek. "I promise I'll do my best."

Bran shook Reese's hand and clapped him on the shoulder. "Thanks, bro. I appreciate everything you've done."

"Just try to stay alive, okay?"

Bran flicked a glance at Jessie and repeated her words. "I'll do my best."

The U.S. Grant Hotel in downtown San Diego was an elegant, five-star, historic hotel with marble floors, molded ceilings, and crystal chandeliers. Potted palms and rosewood furniture decorated the lobby.

"It's gorgeous," Jessie said as they walked into their suite, which was done in the same old-world traditional motif.

"Leave it to my brother."

"I really liked him. He clearly loves you very much."

Bran glanced away, uncomfortable with the sentiment. "Both our parents are dead. My brothers and I...we take care of each other."

"So I noticed." She glanced around the luxurious suite. "They've already brought our bags up. Do you want to shower? You didn't get to take one this morning. Or would you rather eat? You didn't have that much on the plane. I could call room service."

He walked over and eased her into his arms, gave her a gentle kiss. "I'm pretty sure there's a big bathtub in there. I'd like a nice long soak, some food, and then some sleep."

"That sounds perfect."

"Long as you join me. Since you're still recovering, I promise to behave myself."

Jessie arched a brow. "All right. But I'm not making the same promise."

Bran laughed. Grabbing her hand, he headed for the bathroom. It turned out to be a huge marble affair with a separate glass-enclosed shower and big jetted tub. He really needed that soak. And other things…

Six hours later he awoke feeling better than he had in days, Jessie curled against him in a deep, untroubled sleep. With her features relaxed and a faint smile on her lips, she looked beautiful.

She was smart and brave and loyal. She had put herself at risk for him more than once, and he knew she would do it again. The stitches on the side of her head reminded him of the gut-wrenching moments when the plane had gone down and his terrible fear when he had realized she was unconscious and bleeding. Yesterday she could have died.

Something soft unfolded inside him as he watched her, something he had never felt for a woman before. He was afraid to put a name to it, afraid of what it might mean.

He glanced at the clock as he rolled out of bed, careful not to wake her. Five p.m. They had slept most of the day, but there was still work to do.

Grabbing fresh clothes out of the suitcase and his Glock off the nightstand, he padded into the living room, picked up the hotel phone, and ordered coffee and a couple of sandwiches for a late lunch. Then he got an outside line and phoned Hunter Brady.

"It's Bran Garrett, Hunt. I need to talk to you about Mara Ramos." Hunt had been keeping tabs on Ramos since Bran had asked for his help.

"Where are you?"

"San Diego."

"I'm in the office. Just got back from Ramos's apartment. If it works for you, we can meet here."

"Works great, I'm not far away. We need to eat something, then we'll be there. An hour should do it."

"We? You've got Jessie with you?"

He'd been as straight with Hunt, a former police detective, as possible. They had worked together before, and Bran trusted him. "She's here. She's had a rough time, but she's okay. I'll tell you about it when I see you."

Next he phoned Tabby, identifying himself since he knew she wouldn't recognize the hotel number.

"Hi, stranger," Tabby said. "How are things in the Mile High City?"

"Long gone from there. I need you to check out my phone, make sure it's not giving away any secrets, including my location."

Before he'd found the bug in Jessie's purse, Weaver and his crew had tracked her to Dallas, then back to the airstrip in Colorado Springs where they had landed. He figured that was how they knew about his plane, but he had to be sure.

"Your phone's got state-of-the-art encryption," Tabby said. "But I'll take a look."

"Thanks. Anything new on the offshore accounts?"

"Not so far. These guys are really good, but I've still got a few tricks I haven't used. I took a look at your guy Weaver in ADMAX. His first name's Edgar. He's from Georgia, in for a triple homicide."

"Yeah, we found that out."

"So far I haven't run across anything you can use, but I'll keep looking."

"Great. Also, I need you to go deeper on Mara Ramos. I have a feeling she's not who she seems."

"I can do that."

"Make it your top priority, Tab. These guys aren't messing around. Yesterday, they crashed Chase's plane."

"Crap, Bran! Tell me you and Jessie weren't in it."

"I wish I could. We're both okay, but we need this to end."

"I'm on it. I'll call you back as fast as I can." The line went dead. When the doorbell rang, Bran grabbed his pistol, checked the peephole, then stashed the gun out of sight and opened the door.

His stomach growled at the delicious smells coming from beneath the silver domes on the linen-draped cart as the server rolled it into the living room. He signed the tab, tipped the server, then closed and locked the door. He was about to wake Jessie when she walked into the living room, her face washed and her hair pulled into a French braid.

She was dressed in clean clothes, a pair of beige leggings, her brown ankle boots, and the lightweight, short-sleeve, peach knit top she'd had on in Dallas the first time he'd seen her. Hey, even in November it was sunny and mild in San Diego.

He caught a hint of cleavage as she drew near, and arousal slipped through him. Even after the slow, easy, very satisfying sex they'd had in the tub, she stirred his blood.

"How are you feeling?" he asked.

"My head doesn't hurt, and thanks to some very sweet lovemaking, I slept all afternoon. I feel great."

"Sweet, huh? I don't know whether to be complimented or insulted."

She reached up and cupped his cheek. "You took great care of me. Thanks."

He glanced away, a little embarrassed. He'd been worried about her. Apparently she'd noticed. "You ready to get back to work?"

Jessie glanced wistfully over to where her laptop sat on an ornate rosewood desk. "I was hoping to get some writing done today—I still have to make a living, you know. But I'd rather talk to Mara Ramos, if that's what you're planning to do."

"Not yet. Tabby's going deeper, looking for something that might help. I'm heading down to The Max to talk to Hunt Brady. He's been keeping an eye on her. He might be able to give us something."

"Like a typical writer, I'll take any excuse I can find not to face that blank computer screen."

Bran chuckled. "Soon as we finish eating, I'll call downstairs, have the valet bring up the rental car."

She sighed dramatically. "It's good to be king."

Bran laughed as he caught her hand and led her toward the dining table.

THE MAXIMUM SECURITY office in the Gaslamp District was housed on the ground floor of a two-story building in the 400 block of F Street. Yellow and white with a bay window in front and a big wooden arched front door, it shared the structure with a bar called the Tipsy Crow.

Jessie waited anxiously as Bran parked their rental car, a pearl gray Lincoln Navigator, in the parking garage across the street, then they went inside.

The ornate oak desks and green glass lamps scattered around the room felt similar to the Dallas office, though that one had more of a Western vibe. The slightly more ornate decor in San Diego perfectly suited the late-Victorian, nineteenth-century architecture of the historic neighborhood filled with shops and trendy restaurants.

There was a reception area up front, but being after 6:00 p.m., no one sat behind the desk. Three people were still working, a woman and two men. One of the men rose and started toward them across the open space, Hunter Brady, she assumed. Medium height and solid build, he had light brown hair and a jaw mostly hidden by a close-cropped beard.

He was attractive, Jessie thought, which seemed to be a requirement to work at The Max.

The men shook hands. "Good to see you, Bran."

"You, too. It's been a while." Bran turned to Jessie. "Hunt's former San Diego PD. Homicide detective. Hunt, this is Jessie Kegan. I told you about her."

"Nice to meet you, Jessie." His hand felt warm and strong. He had an air of confidence that eased some of her worry.

"Let's go into the conference room where we can talk," Hunt suggested. Located at the rear of the building, the room had a long oak table surrounded by eight chairs up-holstered in dark green leather. Jessie sat down next to Bran, and Hunt noticed the bandage on the side of her head.

"Looks like you ran into some trouble."

Absently she reached up and touched the wound, the area still sore. "Actually, I was lucky to have such a good pilot."

Bran went on to explain about the attempts on her life, the arrest he'd made that had landed him in jail, and the plane crash.

Hunter's mood darkened. "You need to find these guys."

"You got that right." Bran's phone rang, and he pulled it out of his jeans pocket. "Hey, Tabby."

Jessie sat up a little straighter, hoping for good news.

"Phone's safe to use," Bran said as the call ended. "Nothing on Ramos yet, but Tabby's just getting started." His gaze swung back to Hunter Brady. "What have you got?"

"I've been keeping a loose eye on the house the way you

asked. The address in La Jolla is a rental, one-bedroom, one-bath condo. I've followed the woman a couple of times, but she just went shopping. Once she went to a matinee."

"By herself?" Jessie asked.

"Yeah. Seems to be pretty much a loner. No visitors, doesn't meet friends for coffee, nothing like that."

"What about at night?" Bran asked.

"I've driven by a couple of times, never stayed more than an hour. I can set up surveillance if you want, have the place watched 24/7."

"It might come to that," Bran said. "First I want to see what Tabby comes up with. If I haven't heard from her by tomorrow, I'll drive out there. If I can't get something out of Ramos, I'll call Special Agent Tripp and give him her location. Tripp's with the Criminal Investigation Division at Fort Carson. He's got one of Weaver's guys in custody. With any luck, they'll be sweating him hard enough to get some answers."

According to what Bran had said, he hadn't told Hunter Brady about the stolen chemical weapons, just that they were trying to find out who had murdered her dad.

Jessie thought of her father and his relationship with Mara Ramos. What if the woman had seduced him into aiding in the theft of the weapons?

The idea seemed so impossible she immediately abandoned it. Bran didn't believe it and neither did she. Her dad was as honorable a man as she had ever known.

They left The Max and returned to the suite. Jessie spent the evening working on the article she was writing for Kegan's Korner. She had turned in the one she'd written on the problems in Drover City a week ago. Since then, Factfinders had sent her a half a dozen emails asking her for something new.

She wasn't sure how much she could say about the weapons theft at the depot, but she would push the boundaries as far as possible. She needed to get everything organized and documented. She had a hunch it was going to be one of her best pieces of journalism.

She sighed as she closed down her laptop. In order to finish the story, all they had to do was prove her dad's innocence, find the people who had murdered him, and locate the stolen weapons before hundreds of people were killed.

All they had to do was stay alive long enough to get the job done.

CHAPTER TWENTY-EIGHT

Bran lay spoon-fashion with Jessie on the sofa, watching the original Tobey Maguire version of *Spider-Man*. He'd seen it and most of the remakes half a dozen times, but it never got old. Jessie seemed to agree.

After napping all afternoon, they'd been too wired to go to bed. He'd ordered room service, thick New York steaks and Caesar salads, even indulged in a glass of red wine. He was finally ready to call it a night, though sleeping was not his intention.

The credits were rolling as he nuzzled Jessie's neck and softly nibbled an earlobe. "You ready for bed?"

She rolled onto her back and looped her arms around his neck. "If you promise we aren't going to sleep."

Bran grinned and kissed her. "Cross my heart." He made a dramatic show of drawing a cross on his chest and started to get up. When his phone rang, he was torn between disappointment and hope for a break in the case.

Recognizing Tabby's number, he put the phone on speaker and set it on the coffee table. "Hey, Tab, you got something?"

"You bet I do. Mara Ramos's real name is Mahri Rahmati. She was born in Yemen, been in the States since her early twenties. Came here on a student visa and never left. Her fake identity runs deep. Someone went to a lot of trouble to give her a new life in America."

Adrenaline pumped through him. He looked at Jessie, whose eyes were wide and alert. "Yemen," he repeated. "Big-time terrorist activity. Got to be connected to the stolen weapons."

"Could be someone in Yemen was the buyer. I'm looking into it. I wanted to give you what I had on Ramos aka Rahmati as fast as I could."

"We need to bring the army in on this, but I want to talk to her first."

"What if she runs?" Jessie asked.

"Mahri Rahmati disappeared once before," Tabby said. "In 1998, a year after she arrived in the States. She reappeared as Mara Ramos, finished her education, and worked as a schoolteacher most of her life. I connected the two identities using facial recognition…among other things. So far I haven't linked her to a terrorist organization, but I'm looking hard."

Bran scrubbed a hand over the scruff on his jaw. "We won't let her run. We'll figure something out."

"I'll keep you posted." Tabby hung up the phone.

"What are we going to do?" Jessie asked. "If we tell the army, they'll step in and we'll be out. No access. No answers. People will still be trying to kill us, still trying to stop our investigation. If we don't come forward, we could be responsible for a terror attack."

"If we go to the army, we'll be out, all right—or in jail. Tabby didn't get that intel off Facebook."

"We have to do something. We don't have any choice."

"Oh, we're going to do something. We're going to talk to Mara Ramos. Now. Tonight."

Grabbing his phone, he punched Hunt Brady's number. "Sorry to call so late, but we just got intel on Mara Ramos. Her real name's Mahri Rahmati. She's Yemeni, here illegally. Her cover's deep. Very good chance she's involved in terrorism."

"Terrorism? What the fuck, Bran?"

"Long story. Some of it's classified. I'll tell you what I can when I see you." He stood up from the sofa, the phone still pressed to his ear. "I'm on my way to talk to Ramos, but I'm going to need backup."

"You got it. How long before you get there?"

He knew her address, brought the directions up on his cell. "No traffic this time of night. We're twenty minutes out."

"Make it thirty and I'll meet you there."

"You got it." The phone went dead and Bran glanced around for Jessie, saw her walking back into the living room, already changed into a black T-shirt and sneakers to go with the black yoga pants she'd had on.

"I'm going with you."

He was torn. There was no way for anyone to know they were staying at the Grant. She should be safe. On the other hand, leaving her behind gave him an itchy feeling. He'd rather keep her close. Besides, with Ramos's connection to her father, she might get something he couldn't.

"All right, we'll both go."

"I want a weapon."

He frowned. "It won't be legal here."

A half smile curved her lips. "Better to be judged by twelve than carried by six."

Bran laughed, recognizing one of Danny's pet sayings. He knew she could shoot. Hell, she was probably a crack shot. No way would Danny not have taught his little sister how to defend herself.

Since Bran wanted her safe, he retrieved the Smith &

Wesson .38 out of his gear bag and handed it over. "Let's hope you don't need it."

Jessie flipped open the cylinder, which was fully loaded, then flicked it closed and stuck the revolver into her cross-body purse.

Twenty-five minutes later the Navigator rolled past the address of the condo on Via Mallorca. The house was dark. He circled the block and parked down the street. A few minutes later, Hunt Brady's black Chevy Blazer eased up behind them and the engine went silent. They all got out of their vehicles.

"No lights on inside," Bran said. "She may not be home."

"I guess we'll find out," Hunt said.

Bran scanned the area for anyone moving around in the darkness. "Looks clear."

"There's a sliding glass door in back," Hunt said. "Opens onto a fenced patio. I'll head in that direction, make sure she doesn't get out that way."

Bran nodded. He and Jessie moved quietly to the front door, Bran holding his pistol in a two-handed grip pointed up. Standing off to the side, out of the line of fire, Jessie knocked on the door. It was after midnight. They waited and she knocked again. There was a rustling sound inside, foot-steps, then the porch light went on, but the door didn't open.

"Who is it?"

"It's Jessie Kegan, Mara. I need to talk to you about my father."

Long seconds passed. Bran wondered if she'd bolted. Instead, he heard the metal click of dead bolts turning, more than one, then the door swung open. Bran was on her, shoving Mara back inside, Jessie following him in and closing the door. Jessie switched on the light in the living room while Bran cleared the small, one-bedroom condo.

"She's alone," Bran said, returning to the living room.

"Who are you people? What do you want?" In a pale blue plush robe and slippers, Mara stood stiffly. It looked as if she'd been sleeping, her shoulder-length jet-black hair slightly mussed, her face clean of makeup.

"I think you know who I am," Jessie said. "I'm betting my dad showed you my picture."

She swallowed. "Jessie…yes…yes, he did. I don't understand. What are you doing here in the middle of the night? And who is this man?"

"My name is Brandon Garrett. Let's just say I'm a friend of the family. Why don't we go into the kitchen and you can make us a pot of coffee, *Mahri*?" He said the words in Arabic, which he'd learned in spec ops and spoke fluently.

Mara's face went sheet-white, and she swayed on her feet. Bran nudged her forward into the kitchen and set her down in one of the kitchen chairs. He opened the sliding glass door, letting Hunt Brady into the condo.

"I'll make the coffee," Jessie said.

Bran just nodded. It was going to be another long night.

WITH HER GLOSSY black hair, full lips, and dark eyes, Mara Ramos was indeed a beautiful woman. Her olive complexion made it easy for her to pass under a Hispanic alias. But Bran had spoken to her in Arabic, and she had clearly understood.

According to Tabby, she was forty-five years old, ten years younger than Jessie's father. Thinking of the intelligent, vital man James Kegan had been, it wasn't difficult to imagine them together.

"What was your relationship with my father?" Jessie demanded, taking the lead.

"We were…we were seeing each other. We cared about each other."

"Bullshit. You never cared about him. Your relationship with my father was nothing but a scam. You just used him, won his trust, then set him up to take the blame for stealing those chemical weapons."

Seated in a chair at the table while the three of them stood around her, Mara looked frightened and resigned to whatever happened next.

"That isn't true. I loved your father. James was the best man I've ever known."

Caught off guard by the declaration, Jessie fought a fresh surge of anger. "You're a liar. You seduced my father to get his personal information—his social security number, bank account numbers, credit cards, everything you could find that would help pin the blame on him. You gave that information to the men who murdered him!"

"I didn't know they were going to kill him! I loved him!"

Struggling with her shock at the unexpected turn, Jessie fell silent.

Bran stepped into Mara's personal space, forcing her to look up at him. Her eyes glistened with tears. "When did you start planning the setup?" Mara glanced away but Bran caught her jaw, forcing her gaze back to his face. "How long ago, Mara?"

Pain surfaced in her eyes. Bran let her go and she swallowed. "I suppose you could say all my life. I was twenty-three when I came to this country. The people who paid my way also paid for my education, and when my visa ran out, they gave me a new identity. From the beginning they made it clear I owed them a very big debt and that someday they would expect to collect."

"Go on."

She shivered. Her gaze seemed to turn inward, to someplace inside. "The debt I owed was the reason I never had children. I always knew the time would come. I didn't want a family that could be put at risk."

Jessie hardened her heart. Her father was dead because of this woman. Nothing she could say could justify what she had done.

Bran didn't back away. "You keep saying *they*. Who are you talking about?"

"A group I was involved with in Yemen. But it was a long time ago."

"What was their name?"

"They called themselves *jaysh alaslam alyamanii*. Army of Islam of Yemen. But they've changed the name half a dozen times since then. I don't know what they're calling themselves now."

"When did someone from the group contact you?"

"About five months ago. He said his name was Ahmed. Nothing more. Ahmed said it was time for me to pay the debt I owed. He said it was all arranged. I was to move to Colorado Springs, into an apartment rented in my name. It would only be for a few months, he said. While I was there I would meet a man, a colonel in the army named James Kegan. Ahmed told me to get his personal information. I understood what that meant."

Jessie's fury mounted. She ground down on her temper, determined to stay in control. "So you seduced him. You slept with him to win his trust and get him to help steal the weapons."

The woman cringed. "James didn't help them! Your father would never have betrayed his country. That was never part of the plan."

Relief spiraled through her. She felt Brandon's hand on

her shoulder, steady and comforting. He understood the importance of those words.

"So what *was* the plan, Mara?" Bran asked. "You said you didn't know the men were going to kill him."

"No. Ahmed said all I had to do was get close to him, get his personal information. He never said what they planned to do with it, but he made it clear they would kill me if I refused. I owed them everything—my education, my life here, the friends I had made. Everything. James was nothing to me then. It didn't seem like a high price to pay."

"Where did you meet my father?" Jessie asked.

"There was a party for one of James's friends. Someone set it up so I would be invited. I don't know who, but I was welcomed. I was a schoolteacher. There were single men at the party, military men from the base. As the evening progressed, I sought out your father and pretended to be interested in him. He was a very attractive man, and I found him to be likable and smart so it wasn't difficult. He asked if he could see me again and I said yes. We started dating. That was part of the plan."

"Where was this party?"

"Around the pool at the Marriott Hotel."

"Whose party was it?"

"I don't remember. It was a big party, lots of people invited. A twenty-five-year anniversary celebration. I don't remember the couple's name. Perhaps someone suggested the colonel and I would suit. Which we did."

"So you slept with him," Jessie said. "And while he was in your apartment, you stole his personal information."

She nodded. "A little at a time, yes. But even after I had done what they asked, James and I continued to see each other. I knew I should go back to San Diego before things got any more complicated, but by then I was falling in love with him. After he was arrested and charged with those terrible crimes, I understood what I had done."

"And a few days later he was killed," Bran finished.

Fresh tears collected in Mara's obsidian eyes. Her voice cracked. "If I had known, I would never have done it."

Jessie felt a fresh surge of anger. *Was the woman acting? Or could the emotion possibly be real?*

"But you did do it," Bran pressed. "The colonel is dead because of you." He leaned over her, braced his hands on the arms of her chair, caging her in. "Now it's time for you to undo some of what you've done. We need to know the names of the people involved."

Mara shook her head. "I don't know. I only saw Ahmed once. After that, he called me on a disposable phone whenever he wanted to give me instructions."

"Do you still have the phone?" Bran asked.

"No. He told me to throw it away."

"So you have no proof that anything you've just told us is true," Jessie said.

Tears rolled down Mara's cheeks. "No."

Bran glanced over at Hunter Brady. "You get all that?"

Hunt turned off the recorder on his cell phone. "I got it."

Bran turned back to Mara. "You understand where this is going, right? You'll be arrested. There's nothing I can do about that. You're involved in what appears to be a terrorist plot. Someone you worked with is now in possession of enough chemical weapons to kill or injure thousands, maybe tens of thousands of people."

A sound of distress slipped from her throat.

"If you know something—anything that could help stop a possible attack—now is the time to tell us."

She shook her head. "I wish I did. I'm so very sorry."

"I wonder what my father would say if he were standing here now?" Jessie asked, her eyes on the woman's exotically beautiful face.

Mara looked stricken, her dark eyes liquid with tears. "I've asked myself that a hundred times."

Jessie stared at her hard. "Unfortunately, because of you, we'll never know the answer."

BRAN PULLED OUT his cell to call General Holloway's direct number. It was the middle of the night. The call would not be welcome.

"Wait!" Mara rose from her chair at the kitchen table. "I don't want people dying because of me. Maybe there's a way I can help."

Bran cocked a skeptical eyebrow. "And in exchange you want…what? Your freedom? You got a man killed, Mara. You have to pay for that."

"I got the man I loved killed. I will pay for that the rest of my life."

He kept the cell phone in hand, the threat clear. "What are you offering?"

"I have a way to contact Ahmed. He said I should only use it in an emergency."

He flicked a glance at Jessie, who had gone from angry to alert. "Go on."

"I could set up a meeting, tell him that the colonel's daughter came to see me, that she believes I had something to do with stealing the chemical weapons. I could ask him to meet me. I believe he would come."

Bran's gaze returned to Jessie. Mara Ramos had been at least partly responsible for her father's death. The army would lock the woman up and throw away the key. The call was hers. Even more important, once the terrorists knew Jessie was alive and in San Diego, her life would again be at risk.

"It's dangerous," Bran said, spelling out the threat. "They'll know where we are."

Jessie's shoulders firmed. "We have to stop these people. This is the best chance we have."

She was right. He didn't like it, but the longer this continued, the better chance one or both of them would wind up dead—or there would be a terror attack.

He fixed his attention on Mara. "All right, you set up a meet with Ahmed. He doesn't show, we call in the army. You try to run, we call in the army. In the meantime, we stay right here. You do anything we don't like, none of us will hesitate to put a terrorist in her grave."

Her lips trembled. "I won't run."

"If you do this and we find these people, there's a chance you might end up with a lighter sentence, maybe avoid spending the rest of your life in prison."

She swallowed, wiped fresh tears from her cheeks. "I once had a naive belief that terrorism was a way to make things better for my country. I outgrew that belief many years ago. I don't want people to die."

CHAPTER TWENTY-NINE

THEY SPENT THE rest of the night at Mara's condo, taking turns napping on the sofa or a blanket on the floor. The door to Mara's bedroom stayed open while she slept, though Jessie didn't imagine she actually got much rest.

Too wired to sleep herself, Jessie made a fresh pot of coffee and sat at the kitchen table with Bran while Hunt took a turn on the sofa. Bran had retrieved his laptop from the Navigator and set it up on the kitchen table. Jessie had spent an hour looking for info on the Army of Islam of Yemen, but aside from an old reference here and there, she found nothing.

She took a sip of coffee, glad she had brewed a new pot. "I've been thinking about something Mara said."

Bran leaned back in his chair, stretching his long legs out in front of him. "Yeah? What's that?"

"I keep trying to figure out how Mara got invited to a party given by one of my father's friends. She said there were single men there, mostly military. We've always figured the link was through a civilian employee at the chemical depot, but maybe someone in the army is connected to the terrorists."

Bran nodded. "It's possible. On the other hand, big party, maybe somebody knew somebody. Could have been anyone." He sat up in the chair. "But even the chance you're right isn't good."

Jessie sighed. "Seems like every answer we get just creates more questions."

Bran reached over and squeezed her hand. "We caught a break with Mara. Let's see how it plays out."

At 8:00 a.m. that morning, Mara phoned Ahmed, told him her fears, and asked him to come to the house. Ahmed agreed, but said he couldn't meet her till eight o'clock that evening.

The hours dragged as they waited for nightfall. They spent much of the time making preparations, making sure their cars were parked out of sight, checking their equipment. While Jessie retrieved a small bag Bran had assembled and set it down on the kitchen table, she could hear him moving around in Mara's garage. She wondered what he was doing out there, but she had too much on her mind to worry about it.

At one point in the afternoon, she went back to check on Mara, found her sitting in a chair staring into the tiny patio outside the bedroom window. Jessie stopped in the doorway, angry, but curious to know more about the woman.

"You and my father," she began, "you really must have had him fooled."

Mara's dark, troubled eyes swung in her direction. "That's not how it was. Falling in love with James wasn't something I planned. It was an accident."

"An accident," Jessie scoffed.

"That's right. At first I was just repaying a debt. But in order to win your father's trust, I needed to get to know him. I needed for him to know me." Tears welled in her eyes and she glanced away.

"Then something happened," she said. "The more time I spent with James, the more I came to respect him, the more I admired him, and little by little I fell in love with

him. The best day of my life was when James asked me
to marry him."

Jessie's chest felt tight. "Even though he proposed, it
wasn't really you he was asking, was it? It was the woman
you were pretending to be."

Mara wearily shook her head. "I left that other woman
behind many years ago. I thought once my debt was paid,
I would be free. Instead, I lost the only man who ever mattered to me."

Jessie studied Mara's haunted features. It was impossible not to be moved. "My father never mentioned you to
me. Why should I believe you?"

"At this point, I don't suppose it matters, but I'll tell you
this. James and I were planning a trip to Denver. Your father wanted you to meet me. He wanted us to spend some
time together before he told you our plans."

Something shifted inside her, a distant memory of a visit
her father had mentioned. She didn't want to believe Mara
was telling the truth. But she did.

"My father wasn't a fool," she said. "If he loved you, he
must have seen the person you are inside. I'm sorry for the
way this turned out. I'm sorry for both of you."

Turning away, she walked back out into the hall. After
her mother's death, her father had been desperately lonely.
Perhaps in his final days, he had found some comfort in
the arms of the beautiful woman who so clearly loved him.

She swallowed past the painful tightness in her throat
and continued toward the kitchen. When her cell phone
rang, the screen showed General Holloway's contact information.

She held the phone to her ear. "This is Jessie."

"I got a call this morning from Agent Tripp at the CID,"
he said. "Wayne Coffman is dead. Found murdered in his

cell this morning. I'm sorry this didn't work out the way you hoped, but I figured you'd want to know."

Her hand trembled. The only person who could help them get to the man who had orchestrated her father's death was dead. Without Tank, there was no way to pressure Edgar Weaver, which meant no way to catch the men who had murdered James Kegan. Her throat ached. "Thank you for calling, General."

Holloway hung up and Jessie sank down in one of the kitchen chairs.

"What is it?" Bran asked as he came in from the garage.

"Tank's dead. Found murdered in his cell this morning." Her eyes filled. "All that work and it's a complete dead end."

Bran caught her shoulders and drew her up out of the chair. He kissed her quick and hard. "We'll figure it out. Find another way to get the proof we need. Right now we've got to focus on what we need to do right here." He gently shook her. "You gonna be okay?"

She looked up at him and dragged in a shaky breath. "I'm okay."

The men went back to work, getting ready for the confrontation, then arming themselves with multiple weapons. At 7:45 p.m., Bran and Jessie disappeared into the bedroom while Hunt took up a position outside to be sure no uninvited guests tagged along.

The plan was for Mara to invite Ahmed into the condo, the unknown factor being whether she would keep her word or warn him so he could escape.

As the minutes ticked past, Jessie stood tensely next to Bran, who held his Glock in a two-handed grip.

Peering through the crack in the bedroom door, Jessie

could feel the perspiration gathering between her breasts. Eight fifteen and still no sign of Ahmed.

"Maybe he isn't going to show," she said.

"Or maybe he's checking things out, making sure it's safe." They had closed the bedroom curtains, and only a lamp burned in the living room.

Nerves dried the inside of her mouth while Bran looked totally relaxed. This wasn't new to him. She wondered how many times he had faced a deadly opponent.

At exactly eight thirty, a solid knock rattled the front door. Jessie could hear Mara's footsteps padding across the carpet. The locks turned and the door opened.

"Hello, Ahmed," she said, greeting him in English. "Please come in."

"I think it is better that you come with me."

Bran softly cursed. He was out of the bedroom and down the hall in an instant, his Glock leveled at Ahmed. "Raise your hands and keep them in the air! Do it now!"

Jessie watched from the hall, her heart beating wildly as Bran crossed the living room, his Glock pointed at Ahmed's chest. Hunt came in though the sliding glass door, his pistol also aimed at Ahmed.

Bran's eyes were a hard ice-blue as he dragged the man inside and hurriedly searched him for weapons. "I think right here is better," Bran said, closing the door. "That way we can all get to know each other."

Ahmed cast a disdainful glance at Mara, who stood pale and shaken a few feet away. "From the start, they said you were not to be trusted. I told them they were wrong. I was a fool." He was tall and thin with a neatly trimmed heavy black beard. Dressed in black slacks and a white shirt, he was the cliché of a terrorist hiding in plain sight.

In seconds Ahmed's hands were zip-tied behind his back

and Bran had dragged him into the kitchen and into a chair at the table. Hunt kept his weapon pointed at Ahmed's chest.

"I'm sorry," Mara said to the man. "What you did was wrong. I couldn't let you hurt anyone else."

Bran moved into his space. "We need to know what happened to the weapons you stole and you're going to tell us—one way or another. You can make it easy on yourself or hard."

Ahmed's mouth lifted into a smirk. "Do you really believe I will tell you anything? You Americans make me sick. What will you do—waterboard me?"

The look on Bran's face sent a shiver down Jessie's spine. Cold, determined, utterly ruthless. It was unlike anything she had seen before, and it made her doubt everything she thought she knew about Brandon Garrett.

"You sure this is the way you want it?" Bran asked softly, almost politely. It was more terrifying than his anger.

Ahmed blinked, no longer so certain. "I will tell you this. The weapons are no longer in your country. They are gone, and there is nothing you can do to stop what is going to happen."

"Where are they?"

Ahmed closed his eyes and started praying. Bran let him finish. Then he grabbed the roll of duct tape out of the bag on the table, tore off a strip, and slapped it over Ahmed's mouth. The man's dark eyes widened as Bran jerked him out of the chair and hauled him through the door leading out to the garage.

"I borrowed your jumper cables, Mara," Bran said on his way out. "I'll put them back where they belong when we're done." He slammed the garage door shut, the sound vibrating across the kitchen.

Jessie's breathing heightened. Mara's eyes looked wide

and fearful. Hunt said nothing, just settled himself in one of the kitchen chairs. There were only three. One was out in the garage where Bran had taken it earlier. She had thought it was odd at the time.

"What…what is he going to do?" Mara asked.

Jessie glanced at Hunt.

"Don't look at me," Hunt said, shrugging his shoulders. "I don't have the vaguest idea and I don't want to know."

The kitchen fell silent. On the other side of the door, Jessie could hear grunts and the sounds of a brief struggle. In the kitchen, no one uttered a word.

Bran said something. Ahmed gave a muffled reply. There was a sharp snapping sound, then a buzzing noise, then silence.

"What is happening?" Mara asked, a faint Middle Eastern accent now discernible.

No one answered.

The snapping, buzzing sound came again, followed by a muffled shriek, then silence.

"You have to stop him," Mara pleaded, panic in her eyes.

Jessie was thinking the same thing. Except that her father was dead, and Ahmed and his friends had killed him and were now trying to kill her.

More snapping and buzzing, another muffled shriek, then silence. Jessie's heart was thundering so hard she wondered if the others could hear it.

"He won't…he won't kill him?" Mara asked.

"I doubt it," Hunt said. "Too messy. He won't want trouble with the police."

Mara made a sound in her throat.

Time dragged on. When the snapping, buzzing sound came again, Jessie started moving. Her legs were shaking as she crossed to the garage door. How far was she willing to go to get answers that might save people's lives? It was the same moral dilemma people had faced since the beginning of time. She thought of her dad and the honorable man he had been, and reached for the knob just as it turned and the door swung open.

Bran looked at her pale face, reached out and caught her shoulder. "He's fine. A little the worse for wear, but he'll be okay. We need to call General Holloway, have him deal with the situation." Holloway wanted the weapons found. He would know who to contact to deal with a terrorist threat.

Her heart was still throbbing. She thought of Holloway and the phone call she had received that morning. Something about it had nagged her all day. How many people had known Wayne Coffman was their only link to Edgar Weaver? Who knew that Weaver could be the key to finding a major player in the theft of the weapons? Holloway was one of very few.

And Holloway could easily have arranged for Mara to be invited to a party her father was attending.

She cast Bran an uneasy glance. "I don't know…maybe we should call Agent Tripp at the CID."

Bran's gaze zeroed in on hers and locked in silent communication. "Maybe we'd better call them both."

CHAPTER THIRTY

IT WAS FULL daylight by the time Hunt Brady headed back to his apartment and Bran started driving back to their suite at the Grant Hotel. It had taken an hour and a half for MPs from the CID Pacific Field Office in Irvine to reach the house in La Jolla. Then the hours of questioning had begun.

Special Agent Brian Kopecki had taken statements from Bran, Jessie, and Hunt, along with the information that Mara had fully cooperated in helping them capture the terrorist, Ahmed Malik, his full name. After lengthy questioning, Malik and Mara had been taken into military police custody and hauled away.

Interrogations were sometimes handled by the FBI, but the classified nature of the missing munitions meant the pair would be taken by army jet back to Fort Carson.

After Malik and Mara were gone, Agent Kopecki had interviewed the three of them separately, asking an endless array of questions, getting mostly the same answers. But no one knew what had happened in the garage except Bran and Malik. Bran had left no physical evidence, and Malik, wisely, wasn't talking. He didn't want Bran coming after him, as Bran had convinced him he would. Since the information he'd gleaned was more important than the methods he had used to get it, the subject would be dropped.

Special Agent Kopecki was in touch with his superiors, as well as Special Agent Tripp. Someone higher up the food chain, either Tripp's superior, Colonel Larkin, head of the CID, or General Holloway, had ordered Bran, Jessie, and Hunt Brady's release.

So far Bran hadn't had a chance to fill Jessie in on what Malik had told him in the garage, and she had been strangely silent since they'd left the condo.

"All right, what's going on in that beautiful head of yours?" he asked, casting her a glance from behind the wheel of the Navigator as the vehicle made its way back to the city. Both of them were exhausted, but this was more than just fatigue.

Those big green eyes swung to his face. "Did you torture that man?"

He should have known.

His jaw clenched as he gripped the wheel and searched for an exit, flipped on the turn signal, cut between two slower vehicles, and pulled off the freeway onto La Jolla Parkway. Following the GPS map to a spot on the beach, he drove into a lot on a cliff overlooking the ocean and turned off the engine.

"We need to talk," he said, cracking the door and sliding out of the SUV.

As Jessie got out to join him, a brisk wind rolled in off the sea, whipping loose strands of fiery hair around her face. She looked drawn and tired and beautiful. Her black yoga pants outlined the perfect little ass that always turned him on, and he felt a rush of heat he was forced to ignore.

As they walked along the path above the cliffs, waves pounded the rocks below then rushed back out to sea. Gripping Jessie's hand, he led her over to a fence rail at the top of the cliff.

"I understand why you did it," she said, looking up at him. "I'm not condemning you, I just need to know."

But that wasn't true. Same as during the war, people didn't really want to know about the enemy soldiers he had interrogated or killed. They wanted to pretend none of the bad stuff actually happened. That was one of the reasons he never got involved in a serious relationship. He'd never known a woman who could handle the truth. Very few people could deal.

Looking at Jessie, it hit him with the force of a blow that this was the reason the two of them would never work. She couldn't handle knowing the things he'd done and he didn't want to live a lie.

He steeled himself. Better to get it over with right now.

"I hooked jumper cables to Mara's car battery. Then I told Ahmed if he didn't tell me what I wanted to know, I'd clamp them on his balls and light him up."

She made a little sound in her throat. Bran kept going. "I gave him a demonstration. You probably heard the charge going off in the kitchen. Then I asked him where the chemical weapons had been taken. When he refused to answer, I zapped him. When he still refused to answer, I hit him with the juice again."

Her eyes filled.

"He told me the weapons had been driven from Colorado to the port in Houston. They were loaded aboard a ship and transported to Yemen. The name of the ship was *Delfina*. It would have arrived weeks ago. A group calling themselves *sawt Allah*, the Voice of God, has the weapons. But if they'd used them, we'd have heard about it at the time it happened, so I'm guessing they're still in the planning stages. I asked him what they were going to do with the munitions. He said he didn't know. At that point I believed him."

"Because if he lied, you would have shocked him again."

He just shrugged. He hadn't really hurt the wormy bastard. Ahmed wasn't a high-level, highly trained combatant. He'd folded almost immediately. It was the perceived threat that ultimately convinced a guy to talk. Bran had a knack for making someone believe there was no limit to what he was willing to do.

Sometimes there wasn't. As a soldier, he'd done what he'd had to. He didn't regret it. Losing Jessie wouldn't make him regret it now.

He hardened his heart against the slice of pain that told him how hard he had fallen for his best friend's sister. How could he not have seen the truth before now?

He clenched his jaw against the knot squeezing his stomach. From the start, he had known it would never work. He should have been more careful, should have protected himself.

He took a deep breath. There was nothing he could do about it now. No matter how she felt about him, he would protect her. He owed it to Danny—and to himself.

He forced his thoughts back to the job. "I pressed Ahmed to name the man behind the theft of the weapons. The guy had no idea. I asked him about Weaver and the hit on your dad, but again, no idea. He was assigned a job and he did it. That's the way it works with terrorists. No one knows what another part of the cell is doing. The CID will go after the group in San Diego. They might bring in the FBI to help. Eventually they'll probably get the name of the person who bought the weapons through the auction, but that's not going to give us the answers we need."

"You mean the name of the man or men at the top, the people who got the twenty-five million dollars."

"Exactly. But we're getting closer every day. Whoever

it was has got to be very nervous. Which is why we can't afford to stay at the Grant much longer."

"So even after everything that's happened, our lives are still in danger."

"Unfortunately, yes."

JESSIE SAT QUIETLY on the ride back to San Diego that morning. The ache of loss in her chest felt like a heart attack. In a way it was. She was more than half in love with Bran. All the way back from La Jolla, her mind went over the information he had gotten from Ahmed and what he had done to get it.

Torturing someone was a crime. She'd been terrified the MPs would haul Bran off to jail. She had no idea what Ahmed had said to Special Agent Kopecki. Maybe Bran would still be arrested.

On a physical level, she was wildly attracted to him. Every time his amazing biceps flexed, she felt hot all over. But how did she feel about the code of justice he lived by? He'd been a Delta soldier, one of the most highly trained men in the world. Danny had been in the same unit. They operated in secret, did whatever was necessary to protect America.

Still, it was the first time she had ever really had to face what the job required.

Almost from the start, she had warned herself not to get involved with a soldier. She didn't want that life, didn't want to risk that kind of pain. And though he was no longer in the army, Bran was a warrior and always would be.

On the other hand, maybe what she felt for him didn't matter. From the start, she had known it was only a *friends with benefits* kind of relationship. When all of this was over, Bran would be gone.

Her heart squeezed hard, telling her how deeply involved she had gotten.

Her desolate mood turned even darker. Neither of them talked on the way back to the city, Bran's mood apparently mirroring her own. She hadn't meant to hurt him by the censure in her tone, but she knew that she had. Something had shifted between them. They had lost something important, and she didn't think they would ever get it back. Her heart ached so hard she felt sick.

On the way back to the Grant, Bran drove them through a Carl's Jr. for something to eat. With everything that had happened, she had very little appetite, but the future was uncertain. She needed to keep up her strength.

She sighed as they walked back into their extravagant suite. It was probably a good thing they would be checking out soon. She was getting spoiled by the Grant's luxurious Egyptian cotton sheets, twenty-four-hour room service, and opulent marble tub.

As soon as she had showered and dressed, she went to work on the article she was writing, entering the latest information they had gleaned. As long as she didn't go on the internet and just used the word processor, no one should be able to track her.

She worked for a while, but it was hard to concentrate. Bran was typing on his laptop at the opposite end of the table, following leads that Ahmed had given him. Just watching him made her eyes burn. He was pulling away, just as she was, asking the same hard questions. She ached to go to him, have him hold her. But it wouldn't be fair to either of them.

She steeled herself. She had to focus on finding the answers they needed to stay alive.

"Maybe you should call your friend, Tabby," she said,

forcing her mind back where it belonged. "Let her know Tank is dead."

"Good idea. I'll do it right now. I'll find out if she's got anything new." As soon as the call went through, he put it on speaker and set the phone on the kitchen table next to where she was working.

"Hey, Tab, it's Bran. Wanted to let you know Wayne Coffman was murdered yesterday. Which means Edgar Weaver is now a dead end."

"Jeez, Bran, Weaver was your best lead," Tabby said. "That's really bad news."

"Yeah, I know."

"Unfortunately, I've got even worse news for you."

Jessie stopped typing.

"I've been working on the auction site, trying to follow the links backward to where it originated. I was making some progress, but the guy who built it was good, set it up so the IP addresses kept bouncing all over the world. I got as far as Kazakhstan and back to the States—and here's the bad part—I discovered there was a split. The weapons that sold for twenty-five million?"

"Yeah?"

"That money only paid for twelve thousand pounds of munitions. Five million more paid for the other three thousand pounds."

Jessie's gaze shot to Bran, whose jaw clamped down. Her stomach quivered.

"Two different buyers?" Bran asked. "Or the same buyers with two different money sources?"

"My guess would be the buyers are connected in some way, but the money for the smaller batch of weapons came from a different source. But at this point, I can't say for sure."

"I don't suppose you have any idea where the second batch of weapons went?"

"Unfortunately, no idea. I'll stay on it. See if I can narrow things down."

Jessie looked at Bran as the call ended. "According to Ahmed, the weapons were shipped out of the country," she said. "Now we find out there's a chance some of them are still here."

"Yeah," he said. "The question is where?"

TWO BATCHES OF WEAPONS. Bran didn't have enough intel to find the location of the smaller batch, but he knew where most of the weapons had gone.

Sitting down on the sofa, he phoned a number he had never used before. Delta Force Squadron Commander, Colonel Dylan Bryson.

"It's Brandon Garrett, Colonel. A problem's come up. I'm really hoping you can help." He told the colonel about the shipment of chemical weapons that had been stolen and shipped to Yemen, gave the colonel the ship name, *Delfina*, which he'd found registered in Bolivia, and the names of the terrorists who'd been arrested so far.

"The group in Yemen calls itself *sawt Allah*," Bran said. "I don't know what they're planning, but it can't be good."

"Who's in charge of the investigation on your end?" the colonel asked.

"It's murky. General Samuel Holloway, director of Chemical Materials Activity, is the top of the food chain. Weapons went missing under his watch so he's heavily involved. Special Agent Derek Tripp at the CID is heading up the investigation. Long list of others. Lot of folks in the mix but not much progress being made. I'm hoping you can find out what's going on in Yemen and stop an attack before it's too late."

"What's your interest in this?"

"Colonel James Kegan was arrested and charged with the theft. His daughter's my client. You might remember her brother, Danny."

He could almost see the colonel nodding, a lean, athletic, broad-shouldered man with thick dark hair cut military short, and a nose that had once been broken.

"Daniel Kegan. I remember him. Loss of a good soldier and a good man."

Bran felt a sudden tightness in his throat. "From what we've discovered, Colonel Kegan was set up to take the blame, wrongfully charged, then murdered. His daughter began investigating, now she's fighting to stay alive. I'm doing my best to make sure she does."

"She's fortunate to have your help."

"Thank you, sir."

"Anything else I need to know?"

"Unfortunately, there is. We just got fresh intel that the stolen munitions were divided into two different batches. Most of them went to Yemen, the rest followed another money source in the States, which means there's a chance they're meant to be used on US soil."

"Who'd you report this to?"

"That's part of the problem, sir. We're no longer sure who we can trust. And as I said, the latest intel can't be verified."

"I may be able to help with the situation in Yemen," the colonel said. "You have my word I'll do what I can. But domestic terrorism is out of my jurisdiction."

"Yes, sir."

"I'll be back in touch."

The call ended and Bran looked up to see Jessie standing a few feet away.

"You think he'll help us?"

He nodded. "If there's any way he can. He knew your brother. Maybe your father, too. He'll keep his word."

Her eyes found his. "Just like you," she said softly. "If you give your word, you keep it."

His chest tightened. "I do my best," he said a little gruffly. He thought her eyes glistened, but maybe he'd imagined it. He wanted to ask what was going on in her head, but he was afraid he knew.

"So there's nothing more we can do with this new information," she said.

"Maybe we can find out if Homeland has seen any uptick in terrorist activity. I'll call Jax Ryker. He was a navy SEAL. He knows people, maybe someone in Homeland who can help us."

He picked up his cell and phoned Jax, who said he'd make a couple of calls and get back to him.

Jessie shoved her hair back from her face and sighed wearily. "So until something breaks, we're pretty much at a standstill."

"Pretty much," he said. He could tell by the set of her shoulders how discouraged she was.

"I...um...didn't get much sleep last night. I think I'll go in and take a nap."

He wanted to join her, even if they just curled up together and slept, but instead he only nodded. It was time to slow things down, bring his emotions back in check.

From the way his heart was throbbing as he watched her walk away, it wasn't going to be easy.

CHAPTER THIRTY-ONE

AFTER A COUPLE of hours of tossing and turning, thinking about Bran and unable to fall asleep, Jessie gave up and went back into the living room. Bran was stretched out on the sofa asleep. Even with his eyes closed, there was a vigilance about him, a tension in his muscles that said he could come awake in an instant.

She moved quietly over to the table so she wouldn't disturb him. So far the encryption on his computer hadn't been penetrated. The people at The Max were good. Now was her chance to do some research.

When she'd first begun her investigation, Robert De La Garza, the project manager for Weidner at the Alamo Depot, had been her primary suspect, the man at the top who controlled the plant. She'd found nothing to connect him to the theft.

She took another look at him now, his credentials, his experience, the date he'd taken the job. She followed every link she could find. Nothing popped up.

There were two deputy directors under De La Garza, Dwayne Higgins and Nathan Staats. She had looked at both of them, but hadn't gone that deep. Then things had started happening. Her life had been threatened, she'd headed for Dallas, and nothing had been the same since.

She started to look up Deputy Director Dwayne Higgins, then paused.

The one person she had never investigated beyond looking at his biography on the US Army website was Brigadier General Samuel Holloway. Her father had respected the man, and she'd had no reason to suspect him of being involved. But Wayne Coffman's murder still bothered her.

Just days after Coffman had been transferred to the army stockade, he was dead. Weaver could have ordered the hit through his Aryan Brotherhood connections in the prison, just as he had before, but how did Edgar Weaver find out Tank had been arrested? And why wasn't he placed somewhere the Brotherhood couldn't get to him?

Holloway was one of the few people who knew about the connection between Tank and Weaver. She typed in *Brigadier General Samuel Holloway* and the US Army website popped up, showing his photo and page-long biography.

At the sound of footfalls padding toward her, she glanced up to see Brandon yawning and absently scratching his broad chest. With his hair sleep-mussed and the dark scruff along his jaw, he looked so male and sexy she wanted to eat him up. Then she remembered her resolve. At the very least, she needed time to figure things out, try to decide on the right course to take.

Which was all well and good until he stood behind her to look over her shoulder and she could feel the warmth of his powerful body. Her mind flashed with memories of the last time they had made love, and her whole body flushed with heat.

"What are you working on?" he asked.

She mentally shook herself, focused on the question. Hesitated. Bran was military to the bone. Thinking a decorated superior officer might be capable of treason wasn't something he was going to take lightly. Though she had a hunch he might have a few suspicions of his own.

"I'm looking at General Holloway, seeing if there's something I missed."

Bran started reading the words on the screen. "'Division Chemical Officer Tenth Infantry Division, New York and Kandahar. Assistant to director of the Joint Staff at the Pentagon. Commanded the Blue Grass Army Depot for two years before he was also assigned to command Alamo.'"

"His background's definitely impressive," she said, knowing he had only read the bottom few paragraphs aloud.

"Yeah, and so are his awards. Bronze Star, Meritorious Service Medal, Army Commendation, Army Achievement Medal, Kosovo Campaign, Iraq Campaign, War on Terrorism Service Medal, NATO Medal." He looked up. "Do I need to keep reading?"

"I get it. I'm sure it's a big waste of time."

"The thing is, the guy's a highly respected army general. Twenty-five million is a helluva lot, but surely it would take more than money for a guy at that level to commit treason."

"You're probably right," she conceded. Which didn't mean she was quitting. She was a better journalist than that.

Bran scrubbed his fingers through his too-long brown hair, shoving it back from his forehead. "Most likely, I am right. But you're right, too. We can't leave any stone unturned. With Tank dead, Weaver is safe and we've lost our best source. The fact Holloway's crossed both of our minds is enough for me. Keep at it."

She turned back to the screen and continued, going backward in time, further into the general's history, finding his place of birth, information on his wife, his kids, anything that might link him to Edgar Weaver.

An hour later she found it. For a moment, as the pieces fell together, she couldn't believe her eyes. She read the info again, and the pulse in her temple started throbbing.

"I think I found something, Bran."

He rose from the sofa where he was watching TV and at the same time gaming on his cell phone. She noticed he played when he was restless, a way of burning off excess energy, she guessed.

He paced over to where she sat and looked down at the computer screen. "What is it?"

She had two screens up side by side. One was General Samuel Holloway, the other Edgar Weaver. "Both men born in Albany, Georgia. Both attended Weatherbee High School."

His blue eyes sharpened. "So Holloway and Weaver knew each other?"

"It gets better," she said, feeling a second rush of excitement. "Holloway's mother's maiden name was Weaver. Her brother was Cyrus Weaver. Cyrus had two boys—Joseph… and Edgar." She turned to look up at him. "They were cousins, Bran. Holloway and Weaver are *cousins*."

Bran's expression went granite-hard. "Holloway contacted Weaver and arranged your father's death. Someone in the Aryan Brotherhood poisoned him and someone in the infirmary gave him the drug that caused his so-called heart attack."

Jessie came up from her chair. "Then Holloway tells Weaver that Tank is in custody and someone in the Brotherhood kills him."

"Now Weaver's safe and so is the general."

"Holloway is a murderer."

Bran's blue eyes went ice-cold. "That motherfucker is going to be sorry he was ever born."

Jessie reached out and caught Bran's arm, her nails purposely digging in. "You are not taking justice into your own hands. You are letting the authorities handle it."

His jaw worked back and forth. He was wearing the same expression he had worn when he had dragged Ahmed Malik into the garage.

She squeezed his arm. "Are you listening to me?"

He inhaled deeply, then slowly exhaled, bringing himself under control. "I hear you."

"Fine. You let the army handle it."

He released another slow breath. "If that's the way you want it. James Kegan was your father. We'll handle it any way you want."

Relief trickled through her. "Okay. Good. Thanks."

"You realize we don't have enough on Holloway to prove he's guilty."

"Then we'll keep looking until we do."

Bran reached out and gently cupped her cheek. "I'm sorry, baby, for the way this has all turned out. If I could change things, I would."

She couldn't stop herself from going into his arms. She loved him. She rose on her toes and very softly kissed him.

Bran kissed her back just as softly. "I wish things could be different."

She knew what he meant, knew that last night had changed things between them. She swallowed past the tightness in her throat. "Me, too."

Neither of them moved. Then Bran's cell began to ring and the moment was lost.

"Chase," he said, pressing the phone to his ear. "I meant to call you. Lots going on."

Bran filled his brother in on what had been happening and what they had discovered. "Looks like one of the top brass is involved in the theft, a general named Holloway. Not quite sure what to do with the intel. Still don't know exactly who we can trust."

Bran looked over at Jessie. "I'll tell her. Take care, bro." He shoved the phone back into the pocket of his jeans. "Chase said to tell you not to get discouraged. He asked if we wanted him to fly out, give us some backup. I told him no reason at this point. He said if we needed anything to give him or Reese a call."

"He's always there for you."

"Yeah."

"I like your brothers."

He nodded. "They're great. After my parents divorced, Reese got into some trouble. He was in high school, living with my dad at the time. Chase and I lived with my mom. Mom took custody of Reese and moved him in with us. We all lived with her family. Devlin men are law enforcement and military for generations back. They helped Reese get himself straightened out."

"Sometimes people can change."

His eyes never left her face. "Yeah," he said. "Sometimes they can."

IT WAS LATE afternoon when Bran got a phone call from Jaxon Ryker.

"I talked to a friend at Homeland," Jax said. "He set up a meet with someone in the San Diego branch. It's off the record, an agent named Joe Bonnet. He'll meet you at the Bayfront Café in an hour."

"How do we find him?"

"He'll find you."

"Sounds good. Thanks, man."

"You sure taking Jessie with you is a good idea?"

"Not safe for her to stay here." Especially not now that Mara and Ahmed were in custody, which meant members of the local terror cell could be hunting them. And there was Holloway to consider. The man was a powerful enemy. They needed to bring him down and soon.

"Thanks for the help," Bran said. "I'll keep you posted." He turned to Jessie. "We've got a meet with a guy from Homeland in an hour."

"That's great. Maybe he can help us."

"Yeah, maybe. Or maybe we can help him."

THE BAYFRONT CAFÉ was a tourist mecca down on the Embarcadero, with big glass windows overlooking the ocean. It was overflowing with guys in flowered Hawaiian shirts and flip-flops, women in shorts and tank tops. Lots of skin, sunglasses, and baseball caps. It was a warm day, the breeze off the sea cooling the bright sun burning down on the water.

Bran had dressed to fit in and so had Jessie, both of them wearing bill caps and sunglasses. It was just before two o'clock and they still hadn't eaten, so they stood in line and ordered, then waited for their burgers and fries to come up.

Carrying their trays over to an empty table, they sat down and dug in, Bran casually looking for anyone who might be Joe Bonnet. He was trained to notice alphabet agency types, so Bran wasn't surprised when a man with short black hair, a blue, button-down oxford shirt tucked into a pair of tan chinos, and without the hint of a smile, walked toward them.

Bonnet pulled out a chair and sat down. "Joe Bonnet. Ryker described you both. Ms. Kegan was hard to miss."

Nope, not with all that fiery hair.

Finished with her meal, Jessie shoved her tray away. "Nice to meet you."

Bonnet hadn't used his formal agency title, which Bran took as a good sign. Also finished eating, he wiped his hands on a paper napkin and tossed it on the tray.

"We're asking for an information exchange," he said, getting right to business. "What we've got for what you've got. Assuming you have anything at all on a possible domestic terror attack."

Bonnet's dark eyes sharpened. "What sort of information do you have?"

"Do we have a deal?"

Bonnet hesitated. Like all the agencies, Homeland wasn't much for sharing. "I've read your file, Garrett. We're grateful for your service to our country. That being the case, I'll give you as much as I can."

Bran sat up straighter. The noise around them muffled their conversation just enough not to be overheard. "We have intel that three thousand pounds of chemical weapons, stolen from the Alamo Depot in Colorado, were purchased on the dark web. The price was five million dollars. We don't know what the buyers are planning to do with the weapons, and the intel can't be verified." *At least not by legal means.* "But our sources are good. We believe it's true."

He didn't mention the munitions that had gone to Yemen. Colonel Bryson was handling that operation. He was the most capable man Bran had ever known. Bryson could move faster without interference from Homeland.

"Your turn," Bran said.

"US Intelligence agencies have been hearing internet chatter about a specific plot involving a public transportation venue in a major US city. We've narrowed it down to the western part of the country. We don't know who's behind it, what they're planning, or at this point whether or not it's a credible threat. But we're following it closely. Until now, we haven't tied it to the use of chemical weapons. I'll relay that information to all parties."

"And keep our names out of it."

"At this juncture, yes." He handed Bran a card with his Homeland office number, and Bran handed him a Maximum Security card with his cell number.

"Anything else you want to share?" Bonnet asked.

"That's it for now."

"What about you, Agent Bonnet?" Jessie asked. "These people are linked to the murder of my father. Surely you have some idea who they are."

"I'm sorry. Even if we have potential suspects, I'm not at liberty to say."

Bran rose from the table and so did Jessie. "Thanks for the meeting," Bran said. "If we come up with something, we'll let you know." Urging Jessie toward the door, they walked away, holding hands and smiling at each other like lovers. Bonnet slipped quietly off in another direction, disappearing among the tourists as if he had never been there.

THEY WERE BACK in their suite. They had a lot more info and still not enough.

"Okay, so what do we do now?" Jessie asked.

Bran wished to God he knew. "Best plan at the moment, we pack up and head back to Fort Carson."

"Why don't we stay here? Mara Ramos and Ahmed were both living in San Diego. Maybe we'll find something here that will lead us to the second batch of chemical weapons."

He caught her shoulders, bringing her eyes to his face. "We're stretched pretty thin here, Jess. Which would you rather do? Take down the man who killed your father? Or locate the second batch of weapons?"

"Both," she said without hesitation.

Bran shook his head. "We're not Homeland or FBI. I say we let the agency handle the domestic terrorists, which with any luck will lead them to the rest of the missing weapons. In the meantime, we go back to Fort Carson. Agent Tripp is a guy I think we can trust. The CID has no skin in the game, no involvement in the theft. They're just looking for answers, same as we are."

"You could be right. By now, Ahmed and Mara are probably in the hands of the counterterrorist unit, but Tripp has to be looking into Tank's murder. He was under interrogation when he was killed. If we talk to Tripp, explain about Weaver and Holloway and their connection to my father's death, maybe he'll believe the general was also involved in the weapons theft."

"We still don't have proof your father was murdered," Bran said.

Her chin lifted. "Then we'll get it. I've wanted my father's body exhumed from the start. After everything that's happened, we should be able to get permission."

Mulling over the possibilities, Bran started nodding. "So we go back to Fort Carson. We prove your dad was murdered and lay out our case against Holloway. No chance Holloway stole those weapons completely on his own. We bring him down, good chance he'll give up whoever helped him pull the whole thing off. With enough information, the army should be able to track down the rest of the weapons."

"While we're there, we should talk to Charles Frazier again. If we give him the information Tabby came up with on the internet auctions on the dark web and the sale of the missing weapons, maybe he can go back into the Alamo computer systems and find something new that will help us."

"Good idea." Bran hauled her into his arms and kissed her. "We're going to make this work," he said with conviction. And as he held her, the realization hit him that he was thinking of more than just solving the case.

Jessie was the woman he'd been looking for since the day he'd left the army and begun a new life. He might not have realized it, but he did now. He could change for her. All he had to do was convince her.

When she slid her arms around his neck and kissed him back, he thought that maybe he actually had a chance.

JESSIE MANAGED TO withstand the effects of that searing kiss, but it wasn't easy. Forcing herself to end the contact, she stepped away.

"If we're going back to Colorado, I need to pack my things." Bran caught her as she tried to brush past him, tipped her face up, and softly kissed her.

"I'll make the flight reservations."

She just nodded, her pulse once more thrumming. It was insane. After what he had done in Mara Ramos's garage, everything about their relationship had changed. It didn't matter that Brandon was no longer a soldier. He was a warrior and always would be.

She had never even dated a military man, never imagined she could fall in love with one. She had left that life behind when she had left Fort Carson, left her dad, and headed off to college.

She understood a soldier's world, had seen the pain their families suffered, knew that pain firsthand. Husbands and sons who died in combat, brothers who had made the ultimate sacrifice, men and women who would never come home.

Bran might be a civilian, but in the job he had chosen, he faced that same sort of peril every day. Using the harshest means possible to get answers from a suspect didn't bother him. She knew he had killed men in the past, and under the right circumstances would do it again without remorse.

She understood that men like him were necessary to society, but she didn't think she could handle a long-term relationship with a man like that.

On the other hand, Bran had never said anything about his feelings or that he was interested in any sort of permanent relationship. Which meant, one way or another, she was destined for heartbreak.

She forced her mind back to the problems at hand, finished packing and returned to the living room. Just watching the confident, quiet strength of Bran's movements as he crossed the room made her want him.

She needed to be more careful, find a way to separate her body's physical need for him from the need that was building in her heart.

She wondered if there was the slightest chance she would succeed.

CHAPTER THIRTY-TWO

BRAN CHARTERED A PLANE for their trip back to Colorado. Which allowed him to bring his weapons and gear without the hassle of security at a big international airport. Since Jessie wanted to check on her apartment, they were flying into Denver and driving south, but he couldn't get a flight scheduled until the next day.

It was early afternoon when the pilot landed at the Signature Executive Terminal at the Denver Airport, where Bran had a rental car waiting. He drove straight to Jessie's downtown apartment, figuring she had been gone so long and so much had happened the odds of anyone surveilling the building were slim.

"Nice place," he said as he prowled the living room while Jessie went in to pack fresh clothes. The weather was changing, getting colder every day. Today the temperature hovered in the low fifties, low thirties predicted for tonight. Snow had already fallen a couple of times, though it had mostly melted.

He glanced around the apartment, his size making it feel even smaller than it actually was. She had done a good job, used bright colors to liven up the inexpensive beige sofa and chair that looked more comfortable than the outrageously expensive furniture in his exclusive high-rise condo. The pastel-colored pillows on the sofa matched watercolor paintings of flowers on the walls and gave the place a homey feel.

Tugging her carry-on behind her, she walked out of the bedroom in a yellow turtleneck sweater, dark blue jeans, and her ankle boots. She had plaited her hair into the intricate braid that always made him want to pull it apart and run his fingers through it, spread the silky mass around her shoulders.

His groin tightened as he thought about stripping her naked and making love to her in the white wrought iron bed in her bedroom—as if taking her there would somehow be staking his claim. It was definitely not the time for thoughts like that, but his body didn't seem to agree.

He was in deep trouble with this woman. Deeper than he ever imagined. Funny thing was, for the first time in his life, he didn't care.

She surveyed the wilted philodendron on a white wrought iron stand against the wall. "My plants all died." She sighed. "I never had much of a green thumb, anyway, but with Hallie coming by to water them, I thought they might stand a chance."

"When this is over, I'll buy you some new ones." Unless he could convince her to move to Dallas, into his condo. Then he could buy them for her there.

The thought only half surprised him. It hadn't taken him long to realize he wanted Jessie in his bed. It had taken a while longer to figure out he wanted her for more than just sex. He wanted her in his life, wanted the chance to make it work for both of them.

He looked at her and his resolve strengthened. He was Delta. When a man had a goal, he went after it. He just had to figure out how to achieve his mission objective.

"Let me make sure I've got everything I need, and I'll be ready to go," Jessie said.

While she finished up, he checked in with his friend Ty Folsom, who also lived in Denver.

"Thought I'd let you know we're still breathing," Bran said.

"Glad you called. We were worried."

"We?" he asked.

"Me and Hallie. We've been spending a lot of time together." Bran could hear the smile in his friend's voice. "She's due here any minute."

"So I guess things are working out."

"Hallie's great, and Chris and Sarah love her. The kids' grandmother is springing for a trip to Disneyland next week for Chris's birthday. Hallie's coming with us."

"That's great, Ty."

"How about you and Jessie?"

"Working on it," he said.

"Listen, you guys stay safe. Let me know if you need me."

"Will do." Bran ended the call as Jessie walked back into the living room. At the pale color of her face, his worry kicked in and he rose from the sofa. "What is it?"

"I—I found this in the kitchen." Her hand shook as she held up a card with a red valentine heart on the front. "It's… it's from him, Bran. Ray Cummings."

The muscles across his stomach sharply contracted. Careful not to touch more than the corner, he plucked the card from her trembling fingers and flipped it open, read the handwritten words.

Hello, sweetheart,
Dropped by but you weren't home. Don't worry, I'll be back. We still have unfinished business. See you soon!
Love, Jordy

"Jordy…" she said, her throat working as she swallowed. "That's what he called himself. I never knew his real name was Ray until they caught him." Her eyes glistened with unshed tears. She dropped down on the sofa as if her legs wouldn't hold her any longer. "I'm scared, Bran."

Fury burned through him. Jessie had been shot at, fought men twice her size trying to protect him, survived a plane crash, and hiked through a freezing desert.

But this man scared her.

He wanted to tear the bastard apart with his bare hands.

His jaw clenched as he sat down on the sofa beside her, reached over and took her hand. "I won't let him near you, baby. I swear it." He tipped her chin up, bringing her wet eyes to his face. "He comes after you, he's a dead man. You believe me?"

Her lips trembled.

"Do you?"

"Yes…" He pulled her into his arms and held her. He had never felt so completely helpless, or enraged.

When her trembling eased, he set her away, got up and prowled the apartment, careful not to touch anything.

"The lock on the door wasn't broken," he said, surprised at how calm he sounded. "Any idea how he got in?"

She turned toward the bedroom. "There's a fire escape outside the window next to my bed. I like fresh air so I might have left the window unlocked. I never really worried about it. Maybe he got in that way."

The apartment building was older, with molded ceilings and hardwood floors, an electric heater in a faux fireplace in the living room. It gave the place a certain charm, he supposed, and probably the reason Jessie had chosen it. But it was also less secure. He walked into the bedroom and looked at the window, saw that it could easily be opened if the lock wasn't turned, which it wasn't.

He didn't know any of the local police, but he knew sheriff's detective Mace Galen, still had Galen's number in his phone contacts.

He pulled out his cell. "It's Bran Garrett, Detective. I need a favor, information on a guy named Ray Cummings."

"I hear Wayne Coffman is dead," Galen drawled, ignoring his request. "Murdered in his army prison cell. What the hell happened?"

"How'd you hear?"

"A CID agent named Tripp phoned the information in since the sheriff's department made the original arrest."

"Coffman's dead, all right. Unfortunately, he was killed before he gave up the intel we needed."

"They catch the guy who killed him?"

"Not that I've heard."

"Coffman winds up dead and your intel dies with him. Sounds pretty convenient for someone."

"Yeah, it was. Cummings is another matter. Arrested in Denver for serial rape about three years ago. You remember Jessie Kegan?"

"Oh, I remember her. How could I forget a woman who was as big a pain in my ass as you were."

Bran's mouth edged up. "Ms. Kegan testified in Ray Cummings's trial. She helped put him away. He was sentenced to ten years, but he's out and making threats against her. I want to know what the fuck is going on."

"Cummings is in Denver?"

"Broke into her apartment while she was out of town."

"I'll call you right back."

Unable to sit still any longer, Bran got up and started

pacing, moving from one side of the living room to the other. Which didn't take long, considering how small it was.

His phone rang. He recognized Galen's number and answered. "What?"

"Cummings's lawyer managed to get him off on a technicality," Galen said. "With the prisons so full, they were glad to have an excuse to let him out early. They're handing out shorter sentences. Hell, they aren't even collecting bail in some places. Just writing the goddamned criminals up at the station, then letting them go."

"Yeah, well they let the wrong guy go this time. Cummings broke into Ms. Kegan's apartment and left her a threatening message."

"Be careful with the note. Maybe we can get his prints."

"Maybe. Unfortunately, she lives in the city not the county so it's not your jurisdiction."

"I'll call it in. I've got friends in the Denver PD. I'll find someone I know to take the case."

"Thanks, Galen."

"Do us all a favor and try not to contaminate the crime scene." Galen hung up the phone.

Twenty minutes later a knock came at the door. A tall, thin detective with ebony skin and very dark eyes took their statements. His name was D'Marco Porter, and he projected the kind of confidence Bran respected. Porter took a look at the Valentine's card and the window and called in the CSIs to check for prints.

"We'll bring Cummings in for questioning," the detective promised. "See what he has to say."

"Thank you," Jessie said.

"If his prints turn up on the card or in your apartment, he'll be arrested. In the meantime, I have contact information on both of you. I'll keep you updated on our progress."

It wasn't enough to suit Bran, who wanted the bastard's head separated from his shoulders. But for the time being it would have to do.

Leaving the police with a key to Jessie's apartment, Bran drove the rental car south on I-25 to Cutter Aviation, the executive airport in Colorado Springs where he had left Jessie's Honda for their ill-fated plane ride to San Diego.

He used his bug detector to make sure no new GPS trackers had been planted on the car, and they headed for town. Jessie remained quiet all the way. She hadn't said two words since they had left Denver.

"You gonna be okay?" Bran asked as they walked into their latest quarters. Hoping it would cheer her, he had booked a suite on the third floor of the Broadmoor, one of the finest hotels in Colorado. It wasn't cheap, but it had the added benefits of top-rate security and gourmet food.

"I'm all right," Jessie said. "At the moment, at least, Cummings doesn't know where I am. Maybe the police will find his prints and it'll be enough to get him thrown back in prison."

Bran clamped down on a rush of anger that had his back teeth clenching. "Yeah, maybe." But life was never that easy.

"In the meantime, I need to stay focused on why we're here."

No arguing with that.

They took a few minutes to get settled in the suite, which was as elegant as it looked on the internet, with a fire-place in the living room, a four-poster bed, and views of the mountains. He could tell Jessie liked it, and Bran liked making her happy. He just hoped to hell he could continue to keep her safe.

They used the balance of the afternoon to put their latest plan in motion, first calling Tabby to run the idea past her, then Charles Frazier. With Petrov and Graves out of the picture and no immediate threat to his family, Frazier agreed to a conference call between the four of them. Tabby and Frazier, communicating in computer-speak, came up with a fresh approach, and Frazier agreed to take another look at the Alamo Depot computers.

Someone had managed to hide the theft of the weapons for two full weeks before Frazier had discovered it. Using Tabby's suggestions, maybe something would pop that would help them.

At the end of what had turned into a long, exhausting day, Bran ordered room service instead of going downstairs for something to eat. He felt like he was ass-deep in alligators. They still hadn't found a way to nail Holloway, and until they did, they were in danger. The second batch of munitions still hadn't been located, and now there was Ray Cummings.

Bran almost wished that prick would come for Jessie so he could personally eliminate one of their problems.

Instead, he lifted her into his arms and carried her to bed. At least there was one mission he could accomplish before the night came to an end.

JESSIE TOLD HERSELF she should stop him. Letting Bran make love to her was only going to make things harder when they parted. But the heat of his mouth, the way their lips melded so perfectly together, sent desire sliding like liquid silk into her core. Hungry need curled low in her belly, reminding her how good it was between them, making her ache for more.

More kisses, the feel of his hands on her breasts, Bran's hard body pressing her into the mattress, moving deep inside her, driving her to the peak of pleasure. She wanted to feel those things again, and more.

Kissing her all the while, he stripped her out of her clothes, shed his own, and settled her in the middle of the bed. She almost didn't recognize the hoarse moan that slipped from her throat as his lips traveled along the side of her neck, over her bare shoulders, and he took her nipple into his mouth. She could feel his heavy erection in the vee between his legs.

"I want you, baby," he said. "So damn much." His tongue collided with hers in a deep, wet kiss that made her shiver all over. She couldn't resist sliding her fingers into his thick dark hair.

He was kissing his way down her body, mumbling soft words that said how much he wanted her when it happened. When her traitorous mind began to slide backward, away from Bran, away from the present, back to another, darker time when she was trapped, tied up, and unable to move.

Cold hands were touching her breasts, moving like snakes over her skin. She struggled as the hands moved lower, his slick hot lips pressed against the side of her neck, making the bile rise in her throat. She tried to cry out, but the gag in her mouth muffled her cries for help. Dear God, she couldn't bear it—not a moment more.

"Stop!" she screamed. "Get away from me! Oh, God, please stop!"

A dark head shot up, and even in the dim light of the bedroom she recognized Brandon's beloved face.

"Easy, baby. It's all right. No one's going to hurt you. Everything's okay."

Tears rolled down her cheeks as she realized what she had done. That Ray Cummings had intruded back into her life. That she was a victim. That she could no longer trust herself to behave like a normal woman. Not even with Bran.

She started crying and he pulled her into his arms, holding her tightly against him, like a fortress against the evil in the world.

"It's okay, honey. It's okay."

A sob escaped. "I'm so sorry, Bran...so sorry."

He kissed her forehead and drew her even closer. "It isn't your fault. You hear me? It's his. Cummings. I promise you he isn't going to hurt you. I'll kill the bastard first."

She whimpered. It was exactly that kind of thinking that destroyed whatever chance they had of being together. And yet, as she thought of Cummings and the terrible things he had done to the women he'd locked in his basement, the awful things he had meant to do to her, there seemed a rightness to it. A notion that justice would finally be served.

She couldn't think about it now. Not now. Instead, she slid her arms around Bran's neck and clung to him. "I ruined everything," she said tearfully. "It was always so good between us and now I ruined it."

Bran eased her a little away. "You didn't ruin anything." He gave her the sweetest smile. "Worst-case scenario, you get to tie me up again."

An unexpected laugh escaped. She couldn't believe it. Her eyes burned. How could such a hard man be so sweet? *I love you*, she thought. *I love you so much.*

The thought formed crystal clear in her mind, and there was no more denying it. She was desperately in love with Bran Garrett, and losing him would be the hardest thing she had ever done.

Bran shifted her a little but didn't let go. "Why don't we watch a movie? Something boring so we can both get some sleep."

She nodded, her heart squeezing at the way he always looked out for her. "That sounds good."

"Tomorrow's another day," he said. "Things always look brighter in the morning." Then he softly kissed her. Crossing the room unashamedly naked, he grabbed the remote off the dresser.

As she watched the supple movements of his powerful body, Jessie was already thinking of tying him up again.

CHAPTER THIRTY-THREE

NOW THAT THEY were back in Colorado Springs, their first order of business Monday morning was to request the exhumation of James Kegan's body. They needed proof he was murdered. Jessie had believed from the start that a second autopsy would give them the evidence they needed.

They were also meeting with Special Agent Derek Tripp. They planned to present their case that General Samuel Holloway was behind her father's murder and involved in the theft of the chemical weapons.

After the phone call Special Agent Tripp had received from Bran in San Diego and the CID's arrest of two suspected terrorists, Jessie figured Tripp would be as eager for a meeting as they were. But instead of CID headquarters, she made the appointment for the Judge Advocate's office.

She trusted her father's military counsel, Major Thomas Anson. During the dark days after her father's death, Jessie had come to consider Thomas a friend.

Freshly shaved, her father's attorney was even better-looking than she remembered. And he clearly hadn't lost his interest in her. Which Bran could apparently tell. Every time the major glanced in her direction, his jaw clenched. Jessie flicked him a look of warning, reminding him of the reason they were there.

Having arrived early to discuss the exhumation, they

took seats in front of Thomas's desk while he sat back down in his chair.

"When we spoke before," Jessie said, "I asked you to arrange for my father's body to be exhumed. A lot has happened since then. It's even more important now."

"As I said then, Jessie, it isn't that easy. You need a specific reason, grounds to support taking that action."

"I understand. What you'll hear when Special Agent Tripp arrives should give you what you need."

Thomas looked intrigued, but neither she nor Bran were willing to explain until the agent joined them, which was only a few minutes later.

With supershort blond hair shaved on the sides and longer on top, his bearing perfectly erect, almost overly so, Tripp walked in and immediately stepped aside. An older, silver-haired man followed him into the room. A couple of inches shorter than Tripp and a little broader in the chest and shoulders, William Larkin was a full-bird colonel and head of the CID at Fort Carson.

Jessie's already nervous stomach rolled. She found herself rising as the men approached, saw Bran coming sharply to his feet.

"Colonel Larkin." Thomas Anson stood behind his desk. "I didn't realize you would be joining us."

"Special Agent Tripp thought it would be a good idea for me to hear what Ms. Kegan has to say." He turned to Bran. "You must be Captain Garrett."

"Retired. Brandon is fine."

The colonel nodded. "Ms. Kegan. Special Agent Tripp has told me about what took place while the two of you were in San Diego. As you were, everyone."

Tripp pulled a couple more chairs around the desk, and they all sat down.

"Now, if you will please tell me what the arrests of two suspected terrorists has to do with the death of your father," Colonel Larkin politely demanded.

Jessie steeled herself. "It's complicated. Suffice it to say, our investigation into my father's murder led us to members of a terror cell involved in the purchase of chemical weapons stolen from the Alamo Depot. In order to make sense of everything that's happened, I'm requesting that Major Anson, my father's counsel, have his body exhumed so that we may reexamine the cause of death."

"Based on what?" the colonel asked.

She started the lengthy explanation when the door burst open and three MPs stormed into the room.

"Captain Brandon Garrett, you are under arrest for treason in the matter of revealing classified information. Please turn around and place your hands behind your back."

Bran looked at Tripp. "What the hell's going on?"

Tripp looked as shell-shocked as Jessie felt. "I don't know."

"Put your hands behind your back, Captain," a big, beefy MP commanded. "I'd advise you to cooperate. If you resist, it will only make things worse."

Tripp turned to Larkin. "Sir?"

"Earlier this morning I received a call from General Samuel Holloway, director of Chemical Materials Activity. He's asked that Captain Garrett be detained pending investigation into charges of treason."

The MPs moved forward, a wall of solid muscle with one objective in mind.

"No!" Jessie tried to wedge herself between Bran and the men, but he set her carefully away. "Holloway's behind all of this!" she shouted. "He's been working with a man named Edgar Weaver, a prisoner in ADMAX. They're cousins! Weaver arranged my father's murder to keep him from finding the real thieves. Samuel Holloway is the man behind the theft of fifteen thousand pounds of chemical weapons!"

Stunned silence filled the chamber.

"Take him away," Larkin commanded.

"Wait, please!" But the MPs didn't hesitate, just pulled Bran's arms behind his back, locked his wrists in handcuffs, and forced him toward the door.

"She needs protection!" Bran shouted. "Call Ty, Jessie! Ask him to get Colt Wheeler down here!"

For an instant, she was afraid Bran would fight, but even for him, escaping a military base wouldn't be easy, and it would make the situation far worse. The door slammed as the soldiers hauled him out of the office and down the hall.

Jessie was shaking when Larkin's attention returned to her, a dark scowl on his face. "A decorated officer having a relative in prison is hardly grounds for those sorts of wild accusations."

"I—I can prove it, sir. But I need to have my father's body exhumed. Please, Colonel. Brandon Garrett is innocent. Holloway is the man you want."

Thomas spoke up. "Under the circumstances, I don't believe what Ms. Kegan is asking is unreasonable, Colonel."

Larkin's gaze remained on Jessie.

"Please, Colonel."

"All right. Request granted."

"There's one more thing," she said, fighting to keep her voice from shaking. "Two people involved in this were murdered while they were locked in an army prison cell—my father and a man named Wayne Conrad Coffman. Special Agent Tripp can verify Coffman's death. There's a chance the men responsible will come after Brandon, too. I beg you to release him into Major Anson's custody and give us the time we need to prove our claims."

"Ms. Kegan is right about Coffman," Special Agent Tripp said. "He was murdered in his cell. His death is currently under investigation."

The light reflected on Larkin's thick silver hair as he shook his head. "I'm sorry. At this juncture there is no connection between Coffman's death and anything else. Without proof, there's nothing I can do."

His features softened as he looked into Jessie's terrified face. "However. If the autopsy uncovers proof that your father was indeed murdered, I'll reconsider my decision."

"Thank you, sir," Thomas said. He gave a smart salute, which the colonel returned. Tripp walked over and opened the door, and the colonel strode out of the office.

"I'm sorry that happened," Thomas said as soon as the men were gone. "I assure you I had no idea."

Forcing down her fear for Bran, Jessie's anger solidified into an iron resolve. "I want that exhumation, Thomas. How soon can it be arranged?"

"I'm not sure."

"I want it done no later than tomorrow. A man's life depends on it." Turning, Jessie walked out of the office. She didn't bother to close the door.

JESSIE DIDN'T CALL TY. He had two kids who needed him, and she really didn't know Colt Wheeler. She had Brandon's .38 revolver back in the room, and God only knew what other weapons were in his gear bag. If someone came after her, she could protect herself.

She refused to let her mind stray to Ray Cummings. Cummings had no idea where to find her. The help she needed was for Bran. That help was in Dallas. As soon as she reached her car, Jessie phoned Chase Garrett.

"Chase, it's Jessie Kegan." She swallowed and tried to stop trembling.

"Jessie. What's going on?"

"Brandon's in trouble, Chase. We both are." Her voice broke. "We really need your help."

His worried tone shifted to hard-edged and focused. "Is your phone safe?"

"It's…it's a throwaway."

"Where are you?"

"Fort Carson. Getting ready to drive back to the Broadmoor Hotel where we've been staying." Her throat tightened. "They arrested Brandon for treason, Chase. It's just some made-up charge to get him in a cell so they can kill him." Tears clouded her eyes. "Oh, God."

"Listen to me, Jessie. I'll be there as fast as I can. I'll be bringing all the help we need. All right?"

She nodded though he couldn't see her. "Okay."

"Will you be safe until I can get there?"

"I've got Bran's revolver and I know how to shoot. I'll be all right. But Brandon—"

"If anyone can take care of himself, it's Bran. Just get to your hotel room and lock the door. Don't let anyone in, and don't go out until I get there, understand?"

"Yes."

"Everything's going to be all right. I'll be there in a few hours." The line went dead.

Jessie held on to the phone a few seconds longer, a lifeline to the brother she trusted to do everything in his power to help them. From the base, she drove back to the hotel, went up to the third floor, and locked herself in the suite.

She took the revolver out of Bran's gear bag and set it

on the dining table next to her computer. Bran's laptop was set up, too, and he had internet access.

They had gone to Tripp that morning to present information that pointed in one direction. Edgar Weaver, at Holloway's urging, had arranged her father's death. But the discussion had never gotten off the ground.

Jessie brought up the file she had been creating. She went over each detail, stringing the pieces together, along with pertinent facts. She pulled up the pages she had copied from Georgia court records showing Weaver's ties to the Aryan Brotherhood. Janos Petrov, Harley "Digger" Graves, and Wayne "Tank" Coffman, all members of the Brotherhood, had been enlisted by Weaver to put an end to her investigation before Holloway's role could be discovered. Even if they had to kill her.

Petrov had been murdered by Coffman, directed by Weaver. Now Tank was dead.

She put in everything she knew about Mara Ramos, though with Mara in custody, it was information Tripp must already know or have access to. She needed the agent to question Mara about the personal information she had stolen from James Kegan—without his knowledge. Information later used to set up the fake offshore account that made him the scapegoat for the theft of the weapons.

Satisfied with what she'd assembled, she saved the file. She wanted to print the information for Tripp and Larkin, but to do that she would have to go down to the business center. As tempting as it was, she decided to wait until Chase arrived.

Jessie said a silent prayer that it would be soon.

CHAPTER THIRTY-FOUR

IT WAS DARK when Chase arrived in the Garrett Resources Citation at the Colorado Springs Municipal Airport. He had two car rentals waiting. Jason Maddox took the Jeep Cherokee and headed for the Broadmoor Hotel to provide protection for Jessie. Chase and a private military attorney named Russell Addison got into a rented silver Lincoln sedan and drove straight to the base.

The gate guard checked their IDs. In his long-ago military days, Chase had been an army MP. As a military attorney, Addison also had the appropriate credentials.

Unfortunately, once they reached the detention facility, no amount of persuasion could entice the operations officer at the front desk to allow them in to see a detainee named Brandon Garrett.

"I'm afraid visiting hours are long over," said a female staff sergeant named Holmsby. "You'll have to call in the morning and make arrangements to speak to him."

Chase fought a surge of frustration. "Would you at least relay the message that his brother Chase is here. Tell him I'll be back in the morning, accompanied by his attorney."

She cocked an iron gray eyebrow. Holmsby was a stocky, no-nonsense sort of woman suited perfectly for the job. "I can't make any promises, but I'll try."

"Thank you." He shouldn't have been disappointed. He

knew how the system worked. Rules were *not* made to be broken.

They left the base and drove to the Broadmoor. He wished he had better news. He had no idea what sort of relationship Jessie and his brother had, but he had heard the possessive note in Bran's voice whenever he talked about her.

And Jessie certainly seemed to care about him.

"Beautiful hotel," Addison remarked as Chase turned into the long, stately drive leading to the impressive front entrance. "I've stayed here before."

"My brother's tastes have definitely improved since he left the army."

Addison smiled. "From what I read in his file, he deserves a little luxury."

Chase thought of the rugged conditions in Afghanistan and other abysmal spots Brandon had been deployed, as well as their recent adventure in the Colombian rain forest. "That's for sure."

He pulled up in front of the Broadmoor, a grandiose cluster of pink stucco buildings over a century old. With Maddox there, Jessie should be safe.

But worrying about Bran's safety until morning was going to make it a long night for everyone.

BRAN LAY ON the top bunk in his cell on the ground floor of the detention facility. He was alone, which he saw as good news. If someone entered the cell to attack him during the night, he would have more room to maneuver.

His stomach growled, reminding him of his decision to skip the day's meals. Colonel Kegan's lunch had been tampered with. Whatever had been in it had made him sick and ultimately gotten him killed.

No way was he taking that chance.

It was quiet along the row of cells. Lights out, the occasional sound of someone shuffling around in the darkness, but nobody talking. He wondered if he'd have a visitor in the night, and if so, which guard had been paid off and how much money it was worth to unlock the door and look the other way. Or maybe there was a way to remotely unlock the cell doors.

The hours slipped past. He dozed with an ear cocked to the slightest disturbance, an art he had perfected. It was a little past three in the morning when he heard it. The soft snick of the lock, the glide of the heavy door sliding open.

His muscles tensed in anticipation as two shadows moved into the cell. One broad and tall, the other leaner, with long bones in his arms and legs. He caught the flash of a blade in the lean man's hand, but he was ready. He jerked his pillow up as the knife slashed down, felt a sharp sting that was meant to be lethal but dodged the main thrust of the blade. He kicked out at the man's head, connecting hard enough to send the knife flying and the wiry body crashing into the wall on the opposite side of the cell.

The second man was on him, big and strong, a Janos Petrov look-alike with a shaved head and prison tats on his arms and the back of his hands. Bran came off the top bunk feetfirst, kicking the guy in the face so hard his front teeth jammed all the way into the back of his throat.

The big guy clutched his neck, made a gurgling sound, and lurched forward. Bran elbowed him in the face, smashing his nose, sending a spray of blood into the air.

The wiry man was up, swinging a blow Bran ducked. He took the guy out with a chop to the esophagus, then linked his hands and brought both fists down on the top of his attacker's head, driving him into the floor face-first. He lay there unconscious.

The big guy swung a punch, but he was disoriented and badly injured, his broken nose affecting his vision. Bran punched him in the face, elbowed him, kneed him, and he went down. He didn't get up.

Stepping over both men, he walked out of the cell, making his way to the guard station. He was bleeding a little, not too badly. In the guardroom, two men sat behind the glass, watching a pair of screens. Another guard, a woman, stood at the far end of the room. With any luck, they weren't all being paid to look the other way while someone killed him.

The guards raced toward the glass door as he approached.

"I need to speak to Colonel William Larkin, head of Criminal Investigations. You've got two inmates down in my cell. They need medical attention. They were paid to kill me, so I think you had better make that call."

His instincts said Larkin was a straight shooter. A little too by the book, but a man who believed in the law.

The female guard hurriedly picked up the phone while the other two guards sprang into action. The glass door slid open, one of the men grabbed him, spun him around, and snapped on a pair of cuffs.

A medic appeared to apply first aid to the slice in his shoulder, while two more raced back to the injured men in his cell. Then the female guard and one of the men led him down the corridor into a windowless interrogation room.

Better there, he thought, than back in the cell.

Or at least Bran hoped so.

Now he just prayed one of them had actually made the call.

It was four thirty in the morning when Jessie's cell rang, sending a stab of terror straight to the heart. Her hand shook as she grabbed the phone from the nightstand. Hearing the ring, Chase knocked, then opened the bedroom door. Hawk appeared in the doorway beside him.

"This…this is Jessica Kegan." Since she was sharing the suite with two men, she had slept in her yoga pants and a Denver Broncos T-shirt.

"Jessie, it's Thomas Anson. There's been an incident at the detention facility."

She clamped down on a fresh rush of terror, saw the same fear reflected in Chase's whiskey-brown eyes. "Is… is Brandon all right?"

"Colonel Larkin phoned. Brandon was attacked in his cell, Jessie, just as you were afraid he would be."

"Oh, God."

"He's all right, Jess. The two inmates he fought with fared much worse. They're in serious condition in the infirmary. The good news is what happened was enough to convince Larkin to take a look at whatever information the two of you can assemble. In the meantime, he's releasing Brandon into your custody. Apparently he feels that if anyone can keep him in line, it's you."

Relief made her muscles go limp and her eyes burn. She was glad she was sitting on the edge of the bed. She covered the phone. "He's okay," she said, and both Chase and Maddox looked relieved.

Jessie brushed a tear from her cheek. "Thank the colonel for me."

"You can pick him up anytime after 8:00 a.m."

"Thank you, Thomas."

"Also… I should know about the exhumation sometime early tomorrow. I'll call as soon as I have the information." The line went dead, and Jessie looked over at the men waiting to hear the news.

"That was my father's military counsel, Thomas Anson. He says they're releasing Bran this morning. Two men attacked him in his cell. Apparently Bran defended himself with enough vigor to put them in the hospital in serious condition."

Chase released a sigh of relief. "Maybe now we can actually get some sleep."

Maddox chuckled. "Your turn on the sofa."

They were taking turns keeping watch over her, she realized. "I haven't thanked you both for coming all the way out here."

"You don't have to thank us," Chase said. "Looking out for each other is what we do. Get some sleep. We'll see you in the morning."

"Night, Jessie," Maddox said.

"Good night, Hawk."

She remembered meeting him that first day in Dallas, a big man, muscular and handsome, with thick dark brown hair cut short, and blue eyes. He was a bounty hunter, Bran had told her. He'd also said Maddox was former marine spec ops and could do just about anything.

Her stomach contracted as she recalled the events of last night. Maddox had arrived at the hotel just after dark and taken up his duties as her protector. Chase, tall and athletically built, with dark gold hair and a short-cropped beard along a hard jaw, had shown up an hour later.

He'd brought an attorney named Russell Addison, a man in his midforties with slightly receding straw-colored hair. Addison had spent the night in a hotel room down the hall while Hawk and Chase had slept in the living room of the suite.

Maddox had talked about the woman he was going to

marry in just a few weeks. "I think you'd like her. Kate's smart and she's fun. And I know she'd like you."

Jessie smiled. "You like her so I know I'll like her." She could tell he was deeply in love. And Chase had a wife he adored.

Jessie was surprised to feel a stab of envy. She had never come close to a permanent relationship, never felt the kind of connection that would last a lifetime.

An image of Bran Garrett rose in her head. Handsome, intelligent, the sexiest man she had ever met. A man she trusted with her life on a daily basis. She was in love with him. Deeply in love. Whatever happened, she would never regret the time she had spent with him.

She had no idea what Brandon felt for her, but even if he loved her, there was no way she could handle the kind of life he lived. A warrior who survived on the edge, Bran stared danger in the face every day and never backed down. He'd been locked in a cell where he could have died. The thought of losing him was enough to make her physically ill.

It was ten minutes to eight as Jessie stood next to Hawk Maddox in the waiting area at the front of the detention facility. He was acting as her protector again, while Chase and Russell Addison were handling the last of the paperwork for Bran's release.

She couldn't help thinking about the violence Bran had used against his attackers last night. No matter how she looked at it, she couldn't see it as anything other than justified. Two men had died in that prison. If Bran hadn't fought for his life, he would have been the third.

"There he is," Hawk said.

Jessie's heart squeezed as Bran appeared in the doorway and started walking toward her, his brother and the attorney at his side.

His eyes found hers and didn't look away. Then she was in his arms and he was holding her like he would never let her go.

"Jessie…baby…"

She swallowed past the lump in her throat. "I was so worried." She hugged his neck and fought not to cry. Bran was safe. That was all that mattered.

He held her close a few moments more, then pulled away and flashed one of his heart-stopping smiles. "I understand I'm in your custody until this is over."

She smiled back. "So I'm told."

He leaned down and whispered, "So maybe handcuffs this time? Might be more appropriate."

Jessie laughed. But the handcuffs reminded her of Ray Cummings and being held captive. Cummings was still out there. Some of her buoyant mood faded.

"Let's get out of here," Bran said, sensing the change in her as he always seemed to.

They headed outside, into a November day that was dark and gloomy, the temperature in the thirties as they climbed into Chase's Lincoln sedan for the ride back to the Broadmoor, stopping briefly at the armory to pick up Bran's Glock.

They had breakfast in the Lake Terrace Dining Room at the hotel to celebrate Brandon's release: eggs Benedict for her and Chase, pancakes and bacon for Hawk and Bran, and an omelet for the attorney. During the meal, they discussed what could happen next.

"Doesn't look like Brandon's going to be needing your legal services, Russell," Chase said, taking a sip of the aromatic coffee.

"Thank God for that," Jessie said.

"I can stay till things get sorted," Maddox offered, shoveling in a mouthful of pancakes. "Now that Bran's out of jail, the two of us ought to be able to handle things."

Chase had an office to run and a wife waiting at home. But the closer they got to catching the thieves who'd stolen the munitions, the more dangerous it was going to get.

"Bran?" Chase asked.

"If Maddox stays, we'll have it covered." He crunched a piece of bacon and winked at Jessie. "Right, Deputy Kegan?"

Jessie laughed. "We'll be fine."

They were just finishing the meal when her cell phone pinged and Thomas Anson's text appeared on the screen.

Her heart lurched. The exhumation of her father's body was scheduled for one o'clock that afternoon.

CHAPTER THIRTY-FIVE

A BITTER WIND slashed the air and dark clouds loomed over the lawns of the Pike's Peak National Cemetery. Snow-capped mountains rose in the distance, American flags snapped along the roadsides, but all Jessie saw was the sea of headstones in meticulous rows, one after another, hundreds of them. Standing between Hawk and Brandon, Jessie felt cold to the bone.

She watched as a cable at the end of a forklift raised her father's casket out of the ground, then turned and set it on the back of a flatbed truck.

Men tossed straps over the coffin to secure it for the fifteen-mile drive back to the medical examiner's office at Fort Carson. After the attack on Bran last night, Colonel Larkin had made the autopsy a priority. The ME would begin his examination that afternoon.

The wind stung her eyes, and Jessie wiped tears from her cheeks. She had known this would be hard, but she hadn't expected to feel the devastating loss of her father just as fiercely as she had the first time.

Her lips trembled. "I'm sorry, Daddy. I wouldn't disturb you if I weren't sure this is what you would want me to do." Her throat closed up. Her father had only been gone a few months. Part of her still couldn't believe it. "I won't let you down, Dad. I swear it."

Bran squeezed her hand and drew her against his side,

KAT MARTIN   303

steadying her. She took a deep breath, some of her composure returning. As she watched the flatbed drive away, she prayed the autopsy would give them the evidence they needed to prove her father had been murdered.

Then the CID would be forced to look into her accusations that Weaver, the Aryan Brotherhood, and Chemical Material Activities director General Samuel Holloway were connected. Maybe they could find a link to the money from the auction, follow it straight to Holloway's front door.

"Come on, baby. Let's go." Bran's arm went around her shoulders as he urged her back to the Cherokee. Maddox slid in behind the wheel, Bran helped Jessie into the passenger seat, and climbed into the backseat behind her.

No one spoke as they drove back to the hotel. Until they had the evidence they needed, there was nothing to say.

Jessie refused to consider the possibility the autopsy would come up with nothing. Agent Tripp had ordered the Division of Forensic Toxicology to run a new tox screen for various poisons, including aconite, that could simulate a heart attack.

Before they had left the hotel, Jessie had looked it up on the internet, a poisonous tree plant that was sometimes called wolfsbane, monkshood, or devil's helmet. According to Tripp, the ME would be testing for similar poisons, as well as examining the contents of her father's stomach.

By the end of the day or tomorrow at the latest, they should have news.

"WOULD YOU PLEASE sit down?" Hawk grumbled at Bran from his place in an overstuffed chair. "You're wearing a hole in the carpet."

Bran blew out a frustrated breath. "I was hoping we'd get the report back by now." He flopped down on the sofa next to Jessie. He wasn't a patient man—except on a mission when a silent vigil could last for hours. Then patience could mean the difference between success or failure, even life or death.

"Nothing ever happens that fast in the military," Jessie said. "You ought to know that by now."

"Unfortunately," Bran grumbled.

"I'm starving," Maddox said. "Why don't we order something to eat?"

"Now there's a good idea," Bran said.

"You two are always hungry," Jessie teased, smiling.

Bran cast her a heated glance she correctly interpreted as *true, but in my case, not necessarily for food.* He grinned when she flushed. At least she was still thinking about sex. F-ing Ray Cummings hadn't screwed things up completely.

And Bran had enough self-confidence to figure he could make things right again with just a little more effort on his part. He smiled, the sultry look Jessie tossed his way making him even more certain.

Maddox grabbed the room service menu from the desk. He took a quick look, then handed it to Jessie. "Fried chicken for me. What's everybody else want?"

She opened it and held it for both of them to read, but just then Bran's phone rang. He reached over and snatched it off the mahogany coffee table, checked the screen and recognized the contact name.

Bran pressed the phone against his ear. "Sir."

"Captain Garrett, this is Colonel Bryson."

Old habits had him snapping to attention, squaring his shoulders and sitting up straighter on the sofa. "Colonel."

"I have news. I can't tell you everything, but I'll tell you as much as I can. After our conversation, I spoke to Lieutenant General David Tanaka, director of Special

Operations/Counterterrorism Strategic Operational Planning. According to the general, your information was correct. In an effort to gain power in Yemen, a group of rebels backed by Iran began an assault using chemical weapons against Yemeni civilians. Fortunately, we arrived in time to stop a full-scale attack and destroy what remained of the weapons, keeping the number of casualties to a minimum."

Relief filtered through him. But those few casualties would have suffered deadly symptoms, starting with nausea and vomiting, diarrhea, severe blisters, and burns on their skin and mucous membranes. The most critical side effect was a pulmonary edema caused by filling the lungs with fluid, which killed in less than thirty minutes.

"Why gas their own people?" Bran asked.

"They were trying to replicate attacks made by the Saudis in the Saada province in 2015. The rebels wanted the US and the UK to believe the Saudis were guilty of war crimes and intercede against them on the rebels' behalf."

"Were you able to locate the supplier?"

"Not yet, but Army Counterterrorism is on it. NSA and Homeland are also involved. With the information you provided, we know the cell is located in San Diego. Rounding them up shouldn't take long."

"That's good news, sir."

"I managed to keep your name out of it, but know that the army is grateful for your part in this."

"Thank you, Colonel."

Bryson ended the call and Bran turned to Jessie, who waited impatiently on the sofa beside him.

"They found the chemical weapons in Yemen and destroyed them. Casualties kept to a minimum." He filled her in as much as he could on the attack and the reasons behind it.

"When you say '*they*' you mean army Delta, right?"

He just shrugged. He couldn't talk about the actual mission, even if he knew, but given Bryson's involvement, it would likely have been a Delta operation.

Jessie seemed to understand. "So the gas attack was meant to be a false flag. The rebels set it up so the Saudis would take the blame."

"That was the idea. The colonel says NSA and Homeland are working together to find whoever supplied the munitions to the rebels."

She gave a sigh of relief. "That's great, Bran. The majority of the weapons are no longer a threat. Now we just have to prove my father wasn't involved and find the rest of the weapons."

"Yeah…piece of cake."

IT WAS CLOSE to noon when the call came in requesting their presence at the medical examiner's office. Before they left for the base, Bran went down to the business office and printed the information Jessie had assembled.

Then all three of them piled into Maddox's Jeep Cherokee and drove onto the base, parking in the lot in front of the Army Community Hospital complex where the ME's office was located.

Nerves had her stomach jumping as she and Bran climbed out of the vehicle.

"I'll wait for you here," Maddox said. "Keep an eye on the car." He and Bran were both edgy. They were closing in on the bad guys, always a dangerous time.

Or at least they hoped they were getting close.

"Let's go," Bran said, setting a hand at her waist, urging her toward the glass front door.

According to the phone call, a different ME had performed the second autopsy, a double check that would leave no possibility unexplored. The man who greeted them introduced himself as Dr. Terence Chang, a small man with military-short black hair and wire-rimmed glasses.

Off to one side, a man Jessie hadn't noticed rose from his chair. Silver hair gleamed as Colonel William Larkin approached her.

"I wanted to be here when Dr. Chang presented his findings."

Jessie felt a fresh shot of nerves. Larkin's pale eyes were impossible to read, yet it was clear he knew the results. Her mouth went dry. She caught a look from Brandon. This was it. Everything they had worked for hinged on the next few minutes.

"Please have a seat," the doctor said.

She and Bran sat down in front of the desk, but Larkin remained standing.

Chang adjusted his glasses and opened the folder in front of him. "I'll try to put everything in layman's terms." He looked down at the top sheet of paper. "To begin with, an examination of the contents of your father's stomach showed he had ingested *listeria monocytogenes*, the bacteria that causes food poisoning. It was a particular variety that reacts within very few minutes and results in severe nausea."

"The reason he was transported to the infirmary," Larkin put in.

Jessie said nothing, but her stomach was churning. What if they were wrong?

"As you may know, we were given broader parameters this time, a wider range of testing. The tox screen administered showed something different. Traces of calcium gluconate. An equal amount of potassium phosphate also appeared in the colonel's blood."

Chang looked directly at her. "The combination of those two drugs, when administered together, causes a myocardial infarction. A heart attack."

Jessie swayed in her seat. She felt Brandon's hand wrap around hers and hold on tight.

"Pinpoint needle marks were found in the back of the colonel's neck, the injection site of the drugs." The doctor closed the file and his gaze returned to hers. "The official cause of death has been modified. James Kegan's death has now been ruled a homicide."

A sob escaped. Jessie clamped down hard to stay in control.

Larkin took both her hands and drew her to her feet. "I'm sorry for your loss, Jessie. It may help to know that as a result of what happened to Brandon last night and the autopsy results, the CID is bringing General Holloway in for questioning."

She opened her purse and removed the envelope that held the summary of information Bran had printed in the hotel business office. Her hand shook as she passed it to Larkin.

"This is the way we believe it happened," she said. "But we're still investigating, collecting information."

"That's no longer your concern," Larkin said. "It never should have been."

Jessie didn't say that if she hadn't started digging, none of this would have been discovered. Or that she wasn't stopping until her father's name was completely cleared.

"Thank you, Colonel Larkin," she said. "I hope you'll keep me informed as your investigation progresses."

"I'll do what I can. If we have any questions, we'll certainly be in touch."

Meaning the investigation was army business and she wouldn't be part of it.

"After the autopsy was completed, your father's body was returned to its final resting place," Larkin said. "It was my decision to go ahead with that. I felt you had already been through enough."

She nodded, locked down her emotions. Her father's part in this was over and he was back at rest. They had the proof they needed. She was grateful to Larkin once more. They made their farewells and left the office.

Maddox was waiting beside the Jeep, his face filled with concern. "How did it go?"

Since Jessie's throat suddenly tightened, Bran answered for her. "Colonel Kegan's death was ruled a homicide. Now they have to investigate, and Samuel Holloway is at the top of their list."

Maddox nodded. "I'm sorry, Jess."

"Thank you."

Maddox glanced over at Bran. "I don't suppose you two are out of it now."

Bran looked at Jessie. As usual, he knew what she was thinking. "Not quite yet," was all he said.

CHAPTER THIRTY-SIX

THE FOLLOWING MORNING Special Agent Derek Tripp phoned Brandon.

"I thought after what happened to you in that jail cell, you deserve to know where the investigation stands."

"I'd appreciate that."

"Where can we meet?"

"We're staying at the Broadmoor. Why don't you come up to the suite?" Bran gave him the room number and directions.

Half an hour later Special Agent Tripp walked into the living room.

"Nice place." His gaze took in the warm amber sofa and chairs, the manteled fireplace, ornate mahogany writing desk, and views of the mountains.

"Special Agent Tripp, this is Jason Maddox," Jessie said. "A friend from Dallas."

"Jase was marine spec ops," Bran said. "He's up to speed on what's been going on. You don't have to worry about what you say in front of him." The men shook hands, then they all sat down.

Tripp jumped right in. "To begin with, the guard who opened your cell last night has been arrested. He's been charged as an accessory in the murder of Wayne Conrad Coffman and also the attempted murder of Captain Brandon Garrett, retired."

"Good to hear," Bran said.

"He did it for money. So did the two men who attacked you. They, however, are members of the Aryan Brotherhood, which fits your suspicion they were following Edgar Weaver's orders. Unfortunately, so far they aren't talking."

"If they do, they'll be as dead as Coffman."

"I've also had our computer team looking deeper into the offshore account in Colonel Kegan's name. There's a chance we'll be able to find the person or persons who opened the account."

Bran slid a look at Jessie.

"What about Mara Ramos and Ahmed Malik?" she asked.

"Out of my hands. They're being interrogated by Counter-Terrorism."

"And Holloway?" Bran asked.

"I shouldn't tell you this, but we're trying to get a warrant to search General Holloway's office and residence." He rose from the sofa. "I'm afraid that's all I have for now."

"Thank you, Special Agent Tripp," Jessie said, walking the agent to the door. "We really appreciate everything you're doing."

"I'll be in touch." Tripp walked out and Jessie closed the door.

"This is starting to move pretty fast," Bran said.

"About damn time," Jessie said, making him smile.

He checked his watch. The afternoon had slipped away, and there was something he needed to do.

"Once this is over, Hawk and I will be heading back to Texas. I was hoping maybe you and I could talk about a few things before that happens."

Jessie's gaze met his. "Like what?"

Bran looked over her head to Maddox. "You won't feel

left out if I take Jessie to dinner at that fancy restaurant downstairs, will you?"

Maddox chuckled. "I'll manage to console myself with a big steak dinner and an on demand movie right here."

"We won't be gone too long," Bran said.

"If we're going out, I need to change." Jessie headed for the bedroom.

"Put on something sexy," Bran called after her. "I promise not to drool."

Jessie just shook her head. Twenty minutes later, she emerged in a short black dress cut low enough in front to reveal the soft mounds of her cleavage. A pair of black high heels added a good five inches, and her long fiery hair hung loose around her shoulders.

"You look luscious," he said as a rush of heat slid into his groin. She turned to give him a view of the back, showing off the curve of her sexy little ass and great legs. He almost groaned.

"I packed it when we were in Denver, just in case."

"In case what? In case you wanted to seduce me?"

She laughed, but her eyes sparkled.

"You ready?" He had dressed in black jeans and his tweed jacket over a lightweight black turtleneck sweater. The bandage covering the slash on his shoulder was uncomfortable, but the wound wasn't serious and he'd be able to strip off the dressing in a day or two. Jessie had fretted over it and babied him so much getting stabbed had almost been worth it.

She slung the strap of a small black handbag over her shoulder and walked ahead of him out of the suite.

The maître d' at the Ristorante Del Lago seated them at a quiet table in the corner. A man-made lake shimmered outside wood-paned glass doors that slid open in the summer for alfresco dining. The restaurant had a European feel, with terra-cotta tile, heavy wooden beams, warm beige linens, and flowers on the tables.

Bran pulled out Jessie's chair and seated her, then sat down across from her. He ordered a bottle of Chianti, which the waiter brought and poured, then left them to enjoy for a while before making their selections.

Jessie swirled the wine in her glass and took a sip. "Mmm…nice. What's the occasion?"

Bran smiled, took a drink of wine. "Maybe I just wanted to do something special for my favorite girl."

One of her russet eyebrows went up. "Am I? Your favorite?"

He reached over and covered her hand. "You're my only girl, Jess. The only woman I want. All of this is going to be over soon. When it is, I want you to come back to Dallas with me."

"What?" She sat up straighter, her eyes wide with shock. She eased her hand away. "Where did that come from? You've never mentioned anything like that before."

Unsure of himself in a way he rarely was, he ran a finger down the side of his glass. "I'm not good at this stuff. Truth is, I never had a reason to be. I never thought I'd find myself in a serious relationship and never really wanted to be. Not until I met you."

"I can't believe you're saying this."

"Why not? I'm crazy about you, Jess. Surely you can see that. When this is over, I don't want us to end."

Jessie's pretty green eyes filled with tears. "It has to end, Bran. We both know it could never work between us. The kind of life you live? Just because you aren't in the army anymore doesn't mean you aren't a warrior. You're a bodyguard, for heaven's sake. You face danger every day."

"It's not always this bad. Your dad's murder and the attempts on your life…that kind of thing doesn't happen every day."

Jessie just shook her head. "I don't want to live like that, worried every time you leave the house you might not be coming home. I saw what my mother went through. I was there when Danny died. Now my father is gone. I want someone I don't have to worry about."

Something was squeezing inside his chest. It was a different kind of pain than he had suffered before, not a bullet wound that could be stitched up, but an ache that in some strange way hurt even worse.

"It doesn't have to be that way," he said, desperate to make her understand. "People can change. You said so yourself. I can change, Jess. For you. I can be the man you want me to be."

"Brandon…" A tear rolled down her cheek.

"Just think about it, okay? We have a good thing going. Surely you can admit that much. We're good together. Really good."

She swallowed, and he could see she was trying not to break down. "If things were different…if I was different, there is no man on earth I would rather be with than you."

Bran leaned back in his chair. Something was burning behind his eyes. He took a deep breath. "Is it because of what happened in Mara Ramos's garage?"

Her fingers tightened around the stem of her wineglass. "For a while that bothered me. But I've had time to think about it. I trust you to do what's right. You were trying to save people's lives—and you did. This is something else. The life you lead just isn't something I can handle."

Inside his chest, his heart beat dully. He thought of Danny. Maybe he didn't deserve a woman like Jessie.

Maybe he was being punished for living when his friend had died.

"Maybe you're right," he said, his voice suddenly gruff. "We live in different worlds. It was probably just spending so much time together, you know?"

She nodded, wiped another tear from her cheek. "I know," she said softly.

He glanced away, took a long drink of wine. "We should… um…probably order."

She tried to smile, but her lips trembled. "Actually, I'm not very hungry."

"Yeah," he said, closing the menu. "Me, either."

"Hawk's upstairs. Maybe we could take a walk before we go back up. It's kind of windy, but there's a full moon tonight."

"A walk sounds good." He needed a good stiff wind to blow some sense into him, get his head back on straight.

Calling for the waiter, he paid for their wine, then helped Jessie out of her chair. As they walked out the door to look at the moon over the lake, he draped his jacket over her bare shoulders.

They stepped out onto the flagstones, the breeze lifting her long red-gold hair away from her face. Jessie looked up at him. "Don't change, Bran. Not for me or anyone else."

His hand came up to touch her cheek. He drew her into his arms. "Jessie…" He kissed her long and deep, and Jessie kissed him back. Instead of a promise of things to come, the kiss felt like a farewell.

SHE JUST WANTED to go home. Back to Denver, away from all of the intrigue swirling around her. Away from the heartache. Away from Bran.

Lying in bed alone, she turned her face into the pillow

to muffle the sound of her tears. She had never considered that Brandon might have feelings for her beyond that of a temporary lover. Her brother had warned her about him. Bran wasn't a one-woman man.

But tonight…when he had said those things…it sounded almost as if he loved her.

She bit back a sob. Surely it was just working so closely together, as he had said. That and the element of danger. Surely he didn't feel the same sickness in the pit of his stomach that giving him up was causing her.

She took a shaky breath. None of it mattered. She had done the right thing. If they were together, she would be afraid every day of losing him. He had offered to change, but there wasn't a single thing about Brandon Garrett that she would change.

The sob escaped. She loved him so much. Her throat ached. She just wanted to go home. She would talk to Bran and Hawk about it in the morning.

The clock said 4:00 a.m. when her eyes finally slid closed and she fell asleep. Even then, she didn't sleep late the next morning.

As she dragged herself out of bed, showered, and dressed, the need to escape grew even stronger.

"Shower's free," she said as she walked into the living room. Hawk took one look at her puffy eyes and pale face and headed for the bathroom.

"I'll go first," he said, closing the bedroom door behind him and leaving the two of them alone.

Bran didn't look much better, his features drawn, hair mussed, his jaw dark with a night's growth of beard.

"Sorry about last night," he said. "I don't know what I was thinking."

She looked into his handsome, beloved face, and clamped

down on a surge of emotion. "It's just…it's everything that's happened. I think we should let Tripp and Larkin handle things from here. I think…think it's time for us to go home."

Bran just shook his head. "Until Weaver is dealt with and Holloway is in custody, you're not safe."

There was something different about him this morning, a darkness in his eyes, a tough, hard edge in the set of his jaw. She remembered seeing him that way before, but not for some time.

She smoothed the ends of the hair she had plaited into a braid and tossed it over her shoulder. "I don't know how much more of this I can stand."

The phone rang. Both of them glanced around in search of their cells. It was Brandon's. He grabbed it off the dining table. "Garrett."

"It's Charles Frazier, Brandon. I found the bastard. The rotten, no good traitor was right there in my office."

"Hold on, Charles. Let me put you on speaker."

Jessie moved closer. "Go ahead, Charles."

"The man who covered up the theft of the weapons? It was my assistant, Andrew Horton. It looks like he set the whole thing up. He's young and aggressive, one of the brightest computer minds I've ever worked with. He's only twenty-five years old. It never occurred to me he could be capable of something like that."

"How did you find him?" Jessie asked.

"Bran's friend, Tabitha, is a wonder. A genius, really. She sent me some software. We figured a way to put it to work, to link it with the information we had here—and there it was. Andrew's signature all over the dark web auction. He managed the shipments, collected the payments, all of it. He also opened the Cayman Islands account in Colonel Kegan's name."

Hearing information that could clear her father, Jessie felt a surge of hope.

"So Horton was working with Mara Ramos and the terror cell in San Diego?" Bran asked.

"I don't know anything about that. I just know he covered up the theft. He did such a good job it's a miracle I found it in the first place. There's a problem though."

"Yeah, what's that?" Bran asked.

"Horton left on vacation three days ago. He isn't due back until next week."

Bran softly cursed. "He must have been feeling the heat."

"That's what I'm afraid of."

"So how does Holloway fit in?"

"You're convinced he's involved?" Frazier asked.

"Oh, yeah, he's in it up to his lying, murdering eyebrows."

"I'm afraid that's over my head," Frazier said. "Computers are my expertise, not people."

Jessie looked up to see Maddox standing a few feet away, his hair still wet from the shower, damp patches on the dark blue Henley stretched over his massive chest.

"Seems like rotten people have a way of sniffing each other out," Hawk said. "Like they give off the same foul odor."

Frazier made a sound of agreement. "What should I do about Horton?"

"Do you trust De La Garza?" Bran asked. Frazier's direct superior and the head of the civilian side of the plant.

"I believe so. But then I trusted Andy."

"Go see De La Garza. I'll call William Larkin and Special Agent Tripp at the CID. Enough people know, there's no way to cover it up."

"All right, then. That's what I'll do." Frazier hung up the phone.

"Sort of like we're going public," Jessie said to the men standing around the dining table.

"Exactly," Bran agreed. "You call Tripp. I'll call Larkin."

The calls set everything in motion. With De La Garza involved and the CID searching for Andrew Horton, things were moving even faster than before.

It was the end of the day when Special Agent Tripp phoned Jessie back. She put the call on speaker.

"Good news," Tripp said. "Frazier gave us some intel that helped us go deeper into the bank in Cayman. Two more accounts showed up. One in the name of Andrew Horton and one in the name of Samuel Holloway."

"No way!" Bran said. "Those idiots put money in the same bank they used to set up Colonel Kegan?"

"Arrogance knows no bounds," Tripp said. "Horton opened all the accounts the same day. Neither he nor Holloway ever thought they'd be suspects. If it hadn't been for Jessie, they never would have been."

"So the accounts contained millions of dollars?" Jessie asked.

"That's right. Whatever was left after paying whoever was involved. Holloway has been arrested. We haven't found Andrew Horton, but it's just a matter of time."

"What about the rest of the missing chemical weapons?" Jessie asked.

"We'll be pressing for answers. From what we can tell, the second batch of weapons was a little side deal that Horton was involved in, but Holloway knew nothing about."

Jessie felt a rush of anger for her dad.

"We pick up Horton," Tripp continued, "we'll find out

who bought the weapons. Once we know that, we can figure out where they are."

By the time the call came to a close, Jessie's excitement had faded and fatigue had taken its place. Too many long days and sleepless nights. Too much heartache.

"Tripp and Larkin are working the case," she said wearily. "It feels like our part in it is over and it's time for us to go home." She didn't look at Brandon. Bran didn't look at her.

"No reason to stay in Colorado Springs," he said. "Let's pack up and get out of here."

Jessie didn't argue. The urge to go home was stronger than ever.

She wondered if her apartment would actually feel like home when Brandon wasn't there.

CHAPTER THIRTY-SEVEN

HAWK TURNED IN the rented Jeep at the Colorado Springs Airport and caught a direct flight back to Dallas. Bran loaded his and Jessie's bags into her Honda, and they headed for Denver.

All morning Bran had listened to Jessie trying to convince him to leave with Maddox, but that was not going to happen. No matter the torture he felt being near her, he owed it to her brother to make sure she was safe.

He figured Weaver and Holloway were too busy trying to save their asses to still be much of a threat. But Detective Porter had called to confirm Ray Cummings's fingerprints were found on the Valentine's card, on the windowsill, and other places in Jessie's apartment. The guy wasn't even trying to hide the fact he was stalking her. Unfortunately, Cummings was in the wind.

Until he was back in jail, no way was Bran leaving Jessie alone.

They arrived at her apartment late in the day, and he spent the night on her couch. A miserable night thinking of Jessie in bed in the other room. He was used to having her curled up against him, used to her reaching out to him in the night, used to reaching for her. The sex was always incredible between them. He didn't think Jessie would argue with that.

Funny how it had ended, with him wanting more and Jessie just wanting to be free of him. He ignored the ache in his chest.

It was late the next morning, neither of them talking. Bran was tired. Jessie was skirting him, trying to keep her distance. She finally gave up, clamped her hands on her hips and glared at him as he rinsed his coffee mug and set it on the counter in her tiny kitchen.

"You can't just sit in my apartment all day waiting for Cummings to show up."

A muscle ticked in his cheek. "What's the matter? Can't get rid of me fast enough?"

Jessie glanced away. "That isn't it and you know it." She looked back at him. "I know you just want to protect me. We're friends. Good friends. As far as I'm concerned, we always will be."

His jaw clenched so hard it hurt, and something snapped inside him. Gripping her shoulders, he dragged her hard against him. Her eyes widened as his mouth crushed down over hers.

The kiss was rough and demanding, unapologetic. He kissed her until the stiffness went out of her body and she was clinging to his neck, kissing him back.

He eased her away, drawing her eyes to his face. "I'll never be that kind of friend, Jess. I don't want to be, and I don't really think you want that, either." He kissed her again, softly this time. "We're more than friends, even if you won't admit it."

Tears filled her eyes. Turning, she walked a few feet away, then turned back. "You're right, okay? Is that what you want to hear? We're more than friends. I love you, Brandon. It doesn't change anything."

He stared at her for long moments. *She loved him?* He wondered if that could possibly be true. He scrubbed a hand over his unshaven jaw.

"Maybe I never had a chance, you know? Like I was

never supposed to have you. Danny's dead. I'm alive. It wouldn't be right for me to end up with his beautiful sister."

Her hand came out of nowhere, cracking hard against his cheek. "Don't say that! Don't you ever say that again!"

Anger burned through him. "What the hell, Jess?"

"Danny would want you to be happy! I want you to be happy! You deserve it more than anyone I know."

Emotion clogged his chest. "You make me happy, Jess." He reached out and touched her cheek. "Come back to Dallas with me."

Tears rolled down her cheeks. "I can't."

"My condo's big enough for both of us. Hell, it's big enough for you and me and half the neighborhood. We're good together. Say you'll come home with me."

She just shook her head.

Anger seeped back in. "Fine. I'm going for a walk. I need some air. My revolver's on the side table. Consider it a gift. I won't be gone long." He had to get out of there, had to get himself back together. "Lock the door behind me."

Grabbing his down jacket off the coat rack, he shrugged it on over the Glock at his waist and walked out into the hall, heading for the stairs instead of the elevator.

Jessie had said she loved him. Well, he sure as hell loved her. But she didn't want him—not enough.

As he walked out into a cold day and icy wind, his resolve strengthened. He'd made a fool of himself, but he was through with that now.

Pulling up the collar on his jacket, Bran shoved his hands into his pockets and kept walking.

JESSIE HEARD THE doorbell ring. Hallie had called. She was downtown and wanted to stop by. Jessie dried her eyes and went over to check the peephole. Turning the dead bolt, she opened the door.

Hallie took one look at her pale, tear-ravaged face and pulled her into a hug. "It's all right, sweetie. Hallie's here. Everything's going to be okay."

Her throat ached. Jessie sniffed back tears. "I'm sorry. Everything's just so screwed up." She held on to her best friend's hand as they walked over and sat down on the sofa.

"Bran's upset. Everything's a mess. I'm really glad you came over."

"Me, too. Now...tell me what's going on."

Jessie sighed. "Brandon asked me to go back to Dallas and live with him."

Hallie grinned. "That's great!"

"No, it's not."

"Why not? You're crazy about him. An idiot can see that."

"I'm in love with him." Her eyes burned. "God, I love him so much." She wiped at the tears slipping down her cheeks.

"I don't get it. If you love him, what's the problem?"

"The problem is I can't handle the kind of life he lives. Bran's a warrior. He thrives on danger. The jobs he takes? He could be killed at any time. I've had enough of death. My mom, my brother, my father. I want a man who's going to live till he's ninety. Someone who'll be there for me, our kids, and our grandkids."

Hallie squeezed her hand and rose from the sofa. "I'm making us some jasmine tea. Then we'll talk."

Setting out Jessie's antique porcelain teapot and gold-rimmed cups and saucers, she filled the kettle and set it on the stove. When the tea was ready, she carried the tray into the living room, rested it on the coffee table, and poured them each a cup.

"Thanks." Jessie added a lump of sugar and took a sip.

Hallie sipped her tea, then set the cup back in its saucer. "You said you loved Brandon. Does he love you?"

"He didn't say, but…"

"Yes or no."

"I think he loves me. For a guy like him, it was huge to ask me to move to Dallas with him."

"You said before he was too honorable to cheat on you."

She toyed with the delicate handle on the cup. "Danny said he wasn't a one-man woman, but Bran's older now. I don't believe he'd cheat."

"You need to think this through, Jess. You're afraid Brandon's line of work will get him killed. But your mom died of a stroke. True, your brother was killed in the army, but your dad was murdered. It shouldn't have happened but it did."

Hallie set her cup and saucer down on the coffee table. "What I'm trying to say is there's no way to know who's going to live, who's going to die, or when it's going to happen. If you love someone, you have to hold on to them with everything you've got. Hiding yourself away, hoping nothing bad will happen, isn't going to work. You might as well be happy with someone you love for as long as you can."

Jessie just sat there. It made sense. How could it possibly make sense?

"Danny was killed in the same battle as Brandon," Hallie went on. "Danny died. Brandon lived. Your father had been out of the fighting for years. But he still died too soon. Don't you see?"

She looked at Hallie, her heart beginning to thrum with a feeling of hope. "Oh, God. What if you're right?"

"About living and dying? I am right. I can't tell you what you should do, but you need to think about it. Think really hard, Jess. If Brandon is anything like Ty, he guards his feelings. He isn't the kind of man who would fall in love easily, and if I'm right, he won't fall out easily, either."

Jessie's teacup rattled in her lap. "I rejected him, Hallie. I don't think he's the kind of guy who forgives easily, either."

"If he loves you, he'll forgive you." Hallie rose and so did Jessie. "I've got to go. We're on an eleven-thirty American flight to LAX day after tomorrow. I've got a couple of things to pick up for the kids, then I need to pack, get back to Evergreen, and get everyone organized." She grinned. "I'm so excited."

Jessie smiled. "I'm really glad it's working out for you and Ty."

"Me, too. We're already practically living together and Ty wants more. We just seem to click. I've got the greatest guy and two super-great kids—and I owe it all to you."

Jessie walked Hallie to the door, leaned over and hugged her. "Thanks for the advice."

Hallie smiled. "What are friends for?" Turning, she headed into the hall, waving as she hurried for the elevator.

Jessie closed the door and turned the lock, her mind spinning with what her friend had said. She was in love with Brandon. Was she brave enough to risk losing him in order to share a life with him? She couldn't stand the thought of him being killed, but losing him now was nearly as painful. And as Hallie had said, there was no way to know the future.

She was picking up the cups and saucers, carrying the tray into the kitchen, when she heard the sound of shattering glass in the bedroom. *Dear God!*

She knew exactly who it was, and fear shot through her. Setting down the tray, she ran for the side table and grabbed the revolver, whirled and pointed it two-handed toward the open bedroom door.

Her heart was racing, her legs trembling. Jessie steeled herself. Bracing her feet slightly apart, she took careful aim as the man of her nightmares strolled into the living room.

HIS JAW CLENCHED in resignation, Bran climbed the stairs back to Jessie's third-floor apartment. He was done. Finished. He loved Jessie, but it wasn't enough. It was time to go back to Dallas. He'd hire twenty-four-hour protection till Ray Cummings was back in custody.

He topped the last stair and headed down the hall. Who had he been kidding? Getting out of Jessie's life was the best thing for both of them. He was supposed to be protecting Danny's sister—not falling in love with her.

He pulled out the key she had given him and unlocked the door. As his fingers circled the knob, the muffled sound of a man's voice reached him.

"Put the gun down, Jessica. We both know you aren't going to shoot me."

Fucking Ray Cummings. Fury burned through him. Reaching beneath his jacket, he drew his Glock from the holster on his belt. Icy calm settled over him the way it always did, his mind sharpening, senses honing, giving him the control he needed. He quietly turned the knob and eased the door open a crack.

Jessie stood in the living room, his revolver gripped in both her hands. "Leave, Ray. Do it now, while you still have the chance. Come one step closer, I'll pull the trigger."

Cummings stood in the bedroom doorway, six feet tall, dark brown hair, a nasty smirk on his face. He was pointing a big semiauto at Jessie. It was all Bran could do not to just shoot him.

"I've got a gun, too, Jessica," Cummings said. "Put your pistol down and I won't have to use it."

"I'll shoot, Ray. I swear to God I will."

"We both know what happened in that basement. How you wanted it, just like the others. You shouldn't have run, Jessica. If you'd stayed, I would have given it to you, just like you wanted."

"You're insane."

"Put down the gun, sweetheart, and come to Jordy. We'll finish what we started."

Bran kicked the door open with his boot, his Glock aimed center mass at Cummings's chest. "She won't have to kill you, Cummings. It'll give me great pleasure to take care of it for her."

"Brandon…" The hand that held the pistol eased to her side.

"Get out of the way, Jess. Let me finish this."

Her gaze snapped to his. "No, Bran! You can't just kill him!"

Bullshit. He wanted Cummings dead, wanted Jessie safe. His finger tightened on the trigger.

"Don't, Brandon, please!"

She didn't want him to kill the prick. His jaw tightened. He'd told her he could change. He looked at Cummings. Hesitated. Maybe there was another way.

Cummings's hand moved. Bran saw it an instant too late. A gunshot cracked, a thunderclap in the confines of the small apartment. *Jessie!* Then Cummings hit the floor.

Jessie dropped the pistol, turned and ran straight into his arms.

"Easy." Bran holstered his weapon and his arms tightened around her. He didn't let her go. "It's all right, baby. Everything's okay."

She looked up at him with tears in her eyes. "You waited. Why did you wait? You could have been killed."

He kissed the top of her head. "I didn't want to disappoint you."

"Oh, God." She hugged him harder. "You could never disappoint me, Brandon. Never."

He kissed her quick and hard, set her away, and went to see about scumball Ray Cummings. As he knelt to assess the wound, he looked back at Jessie. "Your shot missed the heart. You didn't kill him."

"I didn't miss. I didn't kill him because I wanted to so badly."

He almost smiled.

"I'll call 911." While Jessie went to make the call, he grabbed a towel and used it to slow the flow of blood.

Jessie made another call, this one to Detective D'Marco Porter. "Ray Cummings is on the floor of my living room. He's bleeding from a bullet to the chest that came from my pistol."

Porter said something, then Jessie ended the call and turned to Bran. "The police have been dispatched. Detective Porter is on his way."

Bran pressed harder on the wound. "He's losing a lot of blood. Grab another towel, will you?"

"Or maybe we should just let him bleed out."

This time he did smile. "There's my girl."

Shaking her head, Jessie went after more towels.

Cummings was still breathing when the ambulance hauled his sorry ass away. Porter and another detective took his and Jessie's statements, then, finally, they were alone.

"I shouldn't have left you the way I did," Bran said, pacing over to the window, his hands on his hips. "The bastard could have killed you."

"I don't think so. If anyone was going to die today, it was Ray Cummings."

He turned to look at her. "Yeah?"

"That's right." She walked up to him. "And if you can forgive me for being such a coward before, I'd love to accept your invitation and go to Dallas with you."

His chest clamped down. He started to shake his head. It was over. Jessie was right—it would never work.

He felt her hand on his cheek, drawing his attention. "I know you. I know the man you are. I trust you to handle whatever your job requires. I'm not afraid anymore."

"Jessie…"

"Do you love me, Brandon?"

He couldn't lie to her. Not about something so important. "I should have told you. I wanted to. You're not the only coward."

She smiled up at him. "You're the bravest man I've ever known. You're the man I love. I want us to make a life together."

Something was opening inside him. Something warm that felt like the sun shining on his heart. He wanted what she was offering, wanted it so badly.

He drew her in front of him, set his hands at her waist. "You really think Danny would be okay with us being together?"

Jessie smiled at him so sweetly his chest ached. "If he saw us together, yes, I really do."

The tension slid out of his shoulders and a feeling settled over him that felt like coming home. She wanted to be with him. He could make it work, have the woman he loved. A woman who also loved him.

"So…ah…you're moving to Dallas?"

She smiled. "Looks that way."

Bran felt the biggest grin sliding across his face. Dipping his head, he very thoroughly kissed her.

CHAPTER THIRTY-EIGHT

RAY CUMMINGS WAS on his way back to prison—this time for good, according to Detective Porter. His history of psychiatric disorders wasn't enough to get him released again.

A phone call Jessie received from Special Agent Tripp said Andrew Horton was still on the run, but the CID and Homeland had made some progress on the buyer of the second batch of chemicals.

"Looks like they were purchased by a different branch of the *sawt Allah*. A cell closer to home, we think. We haven't made any arrests yet, but we're getting there."

"Thank you for letting me know," Jessie said.

"If it weren't for you, we'd still be back at square one."

The CID was interrogating Holloway. They were looking for Horton and the rest of the stolen munitions. Cummings was back in prison, no longer a threat.

Which meant it was time to let the army take over, and Brandon could go back to Dallas, a thought that, even a few days ago, would have been heartbreakingly painful. Now, instead of never seeing him again, Jessie was going with him.

"Are you sure?" he'd asked. Standing in her living room, his hands settled on her waist as he looked down at her. "I want you to be happy, Jess. I'll do everything in my power to make that happen, but I need you to be sure."

"I was afraid of losing you. After facing Cummings and

my worst fears, I'm not a victim anymore and I never will be again." She gave him a saucy smile. "Which means you don't have to worry about needing to use the handcuffs."

His lips twitched. "Oh, I don't know about that. I was kind of looking forward to it."

Jessie laughed.

Bran kissed her. "I called Reese, got him to send the jet. It'll be here late tomorrow morning. We'll be going back in style, baby."

"No matter what happens, life with you will never be dull."

"Same goes, honey."

She and Hallie talked several times.

"I hate to see you go," Hallie said, "but you're doing the right thing."

"I know. I feel it every time I look at Bran."

"You're leaving for Dallas tomorrow, right? About the same time we are?"

"That's right."

"Maybe we could meet somewhere in the terminal, get a chance to say goodbye before you leave."

"I would love that. But we're flying back in the Garrett Resources jet." She laughed. "Can you believe they have their own jet?"

"Wow."

"Yeah, I know. The thing is, we'll be flying out of the executive terminal so we won't be close enough to meet. But we're coming back in two weeks. We'll make a date for sure, something with the kids that we can all do together."

"That would be so great."

"Have fun at Disneyland."

The next morning, leaving her Honda in the garage beneath her apartment building, they were packed and ready to leave. They would be coming back after Thanksgiving to load up the stuff in her apartment and officially make the move. As a journalist she could work out of a home office, or maybe she would rent space in an office building so she could meet some people and get to know her way around the city.

Though she would miss the mountains and all of her friends, from a career standpoint, the move was exciting. She figured just story ideas she got from The Max could keep her busy for weeks.

"Time to go," Bran said.

A limo was waiting for the trip to the airport, a big black Cadillac Denali SUV. The driver, a blond man who flashed a mouth full of white-capped teeth, opened the car door and Jessie slid into the backseat.

Bran slid in beside her. "I can't wait to see the look on my family's faces when I walk in with you on Thanksgiving Day."

She was excited to meet the rest of his family and friends. "You really think Chase will be surprised?"

"I think he and Harper will be happy. They seem to want everyone to end up in the married state." His beautiful blue eyes locked on her face. "Not that I'm trying to rush you or anything."

She leaned up and kissed him. "You are the most amazing man. I can't imagine how I ever said no to you."

They pulled into the Signature Executive Terminal and the black SUV rolled to a stop. The driver opened the rear passenger door, then went around to the back, unloaded their luggage, and set it on the asphalt.

Bran's cell phone rang.

Jessie's heart jerked and nearly stopped when emergency alarms all over the airport started shrieking and the entire terminal erupted in chaos.

"BRAN, IT'S TY. I got trouble."

His fingers tightened around the phone. "Alarms are going off everywhere. What the hell's going on?"

"Hostage situation. We're in Concourse A, gate 48, down at the far end. They've got pallets of munitions set all around this end of the terminal. They're wired with explosives, Bran."

"Jesus."

"They took all the cell phones, but I gave them Chris's and hid mine."

"Make sure it's set on vibrate."

"It's done."

"Just keep a low profile and do what they say. I'll assess the situation and figure my best approach. I'm not that far away, but I'll need intel. How many of them are there? Where are they? How are they armed? Anything you can tell me will help."

"I'll call you back."

Bran grabbed his gear bag off the asphalt, tossed it into the backseat of the SUV, and slammed the door.

"Was that Ty?" Jessie asked anxiously, hurrying along beside him. "What's going on?"

"My guess, we've found the chemical weapons."

"Oh, my God." The alarms were deafening. Distant police sirens, racing toward the terminal, had joined the cacophony.

"Ty needs help. I've got to go." Bran kissed her quick and hard. "I love you, baby."

"No! Don't you dare say that to me now! You can say it when this is over!"

Bran just leaned down and kissed her again. With emergency sirens blaring, the limo driver was back in the driver's seat, getting ready to leave. Bran hauled him out of the car and took his place behind the wheel.

"Wait a minute!" the driver yelled.

Bran ignored him. Jamming the car in Reverse, he started backing up when the passenger door flew open and Jessie slid into the seat.

"You can't come, Jess! Not this time! You'll only be in the way."

"Drive," she said, strapping on her seat belt. "I won't go in with you, but those are my friends, too. I'll do whatever you need done."

He swore foully, slammed the SUV into Drive, and the vehicle heaved forward, tires screeching as the Denali blasted across the parking lot, jumped the curb, and charged onto the jet runway leading from the executive terminal to Concourse A.

"Call 911," he said. "Tell them you're at the airport. Tell them there's an army ranger named Tyler Folsom among the passengers in Concourse A who can provide intel on the hostage-takers. Tell them Brandon Garrett, former Special Forces, is heading inside. Get a name, someone you can talk to. Get his direct line and tell them I'll call him back."

She did exactly what he told her. She was calm and completely in control. She was there to help, and he was suddenly glad to have her with him.

"Tell Sergeant Ramirez that Brandon will call him directly," she said, and ended the call. "Ramirez is SWAT. They're en route." She entered the sergeant's number into his cell and set it on the center console.

The SUV roared down the runway. Bran dodged a light jet coming in for a landing, swerving around it as the plane touched down and rolled toward the executive terminal. Nothing else was moving. The small jet appeared to be the last plane cleared, the rest in a holding pattern or being rerouted.

As he neared Concourse A, Jessie went to Google Maps on her cell phone, which displayed the satellite image of the runway they were traveling at breakneck speed, and the layout of the concourse.

"Which gate?" she asked.

"Forty-eight."

She magnified the map. "That's the terminal up ahead. You need to turn left before you get there. That'll put you on the south side of the building. Gate 48 is at the east end, closest to us. You need to be careful they don't see you driving past."

He turned before he got close enough to be spotted through the big plate glass windows, drove west, then turned north again.

"How are you getting in?" Jessie asked.

"Working on it," he said. SWAT wasn't there yet. Airport security didn't have enough manpower to cover the whole place—good news for him at the moment. He needed to get inside unseen.

The terminal loomed ahead. He pulled up next to an Airbus A330 docked at what the map showed as gate 46, and parked the black Denali beneath the wing.

"Get behind the wheel." He got out and opened the rear passenger door, unzipped his gear bag and armed himself: his Glock 9 mil, a .380 S&W semiauto in an ankle holster instead of the .38 revolver still in police custody. A Ruger .45 semiauto backup piece, clipped to his belt behind his back, a six-inch folding knife in one pocket, and an extra 9 mm mag in the other.

His cell rang. *Ty.* "It's bad, Bran. There are at least four pallets of munitions positioned around this end of the terminal, and each is heavily wired with explosives."

"There's probably more." A total of three thousand pounds, the amount stolen and still missing from the plant. Way overkill, to say the least. But the goal of a terrorist was to make history. To destroy the US economy and cause international chaos. "The bad news is those canisters are filled with mustard gas."

"Holy shit, Bran."

"How many terrorists?"

"I counted eight, before three of them disappeared. There's one guarding each of the pallets and one roaming around, keeping track of everyone. They're all heavily armed and carrying AK-47 assault rifles."

"Middle Eastern?"

"Yeah. They're bearded, wearing robes."

"How many hostages?"

"At least two hundred and fifty. People getting ready to board different flights when these guys showed up. With airport personnel, passengers, including women and children, it might be more than that. They've got us sitting on the floor all over this end of the terminal, a bunch of people grouped together in the middle of the corridor."

"Where are you?"

"I got Hallie and the kids as far away as I could manage. We're sitting behind a row of seats on the west end of the group."

"I'm on my way. Don't worry if you don't see me."

Ty made a sound that held a trace of humor. Bran had always had a knack for blending in, becoming practically invisible. With that many hostages, he couldn't go in full

commando. He needed to be just another passenger, someone who didn't draw attention.

Ty ended the call to conserve the battery, and Bran
turned to Jessie, now in the driver's seat.

"As soon as I'm inside, pull back to where it's safe. Get
Ramirez on the line and bring him up to speed. Tell him
I'll have intel when I call. Advise him we're likely dealing
with mustard gas. If I can find a way to get Hallie and the
kids out, I'll need you to be there for transport."

"Just let me know where you want me to be."

He cupped her face and leaned in for a final quick kiss.
"Stay safe, baby." Slinging his gear bag over his shoulder,
he moved away, silently heading for the doors on ground
level below the gates where the passengers boarded the
planes.

Where terrorists now held two hundred and fifty innocent people hostage, the threat of deadly explosives and
chemical weapons hanging over their heads.

JESSIE SAT RIGIDLY in the driver's seat. She'd been able to
hold it together until Bran had slipped away to scout the
area around the terminal before he went in to face the hell
that waited inside.

Now her hands were shaking so badly she could barely
put the car in reverse. He was heading into danger. He could
very well be killed.

Or he could find a way to help Ty and Hallie, Chris and
little Sarah. He could help save hundreds of people's lives.

Her breath trembled out. It was what Bran Garrett did.
He protected people, as he had protected her. He risked his
life for those less able. He was good at it. Better than good.
One of the best in the world.

And she loved him for it. She loved him, and even as

she stared at the possibility of his death inside the terminal, she knew that being with him was worth the risk. As her mother had accepted her father's role as a soldier and loved him every day they shared together, Jessie was prepared to love Brandon every day of their lives.

Taking a deep breath, she steadied her grip on the wheel. Just like Bran, she had work to do. Turning the car around, she headed back the way they had come, careful to keep out of sight until she reached a spot a safe distance away.

There she would wait. Until this was over, she would be there for Bran, the way he was always there for her.

WITH SIRENS HOWLING, evacuation orders blaring, and people trying to get out of the airport, most of those on the lower floor had already fled. Just a few stragglers, shoving through the glass doors, running in the opposite direction, away from the danger.

The lower level entrances were used to bring in supplies and equipment. Bran figured that was likely the way the terrorists had accessed the concourse, as employees who worked in terminal support. Vetting people who worked at the big international airports was a nightmare.

After a check of the area, he returned to the door leading to the lower level. No one remained on the other side of the glass as he approached and shoved the door open. He figured the missing three terrorists were somewhere down here, patrolling the lower level corridors in case of an assault.

He picked a spot out of sight, stripped off his down jacket, leaving him in a dark blue Henley, jeans, and low-topped leather boots. Unzipping his gear bag, he took out his Colt AR-15 full-auto assault rifle, illegal as hell, and set it to bursts of three. He'd never fired it in the States, hoped he'd never have to. The suppressor would cut the sound, but not completely.

Lots of goodies in the bag—spare ammo, flash grenades, tactical vest, his Ka-Bar knife—if he could get back to where he left them. He stuffed a spare .380 mag in the inside pocket of the jacket and zipped it as much as he could, draped the jacket over the rifle, stashed the bag out of sight, and went hunting.

FIGHTING HARD NOT to show her fear, Hallie sat on the floor, her legs curled beneath her, one of the kids on each side, tucked under her arms. Chris's face was pale, his child-size folding wheelchair abandoned a few feet away. Sarah's blue eyes were huge and glassy with tears.

"Everything's going to be okay, sweetheart," Hallie said, giving them both a hug. "Your daddy's here. He won't let anyone hurt you." She had always loved kids. She had fallen madly in love with Ty's.

Sarah looked up at her, her bottom lip trembling. "Those men look really mean."

"We just need to do what they say and we'll be okay."

"Dad was a ranger," Chris said. "He can protect us."

Ty leaned over and spoke to him softly. "I'm going to need your help with that, son. All right?"

Chris nodded solemnly.

"They're the bad guys. We don't tell them I'm a ranger. We don't tell them anything."

"Okay."

Both kids had long ago accepted Ty as their father. It was easy to see how much he loved them. He would die for his family, Hallie knew, which now included her. Her throat tightened. *Please, God, keep all of us safe.*

The kids lapsed into silence. One of the terrorists, the

man she had dubbed Snake because he slipped silently around watching everyone, walked toward them. He was tall and thin, with high cheekbones and slashing black eyebrows. He was young and handsome and wearing a long white robe. Unlike the other two that she had seen up close, he was clean-shaven, while they had short-cropped beards and wore black slacks and white shirts.

Ty eased the phone beneath his thigh as the man approached, a long-fingered hand on the assault rifle across his chest. Long-lashed black eyes surveyed the people huddled on the floor. The absolute power he was feeling registered in every line of his face.

Hallie kept her gaze down and so did Ty, and the terrorist turned and slithered away.

"What do you think they'll want in exchange for letting us go?" she asked Ty.

Something flashed in his eyes before he hid it behind lowered lids. "Maybe they want a prisoner exchange. Some of their guys for us. There's a plane sitting right there. They'll probably make that part of the deal. They get what they want, then we're free to leave."

Hallie managed to nod. But that single glimpse into Ty's mind told her he didn't believe they intended to let them go. They were going to detonate the bombs. The terrorists were planning to kill them.

CHAPTER THIRTY-NINE

BRAN'S CELL PHONE VIBRATED. He saw the number Jessie had entered and hit the button. "Ramirez?"

"That's right. SWAT's here. We're moving into position. What can you tell us?"

He relayed Ty's location at gate 48, intel about the number of terrorists and the pallets loaded with munitions and wired with explosives. Ty's estimated number of hostages.

"What are their terms?" Bran asked.

"The leader's a guy named Sadiq Nazari. Claims dozens of Yemenis are being tortured in secret facilities in Yemen by the United Arab Emirates. He says the US is aiding the UAE with weapons and intelligence. They want the Pentagon to force the Saudis to release the prisoners, some fifty-five of them. That, and he and his men want to fly off in one of the planes parked at the end of the concourse."

"The US doesn't negotiate with terrorists."

"If their demands aren't met, he's going to blow three thousand pounds of chemical weapons sky-high, killing hundreds of people and pleasing Allah."

Bran scrubbed a hand over his jaw. "I'm not seeing this going down any way but bad."

"Near as we can tell, Nazari's the guy in control of the bombs. We think they're designed to be set off by his cell phone. The negotiator will keep him talking as long as he can. My SWAT guys are good, better than good. We're setting up to go in and take these pricks out. We want to do it with the fewest possible casualties. With inside help, we might have a chance to make it work."

Bran spotted a long shadow approaching. "Gotta go." He hit the end button and ducked out of sight, took out his six-inch folding knife and flipped it open.

As the terrorist walked in front of him, he locked an arm around the guy's neck, hauled him back a few paces, and sliced the blade across his throat. He held on until the body went limp, then dragged it out of sight behind a line of equipment. With the hum of the machinery aiding his escape, he moved silently off down the passage.

The corridor stretched ahead. There was a lot of equipment down here, the steady whine muffling his footsteps. It also hid the steps of his quarry. He found a place where he could hoist himself up and look over the false walls to see what lay ahead.

A bearded man in black slacks and a white shirt, an assault rifle across his chest, stood beside two more pallets of munitions, five hundred pounds apiece, the last of the chemical weapons. There were wheels on the pallet, and an iron tongue for towing, which was probably how they'd gotten the weapons into position. The tarp that had covered it lay on the floor a few feet away, leaving the brass canisters exposed. Explosives covered the weapons, connected by a maze of red and yellow wires.

Bran eased back down and found a spot to wait. Noticing a pebble on the floor, he picked it up and tossed it down the corridor. It clattered as it landed, and the bearded man went on alert.

No way to get near enough to use his knife. As the man rounded the corner, Bran fired a quick burst of three, spraying bullets across the terrorist's chest. The guy made a gurgling sound, his legs crumpled, and he went down.

Bran moved on.

JESSIE RAISED HER hands as she got out of the SUV, her cell phone tucked into the pocket of her jeans. SWAT vehicles surrounded the far end of the concourse. Police cars, uniformed officers, SWAT vehicles, people in hazmat suits.

A man dressed in camo and a tactical vest strode toward her, early forties, hard features, bulky in the chest and shoulders, a trace of silver in his hair.

"Victor Ramirez, Denver SWAT. You're Jessie Kegan?"

"That's right."

"Come with me."

She followed him to a portable command center being set up on the tarmac, a huge motor home with antennas on top. As they stood next to the steps leading to the entrance, she could see her breath in the freezing air.

Wishing she had her gloves, she rubbed her hands together to keep them warm. "Have you talked to Brandon?"

"We connected. He's calling me back."

She looked over at the concourse, thought of Hallie, Ty, and the kids, and the terror of being held hostage.

"Anything I need to know about your friend, Garrett?"

She forced herself to focus. "Bran was Delta. He knows what he's doing." She had to hang on to that. She had to trust him to do what needed to be done and come out alive. If she couldn't do it now, there was no hope for them.

"And the guy in with the passengers?"

"Ty Folsom. Ty was a ranger. He's traveling with his girlfriend and his two kids. He won't leave them alone. That'll limit what he can do to help."

Ramirez nodded. He looked up as the door to the command center opened. "You might as well get inside the trailer, out of the cold."

She glanced back at the terminal. She wanted to be ready if Bran needed her, ready for Hallie and Ty and Chris and little Sarah. Unconsciously, her hand slid down to her cell phone. "I'll go inside in a minute."

THE THIRD MAN was shorter than the other two, and older, his beard longer. Bran watched him prowling the corridor, AK-47 strapped to his chest. He opened the door to an equipment room, disappeared inside, and reappeared seconds later. Bran eased back into the shadows, waiting for his prey, patient, listening, hearing the shuffle-glide of his feet on the concrete floor.

Bran counted the seconds, the cadence of the footfalls, calculating the time and distance to his arrival. His quarry paused, carefully checking for anyone who might be hiding. Anyone who might pose a threat.

Come on...come to Papa. He was close now. Bran could hear him breathing. He was nervous. His movements no longer rhythmical, but jerky, uncertain. He had figured it out, knew someone was there, behind a false wall that disguised an air-conditioning unit. The man stopped to aim his rifle.

Bran fired. Three short bursts, chest-high, right through the wall. He stepped into the passage, saw the man lying on the floor but still breathing, finished the job with another short burst. Then he moved on.

Three terrorists down. SWAT could enter through the lower level, spread out and make their way to various metal stairs leading up to the gate level, giving them at least three solid approaches.

He took out his phone to call Ramirez, but it vibrated before he had time to press the contact button.

Ty. "They're getting antsy. Haven't been able to reach the three men downstairs."

"They're enjoying their seventy-two virgins."

Ty grunted his approval. "They're sending a man down to check. He's heading for the stairs across from me, next to gate 47."

"Got it." Bran headed for the stairs next to the supply elevator he figured would be closest to the gate.

This guy wouldn't be as easy as the others. He'd be wary, ready for danger. Adrenaline pulsing. Anticipating the stalk. Eager for the kill.

Which could all be used against him. Bran waited as close as he could get to the bottom of the stairs, just a few feet away, out of sight around the first corner. His prey would just be gearing up, not quite ready for the hunt to begin.

Definitely not ready for it to end.

Footsteps rang on the metal stairs. He counted them down, *three, two, one.* Bran hit him like a tank crashing into a concrete barrier, body-slamming him into the wall, headbutting, plowing a fist into his ribs, breaking at least three. The guy's pretty face hit the floor, caving in one of his cheekbones and knocking him unconscious. Bran finished him with the knife, grabbed the terrorist's cell phone, and faded away.

SERGEANT RAMIREZ STRODE away from his men, back to where Jessie stood near the stairs to the command center, her hands shoved into the pockets of her puffy jacket.

"You were right," he said. "Garrett took out four of the terrorists—half what they had to start with. He's cleared a way for us to get inside the terminal. We're dispatching men now."

Her heart was beating too fast. She could hardly breathe. She took a deep breath and tried to control the fear squeezing her lungs.

"So you're going in?"

"We're moving into position. Nazari is holding on to a cell phone set to detonate the bombs if the Pentagon doesn't agree to his terms. Even if a sniper takes him out, he might have time to hit the send button and the bombs could explode."

Fear trembled through her, came out as a breath of white in the freezing air. So many lives at stake, hundreds of them. Ty and Hallie and the children. Brandon. Her heart squeezed. "What are you going to do?"

"We're setting up a signal that can block cell service for a mile in any direction." Ramirez's jaw hardened. "Nazari can hit the button, but the signal won't go through."

"How long will that take?"

"They're working on it." He looked at her hard. "You believe in God?"

She managed to nod.

"You might ask for a little help. We'll need all we can get to make this work."

Ramirez strode away, and Jessie started praying.

USING THE TAIL of his Henley to muffle his voice, Bran hit the call button on the terrorist's phone, putting him in contact with whoever picked up on the other end.

"The phones do not work well down here," he said in Arabic, tapping the cell and distorting the words so his voice couldn't be identified. "I will check, make sure there are no problems."

He killed the line. He'd bought a little time, not much. It wouldn't be long before they figured out half their men were dead.

He pushed open the service elevator doors and looked inside. The cage waited above, doors open on the gate level. He lifted the strap of his assault rifle over his head and set the gun on the floor, along with the extra magazine, pulled his jacket on to cover his weapons and the blood on his clothes.

Shoving his way into the elevator shaft, he climbed hand over hand up the side to the upper level, then lay on his stomach and crawled on top of the cage. Quietly lifting away the emergency exit panel gave him a bird's-eye view of the concourse.

He could see two of the four remaining terrorists, knew there were two more out of sight. He scanned the area and found Ty sitting on the floor behind a row of seats next to Hallie, the kids tucked between them, opposite the open elevator doors.

Ramirez had kept him informed. SWAT would be arriving any minute, dispersing quietly below, getting ready to make their assault. A perimeter had been set up outside, snipers had at least two of the terrorists in their sights.

Army Special Forces were being helicoptered in, but they wouldn't get there in time. Men from the Alamo Depot had been dispatched to handle the munitions—assuming the terrorists weren't able to explode them.

His phone vibrated. "It's a go," Ramirez said.

Everything happened at once. Shots slammed through the big plate glass windows and passengers screamed as two of the terrorists went down to sniper fire. People started running. SWAT burst onto the floor through the equipment-room doors, firing a barrage of bullets, taking the other two terrorists out.

It was over in minutes. If the leader had pushed the button to set off the explosives, it had been blocked.

Bran jumped down through the open panel in the elevator roof. Just outside the open doors, police swarmed the gate area, shouting orders, herding terrified passengers away from the scene to safety.

Bran spotted Ty and strode toward him, shouldering his way through the mass of humanity rushing to get out of the terminal.

He glanced around. Police and SWAT were everywhere, a group of them directing people down the concourse toward the exits. The bomb squad had arrived. Apparently the devices were rudimentary because the explosives were defused in minutes. Still, it was going to take hours to get the airport back up and running.

"Come on," Bran said as he reached his friend. "We're getting out of here." Ramirez and the mass of law enforcement descending on the building wouldn't like it, but he and Ty had done their part. The rest was just cleanup.

Lifting Chris, Bran set the little boy in his wheelchair while Ty swung Sarah up on his shoulders and reached down for Hallie's hand. Their carry-on luggage sat forlornly a few feet away, but getting to safety was more important.

Bran pushed the wheelchair into the service elevator, and as soon as everyone was inside, he closed the doors. Hallie hit the button for the lower level, and the hydraulic motor started whining its decent.

"Everybody okay?" he asked.

Ty clapped him on the shoulder. "Thanks, man."

Hallie reached up to tearfully hug him. "Thank you."

Bran just nodded. As soon as the doors slid open and

they were headed for the lower level exit, Bran phoned Jessie. "Hey, baby. Any chance you could come pick us up?"

"Oh, my God, are you kidding? Where are you?"

"We're exiting through the same door where you dropped me off."

"I'm on my way. I love you."

"Yeah, me, too." He was saving the words. He wanted to do it right this time. He thought about what Jessie would do if the cops tried to stop her from coming to pick them up. He was pretty sure she'd be there.

Bran wasn't surprised to see the big black Cadillac SUV racing toward them across the tarmac. The vehicle roared up and slid to a stop, the driver's door flew open, and Jessie ran toward him.

Bran swept her into his arms.

IT WAS FREEZING, the icy wind whipping her clothes, but Jessie didn't care. Brandon was there and he was safe. Ty and Hallie, Chris and Sarah were safe. The passengers in the terminal were safe.

Bran's arms tightened around her. His cheek was cold against hers as he buried his face in her hair. She could feel him trembling.

"It's okay," she said. "It's over." She held on tighter, slid her fingers into the soft brown strands curling at the nape of his neck. "Everything's okay."

He took a deep breath and eased a little away, but he didn't let her go. "Sorry. I didn't mean to do that. It always takes me a while to come down after a mission."

"Oh, honey." The darkness was back in his eyes, his jaw rigid as steel. The hard edge was part of him, she now knew, part of who he was. He was meant to do what he did. She knew that now, accepted it.

She wouldn't change him. Not a single thing about him. She loved him exactly the way he was.

She went back into his arms and held him tight. She didn't ask him what had happened in there. He would tell her when he was ready. Or maybe he never would.

It didn't matter. He had done what he had to. People were alive because of what he'd done.

He kissed her softly. "I love you," he said. "So much."

Her heart squeezed at the emotion in his beautiful blue eyes. "I love you, too." She touched his cheek. "Thank you for being who you are."

He looked at her and the tension seeped out of his tall, solid body. Ty and his family were already in the vehicle, the engine still running.

Bran leaned down and kissed her. "Let's go home."

CHAPTER FORTY

JESSIE AWOKE IN a tangle of arms and legs, Bran still sleeping soundly beside her. Lying there in his big king-size bed, her mind went back to the events of the night before, the terrible danger and heart-stopping fear, the pent-up emotions that had led to hours of wild, passionate lovemaking. A night free from any taint of the past.

Jessie smiled and closed her eyes, snuggled a little closer to Bran, dozed again, and didn't stir until just before noon when her cell phone started ringing. She grabbed it off the nightstand, looked down and recognized the caller ID, sat up on the edge of the bed.

"Special Agent Tripp," she said, her voice still a little thick with sleep.

"I've got news you'll want to hear," Tripp said.

Bran sat up yawning, rubbing his bare chest as he swung his legs to the bedside next to her.

"Bran's here. I'm putting you on speaker." She hit the button and Tripp's voice came through loud and clear.

"I heard what you did at the airport, Captain. Off the record, of course." Bran had insisted on remaining anonymous, and so far the army had managed to keep it that way. "Thanks for your help."

"I just did what I was trained for."

"A lot of us consider it far more than that."

Bran said nothing.

"I called to let you know General Samuel Holloway has officially been arrested. He's been charged with treason, larceny, espionage, and a long list of crimes that include conspiracy to commit murder."

"He confessed?" Jessie asked.

"In a manner of speaking. Presented with the evidence and facing the possibility of life in prison without parole, Holloway rolled on Edgar Weaver. He pointed to Weaver as the man who arranged the hits on Wayne Coffman and Colonel James Kegan. He confessed to conspiring with Weaver in an attempt to murder Jessica Kegan and Captain Brandon Garrett."

"That's good work," Bran said.

"From what Holloway told us, he was okay with selling the chemical weapons out of the country. As far as he was concerned, it was just one terrorist killing another. He didn't know about the smaller sale of weapons or the attack planned on the Denver airport."

"Holloway was a well-respected general," Bran said. "Why did he do it? I realize his share of twenty-five mil is a shit ton of money, but still…"

"Apparently, the general wasn't happy with the progress of his career. He was still a lowly brigadier, not the two-or three-star general he was convinced he deserved to be. His wife had left him, his kids were overindulged pains in the ass. His personal life had turned to worms, and he wanted payback for all of it. This way he became a wealthy man, as well as secretly giving the army the middle finger. Just didn't work out the way he planned."

"What about Weaver?" Bran asked.

"Weaver is headed back to the maximum security side of ADMAX—where he'll be locked up twenty-three hours a day for the rest of his worthless life."

Jessie's eyes filled. Bran reached over and laced his fingers with hers. "I hope he and Weaver both rot in hell," he said.

Tripp made a sound of agreement. "Jessie?"

"I'm here."

"I want you to know your father's name has officially been cleared. The army thanks Colonel Kegan for his many years of outstanding service and regrets the loss of such a fine officer."

Her throat ached. "Thank you."

"One more thing," Tripp said. "Last night the police arrested Andrew Horton as he tried to leave the country. He was caught at the El Paso International Airport, trying to board a connecting flight to Guadalajara, Mexico. He won't be seeing the light of day for a long, long time."

Bran squeezed her fingers. "It's over, Jess."

"That's right," Tripp said. "Just let me know if there's anything I can ever do for either one of you."

When the call ended, Bran pulled Jessie into his arms. "Thanks to you, your dad's name has been cleared. He can rest easy now."

And knowing she hadn't failed him, Jessie felt lighter, as if the burden she had been carrying had finally been lifted.

She wiped a tear from her cheek, looked up at Bran, and smiled. "So...after all the excitement, are you sure life with me won't seem boring?"

Bran just laughed. "Not a chance."

EPILOGUE

THE SMOKY AROMA of barbecue brisket, Texas-style, floated on the air. It was a warm April Sunday in Dallas, the perfect time for a Garrett family and friends get-together.

The barbecue was at Chase and Harper's new home in Old Preston Hollow, a charming older custom ranch with molded ceilings, overhanging porches, and lots of paned glass windows. A good house for kids, Chase had said.

Bran stood on the pool deck next to Hawk, Jaxon Ryker, and Jonah Wolfe while Chase grilled the meat. The house was great, but it was the three-acre property less than a twenty-minute drive from the city that had made the sale. Vast stretches of lush green lawn shaded by ancient oaks, brick walkways lined with flowers, even its own little creek.

Beneath the wide, covered patio, Jessie, Harper, Kate, Mindy, and Reese's date, Fiona St. James, were laughing as they set the table with plastic plates, paper napkins, and red Solo cups.

Jessie glanced Bran's way and their eyes met. The smile she gave him was so bright and filled with love it made his chest ache. She was happy. Besides adoring her like a lovestruck fool, he had given her the thing she wanted most. A family.

Her mom and dad were gone, her brother, Danny. But Bran, Chase, Reese, Harper, Kate, Hawk, and everyone who worked at The Max had accepted her as if they had known her forever. They loved her.

And Jessie loved them right back.

She sauntered up to him, slid her arms around his waist, leaned up, and kissed him. "I'm starving. How much longer?"

He flicked a glance at Chase.

"Ten minutes," Chase said.

"I guess I can manage to wait."

Bran grinned. "Maybe I should drag you inside and *entertain* you until the food's ready."

She grinned back and fanned her cheeks. "You wicked, wicked man. Don't tempt me."

He laughed. She was wearing his engagement ring, a perfect diamond solitaire he had chosen to suit her small hand. They were getting married. Jessie wasn't the only one who was happy.

A lot had happened in the months since they had moved in together.

In San Diego, the FBI and Homeland had rounded up the last of the terror cell involved in the weapons sale to Yemen. Because of her cooperation and candor, Mara Ramos had been given a reduced sentence, three years instead of life in prison.

Ahmed Malik hadn't fared so well. He was in prison. *Somewhere*. Probably for the rest of his life.

Unfortunately, the Aryan Brotherhood gang members responsible for Colonel Kegan's death had never been identified. They were already in the army stockade so at least that was something.

Jessie was still writing, digging up interesting cases and trying to find answers. Her blog, Kegan's Korner, was growing by leaps and bounds. But an investigative journalist's job wasn't easy and sometimes, as he had learned, it could be dangerous.

No, their lives would never be boring.

"Brisket's done," Chase announced, stabbing the big

slab of perfectly browned beef and lifting it onto a serving tray. "Let's eat."

Though Jessie seemed happy in Dallas, Bran had been talking to Chase about opening a branch of Maximum Security in Denver. Colt Wheeler was interested. So was Lissa Blayne. Ty was a definite yes, and Jessie was eager to get back to her mountains.

He slid an arm around her shoulders as they walked together toward the table groaning under the weight of cold potato salad, spicy chili beans, garlic French bread, chocolate cake, and bottles of hearty red wine.

Reese sat down next to his current date, a tall, elegant blonde as fair and beautiful as he was dark and good-looking. Fiona was intelligent and friendly, but there was no fire in the way Reese looked at her. Clearly, they would never be more than friends with benefits.

Bran wished his brother could find someone to share his life, someone to love who would love him in return.

But Reese was a loner and not an easy man to handle.

Bran picked up his fork and had just dug into the delicious meal when his cell phone started ringing. The name came up Detective Heath Ford. He pressed the phone against his ear. "Hey, Heath. What's up?"

"Sorry to screw up your day, Bran, but your guy, Stan Wilton, just called 911. Cops are on the way to his house, but you mentioned you'd be working as his body man as soon as the Mavericks got back to Dallas. Stan's back and he's got trouble. Those death threats he was getting?"

"Yeah?"

"Someone broke into his condo and attacked him with a knife. Stan got lucky and managed to get away, but he's pretty shook up. I figured you'd want to know."

The tall, lanky NBA Mavericks' most valuable player

had been getting death threats from what appeared to be a Houston Rockets fan. The cops were on it, but so far they hadn't caught him.

Bran stood up from the table, the phone still pressed to his ear. "I'm on my way. Thanks for the heads-up, Heath."

"No problem. Good luck."

Jessie rose beside him as he slid the phone back in the pocket of his jeans. "Sorry, babe, I gotta go." He leaned over his plate and shoveled in a couple of forkfuls of beef, ignored the tempting glass of Chianti, and washed it down with a drink of water.

"What's going on?" Jessie asked.

"Stan Wilton's back in town. He was supposed to call me as soon as he got here, but he waited. Apparently, someone broke into his place and tried to stab him. Stan managed to get away, but so did his assailant. He needs protection and he needs it now."

He turned to the group who had all stopped eating and stared at him expectantly. "Sorry, guys. Gotta go to work." He glanced at Hawk and Kate. "Can you two take Jessie home?"

"No problem," Hawk and Kate said in unison.

Leaning down, he kissed Jessie long and deep. "I'll call you, let you know what's going on."

She rested her palm against his cheek. "Just stay safe."

He'd do his best. He had a woman he loved to come home to.

He waved as he headed for the bright red Stingray parked in front of the house. Adrenaline pumped as he slid behind the wheel, and his senses sharpened, honing in on the problems that lay ahead. Solving them was what he did. Bran fired the powerful engine and headed into battle.

* * * * *

AUTHOR'S NOTE

I HOPE YOU enjoyed Brandon and Jessie's story. In my next romantic thriller, Reese Garrett struggles with his unwanted attraction to his executive assistant, McKenzie Haines. It gets worse when Kenzie is accused of murder. Worse yet, when Reese risks his position as CEO of Garrett Resources to protect her.

Kenzie won't be safe until the real killer is found so they must work together—the last thing Reese wants to do.

I hope you'll watch for their story; and if you haven't read the other books in my Maximum Security series, *The Conspiracy* and *The Deception*, I hope you will.

Till then, all best and happy reading.

Kat

BEFORE NIGHTFALL

CHAPTER ONE

"Lissa? Lissa, it—it's Julie. I'm really sorry to bother you, but Raymond... Ray's in town. I haven't seen him in years and now he's here. He's on his way over—right now! I'm scared, Liss. He says he wants to see his kids. I don't know what to do."

With the phone gripped tightly in her hand, Lissa Blayne, a private detective at the Dallas branch of Maximum Security, rose behind her desk.

"I'm on my way," she said. "Just hang on until I get there. Where are the kids?"

"They're still in school. They'll be home any minute."

"Okay, just try to stay calm and I'll be there as fast as I can."

Julie Douglas was Lissa's best friend, had been since their freshman year at Pleasant View High School. They were an odd match, Julie born into an upper-middle-class family, while Lissa lived with her single mom, who had barely been able to keep a roof over their heads and food on the table.

Then Julie's family had moved to Houston in her senior year and the two of them had lost touch. They hadn't seen each other until Julie moved back to Dallas three years ago, where their friendship resumed as if they'd never been apart.

Lissa thought of Julie's frantic phone call. They had talked about her friend's disastrous first marriage and her abusive husband, Ray Spearman. He'd been out of her life for eight years. A month ago Julie had started receiving text messages, then a phone call demanding to see the children he had abandoned.

Julie believed he was dangerous.

Lissa believed in being prepared.

Opening the bottom drawer of her desk, she took her SIG Sauer P226 out of the metal gun safe and clipped the holster to the belt on her black stretch jeans. The SIG was Dallas PD standard issue, the same type of weapon she had used when she'd been a detective in the vice division. She'd only pulled it when absolutely necessary, but it always felt like an old friend in her hand.

She headed for the rear of the office, which was done in a Western theme, with lots of oak and burgundy leather, a perfect match for the rugged individuals who worked at The Max.

She detoured by the front desk to speak to the receptionist, Mindy Stewart.

"A friend of mine's in trouble, Min. Can you call Mack Handley at Dallas PD and cancel my three o'clock appointment?"

Being former DPD, Lissa got a lot of cooperation from the department. She was currently working with the mother of an overdose victim who had hired her to find the person who had sold her daughter the drugs.

"Don't worry," Mindy said, pushing her round tortoiseshell glasses up on her nose. "I'll take care of it. Just do whatever you need to."

They were close friends, as Lissa was with the rest of The Max crew—a mix of PIs, bounty hunters, and bodyguards. Most of them were former military or law enforcement, including Chase Garrett, the owner, and his brother, Brandon. Reese Garrett ran the oil and gas company the brothers owned that made them multi-millionaires.

Jaxon Ryker had been a navy SEAL, Jonah Wolfe was former DPD, and Jason Maddox had been Marine Special Ops.

"Thanks, kiddo," Lissa said to Mindy. "I owe you one."

Physically, the two women were exact opposites, Mindy petite and curvy with long dark hair and blue eyes, Lissa five-ten, lean and sinewy, with short blond hair and brown eyes.

Shoving out the back door into the summer heat, Lissa headed for her black Camaro. The color was a definite drawback this time of year, but the sexy design and powerful engine made it worth a little discomfort until the air conditioner kicked in and cooled the red leather interior.

She turned the air on full blast, fired the engine, and shot out of the parking lot, her mind returning to her friend. Julie had met her first husband in Houston, during her first year of college. Ray was handsome, the star quarterback of the Ravens football team, the hottest guy on campus.

Julie had been as impressed as the other girls. Lissa figured Ray Spearman—along with half the guys in school—had been equally impressed with Julie. With her long auburn hair and perfect figure, she had never lacked for male attention.

Ray, a born competitor, wanted to be the guy who scored—and eventually his practiced seduction worked. Julie got pregnant, upsetting both their plans. To make matters worse, both sets of parents had pressed for marriage, which lasted only long enough to produce a second child.

Drugs, alcohol, and Ray's spoiled, abusive behavior finally led to divorce, and not long after, he completely disappeared. Then last month, he had contacted her. Now he was in Dallas.

Julie had been terrified of Raymond during the years they were married. She was even more afraid of him now.

Lissa stepped on the gas.

COLT WHEELER DROVE his black Mustang up in front of the house on Loganwood Street, a simple gray-brick ranch-style with freshly painted white trim.

Until last month, Colt had been a ranger stationed at Fort Benning, Georgia. But injuries from an exploding IED had cost him an eye and left him riding a desk far too long.

He was out now, on his way back to his hometown of Denver, Colorado, to start a new life. But Dallas was along his route, and at least once a year, he stopped by to see the wife of a friend who'd been killed in Iraq.

Liam Douglas had been a ranger in the 75th Regiment, same as Colt. His dying wish was for Colt to look in on Julie and their two kids, make sure his family was okay. Liam had wanted to adopt Julie's children from her first marriage, but he needed the biological father's permission, and the ex-husband was nowhere to be found.

According to conversations Colt had had with Julie, Ray Spearman was a real a-hole. Liam would have made a great dad, but unfortunately he was dead, gone three years, leaving Julie and her kids once more alone.

Figuring he probably should have called first instead of just showing up, Colt turned off the engine, cracked a window for ventilation, and climbed out of the Mustang.

His knock on the door went unanswered. He knocked again, and someone lifted the curtain to see who was outside, then the door swung open.

"Colt!" Julie threw her arms around his neck in an un-expected greeting that put him on alert. "Thank God you're here. Come…come inside. Please."

Her face was pale and he could see the fear in her eyes. "What's happened? What's going on?"

Julie shut the door behind him. She was trembling. "My ex-husband was just here. I haven't seen him in almost eight years." She blew out a shaky breath. "Ray called a little while ago. He said he wanted to see his kids and he was coming right over. There was…there was something in his voice." She shook her head. "Something I remembered from when we were married. I—I didn't know what to do. Oh God, Colt."

His jaw felt tight. "He hit you?"

She took a deep breath. "Not this time, but I thought he was going to."

Colt's jaw tightened even more. He led her over to the beige tweed sofa in front of the TV and urged her to sit down. "Where are the kids?"

"I was afraid of what he might do, so as soon as they got home from school, I sent them over to the neighbor's."

"You tell them their dad was in town?"

"No. They've always been curious, but I've never told them much about him, just that we met in college, it didn't work out, and he left."

He nodded. "You still got that bottle of Jack Daniel's I brought the last time I was here?"

She pressed her lips together but it didn't stop them from trembling. "It's in the kitchen, top shelf in the cabinet over the sink."

"I'll be right back." Colt headed in that direction. He had visited Julie several times since the explosion that had taken his right eye, so the black patch and the scar along his jaw were no longer a shock. Even the kids didn't notice them anymore.

He poured some of the whiskey into a glass and carried it back into the living room. Julie's hand trembled as she took a swallow, then another.

"Better?"

She nodded.

"All right, then. Start at the beginning and tell me what's going on."

CHAPTER TWO

A CAR SAT in front of the house as Lissa approached. A shiny black Mustang. She slowed to look in the living room windows, saw the silhouette of someone too tall to be Julie. Probably Ray.

She kept driving, parked the Camaro in the alley and went in through the back gate, crossing the freshly mown lawn and quietly approaching the back door.

It was locked, so she found the key Julie hid in a planter on the patio beneath a blooming red geranium and used it to unlock the door. She could hear voices in the living room, one definitely male.

Ray. Lissa had hoped to be with Julie when her ex arrived. Now she was walking into what could be a very bad situation. From what Julie had said, Ray had hit her more than once and could be extremely violent. After the divorce, she'd gotten a restraining order against him, but with her ex-husband out of her life, it had expired years ago.

Lissa pulled out the SIG as she eased up behind a wall in the kitchen, then peered around the corner to get a look at the man in the living room. Standing with his hands on a pair of narrow hips and his long legs splayed, he was exactly as Julie had described him. Blond and blue-eyed, with the wide-muscled shoulders of the football player he had once been, though he was taller than Lissa had pictured him.

Julie must not have known about the accident that had taken out an eye and scarred his handsome face, but the black patch he wore did nothing to destroy his good looks—or the danger the man exuded. She could only catch a few muffled words, but there was no mistaking the hostile stance or the fury that oozed from every pore.

Gripping the semiauto in both hands, she stepped into the kitchen doorway, her legs braced slightly apart. "Raise your hands above your head! Do it now!"

Julie jumped to her feet. "Lissa, no! This isn't Ray! It's my friend, Colt Wheeler!"

With her adrenaline pumping, it took a moment for the words to sink in. Lissa waited to be sure Julie wasn't being coerced, then holstered her weapon. She noticed Wheeler had raised his big hands only as high as his shoulders. His good eye, a striking shade of blue, crinkled at the corner, and his lips curved in what could only be amusement.

"Okay to put my hands down now?" he asked, clearly enjoying himself. She wanted to walk over and wipe the smirk off his sexy face.

Instead, she ignored him. "Where's Ray?"

"He was here," Julie said. "But he didn't stay long. When he found out the kids weren't home, he went ballistic." She glanced pointedly at the pottery lamp that had been sitting on the table in the corner, now smashed to bits and pieces on the hardwood floor. "He left just a few minutes before Colt arrived."

Her gaze focused on Wheeler. At least six-two, two hundred plus pounds of solid male muscle. A mustache curved down from his hard mouth to a scarred jaw. With the black patch over one eye, he looked like a total badass. She couldn't imagine her man-shy friend having anything to do with a guy like him.

Julie made the introductions. "Colt, this is my best friend, Lissa Blayne."

"Nice to meet you," Colt drawled, his amused smile back in place, making her temper inch up all over again.

"Lissa's a private detective," Julie hurried to explain, knowing Lissa well enough to recognize her growing irritation. "I called her before Ray got here and asked her to come over."

Colt's amusement faded. He focused on Julie. "Any idea where I can find this guy?"

"No. But I know he'll be back." She sank down on the sofa. "Oh God, what am I going to do?"

"You got a restraining order on him once," Lissa reminded her. "You can do it again."

Julie shook her head. "It took me weeks and cost me a bundle in attorney's fees. And the truth is, it won't keep him away—not if coming here is what he plans to do. Oh God," she said again.

"You don't have to be afraid." Colt remained standing. "I'll stay here a few days, make sure he doesn't give you any trouble." He turned to Lissa. "In the meantime, you're a detective, maybe you can track him down."

"I'll try to find him, but you don't have to stay," Lissa said, thinking the last thing her friend needed in her life right now was a hard-ass like Wheeler. "I can stay with Julie, make sure she and the kids are safe."

"Colt's just visiting on his way to Denver," Julie said. "He needs a place to stay, and the kids and I love having him here."

Somewhere in the back of her mind, Lissa remembered Julie mentioning her late husband's friend, that he was a ranger like Liam. Julie hadn't said their relationship was sexual. But looking at him, Lissa had no trouble believing the man could seduce a somewhat-naive, far-too-trusting woman like Julie.

"Fine," Lissa said. "I'll see if I can track down your ex. Any idea how long he's been back in Dallas?"

"From what he told me, not very long."

"What's he look like?" she asked. "I need a description, something more than an ex-football jock with blond hair."

"He doesn't look anything like he used to. I almost didn't recognize him. His hair's darker and buzzed very short. He's got tats on his neck and arms. I couldn't believe it. He looks more like a criminal than the captain of the football team he was when we were dating."

"Maybe that's where he's been," Colt said. "Maybe the guy's been in prison for the last eight years."

Lissa flashed Colt a look, giving him silent kudos for a good idea. "I'll check it out. Julie, I need you to think back, try to remember everything Ray said. Anything he mentioned might be helpful."

Julie raked back her heavy auburn hair. "Why don't we all sit down in the kitchen? I've got a cold pitcher of iced tea in the fridge. That'll give me some time to think."

"Sounds good," Colt said.

Once they were seated at the table in Julie's sunny yellow kitchen, a glass of iced tea in front of them, Julie went back over the conversation she'd had with her ex.

"I swear, I barely recognized him. Even his voice sounded different, harder, not smooth and coaxing like it was before. I didn't want to let him in, but I was afraid if I didn't it would only make things worse."

"Did he say why he hasn't tried to contact you until now?" Colt asked.

"We didn't talk about it. He just said he'd made mistakes, but he was older now. He'd come to realize a man needed a son to pass down his legacy. He was particularly interested in seeing Timmy."

"He didn't care about Megan?" Lissa asked.

"He said he trusted me to raise her right."

"What legacy?" Colt asked. "Did he mention anything in particular?"

"That was about the time he started to realize the kids weren't in the house. When I told him they went over to a friend's after school, he got so mad he smashed the lamp and stormed out of the house. He said he'd be back and Tim had better be here when he showed up."

Silence fell. Lissa slanted a glance at Colt, whose features looked set in stone. "What else did he say?" she asked.

"He said I still looked pretty. But that was before he got so mad. After that, he said I was still the same useless bitch I'd always been."

"Nice guy," Lissa said dryly.

"You think you can find him?" Colt asked her.

"I'll find him." She glanced at the broken lamp, thought of Ray's violent temper, and hoped it was sooner rather than later.

"You find him, I'll deal with him," Colt said to her darkly. "When I'm finished, Ray Spearman won't ever bother Julie again."

One look into that steely blue eye and Lissa believed him. Unfortunately, as a former police officer, no way could she stand by and let this guy kill Ray. Though there was a very good chance that was exactly what Colt Wheeler had in mind.

CHAPTER THREE

COLT SAT ON the sofa in the living room while Julie and Lissa cleaned up in the kitchen, an excuse, he figured, for Julie to give her friend a rundown of who he was and what he was doing in Dallas.

He looked up as the front door opened and Julie's two kids burst into the living room, home from their time with the neighbors.

"Colt!" Timmy was eleven, a good-looking boy with reddish-blond hair and a gangly frame he was just beginning to grow into. Colt rose as the kid grinned and ran toward him. "Wow, I can't believe you're here."

"Hey, Tim." Colt clamped a hand on the boy's shoulder and they leaned in for a hug. "I swear you've grown six inches since I was here last year."

"I wish. I can't wait to be as tall as you."

He smiled. "Be patient. Someday you will be."

"I hope so. Mom said you quit the army."

"That's right. I needed a change. I'm headed back to Denver to try something new." Something that would challenge him the way the rangers once had.

"Are you gonna stay in town for a while?"

"Maybe a day or two."

"Cool. I got basketball practice so I gotta go. I'll see you when I get home." Timmy took off just as his sister walked in. Megan was a year older, a beautiful young girl with the same fair skin, delicate features, and auburn hair as her mother.

"Colt! Mom didn't say you were coming."

"I should have called. I was driving through on my way to Denver and decided to just drop by."

"I'm really glad you did." Megan leaned over and hugged him. She felt slender and fragile as he hugged her back, but according to her mom, she was tougher than she looked.

"Since you're here, maybe you can come to my school play tomorrow night."

He smiled, lifting the dark blond mustache at the corner of his mouth. "If I can, I will. But there may be something I have to do." With any luck he'd be having a very long, very painful conversation with scumbag Raymond Spearman. "Either way, I know you'll be great."

Megan blushed. "Thanks. I've got to change. Me and my friend Marsha are going to the mall for a couple of hours."

He arched an eyebrow. "What, no homework?"

Megan smiled. "Finished it in study hall."

"Good for you."

As Megan raced off down the hall to her bedroom, he noticed Lissa standing in the kitchen doorway. Just looking at her aroused him, had since she'd stepped into the living room, a big semiauto in her hands, pointed directly at him.

She was wearing a black tank top that curved over small, elegant breasts and black jeans that stretched like skin over the supple curves of her long legs. She was tall, built like a dancer, her muscles lean and strong. She was confident, even arrogant. He could feel it in every look she cast his way.

He wanted to taste that sassy mouth, wanted a lot more than that.

"You're good with kids," she said. "I wouldn't have guessed."

He just shrugged. He knew what people thought when

they looked at him, knew the black patch was even more intimidating than the scar. "Looks can be deceiving."

Lissa shook her head, moving the shiny blond cap of hair he itched to run his fingers through. "I don't think so. I think you're exactly the kind of man you look like."

"That so? What kind is that?"

"Hard and edgy. The kind who's used to having his own way. A man who doesn't take no for an answer."

"You could be right." She was smart, too. She had him pegged just right. He wanted to do a more thorough examination of that graceful dancer's body, but he kept his eyes on her face. "The question is, do you like that kind of man?"

Her mouth tightened. "Depends if he has obligations somewhere else." She had pretty lips, soft and pink, lips a man could sink into. He didn't have time to respond to her question before Julie walked into the living room.

"Marsha's mom is picking Megan up and taking the girls to the mall. As soon as they're gone, I need to take Timmy to basketball practice."

"I've got to get back to the office," Lissa said. "I have some calls I need to make. I'll see if Dallas PD has anything on Spearman. If not, I've got a friend who can dig up info on just about anyone."

"Sounds good," Colt said. "I'll ride with Julie, make sure Spearman isn't out there somewhere waiting for her."

Lissa nodded. "Good idea. I'll see you back here tomorrow."

"I'll have supper ready about seven," Julie said. "Why don't you join us?"

Lissa glanced from Julie to Colt. "You sure you want company?"

He got it then. Lissa thought he'd stopped by for a little action with his dead friend's wife. Just the idea pissed him off.

"I can call," Lissa added. "Let you know what I find out."

Julie smiled. "We'd love for you to join us, wouldn't we, Colt? I'm making spaghetti. Come over a little early and we'll have a glass of wine."

"You should definitely join us," Colt said, just to watch Lissa's temper flare. "Three can be even more fun than two."

Her dark eyes narrowed. There was a hint of gold around the irises that glittered with angry heat. He'd like to turn that heat in a different direction.

"Okay, you've convinced me," she said, clearly determined to protect her friend. "I'll be here a little before seven."

Colt almost smiled. His stop in Dallas was going to be a lot more interesting than he had anticipated. Lissa Blayne was all fiery temper and cool disdain. She heated his blood in a way no woman had in a very long time.

And from the look in those hot brown eyes, Colt figured Lissa felt at least some of the attraction he felt for her. Not that she wasn't fighting it.

Tonight he'd make sure she knew he wasn't interested in more than friendship with Julie and never had been. Nor did Julie have that sort of interest in him.

First he had to deal with Spearman, make sure he was out of Julie's and the kids' lives for good. Then he could focus on Lissa. His body stirred and his groin tightened just thinking about her.

He hoped Lissa came up with Spearman's location so he could make the problem end.

Seven o'clock couldn't come too soon.

LISSA RETURNED TO the office and ran a background check on Ray Spearman. His birth records popped up—born at St. Luke's Medical Center in Houston, only child of Paul and Sylvia Spearman. Attended Woodrow Wilson Middle School and Rutledge High, where he played varsity football.

His criminal record began at eighteen when he'd been arrested for drunk and disorderly. If there were earlier offenses, his juvenile records would have been sealed.

The drunk charges had gone nowhere; Ray had been released on bail and the charges dropped. There was a DUI a year later, charges also dropped. Ray was young and popular, the star quarterback of the Ravens, a local college football team—favoritism happened far too often.

She continued reading, saw that at twenty, a girl named Mary Wilson at the community college had accused him of attempted assault, but Ray had an alibi—two of the football players on his team were with him that night. Again the charges were dropped.

He must have straightened out for a while. Probably about the time he met Julie. She wouldn't have dated a guy who was constantly in trouble. Lissa found Ray and Julie's marriage certificate, and birth certificates for both Megan and Timmy.

The divorce decree was granted in 2008, followed by a string of misdemeanors for everything from resisting arrest to DUIs and assault. In 2009, Ray was picked up for distributing a narcotic substance and spent six months in jail.

Nothing showed up after that. According to Julie, Ray had simply disappeared.

Now he was in Dallas, demanding to see his kids. It was a shame Julie's second husband, a man she had truly loved, had been killed in action before he'd been able to finalize the kids' adoption, which, with Ray nowhere to be found, Liam would have eventually been able to do.

It was heading toward evening when Lissa closed her laptop and started for the door.

"Everything okay with your friend?" Mindy asked.

Lissa sighed. "Not exactly. Her ex-husband has a history of violence and today he showed up at her house—after eight years."

"That doesn't sound good. What are you going to do?"

"I'm going to find him. Then we'll figure a way to deal with him." Or Colt Wheeler would.

Just the man's name in the corner of her mind sent a ripple of heat rolling through her. She had never felt such a primal rush of lust. She had wanted to drag him down to the floor and strip off his clothes, see if he was as hard-muscled and virile as he looked, though she was pretty sure he was.

As she headed out to her car, she thought about the way he had baited her. Now that she'd had time to think, she was 95 percent sure Colt wasn't sleeping with Julie. The two of them were as dissimilar as vinegar and molasses. One of them was hard and remote, the other loving and accessible, two distinctly different people. And though Colt might enjoy it, Julie wasn't the kind of woman to have no-strings sex with a man who stopped by for a quickie once or twice a year. His remarks had been payback for the assumptions she had made, and in a way, she deserved it.

She'd taken one look at Colt's hard, tough exterior and assumed the worst. Julie had said he was Liam's friend from the army. She could see the soldier in every move he made.

Perhaps tonight they could start over on a more even footing. It might be interesting to see where it led.

She checked her stainless-steel wristwatch with its black leather band. Time to head over to Julie's. She ignored a rush of anticipation that should have set off alarm bells and slid into the hot interior of her Camaro. The heat inside exactly matched her mood.

CHAPTER FOUR

DINNER WAS ALMOST READY. The table was set. Julie asked Colt to open the bottle of Chianti on the counter. It was now sitting on the table she had set with white plates on red place mats just to lighten the mood. All she had left to do was pick Timmy up from basketball practice, then come home and finish the salad.

"You ready?" Colt asked.

Julie untied the bright blue apron with the Pillsbury Doughboy on the front and tossed it onto the breakfast bar. "You don't have to go with me. I'll be fine."

"From his appearance here after eight years, we know your ex is unpredictable. He might try to follow you, run you off the road or something. No use taking chances."

Julie wiped her suddenly damp palms on her stretch jeans. "Maybe you're right."

"I'll drive. You can give me directions."

The kids were streaming out of the gymnasium when Colt pulled the Mustang up in front of the school. Timmy had called earlier to tell her basketball practice was running later than usual tonight. Julie and Colt waited in the car until the last straggler walked out, but there was still no sign of Timmy.

"Call him," Colt said. "Find out what's going on."

Julie pushed his contact button, but the call went straight to voice mail. She looked up to see Colt sliding out of the car, and her heart began to pound. As he headed toward the big double doors leading into the dome-shaped gym, she hurried to catch up with his long-legged strides.

"That's Coach Nunez over there." Julie pointed to a lean, sinewy man with olive skin and coarse black hair.

Colt walked right up to him. "Where's Tim Spearman?" Colt asked. "His mother's been waiting outside but he hasn't come out yet."

The coach barely looked up from his clipboard. "His dad picked him up."

Fear slid into her stomach, followed by a wave of nausea. "You...you didn't just let him go off with a man you don't know!"

"Mr. Spearman called this afternoon. He said he was picking the boy up from practice. I checked with the principal's office. There was nothing in the file that said Timmy wasn't allowed to leave with his dad. His father had ID and Timmy seemed excited to see him."

"Oh my God!"

"What's going on?" the coach asked, frowning. "Do I need to call the police?"

"Give us a minute." Colt took Julie's arm and led her a few feet away. "Bringing in the cops right now might not be a good idea. Not until we know what's going on."

Before she had time to argue, her phone rang. She looked down to see Timmy's name on the screen.

"Timmy! Where are you?"

"This is Ray. The boy's with me."

"Ray. Let me talk to Timmy."

"Take it easy. Tim's fine."

"This is kidnapping, Ray. If you don't take Timmy home right now, I'm calling the police!"

"Calm down, Julie, and listen very carefully. Tim's my

son. I have every right to see him, and that's what I'm going to do."

She was shaking. "You...you've been gone eight years. Timmy doesn't even know you."

"Yeah, well, that's about to change."

"I'm telling you, Ray—"

"No, Julie, I'm telling *you*—and you had better listen good. Tim and I are going to spend some time together, get to know each other. You get the cops involved, you'll never see your son again."

A sound came from her throat. At the stark terror in her face, Colt took the phone from her trembling hand and pressed the speaker button.

"My name is Colt Wheeler. I'm a friend of Julie's late husband. Let Julie talk to the boy."

"No cops," Ray said, "or she won't see the kid again."

"Put Timmy on the phone," Colt repeated, tamping down his own fury.

Seconds passed. "Mom...?"

"Timmy! Sweetheart, where are you? Are you all right?"

"Dad came to the school. He said it was okay for me to go with him. He said you knew."

She clamped her lips together, fighting for control. "It's all right, honey. It's not your fault."

Ray came back on the line. "No cops," he repeated. "You got it?"

She looked up at Colt, who nodded. "I've got it," Julie said. "How long before you bring him home?"

"Not sure yet. I'll let you know when I've figured it out." The line went dead.

"Oh my God," Julie said.

"We need to get out of here. Wave goodbye to Coach Nunez as if nothing's wrong, and let's go."

She walked on shaky legs out of the gymnasium and Colt pulled her aside as soon as they cleared the door.

"You need to call Marsha's mother," he said.

"Marsha's mother?" The rest of the blood drained from her face so suddenly she felt light-headed. "Oh my God, you don't think—"

"Tell her to pick the girls up right now. Call Megan first, tell her not to leave with anyone but Marsha's mom."

"I'll call her, but…but the cell service in the mall is always spotty." And just as Julie expected, Megan didn't pick up and the call went to voice mail. She told herself it didn't mean Megan was with Ray, but her heart was hammering so hard she could feel it in her temples.

Fumbling with the phone, she called Ellen Crowley, Marsha's mother. "Ellen, it's Julie. I need you to pick up the girls right now."

"I'm almost there, just a few blocks away. You sound upset. Is something wrong?"

"I—I just need to make certain Megan's safe."

"I'll have her call you as soon as I pick her up."

"Thanks, Ellen." Julie hung up the phone. She looked up at Colt, saw a muscle jump in his cheek.

"We'll get him back," he said. "That's a promise."

Julie wiped at tears she hadn't realized were sliding down her cheeks. Staring up at Colt's hard, determined features, she almost believed him.

DINNER WAS FORGOTTEN. Lissa listened as Julie relayed the events of the evening, including the fact her ex-husband had abducted her son. Megan was spending the night with Marsha, unaware that her brother was missing, giving them time to come up with a plan.

"Colt doesn't think we should call the police," Julie said.

"At least not yet." She was exhausted and shaky. Lissa had never seen her look so fragile.

"He's threatened to run if we bring in the cops," Colt said. "If he does, things could go from bad to worse in a hurry."

"Colt may be right," Lissa agreed. "At this point, there's no reason to believe Ray will hurt Timmy. Tim's his son. I know Ray hasn't been around for the last eight years, but blood is blood. The bigger problem is, will he take Timmy somewhere we can't find him?"

"Oh God."

"Try not to panic," Colt said. "We'll find Ray and once we do, we'll bring Timmy home."

"What if something happens before you catch up with him? A couple of years ago, Timmy had an asthma attack. The doctor said it was a mild case, but if Ray does something that causes another attack, he won't know how to handle it. It could become life-threatening."

Colt quietly cursed. This was getting worse by the minute. "Tim's a smart kid. He'll know you'll be looking for him. Or I will be."

Some of the fear in Julie's eyes receded. "He trusts you. So do I."

"We have to hope he stays calm, does what his father says, and waits for us to find him."

Julie nodded.

"I've got a call to make." Lissa pulled out her phone. "I'll be right back." Heading into the kitchen to use her cell, she phoned Tabitha Love. Tabby worked freelance for Maximum Security. She was a genius at tracking down information on the internet.

"Hey, Tab, I need your help."

"Sure, Liss. What can I do for you?" Tabby was in her

midtwenties, black hair cut super short on the sides and moussed on top. She had tats and a face full of silver: studs, hoops, anything that sparkled.

"I've got an emergency. Young boy abducted by his father. The guy has a history of abuse and he's been gone eight years without a trace. We need to know where he's been and what he's been up to."

She went on to give Tabby all the info they had on Ray Spearman, hoping she could come up with something they could use to find Tim. "First, I need you to ping Timmy's phone."

"What's the number?"

She pulled the sticky note Julie had given her out of her black jeans pocket. "469-555-1238."

"I'll call you back."

Ignoring the fading aroma of spaghetti growing cold on the stove and glancing wistfully at the Chianti bottle on the table, Lissa pocketed the phone and walked back into the living room. "Tabby's going to call me back."

One of Colt's dark blonde eyebrows went up. "Tabby?"

"Tabitha Love. She does forensic computer investigation for The Max. Tab can find out just about anything."

"Let's hope she can come up with something on Spearman," he said darkly.

Lissa used the time to fill Colt in on the background check she had done, including Ray's criminal record. It was ten minutes later when her cell phone rang.

Tabby. She put the phone on speaker and set it on the coffee table, and they all clustered around.

"The call made to Julie's cell pinged off a tower twenty-five miles out of Dallas on I-35E, a little south of Red Oak."

"Wait," Lissa said. "He was already on his way out of town when Julie went to pick up Timmy?"

"I don't understand," Julie said. "Why would he be calling from Red Oak?"

"Another call was made farther south," Tabby said, "on the interstate near Forreston, also to Julie's cell, but it wasn't picked up."

Julie grabbed her phone, saw a missed call from Timmy's number, but the call must have ended before there was time for it to ring.

She held the phone against her heart. "Timmy must have tried to call me but Ray stopped him."

"No calls after that," Tabby said. "The phone was disabled, either turned off or the battery removed."

Lissa flashed a glance at Julie, whose face was pale, her eyes glistening with unshed tears.

"What about Spearman?" Colt asked. "Come up with anything on him?"

"Tabby, that's Colt Wheeler," Lissa said. "Colt's former Army Special Forces. He's a friend. Timmy's mom, Julie, is also here."

"Good to meet you both. I'll be focusing on Spearman, Colt. I'll also keep an eye on Timmy's phone."

"Appreciate it." Colt's deep voice rumbled across the living room.

"Thank you, Tabby." Julie fought to collect herself as the call came to a close.

When Lissa looked over at Colt, he was working his cell, bringing up Google Maps.

"I'm not familiar with the area," he said. "What's in Red Oak?"

"Nothing," Julie said.

"How about Forreston?"

"Not much out there until you get to Waco," Lissa said.

"Just a lot of open country," Julie added. "Ray could be anywhere."

"We need more intel," Colt said. "Ray's traveling south on I-35. He's got a destination in mind. We just need to figure out what it is."

"He was raised in Houston," Lissa said. "Maybe he's headed home."

Colt looked down at the map on his phone. "Doesn't look like the fastest route. Maybe he's taking a detour. Any chance he could be taking Timmy to meet his parents, a high school friend, something like that?"

Julie shook her head. "I don't think so. His father and mother divorced while we were together. His dad remarried a girl twenty years younger. Ray was furious. I'm not even sure Paul Spearman still lives in Houston."

"What about his mom?" Colt asked.

"Last time Ray mentioned his mother, she and the man she remarried were living in Florida."

The phone rang again and Lissa checked the screen. *Tabby.* She hit the speaker button. "What is it?"

"The odds of a guy like Spearman staying completely off the grid for eight years are slim and none. I checked Interpol. Ray Spearman was arrested in Mexico in 2012 for drug smuggling. He spent five years in a Mexican prison. Got out two years ago."

Lissa's glance shot to Colt. "You were right about prison."

"No sign of him in the States until now," Tabby said. "I've got feelers out. I'll have more for you soon."

Colt's gaze went back to the map on his phone. "Mexico," he said, grimly. "The son of a bitch is taking the boy back to Mexico."

CHAPTER FIVE

COLT LOOKED DOWN at Julie, who sat next to him on the sofa, fighting to hold back tears. He cupped her face in his palms, forcing her to look at him. "I'm going after Tim. I'll bring him home. I won't come back without him. I promise you, Julie."

He let her go, and she took a shaky breath. "What about the police?"

"I'll call them," Lissa said, bringing Colt's attention back to her. "I've got friends in the department. They'll get things rolling, put out a BOLO and an Amber Alert. They'll stop him at the border if he gets that far."

"My stuff is still in the car," Colt said. "I'm ready to leave right now. I'll stay in touch, let you know what's happening." He kept his gaze on Julie. "You can count on me to take care of this."

Julie managed a shaky nod.

Colt turned to Lissa. "Stay on your friend Tabby. Anything she gives you, I need to know."

A hard smile curved those pretty pink lips. "That shouldn't be tough to do—since we'll both be in the same car. The only question is—are we taking yours or mine?"

Colt shook his head. "You'll just be in the way."

Lissa actually laughed. "That's not true, and unless you're a fool—which I don't believe you are—you know it. I'm armed. My car's parked out front. I keep a go bag in the trunk. My passport's in it. I'm ready whenever you are."

Amusement filtered through him. She was a trained police officer, and clearly intelligent. She'd be an asset not a liability. And she knew it.

"If you're sure that's the way you want it," he said. "I'm driving."

"Fine." Lissa gave Julie a hug. "The police will want to talk to you. They'll need Timmy's picture." Lissa and Colt both carried photos Julie had given them. "I'll call and keep you posted on what's going on."

Colt leaned down, and Julie's arms went around his neck. "Thank you, Colt. Thank you so much."

He kissed the top of her head. "I'll find your boy. Stay strong until we get back." Colt turned and strode out the front door. Lissa was already outside, unloading her gear from the trunk of her black Camaro, parked in front of his souped-up black Mustang. The sexy visual brought a fresh jolt of heat, reminding him of how she'd stirred his blood the moment she'd drawn down on him in the living room.

He popped the trunk. They tossed their bags inside and he closed the lid, then both of them slid into the car and clicked on their seat belts. The interior was firecracker hot, but she was a Texan so she didn't complain.

"Nice ride," she said.

Colt looked at the Camaro parked in front of them. "Same goes." As he fired up the powerful engine, turned the AC up full blast, and pulled away from the curb, Lissa ran a slim finger over the dash.

"I'm guessing this car isn't exactly factory standard."

He just shrugged. "My dad was a mechanic. I learned a few things, made a few modifications after I bought it."

She flashed a smile that sent the blood straight to his groin. "I like it."

As he drove off down the street, she started making calls. First to a detective at the Dallas PD named Mack Handley, reporting a parental abduction and asking Handley to take the case personally and to use kid gloves on her friend. Next she phoned Julie and told her Handley would be getting in touch.

When the call ended, she leaned back in the seat. "I assume we're taking the same route Spearman's driving."

"For now," he said. "It's damn near a straight shot to the border crossing in Laredo, about four-hundred fifty miles."

"If that's where he's going. Piedras Negras is a few miles closer. He could be headed either place."

"Or somewhere in between. He's got less than a two-hour head start." Colt pulled onto US 75 South, weaving through Dallas on his way to I-35. It was dark, after 9:00 p.m., the traffic at a minimum. "With luck, we can narrow his lead." Colt stepped on the gas.

"You still haven't told me where we're going." Timmy stared into the darkness rushing past the window outside the pickup, a brand-new Chevy Silverado, as it rolled down the highway. It was the same color as its name.

Timmy had thought the truck was cool when his dad had picked him up. He'd thought it was great to finally meet his father. He'd been excited, eager to go with him, get to know him.

Now he felt like a rock sat in the bottom of his stomach and he just wanted to go home.

"We're going on a trip," his dad said. "Think of it as an adventure. You'll get to see places you've never been before."

"Like where?" His dad was a big guy, almost as tall as Colt, with brown hair instead of reddish blond like his own, but they both had blue eyes. His dad had tats. Timmy couldn't believe his mom had been married to a guy with tats. He had to admit, they really made him look cool.

His father's eyes cut away from the road, from the occasional set of headlights speeding toward them. "How would you like to see Mexico?"

His worry swelled. "Mexico? That's a long ways away. I don't think Mom would like it."

"Your mom has been in control of your life far too long. It's time you got to know your father. You're growing up. There are things you need to learn that your mom can't teach you. Things that will make you a man."

Timmy said nothing. He wasn't a man—he was still a kid. He didn't mind that. He figured he'd grow up soon enough. That's what Mom always said.

"How long will it take?" he asked. "To get to Mexico and back?"

"We'll figure it out once we get there."

Timmy fell silent. He didn't say anything else for a while. He didn't know his dad, but he had a feeling it wouldn't take much to make him mad. Still, when his stomach started growling, he decided it was time to speak up.

"I didn't have any dinner. Can we stop and get a burger or something?"

His father cast him a sideways glance. "All right, I suppose we can do that. I'll start watching for a place to pull off."

"I like Burger King or Jack in the Box. They're the best."

His dad's gaze sliced back to him. "You'll eat whatever I buy you and be damned glad to get it. Understand?"

A trickle of fear slipped down his spine. He swallowed. "Okay."

"Good boy. I have a feeling you're going to catch on real fast. You do that, we won't have any problems."

Timmy could feel his breath coming a little too fast. A couple of times he'd had asthma attacks, but the doctor had said they were mild. It scared him, though. First he'd started coughing, then it was hard to breathe. He sure didn't want it to happen again.

They pulled off the road at a truck stop and went in to use the bathroom. Dad bought hot dogs and microwaved them, bought Timmy a Pepsi and himself a cup of coffee, and they got back on the road. The cheese on the hotdog tasted like orange rubber, but at least it filled him up.

"Why don't you get some sleep?" Dad said.

"Okay." He wanted to call Mom. He knew she would be worried when he didn't come home, but when he'd tried to call her before, Dad had taken his phone away and hadn't given it back.

Timmy closed his eyes and settled back in the seat, but his heart was thumping too hard for him to fall asleep.

It looked like he was going to Mexico.

He wondered how long it would take them to get there.

His eyes stung. He wondered if he would ever get home again.

CHAPTER SIX

LISSA WAS NAPPING, the Mustang's powerful engine lulling her into a restless sleep. As she awoke, yawned, and stretched, she caught a highway sign illuminated by the headlights. They were south of Austin, almost to San Antonio.

"I'll drive for a while," she said, adjusting the seat belt as she sat up straighter. "Give you a chance to catch a little sleep."

Colt's jaw hardened. "Dammit, we can't go much farther. Not without more intel. Once we get to San Antonio, there are a dozen different ways to get to Mexico."

Lissa raked her fingers through her sleep-mussed blond hair. "The truth is we don't even know for sure he's heading for Mexico. He could be holed up somewhere in Texas. There's even a chance he's planning to take Timmy back home."

Colt seemed to mull that over. "I don't think so. Spearman's been out of jail for two years. He's had plenty of time to see his kids, but he never showed up. Why now? Something's changed. My gut says a guy who goes to this much trouble isn't planning a friendly little visit with his son. He wants the boy with him. He figures it's time for him to step in and raise him."

Lissa ignored a shiver she attributed to the air-conditioning. "That could explain why he didn't go after

Megan. She's a girl. He has no idea how to bring up a daughter, but Tim is a boy, his heir."

He nodded. "Someone to pass on his legacy. That's what he said."

"Yes, but what legacy? That's the question."

They passed another road sign and Colt's palm slammed down on the steering wheel. "Dammit! We can't just keep driving. We need to pull off, find a place to rest until we hear from the cops or your friend Tabby."

Colt was right. Lissa didn't want to stop, but driving through the night with no idea of Spearman's destination was just flat-out stupid. "There's a little town up ahead. There'll be some motels along the interstate."

"Okay, I'll watch for something."

They pulled onto an off-ramp two miles farther down the highway. Signs boasted of a café and two cheap motels. Colt pulled into the parking lot of a Mesquite Travel Lodge and stopped in front of the office.

It was after 1:00 a.m. They'd been on the road nearly five hours. There was a note on the door, illuminated by the Mustang's headlights. *Office closed till 8:00 a.m... Fill out the form and take a key out of the box. Pay before you leave in the morning.*

She snorted. "I wonder how many people spend the night and don't pay the bill."

The corner of Colt's hard mouth edged up. "Sounds like the lady is a cynic."

Lissa managed a tired smile. "Too many years on the job, I guess."

"Yeah," he said, turning serious. "I know what you mean." He got out of the car, walked over, and opened the wooden box, then reached in and pulled out a form and a single key.

Lissa rolled down the window, felt the rush of hot air against her cheeks.

"Only one left," he said, holding up the key. "You want me to keep driving, find another place to stay?"

She had seen that look on his face before, though he'd mostly managed to hide it. It was hot and hungry, disturbing in its intensity. It made her feel things, want things she hadn't had in far too long.

Her pulse quickened. She wanted exactly what his look said *he* wanted. It wasn't her style to sleep with a man she barely knew, but driving farther wasn't a good idea.

"We can share the room," she said. "If Julie trusts you, I guess I do, too."

"Julie was Liam's wife. She's a friend, nothing more. I want a lot more than friendship from you."

There it was, right out in the open. *He wanted her.* Colt waited for her answer, his hard, hot look never wavering. She took her time. Did she have the nerve to take what she wanted? She could still change her mind.

"You need sleep and so do I. Take the room."

He pocketed the key while she filled out the form. The motel rooms were all in a row, twelve single-story units facing the parking lot. Colt parked the Mustang in front of number ten, and Lissa climbed out of the car into the moist summer night air.

The room was cleaner than she expected. The mattress sagged a little but the spread was freshly laundered, the dark brown carpets recently vacuumed. There was only one bed, but it was a king.

Just looking at it sent her mind into a hot, dark place filled with longing. She glanced at Colt, saw him watching her with that single blue eye, saw the heat he didn't bother to hide. She noticed the way his black T-shirt clung to a chest taut with muscle, the way his jeans cupped a round behind and stretched over long, powerful legs.

His face was the image of hard male dominance, the kind of man who took what he wanted. The kind tough enough to handle the fierce need burning inside her.

She hadn't been with a man in nearly two years. Hadn't met a man she wanted. Not until now.

Still, she knew there would be consequences. With a man like Colt Wheeler there always were.

She looked at him and long-dead passions stirred to life inside her, along with something that made her feel vulnerable in a way she hadn't in years. She didn't like the feeling, and yet she wanted him.

Her mind was made up.

She wondered if she would regret it.

"WE NEED TO get some sleep," Lissa said. Colt followed her gaze to the bed, which dominated the worn, dated motel room. There was challenge in her words, and something in her eyes Colt couldn't read.

For him, sleep was no longer an option. Not with the hunger burning through him, not when he could see she felt it, too.

"Sleep isn't what I need," he said. "What I need tonight is you." He moved toward her, stopped right in front of her. Sliding a hand into shining blond hair as silky as it looked, he cupped the back of her head, hovered over her mouth long enough to give her a chance to say no, then he kissed her.

Full pink lips sank into his, melding so perfectly he groaned. The kiss went from slow and sexy to hot and deep in a heartbeat. Lissa's arms slid around his neck and she kissed him back with all the fire he'd expected. There was no turning back now. Not for either one of them.

He kissed her long and deep, pressed his mouth against the rapid pulse beating against the side of her neck, and heard her moan. He stripped off her tank top, unhooked her bra and tossed it away, filled his hands with her small, pretty breasts.

Perfect, he thought as his mouth replaced his hands, tasting the tight bud at the crest, sucking until it tightened even more. Exactly right for him.

She toed off her sneakers, and he stripped off her black jeans, ran his hand over those firm, slender hips to cup her sexy ass, felt the lean muscles tighten. The rough brush of lace drew his attention to the scrap of silk between her legs. A pale, delicate pink, not red or black, a glimpse of the woman beneath the tough facade.

In minutes he had stripped her naked and followed her down on the bed, pressing her into the mattress. He kissed her, slid his hands over that graceful dancer's body. He stroked and teased and tasted, bringing her to the edge of climax. He wanted to put his mouth between her legs, but for that she would need to trust him, and he sensed that she still did not. At least not completely.

Instead, he left her long enough to strip off his clothes, then returned, tossing a handful of condoms on the nightstand.

She was flushed and beautiful in the moonlight streaming in through the crack in the curtains, long and slender and supple. He wanted to be inside her, ached to take her, possess her in some primal way.

Lying next to her, he returned to kissing her, stroking her, urging her toward the peak again. He felt her slim hands sliding over his skin, urgent now, touching him and making him burn, wanting more, wanting all of him. She shifted till she was on top of him, settled herself astride his hips, leaned down, and kissed him, long, wet, and deep.

"You like being in control?" he asked, clamping down on the urge to grip her hips and thrust himself inside, take what he wanted.

"Yes," she whispered, kissing him. Her white teeth sank into his bottom lip and he felt a surge of heat that turned his erection to steel. She rose to take him into her body and he let her, let her seat herself and begin to move. She was exquisite, all hot-blooded female, everything he thought she would be and more.

"You like being on top?" he asked as she worked him over.

A feminine growl came from her throat. "Yes…"

His mouth edged up. "So do I." Using his superior strength to lift and turn them, he carried her beneath him. Still inside, he thrust deep and hard. Her fingers dug into the muscles across his shoulders and a soft purring sound came from her throat. She liked this, liked a man who took charge. Instinctively, he had known she would.

For a moment, he paused. "The patch," he said. "On or off?" He always asked. Always got the same answer.

She stared into his face. "Off," she said, surprising him.

Women always wanted him to leave it on, to pretend he was a pirate or some demon lover. He pulled the black patch off over his head and stared down at her. Lissa gazed into his scarred face, and everything suddenly changed.

Leaning up, she pressed her mouth to the jagged slice that ran down from above his eye, pressed a soft kiss on his closed, scarred eyelid. She kissed the gash that continued along his jaw.

It was completely unexpected and it reached something

inside him, set something free that he hadn't known was trapped. Pinning her hands above her head, he thrust deep and hard, pulled out and drove into her again. Kissing her savagely, he pounded into her, taking what he so desperately needed and demanding more.

Lissa locked her legs around his hips, giving in to his powerful hunger, arching beneath him and taking what she wanted for herself. She came in a wild rush of pleasure, her lithe body tightening around him. Colt followed her to release, unable to hold back any longer, completely out of control.

His muscles went rigid and his body shook with the power of his climax. It was incredible. Earth-shattering.

It should have been enough, but it wasn't. He wanted more. Wanted her. Wanted everything she had to give.

It frightened him.

Unable to resist, he took her again, slower this time, drawing out the pleasure. Just before dawn, Lissa became the aggressor, taking the lead, wreaking havoc on his body and her own. She was all woman, just what he wanted.

Maybe even what he needed.

He wondered if he was man enough to find out.

CHAPTER SEVEN

LISSA AWOKE IN a tangle of arms and legs beneath a yellow shaft of sunlight pouring in through a crack in the motel room curtains. One of Colt's powerful arms draped over her middle, pinning her to the bed.

A tingle of heat ran through her. Last night had been amazing. With Timmy missing and in danger, it had been wrong to take pleasure for herself. But the feeling of helpless frustration had added to her worry and to Colt's. The sex had started as a means to relieve the stress both of them were feeling. What had happened had become far more than that.

The vulnerability Colt made her feel had unexpectedly surfaced in him. Without the black eye patch, he was simply a man, one with needs the same as her own, one who gave as well as took. She had touched something in him, as he had touched something in her.

In the light of day, she doubted either of them would admit it.

Bright red numbers on the digital clock on the nightstand read 6:00 a.m. Lissa managed to slide out of bed without waking Colt and headed for the bathroom. She quickly showered and dressed, walked out to see him standing there gloriously naked.

Memories of all that hard male muscle, of Colt on top of her, inside her, had her belly clenching. Desire she shouldn't have been feeling again so soon curled like smoke through her veins. Her gaze went to his face. The patch was back over his eye, his armor back in place.

"I need a shower," he said. "Then we need to call your friend Tabby. See if she's got any leads."

Knowing Colt would want to hear what Tabby had to say, she nodded and dragged her gaze away from his broad V-shaped back as he closed the bathroom door. She finished repacking her few belongings, heard the shower go off, then the phone began to ring.

She grabbed it off the nightstand. *Tabby*.

"Tell me you've got something," Lissa said.

"I've got plenty and none of it's good."

"Tell me."

"Ray Spearman is a known drug dealer who works for the Los Zetas Cartel. He's a fixer for them, works with the cartel's connections in south Texas."

Lissa glanced over her shoulder to see Colt walking up behind her, drops of water on the fine gold hair on his powerful chest, a towel slung low around his hips.

She put the phone on speaker. "Colt's here. Go ahead."

Tabby briefly repeated the information, then added, "Spearman was recruited during the time he spent in prison. He's known as El Puñal. It means 'The Dagger,' probably a play on his last name. He's got a compound somewhere in the hills outside Monterrey."

Colt grabbed his cell and quickly accessed Google Maps. He held the screen up so Lissa could see the location of the city.

"If he's heading back home, he would have made the border sometime last night," Lissa said. "Nobody's called to tell me they stopped him."

"From the location of the city, he likely would have

crossed in Laredo," Colt said. "But he could have gone through Guerrero. It's the less-traveled route."

"Nobody stopped him because he's traveling under a fake ID," Tabby said. "According to Interpol, he's wanted under at least four different aliases. He won't be using any of those now."

"What's he wanted for?" Colt asked.

"Besides drug smuggling, gun running, and human trafficking? Raymond Spearman, aka El Puñal, is wanted for murder."

Silence fell.

"So he's wanted in the US?" Colt asked.

"Both Mexico and Texas have warrants for his arrest."

"Anything else?" Lissa asked.

"I'm still on it," Tabby said. "I'll keep you posted." The call ended and Lissa looked at Colt.

"We need to get on the road," he said.

"You're that sure he's heading to Mexico?"

"My gut says so. It's the only thing that makes any sense."

She nodded, because her instincts were saying the same thing.

He tossed the towel away, turned, and started pulling on his clothes. Lissa ignored a sharp tug of lust she didn't want to feel. They needed to find Timmy. The boy was all that mattered.

She wondered if Colt would mention last night, but he was a man, so she didn't really think so. Sex was just part of his life, an itch he scratched. Nothing more.

She told herself that was all it had meant to her and ruthlessly set out to make herself believe it.

THEY'D BEEN ON the road for two hours. Colt gassed up the car and pulled into a McDonald's drive-thru for coffee and

Egg McMuffins, then they were back on the highway. It was three hundred miles from San Antonio to Monterrey, traveling the closest route, which was straight down I-35 until they reached the border.

It no longer mattered where Spearman had crossed. If they were right, he was already in Mexico, already back in his compound. If he was with Timmy, getting the boy out wasn't going to be easy.

Colt sliced a glance at Lissa. They had been carefully avoiding each other all morning. He was tired of it.

"About last night…"

Her gaze swung toward him, surprise clear on her face.

One of his eyebrows went up. "What? You didn't think I was going to mention it?"

She just shrugged. "I figured you might just be in it for the conquest."

He grunted. "If anyone made a conquest last night, it was you."

A faint smile curved her lips. "Is that right?"

"Yeah, and as far as I'm concerned, you can conquer me again as soon as this is over."

She laughed, easing some of the tension inside the car. "We were good together."

He slanted her a glance. "Understatement of the year."

"All right, we were dynamite together."

"C-4, and considering I've had some experience with explosives, I know the difference."

Her golden-brown eyes traveled over the black patch on his face. "Is that what happened to your eye?"

He nodded. "IED took out our Humvee. Killed a couple of our guys."

"Liam?"

"No. He was killed a month earlier."

She returned her attention to the road, watching the miles slip past, the endless flat landscape broken only by an occasional oak or a patch of scattered green shrubs along the interstate. "How do we get Timmy out?"

"Good question. First we need to be sure he's there. We need intel. Once we have it, we'll figure how to get him out."

Her gaze remained on his face, bringing a memory of the way she had looked at him last night, with a concern that hinted at the soft woman inside the tough shell. It made him want to know more about her, made him want to take her again, watch the pleasure bloom on her face when he brought her to climax.

His blood heated and slid straight into his groin. The cold shower he'd taken had done nothing to end the lust dogging him all morning.

"We need a helicopter," Lissa said, drawing his attention back where it belonged.

His mouth edged up. "Funny you should say that. I've been thinking about it since we left the motel. I've got a friend, retired from the Laredo Air Force Base, ex–helo pilot named Alex Romero. He owns his own chopper now, does charters, tours of the area, anything to make a buck."

"Will he fly us into Mexico?"

"We don't need him to fly us in. We need him to fly us out."

"What about your car?"

"We'll buy a junker, leave it down there." He glanced at the road, a little surprised to see scattered palm trees bending in the warm breeze drifting over the landscape.

"We're closing in on Cotulla," Lissa explained. "This is part of the Texas Tropical Trail."

"It's humid enough, that's for sure. Makes you appreciate the air-conditioning."

A smile touched her pretty lips. "Oh, that's right—you're a Colorado boy."

"Born and raised."

"Julie says you're out of the army for good, on your way home."

"That's right. I'm headed for Denver. I've got a grandmother there, the woman who raised me. I'm going home, but not until we get Timmy back."

"I'm not going home without him, either. I'm not quitting until he's back with his mother."

Colt flicked her a sideways glance. "Julie's lucky to have you for a friend."

She smiled. "I'm lucky to have her, too."

Colt had been fortunate to have Liam's friendship. Now he had Julie, Megan, and Timmy. They thought of him as family, same way he thought of them. Aside from Gran, maybe they were all he'd ever have. The thought, slamming into him from out of nowhere, was oddly disturbing. For years, the army had been his home. Now it was as if he needed a compass, or maybe a rudder, to steer him.

He wasn't the marrying kind, he reminded himself. But the truth was, he had just never met the right person. He was hard-edged, cynical, and tough. He'd never met a woman who could handle him. His gaze traveled to the lady in the seat beside him, but he blocked the thought before it had time to surface.

Instead, he steered the conversation back to the problem at hand. "When we get to Laredo, we'll talk to my friend Alex, make arrangements with him to pick us up in Monterrey. We can also buy a car to drive across the border."

"Whatever it costs, I'm in for half," Lissa said.

"Believe it or not, I'm pretty well-set. Didn't have much to spend money on while I was in the army. Sent a little to Gran but she didn't really need it. Invested the rest of what I saved, made it grow a little."

"That's what I try to do."

He nodded. He wasn't rich, but he wasn't poor, either. And whatever it cost to retrieve the boy was worth it.

Less than an hour later, after a phone call to Alex, Colt drove up in front of Romero Aeromotive in Laredo, a small, private and corporate aircraft terminal. He punched in the code Alex had given him and a gate slid back, opening a portion of the chain-link fence surrounding the property.

Colt drove through the gate and continued across the asphalt to a blue metal hangar with an office on one side. He turned off the engine, and both of them climbed out of the Mustang.

The damp heat hit him. The asphalt felt soft under the soles of his low-topped leather boots. He liked Texas, but he wasn't crazy about the weather.

A good-looking Hispanic man sauntered out of the office to greet them, about five-eight, thick black hair, linebacker shoulders, and the thighs of a weightlifter.

"Colt! My friend, it's good to see you!" They embraced and leaned in to bump shoulders.

"Good to see you, too. Alejandro Romero, meet Lissa Blayne."

She stuck out her hand, and in typical Alex fashion, he clasped it tight and engulfed it in both of his. The guy was a charmer, always had been. Colt usually found it amusing. Today, when Lissa flashed Alex a wide white smile, Colt felt a trickle of irritation. Since he wasn't the jealous type, he forced himself to ignore it.

"It's good to meet you, Lissa," Alex said. His voice was

smooth, with a trace of a Spanish accent. "Come inside out of the heat and we'll figure all of this out."

They walked into a cluttered office, over to a metal desk with a computer on top, a wheeled chair on one side and two metal chairs upholstered in blue vinyl on the other. A bulletin board loaded with newspaper clippings about the air force base hung on the wall, along with framed pictures of Alex's blue-and-silver chopper, an Airbus EC 120.

"You want a beer or something?" Alex asked.

"No, thanks," Lissa said.

"Maybe later," said Colt, keeping his options open. For the next few minutes, he filled Alex in on the missing boy, his father, Ray Spearman, and the compound El Puñal owned in Monterrey.

"You need more than just a helicopter, my friends," Alex said. "You need information. We'll fly down together, stay till we get what we need. I have family in Monterrey. And I know people there who can help us."

"Us?" Colt repeated.

Alex shrugged those linebacker shoulders. "Things have been pretty dull here lately. I could use a little excitement."

Lissa brightened. "That would be great, Alex. We could really use your help."

"Things could get rough," Colt warned.

Alex grinned, flashing a mouth full of ivory in a darkly masculine face women loved. "Sounds perfect."

Colt leaned back in his chair, damned glad to have Alex on board. "All right," he said. "Let's make it happen."

The three of them went to work.

CHAPTER EIGHT

LISSA REALLY LIKED ALEJANDRO, who preferred she call him Alex. He was smart and capable and, once they had come up with a plan, determined to make it work.

"We'll leave this afternoon, fly across the border into Nuevo León and down to Monterrey. It's only a hundred and thirty miles, an easy flight in this weather."

"Where do we land?" Colt asked.

"There's a small private airport south of the city. The owner, Benito Cortez, is a friend. He and his family are extremely well connected. I'll call him, ask him to find out what he can about El Puñal. We need a location. Info about the area where the guy lives, and anything else Benito might be able to come up with."

Lissa felt a rush of excitement. She was eager to get started, but she wanted to find out if there was anything new on Spearman or Timmy first. "I need to make some calls, as well. See if there are any new developments before we leave."

Pulling her cell from the pocket of her black stretch jeans, she excused herself and walked out into the hot, humid air. She made the call from a spot in the shadow of a metal building, which provided at least a little shade.

This was her second call to Julie that day. She had phoned from the motel first thing that morning. Ray hadn't brought Timmy home or phoned to let Julie talk to him.

"Lissa…" Julie's voice trembled over the line. "I was hoping you'd call again. Have you found Timmy?"

"Not yet. I just wanted to let you know we're still on the road. We've got a couple of leads we're pursuing. I'll keep you posted. If you hear from Ray, phone me immediately."

"I will."

"I've got another call to make, so I've got to go. I'll be back in touch soon."

"You said you had a couple of leads," Julie pressed.

Lissa didn't want to tell her they were flying into Mexico. She didn't want to frighten her friend even more than she was already.

"Nothing concrete. I'll let you know as soon as we figure out where he is."

Lissa hit the end button before Julie could ask any more questions. Next she phoned Detective Mack Handley.

"I would have called," Mack said, "but I've been waiting, hoping to have something to tell you."

"I guess that means you don't have Spearman in custody."

"No such luck. The guy was long gone before we got the wheels in motion. We've got BOLOs out all over the state, but there are thousands of silver Chevy pickups in Texas. Without a license plate number or something more useful than a man and a boy in a truck, we don't have much chance of finding him."

"We think he's already crossed the border, Mack. We're exploring that angle."

"Meaning you're headed to Mexico? I don't like the sound of that."

"Meaning we're keeping our options open."

"You and the Special Forces guy?"

She and Mack were friends. She had told him she was

going after Timmy, and knowing he would be worried, she had mentioned Colt Wheeler. "Yes. Colt's with me."

She could almost see the burly cop nodding. "Good. Those guys know how to handle themselves. You two take care. I come up with anything, I'll let you know."

"Thanks, Mack."

Ending the call, she finger-combed her hair back from her face, thankful she kept it short, and walked back into the air-conditioned office.

"Anything?" Colt asked.

"No, which means we're probably right and he's already crossed into Mexico."

"There's bottled water and Cokes in the fridge in the other room," Alex said. "Help yourselves while I call Cortez."

Lissa headed toward a door at the rear of the office, Colt close behind her. The lunchroom had a table and chairs, a Formica counter with a sink, and a refrigerator. She pulled open the door of the fridge.

"Coke or water?"

"Water."

She took one for herself and handed a bottle to Colt.

"Thanks." Both of them twisted off the caps and took long, refreshing swallows, then sat down at the table to wait for Alex.

"You ready for this?" Colt asked.

"Ready or not—I'm going. You think this guy, Cortez, can help us?"

"If Spearman's a fixer for the cartel, he's got money and plenty of it. People with money are usually not that hard to find."

"Then why hasn't he been arrested and put back in prison?"

"Exactly the same reason. He's got money. In Mexico, money equals power. *Mordidas* is the name of the game."

"Bribes."

"Exactly. El Puñal pays off the local authorities and lives his life without a problem. That's why he feels safe bringing Timmy into his home."

"Assuming we're right."

One of his dark blond eyebrows arched up. "You don't think so?"

She sighed. "Unfortunately, I do."

Colt tipped up the water bottle and took several long swallows, moving the corded muscles in his throat. She tried not to think of last night, of pressing her mouth against the spot on the side of his neck where his pulse beat under her tongue. She tried not to remember inhaling the scent of salty skin and hot, virile male.

She turned away as her nipples tightened beneath the orange T-shirt she had put on that morning.

Colt rose from the table. "Let's go check out our gear, make sure we have everything we need."

Lissa nodded. She had a feeling Colt knew exactly what was in his gear bag. So did she, but it never hurt to double check.

They headed out into the heat and Colt popped the trunk on the Mustang. He unzipped a long black canvas bag to reveal what looked like enough weaponry to arm a small militia.

He took a Mossberg 12-gauge shotgun out of the bag, grabbed a box of shells and loaded the weapon, then set it on the floor of the trunk. A Beretta M9, standard army issue until this year, came out next. They had upgraded to a SIG Sauer P320-M17, she remembered reading somewhere.

Colt pulled out a loaded magazine and shoved it into

the Beretta. There was an eight-inch Ka-Bar knife in a thigh sheath, a Nighthawk .45, probably his backup weapon, which he loaded, a black tactical vest, and a .38 revolver, which he also loaded.

"Good thing we didn't get stopped and searched on the way down here," she said dryly.

"I'm just transporting the stuff back to Colorado. I'm licensed to carry there, and all of this stuff is legal."

Lissa checked her own weapons, just her SIG P226 and a little .380 she used as an ankle gun. She put the guns in her go bag next to the tactical vest she usually kept in the trunk of her car and had tossed in at the last minute. There was also a pair of camo cargo pants just in case.

Colt grabbed his travel bag, then slung the strap of his black canvas gear bag over his shoulder.

Alex walked out of the office carrying a travel bag of his own. They were all professionals. They carried the stuff they needed.

"Looks like you're ready. The flight plan's been filed. Let's load the stuff into the helo and get out of here before it gets any hotter."

"Good idea," Colt agreed. Clearly the humid Texas weather wasn't his favorite, but Lissa figured Georgia couldn't have been any better. Lissa supposed he was eager to get back to his home in Colorado and felt an unwanted pang in her chest.

She told herself it was ridiculous. They barely knew each other. But there was something about Colt Wheeler that just seemed to fit, a rightness she had never felt with a man before.

Didn't matter. As soon as this was over, he would be leaving Texas. The physical attraction he felt for her wouldn't be enough to keep him there. Since she hadn't had much luck with relationships, it was probably for the best.

The metallic blue helicopter glinted in the hot Texas sun as they drew near. Alex slid open the heavy door and they tossed their gear inside and climbed in, Alex settling in the pilot's seat. Colt tipped his head for Lissa to take the copilot's spot, but she declined.

Flying wasn't her favorite. Better to be in the back where she didn't have to see so much ground beneath them.

It was blistering hot inside the chopper as they strapped into their seats and put on their headsets. Fortunately, Alex speedily went through his preflight check and in minutes the helo blades were spinning, sweeping them up off the ground into the air and out of the airport compound.

Lissa's stomach lifted with the chopper, the fluttery sensation followed by a sweep of nausea. Fortunately, it didn't last long.

Colt's voice came over the headset. "You okay back there?"

"Sure," she said. "Just peachy keen."

He chuckled. "Hang in there. It's only a little more than an hour flight."

"I'm okay. I just prefer being on the ground."

"Yeah, me, too. Unless I'm jumping. Worth the plane ride to get in the air."

Parachuting was part of a ranger's life. She'd wondered what skydiving would be like. The thought had always intrigued her, but she'd never known anyone willing to try it.

She leaned back against the seat, thinking about Colt and how they seemed to fit. She wasn't sure what it was. Maybe just that she didn't intimidate him the way she did a lot of men. It was one of the reasons she'd liked being a cop. The guys on the force respected her strength, accepted it, were grateful for it. It took a while to earn their trust but once she did, they always had her back.

In a way she had hated to leave, but in another way, she'd craved being on her own. Becoming a private detective suited her perfectly. Unfortunately, the civilian side of life posed a far bigger challenge. It was the reason she rarely dated, hadn't been involved with a man in so long.

There just weren't a lot of men she'd been interested in. In fact, make that zero. Until now.

She glanced up as she felt a shift in the air and realized the chopper had started descending. A few minutes later, the struts settled on the ground, sending dust and leaves into the air. The blades began to slow. Lissa clicked her seat belt off and removed the headset as Colt slid open the door.

"Our ride's here. Alex has everything set. Grab your gear and let's go." Colt and Lissa took their bags and jumped out of the helo. Keeping their heads down, they ran a safe distance away.

"Alex is staying to take care of the chopper," Colt said. "He'll be joining us later."

Lissa nodded and they started walking, striding side by side across the tarmac. Colt stopped when he reached a big black Cadillac Escalade SUV. The driver, a young, thin-faced man with neatly trimmed black hair, pulled open the rear passenger door. Colt waited for Lissa to slide into the deep gray leather seat, then eased in beside her.

The big SUV was the luxury model, everything inside first-class. The air conditioner was running so the interior was cool.

"Nice," she said.

"Alex says we've got a sponsor," Colt said. "Benito Cortez has invited us to his house, a place in the hills called

Casa del Cielo. We'll be staying in one of the casitas until we finish our business."

"Seriously?"

He grinned. "Yeah." The grin faded. "Better yet, he's got intel. According to Alex, he and El Puñal are not exactly bosom buds. He's willing to help us any way he can."

"Looks like we finally caught a break."

"We'll know more by tonight. We're dining with Cortez and his wife, Lupita. In the meantime, we can relax in the casita, catch up on our sleep." His gaze zeroed in on her face and she didn't miss the heat in that hungry blue eye.

He still wanted her. And she very much wanted him.

"As far as I'm concerned, sleep is overrated," she said, sending his hard mouth up in amusement, lifting his sexy mustache.

"You're right, we can sleep when we're dead."

She gave him a sultry smile, but as the SUV rolled up into the mountains at the edge of the city, she didn't say more.

Neither did Colt.

Each knew the other was thinking about last night, wondering if it could possibly be that good again.

CHAPTER NINE

BENITO CORTEZ STROLLED out to greet them as the black SUV drove through the wrought iron gates of Casa del Cielo, "House of Heaven," a stunning residence on the side of a hill at the base of the Sierra Madre mountains.

The sprawling white structure was spectacular, a contemporary architectural design composed entirely of sharp-angled walls and huge plate glass windows. The fountain in front was a modern sculpture, and the views out over the city were magnificent.

The driver stopped the vehicle, got out, and opened the rear passenger door. Colt slid out first, reached down, and took hold of Lissa's hand. He ignored a thread of arousal as she followed him out into the bright Mexican sunshine. It was a few degrees cooler here, the air less humid, which suited Colt just fine.

The stout black-haired man walking toward them in a pair of beige chinos and a blue knit pullover wasn't tall or large. He wasn't handsome. At best, he was mildly attractive. There was no arrogance in his stride as he approached, and yet Colt could feel the power the man exuded as if it were a living force.

"Señor Wheeler." Cortez extended a blunt-fingered hand, the nails cut short and perfectly manicured.

Colt accepted the handshake. "Señor Cortez. A pleasure meeting you. We appreciate your hospitality." He turned. "This is Lissa Blayne. She's a friend of the missing boy's mother. Lissa is a private investigator in Dallas."

One of Cortez's black eyebrows went up. "A lady detective." He smiled. "I do not believe I have ever met a female sleuth before." His English was perfect. Alex had mentioned he was well educated.

Lissa smiled and extended her hand, which Cortez warmly accepted. "Thank you for offering your help," she said.

"As my friend Alejandro undoubtedly told you, it will be my pleasure to see El Puñal receive his dues." He waved airily. "But we will talk more about that tonight at supper when you will meet my lovely wife, Lupita. In the meantime…" He turned and an elegant young man in a perfectly tailored ivory linen suit came down off the porch.

"Rico will show you to your quarters. Your bags will be waiting for you. Cocktails at seven. Dinner at eight. There is a house phone in your casita. If there is anything you need, do not hesitate to ask."

"Thank you," Colt said. They followed Rico along a concrete walkway to a separate villa, one of several that hung on the side of the mountain a short distance from the house.

The structure was done in the same modern design, with brilliant white walls, sharp angles, and lots of windows. The inside was a surprise, the rooms brightened by the use of vivid colors. Reds, oranges, and yellows predominated in paintings, accent pieces, and pillows on the sofa, giving the contemporary design a distinctly Mexican flair.

"I will be back at seven to escort you to supper," Rico said, and left them.

Lissa turned in a circle to survey their surroundings and take in the spectacular view. "Wow. This place is amazing." Then she surprised Colt by reaching up and pulling off his patch before she leaned over and kissed him, her lips softening into his, heating his blood.

It was like lighting the fuse on a dynamite keg. Colt swept her hard against him and deepened the kiss, reached for her orange T-shirt and stripped it off over her head. The rest of her clothes quickly followed. As soon as both of them were naked, he lifted her, wrapped her long, pretty legs around his waist, and strode out of the living room, figuring the bedroom was somewhere down the hall.

The sex was mind-blowing. Just as before, their intimacy was profoundly satisfying, touching him in some unexpected way. He told himself it was just the newness of the relationship, but he had trouble convincing himself.

He knew women, had enjoyed more than his share. This was different. *She* was different.

Sated and relaxed, he curled her against his side and closed his eyes. Exhausted from worrying about the boy and his lack of sleep last night, he drifted away.

It was six o'clock when he awoke. Leaving Lissa asleep, Colt grabbed one of the white terry robes their host had provided and went into the living room. An ivory linen suit and short-sleeved blue-flowered shirt draped over the sofa. Next to it, an embroidered yellow sundress with a full gathered skirt had been laid out for Lissa.

Someone had entered the casita and left the garments. He grinned to think of the passionate sounds they must have heard seeping through the walls of the bedroom.

Lissa appeared beside him. "They brought us clothes for tonight?"

"Alex said they dress up for supper. It's a nice tradition."

Lissa smiled up at him. "If I'm going to wear a pretty dress, I need a shower." One of her blond eyebrows arched in challenge. "Would you care to join me?"

That comment didn't even warrant a reply. He took her hand. "Let's go."

STANDING ON A covered terrace overlooking the city, Lissa took a sip of the lime mango margarita Lupita had insisted she try. It was frosty and delicious, the salt on the rim crunchy and tangy on her tongue.

As they enjoyed cocktails before supper, the men drifted off in one direction while Lissa chatted with their hostess. Unfortunately, feeling restless and edgy and worried about Timmy, it was hard to concentrate.

She sipped her margarita, hoping it would settle her nerves. Earlier, Colt had tried to ease her fears by reminding her that Tim was with his father, and though there was no question the boy was in danger, they had to believe the man wouldn't harm his own son.

"There's no use worrying," he'd said. "Cortez has the information we need, and until we have it, there's nothing we can do."

He was right, of course. And the first step was to hear what Señor Cortez had to say.

"You are worried about the boy." Lupita's voice broke into Lissa's thoughts. Señora Cortez was exquisitely beautiful; a woman in her late twenties, tall and slender, with black eyes that tilted up at the corners, giving her an almost Middle Eastern look. She was wearing an ankle-length white gauze off-the-shoulder summer dress, tied with a colorful red sash. Dangling red-beaded earrings hung from her ears, and her feet were encased in red open-toed sandals. She also seemed very sweet and very much in love with her husband.

"His mother is my best friend. She's sick with fear for her son."

"My husband will do everything he can to help." Lupita glanced over to where Cortez spoke with Alex and Colt. "You see, Benito was married before. He lost a son to the drug cartels. His oldest boy, Miguel, craved independence. He began to associate with the wrong people. Benito tried to warn him, but Miguel wouldn't listen. You know how young men can be. He was killed during a fight between rival cartels."

"I'm sorry."

Lupita sipped her drink. "Benito's first wife, Maria, never recovered from the loss. She was sick with grief and eventually passed away. Benito understands the love of a mother for her son."

"Is he acquainted with Ray Spearman, the man they call El Puñal?"

She shook her head, shifting long black hair across her back. "Only by reputation. It is what El Puñal stands for that Benito disapproves of," Lupita said. "The misery he causes as he does the cartel's bidding. The man is known to be ruthless in the extreme."

A shiver slid down Lissa's spine. "We need to get Timmy out of there."

"*Si*, yes, and Benito knows this. As I said, he will do all he can to help." She glanced up to see Rico standing in the doorway, a sign it was time to eat.

"Dinner is ready." Lupita smiled. "You will find your seat next to your man, Colt."

Lissa's head came up, though Alex must have said they were together or they wouldn't be sharing a casita. At least for now, Colt was her man. She wished she didn't like the sound of it so much.

Determined to enjoy the time they had together, Lissa took her seat beside him. Colt reached beneath the table and laced her fingers with his.

"Enjoy the meal," he said softly. "We've got the intel we need. I'll fill you in when we get back to the casita."

Lissa relaxed. Clearly Colt had found out where Spearman had taken Timmy. Being left out of the men's conversation didn't upset her. This was Mexico, a male-dominated
society. And she had gleaned information of her own.

Now they just needed to come up with a plan to get
Timmy away from El Puñal, out of Mexico, and back to
Dallas.

The hard look on Colt's face said it wouldn't be easy.

TIMMY SAT IN an ornate high-back chair at a heavy, intri-
cately carved wooden dining table. His father sat in an even
bigger chair at the end. He called the house his hacienda.
It was like something Timmy had seen in a history book,
with thick beams in the ceilings and red-tile floors. The
walls were white, the rooms were huge, and there were
fireplaces everywhere.

"The house is filled with expensive antiques," his father
had told him proudly. "Be careful not to break anything."

Dad had shown him to his room upstairs on the opposite side of the house, which was built in a U-shape around
a patio with a fountain in the middle. They had driven in
through a big wooden gate in the wall that surrounded the
property.

And there were actual servants! Men in black pants and
white shirts, women in black skirts and white blouses. Dad
made them call him Don Ramon. Timmy figured *Ramon*
sounded like *Ray* in Spanish. *Don* probably meant "king"
or "emperor" or something because that was the way they
treated him.

"Eat your posole before it gets cold," his father said, jarring him out of his dark thoughts.

Timmy spooned in a mouthful and followed it with a
big gulp of water. It was some kind of pork dish, and it was

burning hot. He had never liked spicy food but he was in Mexico now. He figured he had better get used to it.

"Hurry up and finish so you can go up to your room and get some sleep. I've got a tutor for you starting tomorrow morning. We'll see how your school work is progressing, make sure you don't backslide. His name is Señor Garcia and he'll also be teaching you Spanish."

Timmy's chest felt tight. He took a deep breath the way the doctor told him to do when he got upset. He didn't want to start wheezing. He didn't want his father to think he was a wimp.

He managed to nod. His teachers said he talked too much, but now words seemed to stick in his throat.

"What about Mom?" he asked, the question stupidly popping out of his mouth.

"I'll call her in a day or two, let her know you're okay. We'll give her a little time to get used to the idea you'll be staying with me, then you can talk to her."

His head bobbed in agreement, but he felt like crying. He wouldn't be going home any time soon.

He started to slide the heavy chair back.

"You'll ask to be excused before you leave."

He swallowed. "Can I be excused?"

"*May* I be excused, and yes, you may."

As Timmy slid the chair back, crossed the tile floor, and started up the stairs to his bedroom, he wondered if he would ever see his mother and sister again.

CHAPTER TEN

BENITO CORTEZ WASN'T the only useful contact Alex Romero had in Mexico. He had family here, including a cousin who was living in Monterrey. Diego De La Guerra was a former Mexican soldier now working undercover for the government, part of a joint US-Mexico task force targeting the leaders and finances of the drug cartels.

Diego met them at midnight in a little cantina called El Adobe. It was crowded and noisy, a band playing popular Mexican music on a small stage at the back of the room. Smoke drifted up from wooden tables and there were enough tourists mixed in so that two blond Americans didn't stand out.

Alex led them to a table off to one side where a good-looking, dark-complexioned Mexican man with straight black hair pulled into a stubby ponytail lounged back in his chair. A bottle of Dos Equis sat in front of him.

"This is my cousin Diego," Alex said in English, setting the tone for the meeting. He tipped his head toward the two of them. "These are my friends Lissa Blayne and Colt Wheeler."

"Thanks for meeting us," Colt said as they took seats around the battered wooden table.

"You are here for the boy," Diego said, not bothering with small talk.

"That's right."

"It is unfortunate El Puñal brought his son here at this time."

"What do you know about Timmy?" Lissa asked.

A server's appearance put the answer on hold, a young woman with a pretty face, full breasts bulging from the top of a low-cut blouse, and an obvious eye for Diego.

He pointed to his beer. *"Tres mas Dos Equis, por favor."*

"Si, señor." She flashed him a smile, tossed her long black hair, and sashayed off toward the bar. The conversation remained on hold until she returned with the beers, which Diego generously paid for. Casting him a last interested glance, the waitress merged into the crowd in search of other customers.

Diego's dark eyes traveled from Colt to Lissa and back again. "Alejandro has told you who I am. He has vouched for you, so I will tell you as much as I can." The chair creaked as he sat forward. "For almost three months, the task force has been monitoring El Puñal's movements. We knew he crossed the border into Texas, but we did not know he would be returning with his son."

"Why didn't you arrest him when he left the country?" Colt asked. "According to our information, he's wanted in the States as well as here in Mexico."

Diego took a long swallow of beer. "As powerful a man as he is, El Puñal is only a small prize compared to the men we are after. Those men will soon be gathering at Spearman's hacienda to discuss plans to expand the opioid trade in your country, drugs that have been extremely profitable for the cartels. Each man is second in command—*segundo*—to a cartel leader, in many ways even more deadly. This is a chance to end their reign of terror, a chance to save thousands of lives."

"When is the meeting?" Lissa asked.

"That I cannot tell you."

Colt leaned forward. "So let me guess. In a matter of days, maybe a week, law enforcement is planning a raid on El Puñal's compound."

Diego's lips thinned but he didn't deny it. "I have said too much already. I can assure you that getting the boy out safely will be a top priority. My advice is that the two of you go back to Texas and leave the boy's safe return to us."

Colt flicked a sideways glance at Lissa, whose gaze locked with his in silent communication.

"We understand the importance of your mission," she said. "We aren't asking you to cancel your plans. All we're asking is that when you go in, you let us go in with you."

Diego shook his head. "That is not an option."

"I'm a US Army Ranger," Colt said. "Lissa is a trained police officer. Let us help you. We'll follow your orders and stay out of your way. We'll take care of the boy and you'll be able to do your job without worrying about his safety."

"I'm sorry. I am afraid I cannot do that."

Colt leaned back in his chair. "You might want to re-think that position. If we don't go in, neither will you. We could blow the whistle on your whole operation. Leak your plans to El Puñal. You'd wind up with nothing to show for three months of hard work."

Diego's jaw tightened. "You realize I could have both of you arrested and thrown into prison."

Lissa set a hand on Diego's arm where it rested on the table. "We don't want to make trouble for you or the people you work for. We just want to bring Timmy home to his mother."

"The answer is still no." He focused on Colt. "And if you are the man my cousin believes, you will do nothing to interfere with our operation. This man, Spearman, and the men he is meeting are drug dealers and murderers. They destroy life every day, all for their own profit. We will watch out for the boy. I give you my word."

Colt took a long swallow of beer, resignation filtering through him. He set the bottle back down on the table.

"You took a chance just meeting us tonight. We won't repeat anything you've said or interfere in your operation in any way. You have our word on that. But we aren't leaving Monterrey without the boy."

Diego relaxed. "A compromise, then. I know where to find you. I will see the boy is returned as soon as this is over." Rising, he finished the last of his beer, turned, and made his way through the crowd toward the entrance, pausing briefly to speak to the girl with the long black hair. Both of them laughed, and Diego disappeared out the door.

Colt turned to Lissa and Alex. "If they go in with a massive army of men, they'll need to bring Spearman and the cartel *segundos* down. Timmy could get hurt."

"Or killed," Lissa said.

"So what are we going to do?" Alex asked.

"Only one thing we can do. Get Tim out before the task force goes in."

LISSA WALKED IN front of Colt and Alex out of the cantina, and Alex drove them back to the casita. He was staying in the city with a woman, which probably explained some of his eagerness to accompany them to Monterrey.

He would be picking them up in the morning, driving them to San Pedro Garza Garcia, an urban center about eight miles southwest of the city. According to Señor Cortez, El Puñal's compound, which overlooked the basin, sat near the end of a road winding into the Loma Larga mountains.

As soon as they were back in the casita, Lissa used the information Cortez had provided to find the area on Google Maps.

"The place looks like a fortress," she said, studying Google Earth photos on her cell phone, satellite images of the house and grounds. "How are we going to get in?" She glanced over her shoulder at Colt, who stared at the screen from behind her.

"More importantly, how are we going to get out?" He rubbed the back of his neck. "Alex will be here in the morning to drive us up there. Once we get a look at the place, maybe we can find a chink in Spearman's armor."

Lissa hoped so. But the task of getting in and out without being seen seemed impossible.

"In the meantime," Colt said, "it's late. We need to get some sleep."

Lissa cast him a glance. "What about sleep being overrated?"

Colt's mouth edged up in amusement. "True, but we really need to be at the top of our game if we're going against a guy they call The Dagger."

She sighed. "You're right. We've got to stay focused on Timmy." She didn't want to imagine the boy's fear, being with a man he didn't know, worried about his mom and sister, afraid he might never get back home.

Colt must have sensed the depth of her concern. "On the other hand, it's important to get the best night's sleep possible, and I know exactly the way to make that happen."

The glimmer of heat in that cool blue eye drained some of the tension from her shoulders. Lissa managed to smile. Reaching out to take the hand he offered, she let him lead her down the hall to the bedroom.

THE MOUNTAINS ABOVE the metropolis of San Pedro Garza Garcia were rugged: jagged granite outcroppings shoving up from the earth, dense scrub vegetation that included the occasional cactus or palm, and thick deciduous forests.

Luxury homes dotted the lower slopes, the streets lined with leafy trees and colorful blooming flowers, but farther up the hill, the terrain turned forbidding, a hostile no-man's-land.

Using GPS coordinates, they located Spearman's house at the end of the road at the far edge of the city: a huge two-story U-shaped white structure with a red-tiled roof. It was completely surrounded by a ten-foot wall.

The good news was the terrain would provide the cover they needed to get close to the residence without being seen. The bad news was it was going to take a miracle to find a way in.

Alex parked his girlfriend's SUV out of sight in the heavy foliage a quarter mile down the hill and they all got out of the vehicle. Wearing the camouflage cargo pants and T-shirt he'd had in his gear bag, Colt joined Alex and Lissa, who both wore lightweight camo.

Before they could come up with a plan, they needed intel, needed to know what they would be facing. They split up and took off in different directions, each taking a position to watch one side of the house. Careful to stay out of sight, they moved silently through the trees, keeping a lookout for any of Spearman's men patrolling the area.

Colt hunkered down to track the east section of the house and grounds, while Lissa moved around to the west, and Alex took a position at the rear. An hour later, they rendezvoused in a hidden spot in front, where they could observe people and cars going in and out through the main gate.

"Sitrep?" Colt asked Lissa, once they were back in a secure location.

"I spotted two of Spearman's men on foot patrol. They

weren't paying a lot of attention. Clearly they weren't expecting trouble."

"They'll be far more alert the day the cartel higher-ups are due to arrive," Colt said.

She sighed. "I wish we knew when that was going to happen."

"I think Colt nailed it." Alex rolled his beefy shoulders, probably stiff from sitting in one place for so long. "If I read my cousin Diego right, I'd say sometime this week, probably no more than a couple of days."

"Which means we haven't got much time," Colt said. "You pick up anything useful out there?"

"I might have. You saw the rear entrance into the compound on Google Maps, right? A gate that opens onto a dirt lane curving around the hacienda to the main road?"

"We saw it," Colt said. "Couldn't tell much about it from the images we were able to access."

"Could be exactly what we're looking for," Alex said. "Freight and staff go in and out that way, and from what I could tell, it was fairly busy."

"You get pictures?"

Alex held up his smart phone. "Sure did. Sent them to your cell."

Colt nodded. "Let's go back to the casita and make some plans."

Benito had insisted on meeting them when they returned that afternoon. He joined them just minutes after their arrival and he didn't come alone.

"I brought someone who may be able to help us," Benito said as he walked into the tile-floored entry of the guest house. He motioned for the man behind him to come forward. "This is Zachariah Bridges. I think you will find him a man of many talents."

"Zach," the man corrected, reaching out to shake Colt's and Lissa's hands. "Good to meet you." He was in his midforties, whipcord lean and hard-edged, his skin sun-browned to the color of teak. With his dark hair and dark eyes, he could pass for Mexican, but the minute he started speaking, Colt knew he was an American.

"Zach has retired from the federal agency he once worked for," Benito said. "He now makes his home in Monterrey."

Colt looked him over, trying to discern which of the alphabet agencies had employed him. "Thanks for coming. We can use all the help we can get."

"I understand you were at Spearman's earlier today."

Apparently Benito trusted the man enough to reveal their mission. If they wanted to succeed, they had no choice but to trust him, too. "That's right."

"Then you know it won't be easy to get into the compound and possibly even more difficult to find the boy once you're inside. I can help you locate him."

One of Colt's eyebrows arched up. "That so?"

"You're talking about surveillance equipment," Lissa guessed, earning another degree of respect from Colt.

Bridges smiled, sun lines crinkling at the corners of his dark eyes. "I brought some things I figured you could use. Parabolic mic, infrared thermal imaging camera, and best of all—a drone."

"A drone?" Lissa asked.

"That's right, and not just any drone." Zach reached into his pocket and pulled out a device about an inch-and-a-half long that looked like an insect. "Flies right in, gives you a visual on everything that's happening inside the house. Or it can circle the perimeter, keep an eye on what's happening in the courtyard or outside the wall."

Colt's level of confidence rose. With all of them working together, hell, maybe they could actually pull this off.

He turned to the others. "If we set up the mic and thermal camera on the hill, we'll be able to hear what's going on in the house and locate Tim by the size of his infrared image."

"And the drone lets you know where the bad guys are while you're in there," Alex added.

"Which is great," Lissa said, "if we can figure out how to get in."

Alex's jet-black hair gleamed in the light hanging over the table. "I've got an idea that might work. While I was watching the back gate, I saw two different trucks drive in and out. One was a food truck, the other was a UPS parcel delivery truck. There was only a single guard at the gate. He spoke to the drivers, then waved them right through. I have a hunch trucks come and go all the time."

Colt started nodding. "That many people around, they need supplies. And like everyone else these days, they probably buy a lot of stuff on the internet. We get hold of a UPS truck, we can drive right in through the back gate."

Alex grinned. "Easy peasy."

Colt thought of the armed men they'd be facing once they got into the compound. "Yeah. No problem at all."

CHAPTER ELEVEN

SINCE EVERYONE SEEMED ready for a break, Lissa checked the refrigerator, found a six-pack of Jarritos soda, and passed the chilled bottles around.

"The best way out of Mexico is the same way we came in," Alex said, taking a swallow of the lime-flavored drink while Lissa resumed her seat. "I just need to find a landing site close to the house. I saw a promising spot this morning, but I need to check it out."

Colt tipped up his bottle and took a long swallow. "We can't fly out at night, but we won't need to if we breach the compound during the day. We drive in, grab the boy, drive out, and head for the landing site."

"This could work," Lissa said, feeling a rush of excitement.

Colt flashed her a smile. "Yeah, baby, it could."

The endearment and the warmth in his expression sent her heart rate up a notch. Colt Wheeler was everything she respected in a man. And he already meant far more to her than someone she had hooked up with for a few nights of sexual release. Not that she did that often. With Colt it had just seemed so natural, exactly the right thing to do.

Benito leaned back in his chair. "It could work, but there is still a problem."

Colt arched a brow. "You're worried about what Spearman will do when he finds out Timmy's gone."

"*Si*, that is right. Spearman could call off his meeting with the men from the cartels to go after his son. We could be jeopardizing the task force's entire mission."

Lissa's attention swung to Colt. "You think he'd do that? Call off the meeting?"

Colt shrugged. "No way to know for sure. He'll be furious at being outmaneuvered, but he's a selfish son of a bitch or he wouldn't have forced Timmy to leave his home. Guy like that, I don't think he'll put his personal agenda in front of the chance to expand his power base."

Benito seemed to mull that over. "I think you are correct. If we get the boy out of the house and Alex flies you all back to Texas, Spearman may come after his son again, or send someone to do it, but I do not think he will cancel the meeting."

"If the task force does its job," Zach put in, "El Puñal will be locked up in prison, too busy covering his ass—literally—to give his family any more grief." A faint flush tinted the leathery skin over his cheekbones. "Sorry, ma'am."

Lissa just smiled. She'd been a police detective. She knew what happened in prison. In Spearman's case, whatever he got was well deserved.

Benito was speaking. "Everything carries a certain amount of risk," he said, his gaze going around the table. "I think you should proceed with your plan."

All of them agreed.

As another hour slipped past, more details were added. Zach would provide additional equipment, namely an AR-15, which would be hidden in the delivery truck, along with a couple of backup weapons, in case they ran into trouble as they left the compound.

"But you can't just go in there blasting away," Zach said.

"Not if you expect to get out alive. You need to be extremely careful how you proceed."

"Good thought." A corner of Colt's sexy mouth edged up and Lissa's stomach contracted. She reminded herself now was not the time to be thinking about sex, but whenever Colt was around, desire was never far away.

When they were satisfied with the details they had worked out, Lissa and Colt walked the others to the door. Since they would be abandoning Zach's surveillance gear at the location, Benito insisted on paying for it. Likely he was also paying Zach Bridges a hefty sum for his help.

Lissa understood his motivation. Benito Cortez was a good man. He had plenty of money, and he had lost a son.

"Who do you think Bridges worked for?" Lissa asked once she and Colt were alone.

"Considering the spy gear, CIA would be my guess. Now he's retired from The Company and working for himself, doing pretty much the same job he did before."

"Spying on people."

Colt smiled. "Pretty much."

Tonight Zach would be bringing the additional gear they needed, then helping them set up the microphone and camera outside the compound.

Tomorrow, at the end of the day after most of the employees had gone home, they would go in. The few who remained would be tired by then, suffering from the lingering heat and wishing their shift was over.

Alex was in charge of "borrowing" a UPS delivery truck. "I'll take care of it," he said. "I've got a cousin who drives for them."

Lissa and Colt both grinned. Alex's seemingly endless list of friends and relatives definitely came in handy.

EVENING ARRIVED, the hot sun sinking below the mountains behind the house, casting long shadows over the city and creeping toward the jagged peaks to the east.

After supper with Benito and Lupita, during which they carefully avoided any mention of the upcoming mission, Colt and Lissa returned to the casita. It was midnight when Alex arrived in his borrowed compact SUV, while Zach drove up in his dark brown Chevy pickup.

As a precaution, they were taking both vehicles. Lissa rode with Alex, which seemed to annoy Colt, who rode with Zach, giving him a chance to review the operation of the surveillance gear. She wondered at his dark mood. Surely he wasn't jealous. It seemed impossible when their relationship was so uncertain. Still, she couldn't help hoping it was a sign of his feelings for her.

Whatever happened, she would never regret the time she spent with him. She hoped he would feel the same about her. That over the years, he would remember her with warm affection. Though what she felt for him had become far more than that. The thought made her chest feel tight.

They headed for the compound. By the time they were parked out of sight on the side of the hill, the temperature was much cooler. A gentle breeze rustled the leaves on the trees as Lissa moved silently through the foliage with Colt and Zach toward an outcropping of granite she had spotted on Google Earth.

Alex had headed off to a wide, flat, open area he had noticed when they had been there that morning. He wanted to take a closer look, make sure it would work as a helo exfil location, military speak for extraction point.

Careful to stay out of sight, the three of them reached the rocky outcropping, slipped behind a cluster of boulders, and began to arrange the equipment. The rocks provided cover while they set up the parabolic mic, which, according to Zach, could pick up sounds as faint as fingers rubbing together from as far away as fifty meters, about a hundred and sixty-five feet. Colt moved silently off through the brush, finding a place close enough to the house to pick up the sounds inside.

"All set," he said as he returned. Zach would be manning the gear, monitoring the info, and relaying it through the earbuds they would be wearing tomorrow. He would also be controlling the drone, their primary source of information.

He turned on the devices, set the drone loose for a test flight, then they settled in to wait. This late there wasn't much activity. When Zach pointed to a glowing infrared image on the second floor at the far end of the west wing of the house, Lissa's heart took a leap. *Timmy?*

"You think it's him?" she asked.

"Hard to say the way he's positioned."

"In bed most likely," Colt said.

"Can't be sure it's him," Zach said. "But the other images are all larger. I'd say that's likely the boy asleep in his bedroom."

"That's the room farthest from the main part of the house," Lissa said, remembering the photos on Google Earth. "There's a balcony with a wrought iron railing off each room on the upper floor. The rooms all look into the courtyard. But the room at the far end has two balconies, one looking into the courtyard, the other facing the mountains. That one's pretty much out of sight. We could go over the rail, go in through the balcony doors, and bring Tim out the same way."

"I like it," Colt said, nodding. "I'll be driving the truck. If I park under the balcony, you could climb up on top, go right over the rail, and get Tim. In the meantime, I'll keep the people in the house occupied long enough for you to get the job done."

"How will you do that?"

He smiled. "I'm a delivery man, right? I'll deliver some fake parcels, keep them talking long enough to get Tim out."

She started nodding. "That's good."

"I'll also be your backup," Colt said. "If trouble comes, inside or out, I'll be ready."

"Good plan," Zach said. "The trick is to do it without being seen."

Silence fell.

Zach was the first to speak. "You need a couple of stun guns. A guy walks up on you, you hit him. A five-second jolt will put a man down long enough for you to get away. Hit him enough times, he's out for minutes."

Lissa could feel the plan coming together, the way it had before a raid when she was with the DPD. "Can you get ahold of some?"

Zach nodded. "I'll take care of it." He returned his attention to the imaging screen, pointed at a glowing red infrared image moving rhythmically along the inside of the wall, a guard no doubt. The man made several circles, then went into the house through the back door. The parabolic mic picked up a conversation in Spanish with another man, something about a shift change, and the sound of laughter. Their voices were crystal clear.

"Everything's working," Zach said. "Let's cover it up and get out of here."

They threw a small camouflage net over the camera and another over the mic, disguised them with leaves and sticks, then made their way back to the vehicles. Alex joined them a few minutes later.

"Landing site looks good," he said. "Airpark where the chopper's sitting is less than fifteen minutes away. I'll be on-site and ready for evac by the time you get the boy to the LZ."

The words filled Lissa with hope and a goodly dose of fear. Time was running out. The cartel *segundos* would be arriving any day. Once they were there, the task force would be charging in with a massive offensive, a battery of armed men and deadly weapons, storming the place in a barrage of gunfire. Timmy could be killed.

They had to get him out of there. Tomorrow was their best chance. If they failed, all of them could wind up dead.

CHAPTER TWELVE

THE MORNING SUN brightened the horizon when Colt awakened next to Lissa. They had returned to the casita late last night and gone straight to bed, both badly needing sleep. Still, when he'd curled her against him spoon fashion, a flash of heat burned through him, and he went hard beneath the sheets.

Lissa's need must have mirrored his. A soft sound came from her throat and she moved closer, urging him to take her from behind. It was hot, erotic sex, but with Lissa it was always so much more. He couldn't define it. He just knew he needed it, needed her.

He only hoped Lissa felt at least some of what he felt for her. He sighed into the morning quiet. Even if she did, with both of them living different lives nearly a thousand miles apart, he had no idea what to do about it.

Resigned, he got up to shower and dress and Lissa did the same. By late morning, they were positioned on the hill below the compound, the surveillance equipment turned on and working. They needed to know what was happening inside the house, needed to locate Tim and watch his movements.

Timing was everything and the clock was ticking.

They spent the rest of the morning and early afternoon observing activities around the house, counting the number of guards, memorizing their schedules. Tim's smaller image had been easy to identify, and they could even hear his voice. He was upstairs in his room at the far end of the house, getting lessons from a teacher he called Señor Garcia.

Outside the compound, exactly every half hour, a guard patrolled a worn path around the perimeter of the property. Fortunately, the rocks gave them cover and they knew what time the man would be passing by. So far they hadn't had a problem.

They were almost ready. Zach would be working the spy gear and manning the drone while Colt drove the UPS truck, and Alex piloted the chopper. Alex's cousin had arrived with the delivery truck an hour ago and left it parked down the hill in the same secluded spot they had used last night. Lissa would be riding in the back of the truck, hidden among a stack of fake parcels loaded with an assortment of bricks and papers.

All of them were armed to the teeth, a pair of semiautos, six-inch folding knives, and stun guns, but the goal was to complete the mission without being seen.

The sun still burned brightly when they realized they would need to move their original plan ahead. They had to get to Tim while he was upstairs with his teacher, before he left for another part of the house or went down to supper.

They were geared up and ready to go in when Colt's cell phone vibrated. He pulled it out and saw it was Alex.

"We got trouble," Alex said. "Diego just called. A member of the task force spotted us on the hill last night. They were planning to arrest us, but word just reached them that the cartel *segundos* were on the move, on their way to the meeting with El Puñal. Diego relayed a warning for us to back off and let them do their jobs or suffer the consequences."

Colt's glance went from Lissa to Zach. Time had just run out.

"Get ready to move the chopper into position," he said to Alex. "We're going in."

"Copy that. See you at the LZ." The line went dead.

Colt turned. "Cartel's on its way. We're out of time. If we're going, we need to go now."

Lissa nodded. Her chin firmed. "Let's go."

While Zach remained on the hill, Colt and Lissa made their way back into the trees, then hurried down the hill to the UPS truck. Lissa wore her tactical vest under a camo T-shirt, while Colt's vest was hidden under the UPS uniform shirt left for him in the truck. He'd been deployed in South America so his Spanish was better than average. Good enough, he hoped, to get him into the compound.

They each checked their primary weapon, dropped the mag and shoved it back in, checked their backup pieces, a couple of Beretta M9s. The AR-15 and extra mags were hidden behind the driver's seat. Lissa climbed in the back and took her place beneath a big empty cardboard box, and Colt fired up the engine. The truck pulled sluggishly onto the road and began to grind its way up the hill.

It didn't take long to reach the dirt lane that circled around to the back of the house. Dust billowed around them, forcing Colt to slow down, and the road was rutted in places, making the ride bouncy as hell. A few minutes later, he spotted the gate up ahead.

"We're here," he said into the mic attached to the tiny earbud out of sight in his ear. Mexican music played on the radio in the dash, helping cover his American accent as he spoke to the guard. There were two of them now, he noticed. Extra men in preparation for the cartel members' arrival.

Colt stepped on the brake as the guard on the driver's side walked up to the truck.

"Buenos días," the guard said, peering into the interior.

Both men wore short-sleeved tan uniforms, and both of them were armed with semiautomatic pistols.

"Buenos días," Colt replied, smiling. There were plenty of blond Mexicans so his fair skin and hair shouldn't be a problem. The eye patch was conspicuous, but he was wearing a UPS ball cap pulled low across his forehead, which helped. And no one knew who he was, including Ray Spearman.

The other guard looked in through the passenger window, walked to the rear and opened the door, saw the stack of parcels ready for delivery, and slammed it shut.

The first guard waved him through the gate, and Colt drove into the compound. *So far so good.* The next part was tricky, pulling around to the west end of the U-shaped building, then backing up beneath the balcony. He was far enough away the guards didn't seem to notice, or maybe they were used to trucks parking wherever they could find a place.

Colt walked around to the back and opened the door. He couldn't see Lissa but he knew she was in there waiting for their plan to move forward. "Truck's in position. I'm heading for the house now."

Zach's voice came through the earbud. "Everything's a go on this end." Meaning Timmy was still in his bedroom.

"Roger that," Colt said. Reaching up, he adjusted his earbud to be sure it was out of sight.

Lissa lifted the box away and stood up facing him, her pretty brown eyes intense on his face. "Come back to me," she said softly.

His throat tightened. He wanted to tell her how much she meant to him, but now wasn't the time. "Don't wait more than five minutes. If I'm not back, drive out the gate and keep going. They aren't checking the trucks as they're leaving. Just drive out and don't stop till you get to the landing zone."

Her chin firmed. "I'm not leaving you here. That was never the plan."

"Think of Tim and do what you have to. Stay safe." He loaded a stack of fake parcels into his arms, eased the door shut but didn't actually close it, turned, and walked away.

FIGHTING TO BLOCK out Colt's last words and the terror that had gripped her when he'd said them, Lissa opened the truck door enough to check her surroundings. A heavy-set woman in a long red gathered skirt tended a vegetable garden on the far side of the compound. A man in a wide-brimmed straw hat worked in the flower beds pulling weeds. She could see one of the two guards who had been at the gate when they'd driven through, but the other guard must have wandered away.

She looked but couldn't spot him, and nerves burned through her. Slipping out the back of the truck, she climbed the narrow ladder beside the door and stepped onto the roof of the vehicle, keeping as low as she could.

Choosing a spot where she couldn't be seen from the bedroom, she reached up, grabbed the iron rail, and hauled herself over. In seconds she was on the balcony, moving quietly toward the French doors.

She was hoping they wouldn't be locked, doubted anyone in the compound worried about a break-in, but she carried a lock pick just in case.

Flattening herself against the wall, she took a quick look through the small glass panes. The teacher had his back to her. Timmy was facing the door. She stepped out where he could see her, put a finger to her lips to signal him to be quiet, saw the faint jolt of his body as he recognized her.

Lissa carefully turned the door knob. As she had hoped, the door swung quietly open. She drew her pistol as she stepped inside and pushed the barrel into the teacher's back. The stun gun remained within easy reach. She hoped she wouldn't need it.

The teacher stiffened.

"Be quiet and you won't get hurt." She had heard him speaking to Timmy in English, so she knew he understood. "Turn around, Señor Garcia. Do it slowly."

He was a lean man, about her height, with a leonine mane of silver hair.

"What do you want?"

"Put your hands behind you. Do it now, professor."

He did what she told him, and she cuffed him with one of the zip ties in the pocket of her cargo pants.

"Coming here is a death sentence," he said in slightly accented English. "You must know that."

Lissa made no reply, just took a roll of duct tape out of her pack, tore off a strip, and slapped it over his mouth. She used the gun to wave him toward the closet, and Timmy raced to pull it open. He seemed to be recovering from his shock. She knew he was still afraid, but he was also determined to help.

"Get in," she commanded Garcia. "Sit down on the floor and put your back against the wall." As soon as he was in position, she zip-tied his ankles. "We'll be out of here in just a few minutes. Stay quiet and you'll be okay." It occurred to her she might be saving his life. At least up here, he wouldn't be caught by a stray bullet when the task force raid commenced.

She closed the closet door and turned. "Time to go, Tim."

His eyes were huge, a rapid pulse beating in the side of his neck. "I can't believe you're here."

"We haven't got much time."

He ran toward her, and she pulled him in for a quick hard hug. "We're going home. You just have to be brave a little longer."

Some of the color washed out of his face, making his freckles stand out. A wheezy breath whispered out. "Okay."

She thought of the asthma attack he'd had and a fresh rush of fear slipped through her. "Everything's going to be all right. Colt's waiting for us. You just need to stay calm and let us get you out of here, okay?"

He took a deep breath and released it slowly. Some of the strain in his face seemed to ease. "Okay."

With a hand on his shoulder, she urged him out onto the balcony. It was still quiet in the courtyard, the woman working in the garden, the man in the straw hat still pulling weeds in the flower beds. She could see the rear gate, see one of the guards leaning against the wall, smoking a cigarette. He was talking to a woman who must have just come out of the house. Lissa was too far away to tell much about her, aside from her petite size and black hair, but she seemed to be keeping the guard occupied.

Lissa hurried to the railing and turned to Tim. "It's not far to the top of the truck. Just be careful as you climb over the rail."

His shoulders straightened. "I can do it."

"Good boy. There's a ladder next to the door at the back of the truck. When you reach the ground, get in the back and hide behind the boxes. I'll be right behind you."

She took a last glance into the bedroom. The teacher was still in the closet. Lissa followed Tim over the railing to the top of the truck, down the ladder, then into the hot, humid darkness inside the back of the truck.

Five minutes, Colt had said. They were maintaining radio silence as long as he was inside the house. She glanced at Tim, saw the outline of the boy's small body huddled in the dark behind an empty box, saw that he was trembling.

Lissa thought of Julie and how much she loved her son. She thought of Timmy and her promise to bring him home.

Five minutes, Colt had said. *He'll be back*, she told herself, blocking any other thought. But she moved to the front of the truck and climbed into the driver's seat just in case.

Easing down out of sight, she started praying.

CHAPTER THIRTEEN

A KNOCK ON the rear door of the hacienda brought a uniformed guard to the door, a beefy guy with black close-cropped hair. Colt asked if the guy wanted him to carry the stack of parcels inside, and being no fool, the guy motioned him through the door.

"Ponlos en la mesa de la cocina," the guard said—put them on the table in the kitchen. Which Colt did, taking as much time as he could, then both of them returned to the back door.

By then they were chatting, the conversation moving along without a problem, just two guys killing a little of the workday. He told the guard a slightly dirty joke, which seemed to put him at ease, and the guy told a foul joke in return.

Colt managed to come up with a laugh.

Then the guard began casting salacious glances at one of the young serving women, telling Colt that he planned to have the girl on her back by the end of the week. Instead of smashing his fist into the guy's face, Colt forced a grin and wished him luck.

It was time to leave. Colt waved and started walking. He prayed nothing had gone wrong and Lissa and Timmy were safely back in the truck, but he couldn't risk speaking into the mic until he was out of the house.

He had just reached the porch when his earbud crackled to life. "They found the teacher," Zach said, info he'd gotten from the drone. "Get out now!"

Colt picked up his pace. He was stepping off the porch into the courtyard when all hell broke loose.

"They've taken my boy! They've got my son!" It could only be Spearman's furious, booming voice. "Lock this place down! You hear me! We have a breach!"

Colt kicked into a loping run, heading for the truck. The engine roared to life before he reached it. He saw the vehicle pulling out of the space he'd backed into, so he changed direction, and ran for the open delivery-side door instead of the driver's seat.

He was almost there when a tall, well-built guard stepped in front of him, blocking his way. *"Alto!"* he shouted. Stop!

Colt pulled the stun gun, jammed the prongs against the side of the guy's neck, and he went down like a sack of grain. Colt kept running, caught up with the truck as it jolted forward and picked up speed as it rolled across the courtyard. He leaped into the open delivery door.

"Keep driving!" he shouted over the whine of the engine and steadied himself against the bump and sway of the van, relief surging through him at seeing Lissa safe. Relief and something far stronger. "Don't stop, baby. Not for anything or anyone."

Her gaze locked with his an instant before she stomped on the gas and the truck surged forward.

One of Spearman's soldiers ran toward them. *"Cierra la puerta! Cierra la puerta!"* Close the gate! Close the gate!— as he raced across the courtyard, but the gate guard wasn't at his post. The soldier continued running toward them, but Lissa had already reached the gate.

She gunned the engine, the truck burst through the opening and didn't slow, roaring down the dirt lane back toward the main road.

Colt's gaze searched the dim interior of the truck for Timmy, spotted him huddled in the darkness. "We're going home, Tim!" he shouted over the engine noise and a sudden barrage of gunfire. "Just stay down and hang on until we can get you there!"

"I'm okay!" Timmy shouted back, and Colt could hear the determination in his voice.

"Two Jeeps just drove out the back gate behind us," Lissa said, checking the rearview mirror. "They're trying to catch up."

Dust billowed around them, providing a little cover against the shots pinging off the hot metal body of the truck. Colt squeezed Lissa's shoulder, pulled his Beretta, and headed for the door at the rear.

He'd only taken a couple of steps when his earbud crackled to life. "The cartel caravan is turning off the main road into the main driveway leading to the front door of the house," Zach said. "They sent a group of soldiers ahead of the main body, two black SUVs. They took the dirt lane around to the back. You're going to have to go through them to get to the main road."

"Copy that," Colt said. "I'd suggest you pull back, get yourself somewhere safe."

"Roger that. I'm out of here. Good luck." The mic went dead.

Spearman's soldiers behind, cartel soldiers in front. *First things first.* Colt's jaw hardened as he continued to the door at the rear of the truck.

TIMMY HAD NEVER been more scared in his life. At the same time, he felt a rush of determination stronger than anything he'd ever felt before. Colt and Lissa had come for him. They were risking their lives to get him home. He would do whatever he could to help them.

Lying flat on the floor of the truck, he gripped a bar built into the wall, used to secure packages, and watched Colt open the rear door and brace himself, sling the strap of an assault rifle over his head and settle it across his chest.

Timmy's pulse started racing and suddenly he couldn't breathe. His chest locked down, air wheezed out, and a wave of dizziness hit him. People could die today. Lissa and Colt could die. He could die. Then he looked at Colt, standing there ready to fight for him. He thought of Lissa, coming all the way to Mexico to save him, and his determination surfaced again.

Easing in a deep breath a little at a time, he held it, then slowly released it. He did it again and felt his muscles relaxing, his chest loosening. One more time and he started breathing normally again.

Through the opening Colt was using to look out the back of the truck, he could see a couple of Jeeps racing toward them. Metal pinged as bullets slammed into the truck. Colt started shooting, firing off round after round. One of his shots slammed through the windshield of the Jeep right behind them and it veered off the road into a ditch.

Colt kept firing, aiming the gun toward the second Jeep, shooting out the windshield, then hitting the left front tire. The Jeep crashed into a boulder and surged into the air, did a weird slow roll and hit the ground upside down. The UPS truck kept barreling down the dirt road.

Tim felt Colt's big hand on the top of his head as he moved quickly past, heading for the front of the truck.

"You're doing great," Colt said.

"Where are we going?"

"To the helicopter." Colt kept walking.

They were flying back in a helicopter? Excitement poured through him, replacing some of his fear. He'd never flown in a chopper but he had always wanted to.

He shifted a little, turned and raised up enough to look out through the front windshield. Down the road, two big black SUVs hurtled toward them from the opposite direction. The cars slid to a halt, then turned sideways, forming a barrier. All four doors flew open and men poured out and started shooting.

The front windshield on Colt's side of the delivery truck exploded, but Lissa didn't slow down. Colt lifted the strap of the assault rifle over his head, nestled it against his shoulder, and started firing through the shattered glass, sweeping a stream of bullets from one side of the road to the other, a rain of gunfire so loud Tim's ears rang.

Flattening himself on the floor, he closed his eyes, afraid to see what happened next.

LISSA DUCKED DOWN in the seat and kept driving, heading full speed toward the two black SUVs blocking the road. There was only a few feet between them, but if she hit the front of the vehicles just right, she figured she could knock them aside enough to keep rolling.

"Don't stop," Colt said as he dropped a spent magazine on the floor next to her and shoved in a fresh one.

As if he has to tell me. Escape was their only option now. If the cartel caught them, they were dead.

She jammed her foot on the gas pedal and the engine whine increased. Colt started firing again as the truck got closer to the barricade. Men ducked and ran for cover, and Lissa crashed the truck into the parked vehicles, sending them flying off both sides of the road and opening the hole she had prayed for.

She kept driving, heading for the final turn before they reached the road. As she made the curve, the wheels on one side lifted off the ground, and she sucked in a terrified breath. Then the wheels settled back down with a thump. Heart pounding, she turned onto the main road, heading for the landing zone.

No one ahead of them. She shifted into a higher gear, pushing the truck to the limit, praying nothing had happened to Alex and he and the chopper would be waiting.

She spotted the space up ahead where they planned to stash the truck, as close as they could get to the landing zone. Slowing, she pulled over to the side and drove the truck out of sight behind a copse of trees.

"We gotta go!" Colt shouted, hauling Timmy to his feet, then slamming open the back door of the truck and stepping outside. "They'll be on top of us any minute."

Lissa jumped down from the driver's side and ran to the back of the truck to join them. Colt flashed her a look she couldn't read, then they were running, moving as fast as they could through the trees and the thick green foliage.

The clearing loomed ahead. No sign of the helicopter.

"We're almost there," Colt said.

"Where's the chopper?" Timmy asked worriedly, speaking Lissa's thoughts aloud.

"He'll be here," Colt said firmly. "Just keep going."

The sound of vehicle motors coming down the road made Lissa's pulse pound. The taste of fear filled her mouth.

"Keep going!" Colt shouted as they burst into the clearing where the helicopter should have been.

"Where is it?" Timmy asked again, his eyes wide with fear.

Lissa scanned the clear blue sky. In minutes it would be too late.

"There! There it is!" Timmy shouted, pointing at a dark shape in the sky that was growing larger as it drew near.

"Run!" Colt's voice rang with authority, the tone of a man used to being in command. "We need to get over that rise!"

They ran up the hill as if the hounds of hell were on their tails—which they were—and dropped over the ridge out of sight just as Alex settled the helo on the ground a few yards away. The bay doors were open.

Colt lifted Timmy up and he scrambled inside, Lissa climbed in beside him, then Colt jumped in, and the helo lifted away. Lissa strapped Timmy into the middle seat and settled in beside him, while Colt wedged himself into the copilot's chair. They all put on their headsets.

Through the plastic bubble, Lissa could see men running into the clearing below. She knew they were firing, but it was too noisy in the chopper to hear the gunshots. They were almost out of range when a second group appeared, a sea of armored vehicles, men and equipment, pouring into the clearing, surrounding the first group of soldiers.

"Looks like the cavalry has arrived," Colt said and she could hear the smile in his voice. The task force brutally outnumbered the cartel men. A few would resist and pay the ultimate price. The rest would be taken into custody, including Ray Spearman. Timmy would be safe.

"Sorry I was late." Alex's voice came through the headset. "Had a little run-in with some of our friends from the task force. Fortunately, they were called away at the last minute, something to do with El Puñal. I have a hunch Benito Cortez had a hand in it."

Colt laughed. "Perfect timing. Cortez is a handy man to

know." They were grateful for everything he had done for them. Colt turned in his seat to look at Timmy. "You okay?"

He nodded. "Thanks for coming to get me."

"You didn't think I would?"

Timmy smiled. "I was hoping you would. I didn't think you'd bring Lissa, but I'm really glad you did."

"Me, too," Colt said and there was a gruff note in his voice that made Lissa's heart contract.

She tried not to think what would happen when they got to Laredo, only a little over an hour from now. But there was no way Colt would be returning to Dallas and no way she would be going to Denver.

It was over.

They had both known from the start it was only a fling. She needed to accept that, deal with it. Lissa leaned back in the seat, trying to think of a way to say goodbye.

CHAPTER FOURTEEN

THEY WERE ON the ground in Laredo. Lissa and Timmy were heading back to Dallas, back to Julie, who had sobbed into the phone when Colt had called with the news her son was safe and on his way home.

Colt wasn't going with them. He needed to get to Denver, check on his grandmother. He was long overdue and he knew how much she missed him. He had duties, responsibilities. He planned to build a life there.

Why was it that now building a life that didn't include Lissa was the last thing he wanted to do?

They were getting ready to leave Alex's small private airport. Chase Garrett, Lissa's boss at Maximum Security, had gotten word of what had happened to Timmy and was sending the Garrett company jet to pick him up. Tim and Lissa would be flying home in style, but Colt wouldn't be joining them.

His chest felt tight. The jet would be arriving at Laredo International Airport any minute. He was dropping them off then heading on to Denver. At the moment, Timmy was with Alex, getting a last-minute helo-flying lesson. The boy was recovering from his ordeal far better than Colt had expected. He was a strong kid. No matter what happened to his father, Tim was going to be all right.

It was time for them to leave, but first he wanted to speak

to Lissa, hadn't had a moment alone with her since they had climbed aboard the helo.

He glanced away from the chopper, spotted her, and started walking. There were things he needed to say, things he had never said to a woman before. Lissa saw him coming and met him halfway across the tarmac, in the shade of a building out of the sun.

This was it. They wouldn't be alone again once they left for the airport.

Lissa stood right in front of him, looked up at him with her beautiful dark brown eyes. "I came to say good-bye."

He nodded. His throat felt tight. "Me too."

"I wanted you to know that the time we spent together meant something to me. I'll never forget you, Colt."

He glanced away. He'd never forget her, either. He looked back at her, memorizing her face. "You were great out there. I've never worked with a better partner."

She smiled but her bottom lip trembled. "Thank you for saying that."

"I mean it. I couldn't have done it without you."

She looked down then back into his face. "Maybe our paths will cross again someday."

His chest ached. Unless something changed, it would probably never happen. After today, he might never see her again. The thought sent an arrow of despair straight into his heart.

She leaned up and pressed a soft kiss on his lips. When she started to back away, Colt pulled her in and kissed her the way he wanted to, with all the feelings he had for her he'd never said. When he let her go, tears shimmered in her eyes.

"We better get going," she said. "We don't want to keep the jet waiting."

Colt just shook his head. He didn't care if the damn plane waited forever. He wasn't ready to let her go. It occurred to him he never would be. He wanted to tell her the way he felt but he couldn't seem to find the words.

Then he opened his mouth and they just spilled out. "I don't want you to go. I don't want to see you at some nebulous time in the future. Or maybe never. I don't want us to be over, Liss. I don't care what it takes, I want us to be together."

She looked at him as if he'd lost his mind. Maybe he had.

"You know it wouldn't work. Long distance relationships never work."

"Then we won't make it long distance. We'll figure something out. We're both single. Neither of us is too old to change the path we're traveling." He set his hands at her waist and drew her closer. "You know we're perfect for each other. Everything about us fits. At least admit that much. If you don't believe it, tell me I'm wrong."

The tears were back in her eyes and they spilled over onto her cheeks. She wiped them away with the tip of her finger.

"You aren't wrong. I've never met a man who suits me the way you do. It doesn't change anything."

A warm feeling slipped through him. He recognized it as hope. "It changes everything, sweetheart." Colt leaned down and kissed her, softly at first, then more deeply. By the time he'd finished, she was clinging to him as if she'd never let him go.

"Tell me you're willing to try," he said. "At least give me that much."

She looked at him and something moved across her features. Resolve, he thought, or some kind of decision.

"I know it's too soon to say this, but I don't want to leave without telling you. I'm in love with you, Colt. It wasn't what I wanted. It just happened."

The warmth in his chest expanded. "I don't think time is a factor when it comes to love. I've never said the L-word to a woman before, but that's the way I feel about you." He gathered her close, her elegant dancer's body melding perfectly with his larger frame. "I love you, Lissa."

She reached up and touched his cheek. "Colt…"

"Say you'll give us a chance."

Fresh tears surfaced. "I can't believe this is happening, but…yes. Let's find a way to make it work."

Colt kissed her softly. "Thank God I wasn't stupid enough to walk away."

Lissa's laughter rang sweet in his ears, and Colt smiled, feeling as if the dark cloud over his head had just been replaced by the sun.

"Okay, so you're flying back to Dallas and I'm driving on to Denver. But as soon as I get things wrapped up, I'm coming after you. We'll figure out a way to be together. We won't let anything or anyone stop us."

Lissa grinned. "One thing I've learned about you, Colt Wheeler. When you're on a mission, you don't quit until you've gained your objective." She leaned up and kissed him. "I'll see you in Dallas."

There was more he wanted to say, but when he turned, he saw Alex and Timmy walking toward them. It was time to go.

Instead of a feeling of loss, a smile lifted the corners of his mouth. He wasn't saying goodbye this time, only a brief farewell.

Colt reached for Lissa's hand. It felt exactly right in his as they walked toward his Mustang for the short ride to the airport.

EPILOGUE

LISSA WAS BACK in Dallas, back at work at The Max. Timmy was home, back in school, handling the trauma of his abduction with the resilience that only comes with youth.

The day after Lissa's return, Alex Romero had called to update her on the outcome of the task force raid, letting her know that Ray Spearman, aka El Puñal, had been arrested. He was facing more than a dozen criminal charges, and because the Americans were involved in the arrest, he was certain to go to a high-security prison, and he wouldn't be getting out any time soon.

Business was good. She'd been able to find the drug dealer who'd sold impure heroin to the daughter of one of her clients. He was cooling his heels in jail, exactly where he belonged. She'd also helped an abused wife get evidence against her no-good husband, which had resulted in custody of her two young children. Life was good.

Lissa looked up as the door whooshed open and a tall, broad-shouldered man walked into the office. Gleaming blond hair, black patch over his eye, roguishly good-looking, Colt was here.

She rose and started toward him. In Laredo, she'd told him she was in love with him. She had only fallen harder in the weeks since that day. This was his third trip to Dallas. He'd been in town since yesterday, planned to stay another week. He was willing to move to Dallas full-time, he had said. Chase had even offered him a job.

But Lissa wanted to wait. She owed it to Colt to consider the possibility of working in Denver. They would be making a trip there soon. It really didn't matter where they wound up as long as they were together.

One thing was certain. They were sticking. They were going to make a life together. There was no doubt Colt was the man for her and she was the woman for him.

When she reached him, he opened his arms and she walked right into them. It was a perfect fit.

Colt kissed her and she could taste the hunger that always sparked between them. "You ready?" he asked, his voice a little gruff.

It was lunchtime and she was starving, but looking at him made her want something more than just food. "Where are we going?"

"I bought takeout. I thought we'd eat at home." And there was the added benefit of having the privacy they needed for what both of them were clearly thinking.

"Sounds purrfect," she said with a playful feline growl.

Colt flashed her a grin as they walked out the door. There was no mistaking the heat in his gaze, and desire slipped through her.

It was going to be a long, hot afternoon.

* * * * *

New York Times *bestselling author Kat Martin concludes the Maximum Security series with her most thrilling novel yet*—The Perfect Murder.

Reese Garrett runs his oil company with efficiency and iron control. But when a mysterious helicopter crash interrupts a routine business trip and lands Reese in the hospital, he can't help but wonder if something more sinister is at hand.

As Reese's personal assistant, McKenzie Haines has always admired her boss's leadership. A single mother, Kenzie works hard at the job she loves to take care of her son—so she's shocked when she hears that her ex-husband, Lee, is filing for sole custody of the boy. Lee has been estranged from the family since he and Kenzie divorced; Kenzie knows Lee only wants to leverage their son for his future political career.

With environmental protests mounting against Garrett Resources, Reese finds himself the subject of every headline…until Lee is discovered dead and Kenzie is named the prime suspect in his murder. With a killer at large, and Kenzie and Reese in serious danger, they'll have to join forces with Reese's brothers at The Max before anyone else falls victim to the perfect murder.

Watch for
The Perfect Murder
by Kat Martin
coming July 2021 from HQN Books!

$$\begin{array}{r} 261 \\ 150 \\ \hline 111 \end{array}$$

$$\begin{array}{r} 291 \\ 151 \\ \hline 140 \end{array}$$